NOWHERE TO RUN

Mike didn't like it, Archie's being so calm. Maybe it was time to reconsider option number one—running off into the woods. But then he saw a state trooper's car pull into the lot at Galston's Motel. It stopped in front of his room. They were looking for him already. If Mike ran now, he wouldn't get far.

Archie stepped out of the truck. "Come on. Don't have all night." They went around to the back. It was a big duffel bag he'd put in there, a new one with lots of zippers and extra compartments. He dragged it onto the tailgate and opened one of the side pockets. Mike couldn't read anything on his face. "Billy says you were out on East Shore near my house this afternoon, round three o'clock."

"That's right, I was walking—"

"His secretary, Patsy DeBruhl, saw you." Archie sighed and pulled his hand out of the bag, holding a pistol, blue and scarred and ugly. He waved Mike back from the truck and closed the tailgate. "Seems you were born under an unlucky star, Michael...."

Other *Leisure* books by Rob Palmer:

NO TIME TO HIDE

ROB PALMER

EYES OF THE WORLD

LEISURE BOOKS NEW YORK CITY

For Theresa, as always.

A LEISURE BOOK®

May 2008

Published by

Dorchester Publishing Co., Inc.
200 Madison Avenue
New York, NY 10016

ISBN 10: 0-8439-5676-3
ISBN 13: 978-0-8439-5676-4

The name "Leisure Books" and the stylized "L" with design are trademarks of Dorchester Publishing Co., Inc.

Printed in the United States of America.

10 9 8 7 6 5 4 3 2 1

Visit us on the web at www.dorchesterpub.com.

EYES OF
THE WORLD

CHAPTER ONE

Lime Key

Mike Stanbridge kept a photograph tucked in his bedroom mirror. He stared at it as he pulled on his swimming trunks. He'd taken it eighteen months earlier, using a Polaroid camera set on auto-timer. It was in Hawaii, at a sprawling beachfront home on the Big Island. He could remember exactly the clean smell of the air and the sound of the raindrops pelting the trees outside.

There were two people in the picture: Mike and a woman. They sat on a rattan sofa, his hand in her lap, her head against his shoulder. Their smiles were contented, and, though she wore only a silk robe, the pose seemed casual, not sexy. She wore no makeup; her blonde hair was uncombed. Just risen from bed. A couple on a second honeymoon, perhaps. But, no. There'd been no honeymoon for these two. She was married to another man.

Her name was Carolyn Connor, and she was, without a doubt, the most famous woman in the world. Lynnie (as she was called by the few billion people who cared about such things) was president of the United States.

They had argued a bit about the picture, and that was

why he'd settled for the Polaroid. There was no digital file, no film to be developed, no negative. Just the snapshot for Mike to keep.

His gaze lingered on the photo, on Lynnie's face. Leaving it out where someone might see it was risky. Sure, other politicians had had affairs, flings really. Mike knew the scorecard: Bill and Monica; Gary Hart and Donna Rice; Wilbur Mills and his Argentine Firecracker. Some had survived, kept their careers alive. But this thing between Mike and Lynnie was different. If the story—the *whole* story—behind that picture unraveled, Lynnie Connor's carefully constructed world would come crashing down.

So why keep the picture in the mirror? So he could look at it every time he came into the room. He'd read about people who needed special lamps in the winter, to make up for the lack of sunlight. For Mike, it was Lynnie who kept his battery charged.

Smiling, he patted the photo and went into the bathroom for his skin cream. The ointment was his own concoction of cocoa butter, aloe, and vitamin E oil. He needed it to keep his skin moist. Otherwise the stiffness and itching drove him crazy.

Through the window over the whirlpool tub he could see the Atlantic, milky blue today. Ismail Hussani was out in his bonefish skiff, a long-billed cap pulled down over his eyes, his fly rod flicking back and forth. Ismail was a perfect neighbor for Mike, quiet and studious, never prying, and, like most residents of Lime Key, Ismail was rich. Most residents, that is, except Mike.

Mike was here as a house sitter. The owners lived in London and had only visited twice since they bought the home four years earlier. Their taste was a little over-the-top for him—Roche-Bobois furniture, original Miró paintings, antique Persian rugs—but the place was way beyond tolerable. Before coming here, Mike had had his own home in the Miami suburbs. One weekend he saw the "house sitter wanted" ad and something clicked in his mind: the slow pace in the Keys; living free-form for a while. He sold out and moved down and hadn't regretted it for a minute. Over the microwave in his kitchen he had a sign, one his father had made for him before he died: NEVER OWN ANYTHING YOU NEED TO PAINT OR FEED.

Lime Key wasn't a separate island but a tiny section of Key Largo, a walled-off enclave of twenty stucco mansions with pea-gravel yards off a winding concrete driveway. There was a security gate, complete with armed guard. Four men worked full-time keeping up the grounds. Getting hired as a house sitter there might have been difficult, but Mike had the right qualities. "He's a lawyer," the property manager told the owners, "but he doesn't have his own clients. Does work for a big firm up in Miami. He'll be perfect."

The newspaper was out on the stoop. Mike checked the front page: no picture of Lynnie. There was an article about the campaign. The election was only a few weeks away. He scanned the lead paragraphs. Lynnie was expected to do well in the final two debates. . . . Still up in the polls . . . Mike yawned and tossed the paper on the kitchen counter. It was Lynnie he was interested in, not politics.

The sun was on the east deck. As he sat down the glass door at the next house slid open. Music spilled out. Sixties' rock, the Raspberries or the Association, Mike wasn't sure which. Wally MacMasters, Mike's other neighbor, stepped out. Mike had an urge to head back inside, like a turtle into its shell, but this afternoon he needed to start work on a brief for that law firm up in Miami. He'd be locked away for four days, no phone, no distractions. He needed some time outside.

Wally was a Canadian, a big man who'd made a fortune manufacturing plastic garbage cans. Shortly after his fiftieth birthday he sold out and retired to Florida. Today, as usual, he had a woman with him, a chesty young thing in a string bikini. Both were drinking piña coladas from parfait glasses. It was just after ten in the morning. Wally waved at Mike and pointed at the woman. "*Chris*ta!" Mike had seen Wally do the same thing with his car. Point. "*Jag*uar!" And the obscene statue he kept in his living room. Point. "*Pre*-Colombian!"

Mike nodded and bent over, dabbing ointment on his leg. Christa watched, holding the deck railing because she was a little tipsy. She worked in the men's department at Macy's at Dadeland Mall, south of Miami. Sizing up men was her job. That's where she'd met Wally. One day he breezed in, tapped her on the shoulder and said, "Bomber jackets, I'll take two. One black, one brown. Wanna have lunch with me?" Not much to figure out there. But this neighbor—this Stanbridge character—he was a lot more complicated.

He had neatly trimmed salt-and-pepper hair and a face that was perfectly handsome—not cute or adorable, just the sort of handsome that played well in the movies. His eyes were like the ocean, sparkling blue, underlaid with something smoky. He was tall, well over six feet, but so thin he appeared slight—the dead opposite of Wally. What really caught her attention were the scars. They ran in a mass up Mike's right side and back, from knee to shoulder. There was one on his neck, a narrow purple streak that probed like a tentacle to the base of his jaw. There was a girl in the perfume department at Macy's with scars like that on her arm. Burn scars.

Christa knew she shouldn't stare, but she couldn't help herself. Still rubbing the cream in, Mike glanced up into her eyes. His expression was placid, a hint of dry humor. He knew what she was thinking: *God, how can you* live *with that?*

Christa started to mumble an apology but cut herself off. It's his fault, coming out here, just swim trunks on. Irritated, she turned away from him.

Mike closed his eyes and settled back, hoping they'd get bored and go inside. No dice. Wally, four coladas to the wind, wanted to dance. And Christa was some dancer, lithe and quick. Before long Wally collapsed onto a bench, panting. He hooted in appreciation.

Mike opened his eyes. Christa was watching him, shimmying. *See? Who's staring now?* He started to get up, go inside, and one-two-three she slipped her hands up her back, undid her bikini top, and tossed it aside.

Wally put his hands out as if warding off a ghost. "No, honey, put 'em back! Somebody'll call the cops or somethin'!"

Mike chuckled and shook his head.

Christa's face had gone grim. Jerks—laughing at her. She grabbed her top and stormed into the house. "Honey?" Wally called after her. "Wassamatter?"

She didn't answer, and Wally made no attempt to follow. He wagged his head from side to side, a way of saying *who knows?* He lifted his glass to Mike. "Wanna come over for some cocktails?"

"No. I need to swim and then lock down and do some work."

Wally wagged his head again. "Workin' man's blues. Yours sure must be interesting. I've never seen anybody go underground like you when you're busy. When I was in it—Who's that?"

"What?" Mike said, smiling. He was used to Wally's practical jokes.

"That man in your kitchen."

Mike turned in time to see someone with a green knapsack disappear into the bedroom. He bolted after him, knocking his chair over on the way.

They squared off next to the bed. The man had a silver wand in his hand, attached by a hose to a metal canister in the knapsack. The logo on his greasy watch cap said BUG/OUT. He gave Mike a perfunctory salute with the wand and said, "Yeah, what?" His name was Mel, according to the stitching on his shirt.

"How the hell did you get in here?"

"Front door. You the new owner?" Mel's accent was throaty and lazy, trueborn Florida cracker.

"House sitter. You've got a key? You come in here all the time?" Mike had edged around so he was blocking the photo on the mirror.

"Not all'a time, like I'm gonna be eatin' your bean dip or nothin'. Just need t' keep the palmettos down." Palmetto bugs were the Florida version of cockroaches—two inches long, big enough to crunch underfoot.

"I moved in in July," Mike said. "You've been here since then?"

"We come every month," Mel said. He bent close, lowered his voice. "But I might'a missed the last few times."

Mike backed against the mirror, covering the photo. It was a dumb maneuver. The picture came loose and drifted to the floor. Mel retrieved it without a glance. "Well, I'll just zap the little boy's room here and the one downstairs and be on my way." He pushed into the bathroom while Mike gave a nod and slipped the picture into the pocket of his swimsuit.

After Mel left, Mike paced the upper floor—bedroom, living room, den. He could feel the Polaroid in his pocket. When he got to the kitchen, he looked out across the deck. Wally had gone inside.

Mike slid the glass door closed and locked it. He checked the other doors. All secure. Then he went downstairs to the family room. In the corner was a fireplace, a neat adobe half-oval, never used.

He hated fire so much his hand shook just reaching for the matchbox. He placed the photo on the bricks and slipped a lit match underneath. The edges curled and began to char. The figures—Mike and Lynnie—drew together, merging, disappearing. When nothing remained but ashes, he doused them with water, then cleaned everything up.

It was nearly noon when Mike started his swim. The tide was so far out the water at the end of the dock was only knee-deep. He waded straight out to sea. Because of his scars, Mike had a slight limp, and he always enjoyed the partial weightlessness of being in the water. After a hundred yards he approached Ismail's skiff. "Hey," he said quietly, not wanting to spook the fish. "Catch anything?"

"Rays," Ismail replied, tilting his head to the sun. "Catching rays."

Come to think of it, Mike had never seen Ismail bring in a fish. "Sounds fun. Watch out for white whales."

Ismail laughed softly. "Backgammon tonight?"

"No, I've got to work."

"Big case?" Ismail said.

"Complex—and yes, a lot of money involved."

"See you when you come up for air, then."

"Good luck with the fish."

"Be careful out there, Bridge. Current's strong today."

Bridge. People called him that, though he never encouraged it. Bridge to where? For what? Bridges were things people didn't think about until they collapsed.

He swam smoothly, aiming for tiny Tavernier Key a mile and a half offshore. He thought about the brief he was going to write. A jurisdictional case, the law simple, the facts complex. He had the argument worked out in his head but needed to review the files—boxes and boxes of files. He tried to stay focused on the work, but inevitably, like the quiet spill of the waves, Lynnie came into his mind. Maybe he shouldn't have burned that picture. He could have hidden it; a safety deposit box, maybe. But what would be the point? He'd had the picture to look at, not save for old age.

He jumped up the pace a bit, making his muscles

strain and his lungs ache. Too late for that picture now, but he might take another one, next week. That was why he had to hurry and finish the brief. In five days he was going to Blaine, the village in the Adirondacks where he and Lynnie had grown up. It was her forty-third birthday, and the whole town was turning out for a party. She'd promised Mike some private time together. That was during their last phone conversation, three weeks ago. They spoke once a month, on a prearranged schedule. She was the one who placed the calls, not him.

He kept up the bruising pace, enjoying the rush of water over his skin. He thought of the rain in Hawaii; he thought of the smell of Lynnie's hair. He was so focused he didn't notice the shark until it was right beside him, a powerful gray mass, cool eyes judging his size and strength. He must have passed the test for, with a flick of its tail, it disappeared toward deeper water. All this happened in the time it took Mike to make a single stroke.

He might have quit then, gone home with a story to tell. Instead he forged on, not missing a beat. If the shark returned, there was nothing he could do about it. Simple fate. His mind stayed with Lynnie—her smile, her voice, the sigh she sometimes made far in the night, in the middle of a dream. Just five more days.

CHAPTER TWO

North Country

Archie Pascoe drummed his fingers on the propane tank outside his back door, trying to show how impatient he was. He would have looked pointedly at his watch, but he was leaning against the handrail. If he shifted his weight, the rail might give way and send him tumbling into the yard. Game five of the World Series was due to start in a few minutes. He should be getting his beer and salami, settling in for the fun. Eve should have figured that out.

Eve was Archie's neighbor, and one of his few friends. Reverend Eve Tessmer. They lived on East Shore Drive in Blaine, New York. Both were seventy-three years old and long retired, but their personalities still matched their former jobs. Archie had been assistant principal at Blaine Central High School, an eagle-eyed, give-no-quarter disciplinarian. He'd called his office in the administration wing "The Gulag." Eve, pastor at the Mid-County Methodist Church, was a practical evangelical, praying for traffic lights on Main Street, new snowplows for the county roads. She also had an ecumenical streak. Shortly before her retirement, she invited a rabbi and a Buddhist monk down from Montreal to speak during the Sunday service. Four Methodist families became Presbyterians that week.

Eve was an organizer, too, and that's what she was on about tonight. Archie drummed his fingers, and she chattered away. Eve was the one who'd come up with the theme for Lynnie Connor's birthday celebration, and she was determined that everything come off perfectly. "Lynnie *is* president, isn't she? Blaine's *most famous* citizen? And all the press *will* be in town, right?" Archie nodded, but he was having trouble paying attention. "Then why won't Marvin Hoxie *listen* to me?"

Marvin Hoxie. Archie knew something about this. He shifted so he could hear the television better. Good—no national anthem yet. Marvin Hoxie was mayor of Blaine. Three nights ago, at a meeting of the planning committee for Lynnie's visit, Marvin and Eve had gotten into a squabble about parking arrangements. Eve wanted more space set aside for the press corps, which meant others would have to leave their cars outside of town and be shuttled in by bus. Marvin was against the idea, but, instead of arguing, he decided to play dumb. "Evie, now you've lost me again." It was the third time in five minutes he'd said that.

Finally Eve exploded. "You're lost, Marvin? That makes sense. You couldn't find your own butt with a Seeing Eye dog." That brought a few titters, followed by uncomfortable silence. Eve had been working too hard, worrying too much. She needed to let others take some of the load. Sarah Jenkins, the village treasurer, told her so, then and there. Eve was later seen sitting on a bench in the village park, crying.

Archie had to agree with the mayor about the busses. Blaine couldn't afford that. But he knew if he said so, he'd be in for a fight. "Marvin'll find out soon enough if you're right. Along about dawn on Thursday."

Eve sighed. "Only four days. Not nearly enough time. And I've got this new problem with Arizona." She waved the stack of papers she was holding.

"Arizona?" Archie said, tilting his head again to catch the television. A Budweiser commercial. Not a good sign.

"I still can't find anyone to be the guest for the first year."

Lynnie's birthday party had a This-Is-Your-Life theme, with one guest representing each of her forty-three years. Lynnie had grown up in Blaine, but she'd been born in Arizona. Eve had complained all along about how hard a time she was having finding someone there who had known the family.

Wait. There was the anthem. "So what?" Archie said, his gruffness coming through. "Forty-two people on the stage instead of forty-three? Who's gonna notice?"

"I will," she mumbled.

Archie looked down and was shocked to see she was near tears. "No," he said. "Don't start that." Years ago, in The Gulag at school, he hated it when the girls cried. He once got so frustrated with a blubbering sophomore, a girl perpetually late for morning homeroom, that he told her she sounded like a pig. He never apologized to her, but he felt so badly he got blind drunk, swilling cheap blackberry brandy right there in his office.

He scuttled down the steps. "Calm down. We'll come up with something."

She sniffed. "I'm out of ideas. I talked to everyone I could think of out there. I thought I had a line on somebody, but it was a dead end. I even called that Aron Aubrey in Manhattan again. He must know someone from back then, and he owes me a favor. Instead he got short, said to stop *bothering* him. Only *four days* left, Archie!"

Archie took the stack of papers. "This the stuff from the Arizona file?"

She nodded. Eve had files all over her house, one for each year of Lynnie's life.

He said, "What if I look through it? Maybe I'll hit on something." Another nod from Eve. "All right, I'll get to it. We can talk in the morning."

She smiled at him, her lips quivering with pent-up emotion. "Bless you, Archie."

He hated that, too, but he smiled back. He watched her walk away, leaning heavily on her cane. She used the cane all the time now, and she'd lost quite a bit of weight. Her hair was pulled back in a ponytail, gray and shaggy, too big for her head. Getting old, Archie thought. We're all getting so damned old. He hurried inside. *Cripes.* One down in the top of the first already. *Cripes.* He tossed all thoughts of Eve aside and plopped into his recliner.

The next two hours passed slowly for him. In seven innings, the Yankees had moved up 10–3 over the Cubs. Archie didn't care one way or the other for the Cubs, but he couldn't stand the Yankees. Like a lot of upstate New Yorkers, he thought the Yankees hogged too much of the spotlight. Always some new soap opera there, and more money than Croesus. That pissed him off, like the Yanks were always trying to buy respect. The Cubs had batted

.301 as a team that year. Amazing. Now, through the first four games of the Series, they were hitting a rousing .215. Typical NL Central crap. Looked gorgeous on the way to the prom, but couldn't dance for shit.

Archie blinked and sat up. In the fifth inning he'd punched the mute button so he wouldn't have to listen to the play-by-play. Now he was sure he'd heard something outside, down the hill by the apple tree. A friggin' deer. He set his beer on the floor and stubbed out his cigarette. Getting up from the chair took real effort. Archie weighed over three hundred pounds. From the table by the back door he grabbed a slingshot and a handful of steel marbles. The steps squeaked as he descended to the yard. It was past ten, and the woods were silent. His breath drifted away in a spectral cloud. No deer by the apple tree. He went around to the front. None there, either.

Archie was about to head inside when he heard another sound, the metallic *thiick* of a car door pulled softly closed.

Blaine, the town, was located at the north end of Blaine Lake. As its name implied, East Shore Drive ran along the east flank of the lake, to a dead end at Simmons Creek. At one time, dozens of families had lived year-round on the Drive. Now it was just Archie and Eve, the rest of the houses having been bought up by "summer people," downstate lawyers and doctors and university professors who came in June and left by Labor Day. All the camps were closed up now, so who would be here? Kids out parking. A little upholstery polishing.

Archie smiled as he thought it over. He could grab 'em by the scruff of the neck, drag 'em to the phone, make 'em call their folks. Nah. Probably just get sued. Anyway, too much of a hassle. He looked at the slingshot in his hand. Maybe he'd plink out a taillight or two, make some teenage Don Juan explain *that* to his daddy.

He moved onto the road, a lumpy dirt track that by

Thanksgiving would be socked in with mud and ice. There was the car, twenty yards away, a big white sedan. He raised the slingshot, but before he could take aim, the car glided away into the night, quiet as a forest animal.

Strange, Archie thought. Didn't turn his headlights on. *His* headlights. A man, not a boy. Archie was sure of it. And he was alone. Could have been somebody out trying to jack a deer. Put out bait, wait a bit, then blast away. Funny place to do it, though, right by a couple of houses with lights on. Besides, it was the middle of hunting season. Why not go out in the woods and shoot one, legal-like? Archie stared at the now-empty road, then shook his head and turned for home.

It was hard going, uphill on the slippery woodchip path. He stopped to catch his breath, still thinking about that car. Something was nagging at him there. He couldn't put his finger on it. He sucked in a lungful of air and chugged on.

Inside he checked the game. Still 10–3. He put the sling-shot away and got a fresh beer. The kitchen faced west, toward the lake. He could see Eve's place down there, the upper half. The rest was cut off by the hill. Except for the porch light, the house was dark. Archie checked the time and frowned. She'd be listening to the radio now, her news and talk program from Burlington, every night from ten to midnight. But the lights were out.

He picked up the phone and dialed. Ten rings, no answer. As he set the receiver back on the cradle, a quick shiver ran through him. A premonition.

Pumpkins—that was the first thing Archie noticed as he swung open the gate in Eve's picket fence. Four jack-o'-lanterns on her porch steps. All that work and there probably wouldn't be a single trick-or-treater out that way this year. Something rustled on the roof. It was a bat, scooting through a crack in the attic vent. They nested up there, dozens of them. Eve didn't care. All

God's creatures, she said. Archie swung the gate shut and carefully reset the latch. He knew he was stalling.

He banged on the door and called, but went in without waiting for an answer. The front porch—Eve's sunroom—was lit by the lamp over the steps. There was a coffee mug on the TV tray by the rocking chair, and an uncapped bottle of rye whiskey. Eve's cane was hooked over the arm of the chair. The mug had the presidential seal on it. Lynnie Connor still kept in touch with the folks back home. She'd sent that mug to Eve last Christmas.

Archie went straight to Eve's bedroom, on the first floor in the rear of the house. He stopped in the doorway and didn't call out. Eve lay in bed at an out-of-kilter angle, too still to be breathing. Dead.

He moved closer, until he was standing over her. She was on her side, facing the wall, one shoulder exposed at the top of the sheet. Moonlight spilled through the window, enough so he could see her face. Her eyes were halfway open.

His mind was spinning, but Archie was already beginning to piece together what had happened. She'd been listening to the radio and started to feel sick. She got ready for bed, but before she could fall asleep the stroke came. He was sure it was a stroke. She'd had two already—that's why she used the cane. In spite of the strokes, he'd always figured it would be Eve who'd find him like this, not the other way around.

Archie wiped the tears from his eyes. Before he called the rescue squad, he'd see she was comfortable, not all tangled up like this. As he tugged on the covers, a piece of paper fell off the nightstand. He bent for it, and Eve continued to roll, her empty eyes swinging across the room. Archie grabbed her elbow to stop her, and then he froze.

There was a wound in her temple, star-shaped, an

erupting volcano half as big as a fist. There was a smear of blood on the pillow. Her right arm was tucked beneath her. A revolver lay in her hand. Archie could smell the gunpowder now. The smell had been there all along, but his mind had refused to believe it.

Then a pain gripped him, a sudden pressure in his chest as if God Himself had taken hold of his heart and was squeezing. Archie staggered out the door and down the hall. He couldn't get a breath; his heart was thundering. Another door. The back porch, a tangle of boots and mops and brooms. Outside, but still no air.

He sat down—*flump*—on the path that led to the lake. From his pocket he took a small bottle. His hands were shaking so much that, once he had the cap off, pills flew all over his lap. He grabbed one and slipped it under his tongue. The nitroglycerin burned, and, though he knew it hadn't had time to take hold yet, he was able to get in one strangled breath, and another.

Angina. Nine years with it now, and this was the worst attack ever. Made sense, seeing Eve like that. He steadied himself, pushing his mind to neutral ground.

Out in the lake he could see the black bulk of Rock Island. He'd fished the island many times. A good bass spot off the south end. He'd taken a trophy lake trout a quarter mile north. Bill Varik drowned at that same spot. He'd known Bill from the Elks Club. Archie let his thoughts slew around to the last time he'd been at the Elks.

Two nights ago, he'd gone in for a beer and a game of darts. Wayne Hoxie was behind the bar, the mayor's brother. He was the one who told the story about Marvin and Eve and the Seeing Eye dog. As the laughter died away, Wayne cast a stage-right glance at Archie, the only one who might defend Eve. The rest of the audience waited. Wayne circled his finger next to his temple. "Poor Evie. The Good Reverend Screwloose."

Archie closed his eyes and listened to the quiet *shush* of waves against the shore. The pain in his chest was gone. Now he could think about her.

The signs were obvious. The gun in her hand, the wound. The barrel must have been right against her head when the shot was fired. Suicide. Clearly suicide.

No, dammit, not clear at all.   .

Archie started to pick up the pills and put them back in the bottle. Sure Eve was upset. Seems she'd been that way since her second stroke. And maybe she was drinking more than she should. This party for Lynnie, too. So much pressure there.

"No." Archie said it out loud this time. "Never." Eve Tessmer wouldn't turn a gun on herself. *Couldn't* do it. Leave too much of a mess for someone else to clean up. Him.

Archie looked across the lake again, past the island to the lights of Blaine. That night at the Elks Club. "The Good Reverend Screwloose," Wayne Hoxie had said. Archie glared at him so hard that Wayne slunk off into the back room. Then Archie tossed his darts on the bar and marched angrily into the night. Before the door slammed behind him, the murmurs started up.

The people of Blaine wouldn't have any trouble passing judgment on Eve Tessmer. She'd always been a bit . . . different. Never married. Living out there on the lake all by herself. And the way she ran the church. That was a scandal, really. Too bad, they'd say. Poor Evie. If only we'd seen it coming.

Archie was kneeling now, sifting through the grass to get the last of his nitroglycerin. He glanced again at the lights of the village. Cold yellow dots like the eyes of birds. Watching.

He rattled the pills in his hand. What did he care about them? He had an extra bottle at home. Then it came to him. He wasn't going to call the rescue squad or the police or anyone. He was going to take that revolver away and make them *prove* it was a suicide, if that's what it was. The pills—he was picking them up because he didn't want anyone to know he'd been there.

It made his pulse quicken again. Breaking the rules was not something Archie Pascoe did lightly. But think what would happen if he let somebody find that gun. What with the rumors that would be flying, the cops would jump to the easy conclusion: got depressed; blew her brains out. Case closed. Cops, hell. Half-wit village police chief. The state troopers weren't much better. They'd be too lazy to look into the things that were out of place here.

That cane, for instance. With her leg the way it was, Eve couldn't walk without it, and yet the cane was on the front porch, and she was in bed. That revolver, too. Where did that thing come from? Hadn't she always preached gun control? Then there was the car, the bastard in the big white sedan. Yeah, there were a *lot* of things out of place here.

Archie stood up, pushing with both hands on his knee, fighting his weight. He reached for the doorknob, and stopped.

In his mind's eye he could see that white sedan. The license plate. New York plates had a blue banner at the top and bottom. On that plate there were no banners, just simple dark letters on white, and a flag logo in the background. It was a government car. A U.S. government car.

That brought a cold prickle to the back of his neck.

Archie's eyes narrowed, and he squared his shoulders. He pulled open the door and moved quickly down the hall. He felt as if he were back in The Gulag at school. He'd even up the damn score, settle somebody's hash for sure. And God help anybody who got in his way.

CHAPTER THREE

Biscayne Boulevard

Barchic & Soames had its offices in the CentroBank Tower on Biscayne Boulevard in downtown Miami. It was a glass-box building set catty-corner to the street to give a better view of the waterfront. The lobby was cool pink marble, empty except for two thirty-foot royal palms in pink planters. Mike Stanbridge rode the elevator alone to the twenty-second floor.

It always felt odd to him, coming back to his old firm. He'd been a partner here for ten years before switching to "of counsel" status. That was nine months ago. With Lynnie Connor in the White House, he needed extra space. It was a relief to keep the television off and not read the newspapers, not hear her name on everyone's lips. Lime Key gave him a break from all that, but it was too quiet sometimes, like suspended animation. The trips he made to Miami kept him in balance.

Mike still had an office at the firm, but he didn't feel comfortable just waltzing past the receptionist. He told her to let Randy Barchic know he was there and took a seat in the reception area. On the table was a newspaper, open to the sports page. The headline said, CHICAGO IN GRAND-SLAM COMEBACK. The subhead was: 11 RUNS IN 9TH GIVE CUBBIES 14–10 VICTORY. That was Sunday, two days ago. It hadn't made Monday's paper because it was a night game.

"Yanks'll get 'em yet," someone said. Smiling, Mike looked up at Monica Ayres. She was Randy's administrative assistant. Monica was originally from Atlanta, and she hadn't lost the accent. "How ya been, Bridge?" Before he could reply, she added, "Too busy to answer your e-mail, I guess." That was a sore spot between them. They had a business to run, and sometimes they needed to get in touch with him.

"Nag, nag," Mike sighed.

She swatted him with the accordion file she was carrying. "Watch your mouth." They started toward Randy's office. The walls were oiled teak, lined with Currier & Ives nautical prints. Monica said, "Somebody's been trying to get hold of you, from up there in Chill-Blaine or wherever you're from. I told him you'd be—"

She was cut off by the sound of laughter. A huge man backed into the corridor. He tossed a crumpled piece of paper—a basketball shot—into his office. "*Crud*," he sputtered.

Randy Barchic had been a star center for the University of Miami football team. He went on to the New York Giants, but got injured and had to give up the game. He came back to Florida, got a law degree, and started Barchic & Soames. "Boat cases, that's what I want," he told his friends. Admiralty. Maritime law. Law of the sea. It was all the same to Randy. Boat cases. He loved the ocean, so much so he had two boats of his own, nearly identical fifty-four-foot Hatteras cruisers. He kept one in Miami, the other in New Orleans for "weekends out."

Randy squawked when he saw Mike and cuffed him on the back. "Buddy-boy! C'mon in. Playin' Horse, we were. Manda 'n me."

Manda was Amanda Hespillier. She was a junior partner with the firm. She had African hair trimmed tight to her skull and café-au-lait skin. Her family was from one of the meanest sections of Little Haiti, on Miami's north side, and she always seemed to be trying to kick that dust off her heels. Even in the middle of a game of Horse, she was quietly dignified. Mike needed to talk to her and Randy both about that brief he'd been working on.

It was a maritime case, but not the kind Randy loved, or Mike. Twenty months ago, during a storm off Ascension

Island, two ships had failed to pass in the night. Both sank, and now everyone was suing everyone—ship owners, ship managers, insurance companies, cargo owners, crew members. The first of those suits had been filed in Federal District Court in Miami. Randy's client, one of the ship owners, wanted the trial moved to the Netherlands. The first step was to get the court in Miami to dismiss the case. Mike had prepared all the pleading papers, including a long Memorandum of Law. Amanda was to argue the motion before the judge.

But Randy never put business first. "You see this?" he said, tossing a copy of *Time* magazine on his desk. Monica slipped out, closing the door behind her, while Amanda took a seat on the sofa.

On the magazine's cover was a cartoon of Lynnie Connor and her opponent in the presidential race, Carl Bryce. Lynnie was riding a unicycle on a high wire; Bryce stood below, dressed like Elmer Fudd. He had a popgun in his hand. The string on the cork was much too short to reach Lynnie. She was smiling, breezing along above it all.

Whenever Mike saw something like this, he felt a sense of impossibility. This was a joke, one of those make-believe computer enhancements they sold in malls. Lynnie Connor on the cover of *Time*. Right. And for ten bucks they'll put your face on Shaquille O'Neal's body. No . . . it's her. The president and Lynnie, one and the same.

"The debate last night, you watched it?" Randy asked. Mike shook his head. He'd been working. Besides, he never watched Lynnie debate. If she competed in Roller Derby, he wouldn't have watched that, either.

"Over before it started," Randy said. "Remember on Sunday, Bryce made that stupid comment of his?"

Mike shrugged. He'd heard of none of this.

"OK," Randy said, "on Sunday this newspaper reporter asked Bryce what he thought of Connor's China policy. Bryce mumbled something that sounded like 'dumb bitch.' " He shot a look at Amanda. "Oops. 'Scuse my French." She gave an indulgent nod.

Randy grinned. "What Bryce didn't know was there was an open mike only a few feet away. So, yesterday it's everywhere—Internet, radio, TV—and Bryce's people are trying like hell to explain. Bryce was talking about the reporter, they say, not blessed Lynnie. Bryce had said 'dumb snitch,' not 'dumb—' Not the other. What a circus."

Randy was pacing now, getting into the story. "So last night at the debate, the two of them come on stage. The microphones are on, but they aren't at their podiums yet. Connor smiles at Bryce and asks did he see the ball game last night. He nods. She says, 'What'd you think of the Yanks' manager going with a new pitcher in the ninth?' Bridge, you could see it. Bryce knew exactly what was coming. He looked at the floor while she turned to the cameras and said, 'That was a dumb switch.' Probably seventy million people laughed out loud."

"It may be funny," Amanda said, "but it won't help her standing with women." The two men looked at her. "Women don't react positively to sports jokes. It makes them feel excluded. The polls all say so."

"They got polls on that?" Randy said. He turned away, staring out the window at the silver throat of Biscayne Bay. "Hell, what would Connor care anyway? Her standing with women is out of this world." A poll a few weeks earlier had shown Lynnie Connor with a phenomenal seventy-one percent approval rating among women. Men weren't so taken with her, but even with them her favorable rating was in the low forties. "She can afford to give a few points," Randy said. "She's unbeatable."

Amanda usually didn't argue with him, but today she pressed her case. "Not unbeatable. Connor's been in office less than a year. People don't know her that well."

"What could hurt her?" Randy said, still facing away. "That mudslinger that Jon Ferrar hired?"

Jonathan Ferrar headed an East Coast media empire called PrimeMedia. He was way down on Randy Barchic's list of favorite people. Barchic & Soames wasn't just a maritime firm, they did a lot of corporate work, too. For years they had represented Ferrar's Florida interests, which included a string of radio and television stations. Then, with no warning, Ferrar had transferred all the work to a law firm in Tampa. He didn't even have the decency to phone Randy to explain why. And Randy, looking over the Barchic & Soames books, had had to lay off fifteen good lawyers.

PrimeMedia was a lot bigger now than it had been in those days, a top player on the world stage. Recently Ferrar had been butting heads with Lynnie over a proposal she'd made to change the federal communications laws. "Family-Friendly Airwaves" she called it. Ferrar had been furious and had said he thought America needed to know a lot more about "this woman who would be Queen." He put his money where his mouth was, hiring a hotshot investigative reporter to write an unauthorized biography of her. Ferrar's newspapers were going to publish advance excerpts from the book before the election. That had Carl Bryce's supporters salivating.

Randy went back to his desk and tapped the *Time* cover. "See? In white. Every time she goes out in public she's dressed that way. America's getting primed for a big church wedding, and Lynnie Connor's the blushing bride. Jon Ferrar can't do any damage now."

Mike heaved a sigh. He had no patience for this kind of talk, political shadowboxing. But Randy was only repeating what he'd read in the newspapers. A senator from Oregon had said, "If you fence with Connor, you're liable to bleed to death before you know you've been cut." The papers in Europe called her "The Silk Tactician." To Mike, this was nonsense. The image-making, that was just a show that went on around her. Lynnie was all about action, not strategy.

Randy plopped into his chair. "One debate left. I can't wait for the fireworks." He rocked back so he could put his feet on the desk. "So, you're going to see her? What, Thursday?" Mike nodded. "You'll get a chance to talk?"

"Probably," Mike said cautiously. It was common knowledge he and Lynnie were old friends. He had to be careful not to imply it was more than that, and he always hated these little evasions.

"Real face time with her?" Randy asked. "Or a crowd scene?"

Mike sensed a change in atmosphere. Randy wasn't looking at him, but instead was polishing a spot on his shoe with his thumb. His expression had gone blank.

Amanda stood up. "I have to return a phone call. Stop by my office when you're ready to talk about that brief."

As the door clicked behind her, Randy pulled his feet off the desk. "She's somethin', isn't she? You know, she was top of her class at Penn."

"I didn't know that," Mike said after a moment.

"Yeah. Sharp as a tack."

"Sure," Mike mumbled. He'd always felt Amanda was bright, one of the brightest in the firm. He'd told Randy that. So why were they talking about it now?

"Bridge, I need a favor," Randy said softly.

So that was it.

"What?" Mike said, trying not to sound irritated.

Randy made his pitch. The U.S. Attorney in Miami had announced he was retiring. Amanda wanted the job. She'd be great, too. Hard worker. A real organizer. And we just agreed she was bright, right?

Randy was getting wound up, throwing his arms around. "She understands that it's more than just running an office full of people. You heard her. She knows the policy angles."

"Right," Mike said flatly. That explained all the talk about politics.

"A word from you with the president," Randy said. "That's all Manda'd need to put her over the top."

"It would be good for the firm, too," Mike said. "Lots of publicity. A friend in a very high place."

Randy grinned. "Hey, it's the way of the world. I didn't invent it."

Mike shook his head. "Amanda can use my name anywhere she wants. If somebody from the Justice Department calls, I'll give her a top recommendation. But I can't talk to Lynnie about this." He couldn't explain either: that he and Lynnie had an unspoken rule—when they were together, it was just the two of them, no outsiders, no favors. Their time was too precious.

"Huh," Randy said, not a question, but more a declaration of surprise. Neither of them seemed to know what else to say, so they stared out the window. A county patrol boat cut south through the bay. Across Miami Beach, lights were starting to wink on. It was getting late.

"I suppose I'd better go talk to Amanda," Mike said.

Randy nodded, his face thoughtful. He waited for Mike to reach the door before he said, "Do you think about her much? Lynnie, I mean." Mike didn't reply. "It's amazing, really," Randy continued. "The *president*. Imagine what she can do. Start a war. Make or break people. Hell, just a twitch of her finger and she could make everybody in this building rich."

"Randy, you're already rich."

Randy gave a shallow laugh. He dug his hands into his pockets and turned again to stare out the window.

When Mike finished with Amanda, he went to his office. He banged the door shut and tossed his briefcase on his desk. He'd told Amanda the same thing he'd told Randy: she could use him as a reference for the U.S. Attorney's job, but nothing more. Amanda had been gracious, but she'd wanted an explanation. Anything Mike might have said would have been a lie, so he just stared at her as a cold awkwardness fell between them.

"If you're really gonna kick that chair, aim for something soft."

Mike sighed, then laughed. Monica was peeking in at him. "Hey—come on in."

She did, and set a stack of message slips on the desk. "You look tired, Mike."

"Work," he said, shrugging with his hands.

His tie was crooked and she gently straightened it. Monica not only sounded the part of a Georgia belle, she looked it. Blonde hair in a pretty layer cut. Blue eyes. Perfect skin. A body not too soft and not too hard. Without thinking, men opened doors for her and pulled out her chair when she went to sit. She liked it that way.

"You work too hard, then."

"Nah. Life of leisure down in the Keys."

"And no need for central heating!" It was an inside joke. At the firm, only Monica knew that Mike wouldn't turn on the heat, no matter how cold it got. That was one of the legacies of his burn. Central heating meant fire danger. He steered clear of it.

He pointed at the message slips. "Did he say who he is? I don't recognize the name."

Monica shook her head. "Just called, over and over, asking for 'Mr. Stanbridge.'" Her accent got goofy here, deep and breathy. "I thought he was gonna be obscene the first time, the way he panted. Like, 'Whatcha wearin', honey? Are your panties *real* tight?'" She tweaked Mike's tie again while he laughed. "You gonna stay at Randy's tonight?"

"If he doesn't kick me out—or I don't kick him out."

"Boys, boys," Monica said, heading for the door. "I'll be leavin' in about half an hour. Want to walk me to my car?"

"Sure thing," Mike replied. He reached for the phone.

Mike and Monica had spent one weekend together—after ten years as friends—and it almost ruined everything for them. They went to Cape Canaveral up the coast. While they were driving there a small tropical depression in the Atlantic took a big step up to hurricane status. The storm-warning flags were already up when they pulled into their hotel. The hurricane passed them by, but maybe it would have been better if it hadn't.

The problem was, Mike couldn't commit. It wasn't the physical part; he just couldn't get his head with the program. He and Monica would wrestle around, mess up the sheets, but she could tell he was distracted. The heat would dissipate. After the third try, she'd gotten up from bed. She was a gorgeous woman. This didn't happen to her. "You want to tell me what's going on?"

"No," he'd said, staring at the ceiling, his mind full of Lynnie. "I don't think I can do that."

Saturday morning, Monica packed her things and took a bus back to Miami. It was four months before she forgave him enough to start talking to him again.

Mike came back to the present. Somebody had finally answered the phone. "Yuh?"

"Archibald Pascoe, please," Mike said.

"Yuh, what?"

"This is Michael Stanbridge in Miami. You called me"—he counted the message slips—"eight times yesterday."

"Uh-huh. You don't know who I am, do you?"

"No, I'm sorry, I don't."

"Think it through . . . Torch."

Torch. Only one person had ever called Mike that, and only once. It was in a grubby office with a sign on the door that said, THE GULAG. Mike realized his fingernails were digging into the arm of his chair. "Mr.—Snooky Pascoe?"

"Uh-huh," he said. "That's the way they remember me—Snooky."

Mike would put an end to this "Snooky" business right now. "Sorry about that. So what'd you want to talk to me about?"

"Isn't that just like you young punks," Archie said. "Here I go to the trouble of tracking you down, and you don't even give me a 'How-you-doin', Mr. Pascoe?' "

Mike wasn't going to apologize again, and he wasn't going to call him *Mr. Pascoe*. "Archie, was there something in particular you wanted?"

"You know Eve Tessmer?"

"Of course," Mike said.

"You talked to her recently?"

"Sure, about Lynnie Connor's party. Eve called me back in July—"

"You know she's dead?"

"Sure," Mike said. "I—What?" It had gone right by him. "Dead?"

"That's right," Archie said. "Murdered. Right out here at her home. We're still on East Shore Drive. You remember?"

"Right. East Shore Drive. Murdered. How? Do they know who did it?"

Archie let a few seconds pass before he answered. "We're workin' on that. Listen, you'll be gettin' into town tomorrow, I figure. The memorial service is then. Three o'clock at Mid-County Methodist. You come t' my place about two thirty and we'll go together. Got it?"

"Yes. Three o'clock, two thirty. But what's this got to do with me?"

"I take it nobody from up here has talked to you yet?" Before Mike could respond, Archie said, "Two thirty, then," and hung up.

Mike was still staring at the phone when a knock came at his door. Monica stuck her head in. "Ready to leave. I hope it doesn't rain. I need to stop—Mike, are you OK? You look like your dog just died."

"Sure," he said after a moment. "I'm fine."

They had to wait for the elevator. Mike stared at their reflection in the polished steel doors. "I'll be damned," he muttered. "Snooky Pascoe."

CHAPTER FOUR

North Country

Flying north the next day, Mike was again irritated with Randy. After he'd walked Monica to her car, Mike had driven to Randy's house, a six-bedroom Italianate villa in the Gables. Randy was there alone, barbecuing chicken. The World Series had moved on to New York, but the game was cancelled because of rain. So they ate their barbecue, drank some beer, shot a little pool. All in all, a fine time.

Then in the morning, while he was driving Mike to the airport, Randy let the other shoe drop about Amanda. One night they'd been together at the office, working, fooling around. Playing Horse. Randy's cheeks colored a bit. And they . . . He wanted it; she wanted it. These things happen. You never start out figuring you're going to end up in the sack. Or maybe you do, he mused. Going on four months now. Everything was cool around the firm. Nobody knew.

"But still, it would be convenient if Amanda got a new job," Mike said.

Randy blushed again. "No, that's not why—It's not like I've got a sexual harassment thing going. Hell, maybe it's the other way around. Manda's always got to come out on top in everything. I mean *everything*. I tell her, let's try something different. Standing up. Or you kneel down and I'll—"

"Stop," Mike said, "right there." Randy started to pull over. "Not the car. Drive the damn car. But don't say another word until I'm gone."

At the airport, Mike jumped out and grabbed his bag.

Randy leaned over, clutching his sleeve. "Hey, Bridge—thanks, you know? For listening."

Mike stared out the window of the 737 at a long crisp stretch of Long Island shoreline. *Thanks for listening.* Randy had said that to him before, a few months prior to his divorce. There'd been a woman involved then, too. When Randy was done pouring out the story—the usual mess of made-up weekend conferences and motel clinches—Mike had asked Randy what he wanted him to do. Nothing, Randy said. Mike got angry: he liked Randy's wife. Why dump this on me? Randy didn't answer, just patted Mike on the right side of his chest, where his burn scars were the worst. It wasn't until later that Mike figured it out. Randy came to him because of his scars. All you've been through, Bridge. You understand what it feels like to have your world turned inside out. When Mike got home that evening, there was a message from Randy on his answering machine. *Just . . . thanks for listening.*

Years before, while Mike was in rehab after being burned, he'd had a few sessions with a psychiatrist. Let's not talk about sports today, the doctor said during the third visit. Let's cut the crap entirely. What's eating you, Mike? Tell me. Mike stared at the man's desk. "I don't think so." He rose and hobbled out of the office and never went back. That was when Mike started hoarding his secrets. They haunted him sometimes, but he wouldn't burden other people with them. Times like this, after talking to Randy, he wished everyone would do the same.

Mike had to change planes at Logan Airport in Boston. The place was awash in Lynnie Connor. She was in town today, stumping for herself and a gubernatorial candidate. Her face was on the front of every newspaper. Besides *Time*, she had the covers of *Newsweek* and *U.S.*

News & World Report. She was there on *People*, too, *Redbook*, even the *New Yorker*. Mike watched a clip of her on CNN. She was coming out of some building, smiling, waving. The Secret Service was holding the crowd back twenty feet. Still, people called out and reached for her, hoping she'd just turn her eyes on them.

Mike's connecting flight was to Plattsburgh, on the New York side of Lake Champlain, hard by the Adirondacks. On the way to the gate he bought a copy of the *Globe*. The clerk at the kiosk had a flat east-European face and a hunched body. He looked to be a hundred years old. Handing over the change, he rapped the newspaper, next to Lynnie's picture. "She doin' OK, now. Kickin' some Chinese butt!"

Mike nodded and smiled, but the good feeling quickly died. There was an article below the fold about Winston Garrett. Garrett, from his ranch in Colorado, had announced he was supporting Bryce, not Lynnie Connor, in the presidential race. That wouldn't have rated front-page coverage if not for who Winston Garrett was: a year earlier, he'd been president. Mike rolled the paper up and slapped it on his thigh. He'd wait and read the article during the flight.

The airplane was a fourteen-seat prop-job, noisy and drafty. There was only one other passenger, a woman. She sat in the back row, huddled under a floppy felt hat. Mike watched the plane's shadow dodge across the warehouses at the end of the runway, and then he looked down at Winston Garrett's picture. It was an old file photo, taken the day Garrett resigned.

Garrett had had a relatively easy race for the presidency. The only dicey part came when he picked Lynnie to be his running mate. She was a first-term senator from Virginia then, not well known nationally. But Garrett knew something about modern politics that others were slow in grasping. It used to be that the presidential ticket had to be balanced geographically. Now, Garrett said, personality balance was more important. Somebody rough and somebody smooth. A man and a woman. Garrett and Connor.

Garrett liked running for president, but, as Lynnie had told Mike, he didn't enjoy having the job, even after three years in office. No fire in the belly, she said. He rarely came out in public. He fought with the press and his own cabinet. Still, he governed well enough. If he had run, he probably would have been reelected. That wasn't in the cards, though. It was the White House doctor who gave him his exit papers. Garrett was diagnosed with stomach cancer. Ironic—he really did have fire in his belly.

The day the doctor told him, Garrett wrote a one-paragraph speech, marched to the briefing room, and read it off. He was sick and thought it best if he resigned. Vice President Connor would take over. He had every confidence in her. He was going back to Colorado for rest and treatment. He smiled as he said all this, evidently grateful to have a reason to quit.

Lynnie's first test was choosing a new vice president. She followed Garrett's lead and went for personality balance, picking Andrew Hoyt, a Philadelphia congressman, a former union organizer and a down-and-dirty street fighter. Her relationship with Hoyt hadn't been good, but everything else Lynnie touched seemed to turn to gold. Until three months ago, when the crisis with China started.

China had a new leader, too, and he thought the run-up to the U.S. election would be the perfect time for his country to regain control of Taiwan. He sent ships to blockade the island, a move he said was justified by "the illegal military buildup" there. Lynnie acted without hesitation—without consulting Congress, either. She ordered an around-the-clock airlift of U.S. soldiers to Taipei. And she went there herself. She dressed in fatigues and reviewed the troops. She reminded them that she'd served fourteen years in the Navy. She knew they were nervous; she knew they were ready to do their jobs. Three tense weeks later, the Chinese ships withdrew, but not before the leaders in Beijing made it clear they'd return to fight another day.

Now Winston Garrett had thrown in his two cents. That cancer of his was supposed to kill him, but it hadn't. For the most part, he'd kept his opinions to himself, but on China he had to speak out, he said. Taiwan wasn't important strategically. Besides, the problem could have been solved without all the saber rattling. Garrett felt America needed a steadier hand on the reins, and Carl Bryce was the only other hand in sight.

Mike was calculating the damage this would do to Lynnie when his eye fell on a sidebar article titled, "Devon on China." Devon Connor was Lynnie's husband. He was a former Navy chaplain who was always off somewhere doing good works; these days it was at a refugee camp in central Africa. Mike had never met him, but in every photo he'd ever seen, Devon had the same vague visionary expression, Peter O'Toole playing Lawrence of Arabia. A reporter had asked Devon what he thought of Winston Garrett's comments on Lynnie and the situation in Asia. "Winston is a great American," Devon had said. Then he'd pointed at a nearby orphan. "We could use his help here. It's a wonderful place to learn humility."

"Score one for Saint Devon," Mike muttered. Someone laughed and Mike realized that the woman with the hat had moved up to the seat behind him. Embarrassed, he flashed a smile at her. Out the window he could see water again, the dreary gray of Lake Champlain. It looked cold enough to be frozen, but it wasn't.

Winston Garrett's announcement was bound to hurt, might even change the momentum of the race. Mike remembered the *Time* magazine cover he'd seen in Randy's office, and the conversation they'd had. Less thàn two weeks until the election, and the polls looked good. But Amanda Hespillier had been right. Lynnie Connor was not unbeatable.

It was windy in Plattsburgh, and the plane came down like a Ping-Pong ball with a lot of English. Then they were on the tarmac, taxiing toward the terminal. A ground-crew worker wearing coveralls and a balaclava trotted out to meet them. Just seeing him, Mike huddled deeper in his overcoat.

At the Hertz counter, the clerk took Mike's credit card and license and began filling out his forms. The woman who'd come in on the plane with him was nearby, talking on her cell phone. She was in her mid-thirties, dressed in a long leather coat, very chic. She'd taken off her hat. Mike stared at her hair: straight and pure blonde, laid out in a shimmery sheet over her shoulders. Her eyes swung up to meet his. She smiled at him before she turned away.

·In the parking lot, the wind was so strong Mike didn't hear her calling until she was right beside him. He stood up, smacking his head on the open trunk door.

"Ouch. Oh, ouch," she said. She lifted her hand as if she might try to rub it, but stopped an inch short. "Sorry. I—My car. I was going to rent one, but they don't have any left. People going to Blaine to see the president, I guess. She—the woman in there—told me that's where you're going. Could you give me a lift?"

He might have said no. He had a lot on his mind, and you never knew about people. But it was a bleak spot, what with the cold and the bare trees. Then there was that sidebar article in the paper, and the photo: Dapper Devon Connor and his Godly Grin. It was enough to lay Mike low in the best of surroundings. "Sure, hop in," he said.

CHAPTER FIVE

Her name was Joy Leiffer, and they'd been together less than ten minutes when she told him she'd lied to him. "About the car," she said. "It's this thing I do with my expense account. Don't rent the car, but get reimbursed anyway. Oh, and my boss knows. It's no big deal."

Mike's hands tightened on the wheel. Another mean secret—with Randy that made two already today. But why sweat it? Apparently she did this all the time and probably admitted it to whoever gave her a lift. "What do you do?" he asked. "Your work?"

"Press corps." She waved her hand vaguely, as if it were too boring to talk about.

They dropped off the highway onto a secondary road and soon were deep in the mountains. The sky was socked in, grim gray clouds that hung in bands like weeping sedimentary rock. Still, it was beautiful here. The hills rolled up before them, tree-covered, round-topped, timeless. They crossed the Au Sable River, its water dancing in white flumes at the base of a rock-lined gorge. There were dozens of lakes and ponds, glassy smooth, reflecting the green curtain of hemlocks and firs that crowded the banks.

They passed through the upland villages—Jay and Lake Placid and Saranac Lake—and Mike recalled something his mother had once said: The North Country would be lovely if people didn't live there. The same was true of most cold-weather places. The streets were pocked and the sidewalks heaved by frost. The houses all seemed to have a decrepit porch or two hanging off the rear, their own little ghettos. Many places had signs in front: DEER DRESSED; HIDES TANNED; MAPLE SYRUP HERE!; YARD SALE. All as permanent and big as billboards.

Just past Saranac Lake they came upon another pond, pretty enough to be from a fairy tale. Joy said, "That's lovely. I wish my camera was charged up."

Mike stopped the car. "Mine will work." He got out and retrieved his Polaroid from the trunk.

Joy laughed. "Do they still make those things?"

"Sure. I keep it for—" He caught himself. "It's easy to use."

She snapped the picture, and they stood at the roadside waiting for it to develop. "Hey, you're shivering," she observed. She gazed up at him. Her smile was almost as pretty as her hair. "Let's get back in the car."

Mike didn't want to tell her about his scars, that the damage to his skin was the reason he couldn't tolerate the cold, so he only said he should have brought a heavier jacket.

Until then they'd spoken little, but the foray with the camera broke the logjam. "You must be from around here," Joy said. "You know the roads, and you knew what kind of tree that was back at the pond. Tamarack? I've never heard of it. And you tuned the radio right to that station. This oldies garbage—sorry, I think it's garbage—you like."

She was right about the music, an odd mix he felt at home with: Jackson Browne, Iron Butterfly, the Beatles, even somebody doing "The Girl from Ipanema." He motioned ahead of them. "We'll come to a small college in three or four miles. My father worked there."

"Do your parents still live around here?"

"No. They died a few years ago, in South Carolina. They lived there for a long time."

"What brings you back, then?"

They were passing a house with a row of signs. WHITE FOR ASSEMBLY. RE-ELECT JUDGE BYRNES. The last one said, in simple block letters, CONNOR - HOYT.

Joy stared at him. "Hold on. You're going to Blaine for

Connor's birthday thing. You're the right age. You *knew* her!"

He smiled. There was no reason to deny it. Tomorrow he'd be on stage with forty-two of Lynnie's other friends, for the whole world to see. "We grew up together. Same class in school."

"Were you close to her? It's a small town. Like her boyfriend or something?"

Mike had this all worked out. He'd told the story a thousand times. "My sister and Lynnie were best friends."

Joy clapped her hands. "Really? This is great! Your sister, is she coming, too?"

Mike paused a split second before he answered. "No, Jen's dead."

The news didn't slow Joy down any. "Oh, sorry. Do you keep in touch with her? Connor, I mean, not your sister."

Mike laughed. "I figured that. Lynnie sends me a Christmas card every year. I do the same." The politicians called it spin. Give the facts, but only the facts you want them to know.

Joy was almost bouncing in her seat. "'Lynnie.' You *called* her that. This is unbelievable. Answer some questions, will you? Was she the kind of kid you thought could grow up to be president?"

"Yes, she was," Mike said.

"Why?"

"She always seemed to know exactly what she wanted. There aren't many people like that—no hesitation, all forward motion."

"Like what? Give me an example."

He had a story ready for this, too. They'd flown a kite together once, one of those stunt jobs that could do loops and figure eights. Mike was content just to keep the thing up, fighting the fickle wind. Lynnie grabbed the controls from him. "C'mon, let's see what this baby can do!" Inside of a minute she was putting it through its paces, twisting, climbing, stalling, diving.

"So what happened?" Joy asked. "Did it crash?"

Mike fiddled with the key ring. "No," he lied. "It didn't crash."

"Mmmm," Joy said. A minute or so passed, and she switched off the radio. "How about her husband, Devon the Magnificent. What do you think of him?"

Mike shook his head. "I only know what I read in the papers."

"But the rumors—do you think he's gay?"

"No." The word landed between them like a dead fish. *Plop*.

The silence didn't last long. Joy was good at keeping a conversation going. "I met Devon once, in Calcutta at a conference on drug trafficking. I was tagging along, a free trip to India, really. One morning I went out to this little restaurant for breakfast. There was Devon, all by himself, no press, no Secret Service. I have no idea how he got there. I asked if I could sit down—just the two of us. 'Why not?' he said. We had this amazing platter of fruit. And there is *no one* who knows more about poppy farming in Afghanistan. He talked nonstop. I think we would have been there all day if the Secret Service hadn't come looking for him. And were they ever ticked off. Put me in a car and questioned me for half an hour: Who was I? What did Devon say to me?"

Mike had heard about this sort of thing—Devon sneaking off on his own, way off the reservation. It annoyed Lynnie as well as the Secret Service. "You liked him," he said, trying to keep the tightness out of his voice.

She stared thoughtfully at him. "He's not what you'd expect, that's for sure."

Mike decided to change the subject. He asked Joy if she'd heard there'd been a murder in Blaine. He was wondering if the national media had picked up on it.

"No. Who was it?"

He told her about Eve Tessmer: that she'd been the minister at his church (Lynnie's church, too); that she'd been the one who came up with the idea for Lynnie's birthday party.

"Small town," Joy said. "A murder will be a big thing." She thought this over for a few seconds before moving on. "You must have known her pretty well."

"Not really," Mike answered. "We went to church only because my mother thought we should. Sat in the last pew; weren't really involved." Then his lips turned up in a private smile. He remembered a Fourth of July picnic. He was only six or seven. Eve Tessmer had taught him to throw a Frisbee. Now, he wondered, where had Eve learned to throw it? Probably out practicing on her own. That's the kind of thing she'd do. "There was a service for her at the church today," he said.

"Too bad you couldn't get an earlier plane so you could be there. But then we'd have missed each other. Kismet, right?"

"Right." Mike smiled along with her.

Actually, he might have caught an earlier flight but decided against it. Mike would have gone to the memorial service. But go with Snooky Pascoe? That was a total nonstarter.

A hundred yards short of the ENTERING BLAINE sign, Mike pulled the car to the shoulder. The town was still hidden behind the crest of Knob Hill. Joy watched him stare into the distance. "Been a while?" she asked.

"Twenty-five years. I guess that qualifies as a while."

Twenty-five years, and Mike still could picture the town. Main Street hugged the north end of the lake; the residential areas fanned out up the hills. Smack in the middle of things was Town Hall. Nearer at hand, a half mile ahead, was the high school. Around the corner from the school, on Grove Street, was the home where he'd grown up—or what was left of it. That was where he'd been burned, and he hadn't been back since that day. He kneaded the steering wheel, feeling clammy inside his shirt. Blaine he could face, but not his home, not yet.

He turned onto a dirt road that led high along the ridge, thus avoiding the school and Grove Street, but giving them a good view of the town. They could see the three churches and the bank; the pulp mill and gravel quarry (both closed now); and there, on the far side of the lake, a new housing development and an even newer strip mall. "Look," he said. "Progress—a McDonald's!" In his nervousness he laughed too loudly. Joy indulged him by laughing, too.

Mike assumed she was staying at the Blaine Loj, the only decent hotel in town. It had been owned by Lynnie Connor's father. When he pulled into the parking lot, Joy looked at the big white facade and said, "Not this place for me. Where are you staying?"

He shot her a glance. "This thing with your expense account, do you—?"

"No, Mike, I don't share rooms so I can cheat on my expense account." She gave him a smile that could only be described as coy. "But it's nice that you asked, sort of."

As it turned out, they both had reservations at Galston's Motor Inn, a low weatherboard motel that faced the lake at the end of Main Street. The clerk was a teenage girl, absorbed in a television game show. She slid their keys across the counter and waved them toward their rooms. They were halfway there before they realized the two units were next to each other. "Kismet?" Joy said again. She was twitting him, a quick needle because of the expense account crack he'd made. He wasn't embarrassed, though. She was an easy person to be with. She opened her door and rattled her key, a cheery farewell. "Thanks for the lift!"

Mike stood for a while looking at the lake. The wind was up, and whitecaps rode the waves in long foamy bands. Seagulls hunkered around the pilings of the village dock. A man named Shirl Maxon used to give seaplane rides there. Maxon would be retired now, or dead.

Farther up Main Street, in the park, men were hammering the last boards in place on a large temporary stage. Behind the stage stood a maple tree that, miraculously, still bore a fiery display of autumn leaves. The lampposts along Main were wrapped in red-white-and-blue bunting, likewise the municipal trash cans. That was just like Blaine. No putting on airs here. A little extra color was all they needed to welcome home the most powerful person on earth. Mike checked his watch. Seventeen hours to go. He turned and went inside.

The first thing he noticed was the flashing light on the telephone. He dialed the front desk. Hang on a minute, the girl said. She hit a button and Archie Pascoe's voice barked out, "Michael, where the hell are you? I told you two thirty. You think this is some kind of—"

Mike set the phone down, sighing, "Wonderful."

From the window in the back of the room, Mike could see a row of Victorian houses, some bright and neat, some tumble-down, and, higher on the hill, a set of football goalposts at the high school. This time of year when he was a boy, he often sat in his bedroom, watching the older boys practice on that field. He stared a moment, lost in time, then snapped the curtains closed so he wouldn't have to look anymore.

He began to unpack and pulled open the closet door. The smell of balsam hit him like a slap. There was a small pillow on the closet floor, full of shredded balsam needles—North Country potpourri, a pungent odor like lemon and pepper and something sweet. Mike's mother had kept a balsam pillow in every room of their house. Smelling it now, he was back there again, the memory more vivid than any he'd had that day. The old kitchen. The living room. The stairs.

He stepped back from the closet. The light was still flashing on the phone. The girl at the desk had forgotten to turn it off. OK, if Snooky Pascoe wanted him, Snooky Pascoe could have him.

On the way out he grabbed the pillow from the closet, then stopped by the office. "Keep this out of my room, please," he said, tossing it on the counter.

The girl didn't lift her eyes from the television. "Sure." She tucked the pillow behind her. Her backside would smell like balsam for a week. Mike got in his car and headed for East Shore Drive.

CHAPTER SIX

When he was young, Mike often rode his bike along the lakeshore. He'd go to Ebbet's Bay to fish, or check out the beavers at Simmons Creek, or ride one of the trails into the woods. He knew every curve in the road, every house. From what he could see, Archie Pascoe's place hadn't changed any. It was set in the trees, tall and blocky, topped by a gambrel roof. Dusk was settling in, but the lights were out. Then, through a window, Mike saw a flicker, a candle or the flame of a match. He climbed the steps, and, before he knocked, Archie called, "Yuh, c'mon in."

It was so dark in the living room Mike wouldn't have known Archie was there if not for the glow of his cigarette. Mike thought of The Gulag at school. Archie kept the lights out there, his own version of purgatory. "How are you, Archie?" He didn't reply, so Mike added, "Sorry I missed Eve's service." Still no answer. "So why did you want to see me?"

Archie finally made a noise, a snort, maybe a short laugh. "You look good, Michael. Prosp'rous. Nice coat, an'way. An' drivin' a nice car. You a lawyer still?"

The way Archie was slurring, Mike wondered if he was ill. His eyes were adjusting, but all he could make out was the murky form of the chair Archie sat in. "Yeah, still a lawyer. You mind if I turn on a light?" He hit the switch before Archie could say no. Mike blinked, startled by what he saw.

Archie had a wadded handkerchief in his lap, and his nose was bright red from weeping. There were eight open beer cans on the floor. OK, he'd just come from a funeral. Getting drunk, crying a little—that was normal enough. It was Archie's size that surprised Mike. He'd always been big, with a thick chest and hefty gut. But the man Mike saw was nothing like that. He was grossly fat, round and buttery. He must have guessed what Mike was thinking, because he said, "Yuh, iss me." This would have been pathetic, except for Archie's eyes, small black dots, unfocused now but still hard looking. Mike remembered those eyes. Like the eyes of a weasel.

Archie stood up and jammed the cigarette into the corner of his mouth. "Need some coffee." He marched toward the back of the house. "You stay put," he called over his shoulder. "Sit down or somethin'." Mike followed anyway.

The kitchen was spotless. There were silk flowers in a basket on the refrigerator. On a shelf over the stove stood an impressive spice rack with pewter containers, and two large crockery jars labeled "Wine" and "Oil."

Archie struck a match and lit one of the burners. The flame shot high before settling down. Mike felt a tightening in his chest, the same as he did whenever he was around fire. Archie's eyes darted over to him. He gave a dark smile. "So . . . Torch," he said.

In school, Mike had steered clear of Archie and The Gulag, except for one time. He and some friends were fooling around, unsupervised, in the chemistry lab. Using a piece of plastic, string, and a Bunsen burner, they made a tiny hot air balloon. Things got out of control and a tile in the ceiling got scorched. Mike was the only one to confess. When Archie got him alone, he came up with that nickname—Torch—and hammered at him with it, hoping to bait Mike into giving him the names of the others who'd been in on the prank. Mike wouldn't tell and had taken the punishment alone. *Torch.* Prophetic, as it turned out, because it was only two months later that Mike's house caught fire and he ended up burned over sixty percent of his body.

"Chem lab," Mike said. "You remember that?"

"Sure do. Your house, too. Seems you healed pretty well."

It had been a long day, and Mike was suddenly weary to the bone. "Archie, what did you want to talk to me about?"

Archie took an old-style percolator out and added water and coffee and put it on the burner. Then he sat down at the table. His hands seemed naturally to rest on his belly, as if gauging its size, or simply holding it in place. "Eve," he said. "I was—" Normally he was quick when he talked, one word rattling after another, but the beer had left him fuddle-headed. "I wondered about your phone number. Eve had it."

"For Lynnie's party," Mike said. "Eve mailed me a letter with a form. I sent the form back, with my phone number."

Archie's weasel eyes were starting to focus, sparkling a bit. "And she had your office number, too, and your cell phone. How'd she get those?"

Mike said, "My office number she could get from one of the lawyer's directories, or the Internet, or directory assistance. I don't know about the cell number. That's unlisted. What difference does it make? Didn't she have phone numbers for all the guests for the party?"

"She did," Archie said, "except she kept yours separate—special-like. I'm trying to figure out why that was."

"What do you mean 'special-like'?"

"Tell you what," Archie said, rubbing his forehead. "Get some cups for the coffee, OK?"

There were mugs hung on pegs next to the stove. Mike went over, keeping his distance from the lit burner. "What do you mean 'special-like'?" he repeated.

"Never you mind," Archie muttered. Then he raised his voice. "Hey, silly, not that one. That's chipped. The green one lower down."

Mike shot him a look. He should have kept his eyes on what he was doing. The mug hit the crock labeled "Wine," which toppled over, spilling viscous yellow liquid. Some splashed on the burner, sizzled, and burst into flames. The fire raced backward across the puddle.

All so fast.

Mike knew he should do something. He could turn on the tap at the sink, hose down the counter. He couldn't move.

Archie was roaring, *"Jesus! Jesus!"* He tossed Mike aside—halfway across the room—then reached into a cupboard for a bag of flour, which he dumped on the flames. Oblivious of the heat, he spread it around, patting until the last spark was out.

Archie spun around, red-faced and panting, but he was standing taller than before, feet apart, a tower of a man. He was cold sober now. *"Moron!"*

Mike's stomach was churning. He wanted to throw up.

"Wha'd'ya tryin' to do?" Archie squalled. "Flambé your own dick?"

"No," Mike said. "Tried that when I was a kid. No good." He tried to smile, but he was too sick. He was furious with himself, too. Dammit, he'd argued cases before the U.S. Supreme Court. He'd run a kayak on the Yough River in Maryland, class V rapids. He'd once, on a bet with Randy Barchic, sailed a boat solo from Charleston to Bermuda. But bring him back to Blaine, show him a little kitchen fire, and he quailed and moaned like Scrooge with the Ghost of Christmas Future. Yes, he actually had moaned.

"What . . ." Mike's eyes were still riveted on the countertop. "What was that stuff?"

"Bacon grease and applejack—apple brandy. I make— I *made* a decent candied yam with that." Archie stared at the smoke hanging by the ceiling. "Well, shit," he said. And for good measure he added one more, "Jesus."

Mike was finally able to turn away. "I'm sorry. I should have been more careful." Archie glared at him. "I'm *sorry*," Mike repeated defiantly.

"Right," Archie grumbled. He took a spatula out and began scraping the sludge from the counter. Mike found a broom and dustpan in the pantry and swept the mess off the floor. Archie uncovered a dark blister on the Formica, but the stove and sink were undamaged.

About then they heard the crunch of car tires on gravel. Lights flashed across the window. Archie glanced outside before heading for the living room. "Injuns, Michael," he said, dusting flour from his hands. "Maybe you'd better circle the wagons."

Mike stepped over to the window. A man dressed in a tight-fitting uniform was climbing out of a white car labeled CHIEF OF POLICE. Mike recognized him: Billy White, one of his old baseball teammates. Billy hadn't always lived in Blaine. He was raised through the seventh grade in Hogansburg, on the St. Regis Mohawk Indian Reservation near the Canadian border. Billy wasn't an Indian. His father happened to run a gas station there. Still, to people in the North Country, if you were born in Hogansburg, you were a Mohawk. All through high school he was called Indian Billy. Coming through the darkness from his police cruiser, he looked the same as Mike remembered, short and aggressive, his body like a pit bull's, the torso built up, the legs trailing behind, skinny and out of proportion.

In the car, Mike caught a glimpse of movement, a passenger. He couldn't tell if it was a man or a woman. Whoever it was waved. Mike waved back, tentatively, and went out to the living room to find out what this was all about.

Archie and Billy White were standing on the porch. Billy was talking. "BLT, you say?" He sniffed. "Hell, old man, smells like you got a whole *pig* cookin' in there." He saw Mike and winked. "Been into the beer, too, I'll bet. Maybe I'll have to run you in. Need a permit to have a luau."

"Fuck you, Billy," Archie said.

"And thank-ye kindly," Billy replied. He held out his hand. "Mike, good seein' ya. Archie told me you'd be out this way tonight."

Mike looked at them both. Archie gazed blankly at him while Billy pushed his officer's cap to the back of his head. He should have left it alone. He'd recently gotten a hair transplant. That, or he had the oddest set of cornrows Mike had ever seen. Billy said, "So, can we go inside?"

"Nope," Archie said. "Talk out here."

Billy screwed his face up, as if he were in pain. "All right. Mike, did he tell you about the phone numbers? The ones Eve Tessmer had?"

"Yes," Mike said. "Eve had my phone numbers. I don't see what—"

"It's not that she *had* your numbers," Billy said. "It's *where* she had them."

Mike glanced at Archie again. "A special place, he told me."

"Right," Billy said. He sneaked a finger under his hatband and scratched his new hair. "She was found by Mary Hodges. Cleaning lady—you know her? No? Doesn't matter. Eve was shot once in the head. In bed. She was nude. Up to that point, not that much out of the ordinary for your run-of-the-mill rape or robbery or whatever. Not that she was raped, by the way. She wasn't. Anyway, she had something with her. A piece of paper, beside her bed. Even had a little of her blood on it. And what else do you think was on that paper?"

"My phone numbers," Mike said, finally catching on.

"Right," Billy said. "The only thing I can figure is that Eve was trying to get in touch with you. Did she call you that night, Mike? That'd be on Sunday."

"No. The last time I talked to her was over a week ago. Was it her handwriting on the note?"

"Yeah, we had the BCI run it through the crime lab in Albany. Eve's handwriting, all right." Billy shook his head slowly. "So I guess we're still stumped. Arch, look, I tried." Then, in a stagy aside to Mike, he said, "Archie doesn't think we're doing our jobs too well on this one." He backed down the steps. "Hey, Mike, you see that game Sunday night? The ninth inning the Cubs had?"

"I was working. Missed the whole thing."

"Working on Sunday? Too bad. Great game. You were at your office, then, so if Eve called—"

"No." Mike came forward to the edge of the porch. "I was at home."

"Oh? Must be tough, trying to get work done with the wife and kiddies underfoot."

"No wife, no kids, Billy. I live alone."

Billy gave a slow smile. "Somehow I expected you wouldn't be married. So, you were alone on Sunday?"

Mike's voice became flat. "Right. Alone. All the way down in Florida."

"Hey, don't get mad. You know me—" Billy dropped into his old catcher's stance, pointing to an imaginary first, second, third. "Coverin' all the bases." He stood up again. "Florida, huh? Neat place. Beach babes. Mickey Mouse. Last month I had to go down there, delivering some evidence in a car-theft case. Jacksonville. Seventeen hours and I was home again. It's a mighty small world. Well, look, I've taken enough of your evening." He started toward his car. "You're staying at Galston's, right?" He waited for Mike to say he was. "Good, we can talk again tomorrow, need be."

The passenger—Mike still couldn't see if it was a man or woman—popped the door open for him. Once he had the engine running, Billy rolled down his window. "You two gents be careful with that pig!" He tromped on the accelerator, and the car rumbled backward to the road, spewing gravel along the way.

"Blaine's finest," Archie said. He spat into the darkness.

"You had him come out here to talk to me?" Mike said.

"Yuh, that I did," Archie replied.

"You could have told me, you know." Then Mike shrugged it off and reached for the door. "Come on, let's finish cleaning up."

"No." Archie held him by the wrist. "You stay the hell away from my kitchen."

"I told you I was sorry. It was an accident."

"Yeah, maybe you have too many accidents." Mike shook his arm free and squared up to him. Archie was first to look away. "Hell with it," he said. A moth fluttered between them, then up, circling the porch light. "Right," Archie said, his voice quieter. His eyes followed the moth. "There's something I want to show you, over at Eve's place."

"No, I've had enough. I'm going back to town and get something to eat, then to bed."

Archie's eyes snapped down on him, cold, black marbles. Mike recognized that look and decided he might as well give in. If he didn't, Archie was likely to grab him and try to drag him to Eve's house. Mike bowed at the waist. "After you, then."

In the driveway, Archie stopped to kick gravel back into the ruts Billy's car had made. "Dumb fucking Indian," he muttered.

CHAPTER SEVEN

"Thanks for not telling Billy about the fire," Mike said to Archie. "He'd have given me untold grief." They were walking toward Eve's house. Water trickled softly in the ditch at the verge of the road.

"Why tell him any . . . thing?" Archie said. They were mounting a rise, and he was wheezing. "Clayheaded yo-yo."

"There's an expression I haven't heard in a while," Mike said. Clayhead was the Mohawk term for a fool. "What's he doing messing with a murder investigation, anyway? The state police should be handling it."

"Politics," Archie said. He stopped and gulped some air. "Billy's running for the state legislature. Look good solving the case, he figures. Get a few extra votes."

"So he's the one. White for Assembly—I saw a poster in a yard in Saranac."

"That's him," Archie said. They started walking again. "Like you say, the BCI's in charge of the case. Bureau of Chickenshit Investigation." Mike smiled. The Bureau of *Criminal* Investigation was the investigatory branch of the New York State Police. Archie continued, "The day they found her, the BCI sent out a bunch of men. Five, six troopers, three plainclothes. The one in charge was something. Up from Albany, tall guy with a squeaky voice, shaved head. Had a big jar of gherkins with him. Spent the whole day wandering here and there, stuffing sweet pickles in his face. He seemed smart enough when I talked to him. He even sent men out to make plastic casts of the tire tracks in the road. That was Monday. Then Tuesday—yesterday—he disappears, hauls ass back to Albany. Had enough of the boonies, I guess. Billy tells me they haven't got any leads. Nothing except your phone numbers."

"My phone numbers aren't a lead," Mike put in firmly. They walked in silence for a moment. "Running for office doesn't seem like Billy's sort of thing. Why's he doing it?"

"He gives the usual bullshit reasons—good of the community and all. I think it's simpler than that. He doesn't like police work. Be a lot easier if he'd quit being chief and run the Loj full time."

"The Loj?"

"Blaine Loj. Billy and his wife bought it from Lynnie after her father died."

"I didn't know that," Mike said. He thought about the zen of small towns. Lynnie connected to her father; her father connected to the Loj; the Loj connected to Billy. Everything connected to everything.

They could see Eve's place now. Thirty years ago, she had hired Mike to shovel her driveway. The going rate was ten dollars a month and all the hot chocolate he could drink. She'd only had him the one winter, moving on to someone else the next year. Spread the work around, she'd said. Give everybody a chance. She was a rare bird, a North Country socialist. The driveway looked a lot shorter now than it had on those snowy mornings of his boyhood.

In the front yard were three white pines, so huge that the house—a simple postwar-era bungalow—seemed hidden beneath them. Around the trees was a strip of orange police tape. There was more tape crisscrossing the door. The jack-o'-lanterns had been set out of the way in a teetering pile.

Mike expected they would look around the outside, maybe peek in through the windows, but Archie climbed straight up the steps and slapped the tape aside. Mike decided not to tell him to be careful. If anyone checked, they'd find Archie's fingerprints, not his. "Eve only had one relative, an aunt in Alabama," Archie said. He reached out beyond the limit of the steps and pulled a key from a crack in the clapboards. "She's nearly ninety, too sick to come for the service today."

As he flicked on the inside light, he motioned Mike through the porch and the parlor. The place was cold and damp, like a cave. Mike rounded the corner, into the kitchen. A distant memory hit him, and he stopped in midstride. Eve kept her cat-litter box there, beside the refrigerator. He'd stepped in it two or three times, coming in after shoveling her driveway. He looked down and there it was, a waiting land mine.

"She still had her cats?" Mike said.

Archie was staring at him. "Only one left. Mary Hodges took it." He sat down at the kitchen table. "You mentioned Eve called you. What did she want to talk about?"

Mike sat across from him. "The party. She called maybe a half dozen times. You know, she had that This-Is-Your-Life theme. She was having trouble getting the guests lined up, especially one from Arizona. So she—"

"Arizona?" Archie said. He sat forward, his interest piqued. He seemed to have forgotten all about showing Mike something in the house.

"That's right." Mike wasn't sure how much Archie knew of Lynnie's background, so he filled him in. "Lynnie was born there, a place called the CC Ranch, near the Mexican border. Her mother died a year later, and her father pulled up stakes and moved here. Most of his family was in England, but he had a cousin near Schenectady. That's why he chose this part of the country. After he moved, he sold the ranch off in pieces, but he kept the house and barn and pond, the whole central area. The land had been in Lynnie's mother's family for generations. Every summer Lynnie and her father went out to visit. In the fifth grade, my sister and I got to be good friends with Lynnie. Her dad invited us to Arizona with them, four summers in a row, a month each time. Eve remembered those trips—we were gone from church, so she knew what we were up to—and that's what she wanted to talk about, to see if I knew anyone she could look up and invite to Lynnie's party, somebody who'd been there the year Lynnie was born."

"Did you give her any names?" Archie asked.

"A few. One in particular. The ranch foreman, Oscar Martinez. He lived there, looked after things for them. I told Eve about him, but she never had any luck tracking him down."

"What about medical people?" Archie said. "That was the tack Eve was working. She figured the family had to have a doctor somewhere. Might still be alive."

"She mentioned that to me, but I didn't know anything that would help her."

"You think Eve could have asked Lynnie about any of this?" Archie said. "From something Eve told me, I think they talked. Not a staffer, but Lynnie herself. Lynnie knows about the party—just not the This-Is-Your-Life theme, all the guests Eve invited."

Mike twitched the zipper on his coat. "I don't know," he said. "They might have talked." But he did know. A few weeks earlier, when he and Lynnie had their monthly phone conversation, Lynnie had mentioned she'd had a call from Eve Tessmer. "That sweet thing," Lynnie called her. But if he told Archie, he'd have to explain how he knew.

The slippery sparkle had returned to Archie's eyes. "Bein' assistant principal, I learned a few things. Some people fidget when they lie. Some get real still, like they're afraid if they move they'll give something away." He looked straight at Mike. "I'd say you're a fidgeter."

They passed a few seconds staring at one another. It seemed to Mike that the whole evening had been heading in this direction, Archie trying to trap him somehow. But what should he expect? Here was a man who used to hide in the janitor's closets in the restrooms at school so he could catch boys smoking. Mike laughed harshly and stood up. "I guess I'll take a look at where it happened."

"Don't need to," Archie grumbled. Mike went anyway, just to get away from him. It didn't work. Archie followed with slow, reluctant steps.

The hall lamp was enough for them to see by, so they left the bedroom light off. The mattress was gone, and there was a bloodstain on the wall next to the bed frame, a ragged triangle the color of rust. There were a few other spots on the floor. Everything else seemed normal. Even the alarm clock was running, the alarm set to go off at 6:00 A.M. Mike hit the button to turn it off. He used his knuckle, thinking, *no fingerprints*.

"Not a rape," Mike said, "but Billy mentioned she was nude. Did he have any idea why?"

"That's the first he's said anything about it," Archie replied. He was distracted, picking at the paint on the door frame. "I don't know. Some people sleep that way."

A noise interrupted him, and they both looked up. It was a bat, flitting out from behind the door. "Damn things get in from the attic," Archie said. His voice was tight. In the corner Eve had a sewing table, and on it was a yardstick. Archie took the stick and swung at the ceiling. "Shouldn't be in here, ugly little monsters." The bat was too quick, but Archie kept flailing, smacking the wall, the bed, the chest of drawers. He hit the mirror and it cracked straight down the middle. "God*damned* little monsters." Archie swung harder, crazily; the bat zipped around, always out of reach.

Mike had retreated to the hall, but now he stepped in and grabbed Archie by the arm. "Leave it. Eve wouldn't have cared. Come on. Let's get out of here."

Mike shut the lights off as they moved through the house. On the steps, they stopped so Archie could lock up. His breathing was labored again. He rubbed his left shoulder, then pulled out his vial of pills and popped one under his tongue. Mike was eying him. "Only angina,"

Archie panted. "Be right . . . in a jiff." He put the key back in its hiding place. "We can walk now." They turned away, leaving the police tape in tatters.

Mike's rental car was parked in Archie's driveway, and they made it all the way there before either of them spoke. Mike would have simply told him good night and driven away, but something Archie had said was bothering him. "You wanted to know if Lynnie had talked to Eve. What makes you think that would be important?"

Archie was at the steps, one foot up, one foot down. "Something I saw the night she was killed—a car out in the road."

"That explains why the BCI took tire impressions. How does that tie in with Lynnie?"

Archie climbed to the porch. "I didn't see the numbers, but the car had U.S. government license plates."

"So?" Mike said.

"So only this: There's got to be a reason Eve was killed. I don't know what yet, but that government car was in on it. And when I start thinking about the government, I start thinking about Lynnie."

Mike couldn't hold back a laugh. "If it had been one of those joke license plates they sell in Lake Placid, that say 'North Pole, USA,' you'd think it was Santa Claus who killed her?"

Archie stood there, backlit by the porch lamp, as sturdy as the pine trees in Eve Tessmer's yard. "I know what I saw, Michael, that's all." He looked at his wristwatch. "Game's gonna start soon. Want to come in and watch?"

"No, thanks," Mike replied. He was halfway into his car when he decided to ask the question that was still nagging him. "You took me to Eve's place to show me something. What was it?"

Archie made that same snorting sound he'd made when Mike arrived, maybe a laugh, maybe not. "Meow," he said. He turned and went inside.

CHAPTER EIGHT

"Meow," Mike muttered as he drove away. It was a damn trap. Archie had taken him to Eve's place to see if he'd step in the cat-litter box. Maybe her killer had stepped in it. If Mike did the same, that would show he was either a slow learner or not the one who murdered her. And he'd danced around it as gracefully as Fred Astaire.

Mike shook his head, trying to imagine what was going on behind those weasel eyes of Archie's. Some conspiracy theory—Lynnie and Mike and a U.S. government car. It was so ridiculous Mike wanted to laugh, but he remembered Archie careening around Eve's bedroom with the yardstick. So much pent-up anger could do a lot of damage.

Mike came to the intersection with Main Street and was surprised to see a long line of cars trickling down Knob Hill. People coming to see Lynnie. By morning the town would be bursting at the seams. The traffic light changed, bringing the parade to a halt. He made the turn and rolled past the park. The workers had erected a sign over the stage: BLAINE WELCOMES THE NORTH COUNTRY'S FIRST LADY!

First Lady. People started calling Lynnie that after she won her senate seat in Virginia, that state's first woman U.S. senator. "First Lady Senator" was shortened to "First Lady," as if, one way or another, she were destined for the White House. A cheeky reporter had asked her husband what that meant to him. If she was First Lady, did that make him president, around the house at least? Devon, with his usual vague aplomb, had replied, "It might mean Lynnie is man enough for both jobs." A picture floated up in Mike's mind, flickering like an old newsreel: Devon working in deepest Africa, tending some orphan boy's skinned knee, then patting the tyke on the rump and sending him off to play.

Devon again. The thought of him thoroughly curdled Mike's already sour mood. He pulled into the parking lot at Galston's, and immediately checked the window of Joy Leiffer's room. The light was on.

He decided to ask her to dinner. She'd probably already eaten but might come along for some friendly conversation. He knocked; no one answered. Kismet, Joy had called it. She was joking, but deep down Mike believed in fate. What burn survivor didn't? If an evening with Joy wasn't in the cards, he'd make do with his own company.

He unlocked the door to his room, and a slip of motel stationery fell from where it was wedged behind the jam. He read it standing on the threshold.

> *I'm at Ralph's Tavern across the street.*
> *—Joy*

Mike smiled. She was a smart woman; she knew what he'd think. *Was there really joy at Ralph's Tavern?*

Ralph's was a big place, half bar and half restaurant. The inside was done up like a woodsman's lodge, with outdoor gear on the walls and a phalanx of stuffed animals mounted on pedestals, from bear to bobcat, leopard to lynx. It was noisy, too, jammed with middle-aged men in wrinkled sport coats; a few women with oily hair, jeans, and sweaters. Reporters, Mike thought. No one else on earth could look so cynical and weary, even when drunk.

Joy sat alone at a table in the corner of the bar, like Wild Bill Hickok, back to the wall, ready to repel attackers. She saw Mike and gave him a big wave. As he approached, her expression became stern. "You lied to me."

"What?"

"*You* are a hero." She almost shouted it.

Embarrassed, Mike looked around. The group at the next table was staring. "What are you talking about?"

"Have you eaten yet?" she asked. When he shook his head she took him by the arm and led him into the dining room.

The booth she chose was again in the corner, and within seconds a young waiter arrived and tossed down two menus. Without opening hers Joy said she wanted pasta, tortellini with white sauce if they had it, spinach tortellini. Yes, said the waiter, no problem. And a glass of the house white wine, she added. Mike asked for the same thing, but beer instead of wine. The young man gathered up the menus and left.

Joy was rummaging in her pocketbook. She shrugged, apparently not finding what she was looking for. "*You* are Michael Stanbridge."

"Right. We did the introductions earlier."

She raised a finger to his throat, to the purple tentacle of scar tissue. "No, *the* Michael Stanbridge."

Now he understood. "Yes. What, you remembered some old newspaper article?"

"All of them. I've read every single article on you, I'll bet. My job, you know. But I didn't make the connection until an hour ago." She was leaning forward, bubbling with energy. "You saved Lynnie Connor's life."

"Yes, I did," Mike replied simply. "A long, long time ago."

"The national press—back when Garrett picked her as his running mate—made out like you weren't even hurt. It was this special thing that happened to Connor when she was a kid, one of those life-changing events. *She* got burned; she healed; she learned some mystic lesson about life. Then I came up here and read the articles in the local papers and—"

"From way back then?" Mike asked.

Joy waved her hand, cutting off that line of discussion. "Research. Background stuff. But you were really hurt.

You almost died. What were you, seventeen? Tell me about it."

"It was a week before my eighteenth birthday." Mike paused, holding a quick debate in his mind. It was natural that she'd ask. Still, this was something he didn't feel comfortable talking about. He looked out the window at the black expanse of the lake. "If you've read the articles, you know all there is to know."

His parents had gone to Plattsburgh that day, to a Harlem Globetrotters game, and they couldn't get home because of an unexpected snowstorm. Lynnie came over in the afternoon to see Mike's sister, Jen—to see Mike, too. They played cards, made dinner. With all the snow, Lynnie decided to stay the night. Her father didn't mind.

The power went out about midnight, and Mike lit a fire in the fireplace. They went to bed not long after—the girls to Jen's room, Mike to his own. Around two o'clock, a roaring sound woke him up. The chimney had caught fire, and the fire had broken through to the walls. He made his way to his sister's room. There was a lot of smoke at that end of the house, and the two girls were groggy. They wouldn't wake up. He grabbed Lynnie and got her out, but Jen . . .

"You and Jen were twins," Joy said.

Mike kept staring out the window. "That's right. You wouldn't have known it to look at us, though, or talk to us. We were pretty different."

"Still, it must have been bad, losing her like that."

His head snapped around so fast his whole body twitched. "What? Oh. I thought you said something else. Yes, it was . . . bad."

"Tell me about her. What was she like?"

"Quiet. She studied hard. Wanted to be an astronomer. Already had her college and grad school picked out. She was . . ." Words seemed to escape him. "My sister, that's all."

Joy laid her hand on top of his, then jerked back, startled. This had happened before to Mike, with almost every woman he'd ever been with. His hand had been burned that night, but there was no visible scar, only a change in texture so it felt cold and smooth, like plastic. It was one of the mysteries of skin grafting. Every spot healed with its own character. Joy recovered better than most. She took his hand again, rubbing her palm over it. "I'm sorry," she murmured.

The waiter arrived with their food—salad, bread, drinks, pasta—everything at once. For several minutes they ate in silence.

"There was an inquest," Joy said, looking down at her plate. "I didn't understand that. It was a chimney fire, an accident. Pretty obvious, right?"

"They had their reasons," Mike said. The reason was the fire in the chem lab at school. Mike was a known fire-bug. Had he set the fire at home on purpose? The inquest determined it was an accident, but only after putting his parents through a week of humiliation. "I didn't even know it was going on. I was still in the hospital at the time."

Joy reached for her wineglass but didn't take a drink. "How did it feel, coming back here after that?"

"I never came back. From the hospital I went on to physical therapy, all of it in Syracuse. Then straight to college."

Joy rubbed his hand again. "You kept in touch with Lynnie, didn't you? I mean, a couple of kids go through something like that, they have to be close later."

Mike poked at his salad with his fork. "It was years before I saw Lynnie again."

"Really? I imagined a big scene: you getting out of the hospital, and she's there to meet you; a big kiss." Mike's hand stiffened, and Joy gently pulled free. "You walk off into the sunset together, a Hollywood ending."

"Nothing like that," Mike said. He set his fork down, through eating.

Joy took a sip of her wine. "Did you see the news to-day about Devon?" Mike shook his head. "He was coming back from Africa, talking to the reporters on the plane. He said he was disappointed with the UN position on African refugees. He wants a new management team, from the secretary-general on down. Before he landed, there were denials from the State Department, the White House. I guess he takes this 'First Gentleman' thing seriously."

Mike didn't smile, and she said, "Talking about him makes you nervous, doesn't it?"

"Not really," he said.

"OK." Her hand returned, one fingertip caressing his knuckles. "It must be something else then." Her look was direct, a little mischievous. "So, Mike Stanbridge, what's your story?" She touched his ring finger, the empty spot there. "Married? Have a girlfriend?"

He couldn't help but smile now. "And why would you ask that?"

Her eyes danced. "Do you like baseball? We could catch the end of the game."

Mike looked into the bar, at the big-screen TV.

Joy shook her head. "Uh-uh." She nodded toward the street and their motel.

Mike signaled the waiter. "We're ready for the check."

A few minutes later, as they crossed the street, she took his arm. "A real hero," she said softly. He knew it was only a joke, but it made him smile.

She reached for her key first; they would use her room. Standing behind her, Mike found himself staring at the yellow halo of her hair. Then he heard a noise, a spurt of squeaky speech. Joy's hand was in her purse. "My pager," she said, too quickly.

Mike stepped up beside her. "Really? It works way out here in the sticks?"

"Sure." Again her voice was too quick.

He reached into her purse. "Mike, what are you doing?"

He pulled her hand out. She was holding a recorder, an expensive digital model, complete with touch screen.

"You had this on while we were eating?"

"Mike—"

"Who are you?"

"Mike, you're hurting me."

"Who *are* you?"

"Mike, I—*Ow.* Please. Look, OK. Let go." He squeezed harder, enough to bring tears to her eyes. "OK, I'm not a reporter. I'm with the campaign."

"Lynnie? No—Bryce. You work for Carl Bryce."

"Opposition research for his campaign. I—" She wiped the wetness from her eyes. Then the words tumbled out. "It's got nothing to do with you. It's a job, that's all. And Connor—I like her. I wanted to work for her, but she's got the A-Team. First class all the way. I didn't have enough experience. So I'm with Bryce. His people are desperate. I follow Connor around, dig into her past, check out everything she does. I didn't really connect you to her until tonight, when I was going over some old notes. I didn't mean to pry. It's only my job."

Mike wasn't squeezing so hard now, and Joy moved closer, pressing against his side. "The recorder was mean, I know. But I turned it off just now, so we'd be alone. See? *See?*"

He saw that the touch screen was dark. He pulled it out of her hand, hefted it, and strode into the parking lot. He'd been a fair left fielder for the Blaine Central High team, and, though his body wasn't anything like it had been then, he still had a good arm. He took a step and whipped it, high and long. It skipped off the roof of Ralph's Tavern and into the field of thistles beyond. He kept on walking, across the lot to his car.

Joy stood in the doorway to her room. He couldn't tell if she was crying, but her voice sounded as if she were. "*You creep,*" she screamed. "*You lousy creep!*" He drove away, wishing he had plugs to put in his ears.

CHAPTER NINE

That's something new, Mike thought, drumming his fingers on the steering wheel. He'd talked to lots of people about Lynnie before, but no one had ever tried to seduce him to get information. Seduce? That probably wasn't fair. Joy had only invited him to watch the baseball game. And she had turned off the recorder. Still, he couldn't help being furious. Something she'd said really stung him: "It must have been tough, losing her like that." What he heard was "choosing." *Choosing* her like that. A thousand nights since the fire he'd lain awake thinking that. Two girls; choose one. Lynnie lives; Jen dies.

That was why he'd driven here, to the Blaine high school, to think about Jen. He was parked by the football field. In the distance, beyond the far end zone, he could see a chain-link fence and, past that, a shadowy spot, a hole in the ground where his home had stood. He'd inherited the lot from his parents; like them, he couldn't bring himself to sell. Mike tried hard to conjure up Jen's image, to remember her voice. They'd played together here, walked home from school together almost every afternoon. There had to be some memory. Nothing came. He looked away and his thoughts veered off—to Lynnie. Lynnie was in Boston tonight, staying in one of the big hotels. He couldn't recall the name. He pictured her there. She hated hotel beds, often pulled the blankets off and curled up on the floor.

Mike had told Joy the truth when he said he hadn't seen Lynnie for a long time after the fire. It was twelve years, almost to the day. Early on, while he was in the hospital and in physical therapy, he refused all contact with people from Blaine—even Lynnie. *Especially* Lynnie. Skin graft by skin graft, he was building a new body;

so he would build a new life. That was childish thinking, but he was only a child then. Forgetting Blaine rapidly hardened into a habit. The town was so far in the past it almost didn't exist for him anymore.

Still, through his years in college and law school, his mother kept him up on Lynnie's progress—and it was something. She was the first woman elected president of her college student assembly. On graduating, she joined the Navy. That was a surprise to everyone. It was the 1980s; the military was a backwater, still suffering from the shadow of Vietnam. Lynnie decided on flight school. As Mike would have guessed, she was a natural pilot, taking on everything they threw at her and more. She had a couple of shipboard tours; she spent the first Gulf War humping C-130 transport planes into Saudi Arabia and running reconnaissance flights over Iraq. Every fitness report was more glowing than the last. There seemed to be no limit to how high she could go.

Mike's mother filled him in on all this whenever she came to visit. (He wouldn't go back to the North Country, no matter how hard his parents tried to convince him.) He listened politely, his manner offhanded. "Flying jets now, huh? Back in the Middle East? How's her father doing?"

Then one Thanksgiving when his parents were visiting in Miami, Mike's mother showed him a newspaper clipping. Lynnie was getting married, it said, to a Navy chaplain. There was a picture of them, both in uniform, Devon's eyes round and blank, the epitome of a space cadet. Mike only glanced at it before shoving it back across the table. "Great, Mom. Here, you keep it." She folded it into her purse. "Connor, his name is. He's a Methodist, just like—" Mike shook his head. "Let's not talk about her anymore, OK?" His mother didn't understand, but, as always, she went along. From then until she died, she said nothing more about Lynnie.

Mike lost thirteen months to his burns, to the work of

healing. Following that, his own career moved along pretty much according to plan. He graduated from college with honors and went on to law school at Columbia. From there he signed on with Randy Barchic's firm in Miami. It was a natural fit. Mike liked Randy from the minute he met him, and he wanted to practice maritime law. Mike worked hard, got good cases, moved up the ladder.

One day he got a call from a civilian employee of the Navy. They were planning a seminar on ship charter contracts. Could Mike come and speak? He checked his calendar, found he had a meeting already scheduled that day. He scratched a line across the page and told the Navy man, yes, he could fit it in. How different his life might have been if he'd said no.

The seminar was in Washington, and Mike arrived at the last minute because his plane had been held up by bad weather. He was sweaty and frazzled, and was irritated when, as he began to introduce himself to the other members of the speaking panel, someone tapped him on the shoulder. He turned and saw Lynnie and nearly fell backward over his chair. Lynnie had been a good-looking girl. Cute, people called her, until she developed to the point where cute wasn't adequate. Now she was stunning. And confident, too. Seeing his distress, she took his hand (which lay limply at his side) and shook it. "Mikey, wonderful to see you." She leaned close, her hair brushing his cheek. "Let's have lunch." He just nodded dumbly.

To this day, parked by the Blaine high school football field, he couldn't remember anything about the talk he gave. He did recall exactly where Lynnie sat—third row, fourth seat from the end. At the lunch break, she came to collect him, and they went out into the noontime bustle of Washington. They walked up K Street into Georgetown. She told him that their running into each other wasn't an accident. She'd recently been transferred to the Pentagon from San Diego. The day she arrived, she saw an announcement about the seminar. Mike was listed as one of the speakers. She took the announcement to her boss, and, though it had nothing to do with her job, convinced him to let her attend.

Lynnie picked the restaurant, a Cuban place with anti-Castro posters on the walls. Mostly they talked about politics. Mike was surprised by how much she knew, all the nuances. Not once did they mention Devon. Between them he was already taboo. Lynnie was careful in her speech, and sometimes she turned away, forming a sentence in her mind before she spoke. Mike stared at her then. She was everything she'd been as a girl but more so, her lips fuller, her cheekbones more pronounced, her neck and hands longer and more graceful. They decided to play hooky from the seminar, spend the afternoon together.

It was when they left the restaurant that it happened, though it could have come at any time. As they stepped onto the sidewalk, a man jostled Lynnie. Mike grabbed her to keep her from falling. Then slowly he put his other arm around her. For a half minute they stood like that, studying each other's faces. This was a new experience, their first hug. Back in Blaine, there had been a hefty spark between them, but they never acted on it. Instead they circled and circled, like wrestlers afraid to go for the clinch. Now, finally with a chance to hold her, a tumult of questions flooded Mike's mind. Why had he been so eager to speak at this seminar? Because it was Navy, and, in the back of his mind, he connected that with Lynnie? Why had he gone into maritime law in the first place? He hadn't even set foot on an ocean-going boat until he was twenty-three. And why was it that every woman he'd ever dated had blonde hair? Was Lynnie's height? Had blue eyes like hers?

Lynnie flung out her hand, and a taxi pulled to the curb. She pointed for Mike to get in. Where to? he asked. I want to show you something, she said.

They went directly to the Cherry Blossom Motel in Arlington. They did not pass Go; they did not collect two hundred dollars. Lynnie registered them. She had stayed here before, on a business trip from San Diego. They gave a discount to Navy personnel, she explained. Mike, meanwhile, looked over the travel brochures by the door. Truth was, he was afraid to stand any closer to the registration desk. Lynnie always had a plan, always knew where she was going. He didn't want to know if she had reserved the room in advance.

Soon they were alone, the door to the room shut, the curtains drawn. Neither of them seemed nervous. Lynnie pulled off her tunic and loosened the ribbon tab at her throat. She undid the two top buttons on her blouse, then moved closer to him. "Here, you do it." Mike unfastened the rest of the buttons. The fabric sang as she pulled the blouse free and slipped it off her shoulders. Her bra was old-fashioned and modest, the cloth thick and bright-white. She lifted his hand—his burned hand—kissed the middle of his palm, then placed it in the small of her back, where it would go if they were dancing. She moved sideways until they were in front of the mirror. "There," she whispered. "That's what I wanted to show you."

He looked in the mirror and shook his head, not understanding. Smiling, she shifted his hand away. Mike was so shocked by what he saw that he gasped. Lynnie's back was mottled with scar tissue, grainy, tan in color—all except for that spot at the base of her spine. There, burned into the flesh, was an outline, a thumb and two fingers. It was like the rock paintings made by the Aboriginals in Australia, blurred but unmistakable. He stared into the mirror and he was seventeen again: lifting her, barely conscious, from her bed, both of them choking on the smoke; thumping down the stairs while groping to hold her rag-doll body. The fire caught them in the living room, a jet of orange flame that shot the length of the room. His hand must have been in just that spot, and left that imprint. He dumped Lynnie in the snow in the front yard and stumbled back inside. Not in time. Jen's bedroom, the whole upstairs, was a roiling fireball.

Tears welled up in Mike's eyes, from sadness at remembering the fire, from amazement at what he saw in the mirror. Lynnie arched up to kiss him, and, as they kissed, she unfastened her bra and stripped it off. She pushed him away so she could look at him, and then she glanced over her shoulder. His hand had again slipped into the hollow of her back, filling its outline perfectly. "See?" she whispered. "Made for each other."

They stayed in the room all that afternoon and night, and that was when Mike learned how much she hated hotel beds. The floor suited them fine. In the morning they lay together on the carpet, he on his back, she on her stomach, probing each other's scars. Ooo, that one's big. How many grafts? How did they fit the compression wraps—around the neck? Do you still use skin cream? I've got a special mix. I'll give you some the next time I see you.

The following years were, for Mike, like a long, slow fall down Alice's rabbit hole. He and Lynnie met in a wonderland of places—Kitty Hawk, Sarasota, Philadelphia, Galveston. Twice they visited the ranch her father owned in Arizona, the place where she was born. All that time, Devon was stationed in the Pacific (eventually they did get around to talking about him). Lynnie was promoted to work directly under the Chief of Naval Operations. The new job kept her busy, but she was still able to get away from Washington at least once a month. Would she have left Devon and married Mike then? Years later, Mike could only wonder. He didn't ask, and she didn't mention it either. He needed a lot of space, time on his own, and she seemed content to leave things as they were. He sometimes wondered what she got out of their relationship, why she kept wanting more. Maybe it was what she had said, that they were made for each other. Like Mike, she was a burn survivor. Perhaps she had a fatalistic streak like him, too. That was hard to believe, though. She was so directed, so certain of herself.

One summer afternoon, Lynnie called him at his office. Watch the news tonight, she said. Which news? he wanted to know. Any channel—national news. He switched it on when he got home, and a few minutes later was startled to see Lynnie, dressed in civilian clothes, standing next to the president. They were at the White House, in the Rose Garden. It was sweltering; everyone but Lynnie was sweating. The president introduced her, and she made a brief speech thanking him for choosing her for such a challenging job. She'd been appointed Director of Drug Policy. One of her jobs at the Pentagon had been heading up a drug-abuse task force for the military. Now, with this new position, Lynnie had rung up another first. No woman had ever been national drug czar before. She had to resign from the Navy, but she felt she'd gone about as far there as she could. She told Mike this the next time they got together, three months later.

Three months—that was their new pattern. Lynnie was busier than ever. Mike chafed at this, but he went along, hoping someday things would again settle down for them. But life, for Lynnie, had turned into a whirlwind. Newspaper and TV interviews. Congressional hearings. Trips to Asia and South America. Then Devon came home from the Pacific. A month later, Lynnie announced her candidacy for the Senate. Mike watched that speech on television, too, sitting with Randy Barchic in a Miami sports bar. Lynnie's star was definitely on the rise. How long would it be before she was completely beyond Mike's reach?

They managed to see each other a dozen times while

she was in the Senate, only twice in the three years she
was vice president, not once since she took over the top
job from Winston Garrett. Their last meeting, in Hawaii,
had been difficult. Devon wasn't a problem. He was away
in Bangladesh, hip-deep in good works. It wasn't the
place they stayed either. The Big Island beach house was
beautiful. But they were forced to hole up in Lynnie's
suite of rooms, lest one of the media people who followed
her see them together. They made love like clockwork,
gently now since they'd had so many years together.
They slept and read the newspapers and talked. An hour
before he was to leave, they went out on the porch to listen to the rain. They had to adjust the blinds so no one
could see them. Mike set up his Polaroid and took their
picture. Sitting shoulder to shoulder, they watched it develop. "Marry me," he said. He hadn't planned this. It
just tumbled out, seeing how peaceful they were in the
photo, how well they fit together.

"My job, Mike," Lynnie said. "I can't—" She began to
weep. Mike wanted to speak, but she covered his mouth
with her fingertips. "No, hush. All the time I feel so self-
ish. We see each other once a year, that's all. There's the
phone, but what good is that? You don't even like to talk
on the phone." She brushed her tears away with her
knuckle, but they were coming too fast to keep up with.

"Lynnie, it's all right. Forget I even said it."

She pulled away from him and put on a bleak smile.
"Forget a marriage proposal? Give a girl a break." She hesitated, then plunged on. "But you're right about that—
about getting married. It's time for you, long past time.
Find someone, Mike. Have a real life, kids. You should. I
want that for you." She seemed certain of this: done deal,
decision final. Then she leaned over, putting her head on
his shoulder again. "I love you. Don't leave me," she whispered frantically, contradicting everything she'd just said.

Mike tried to think it through on the plane trip home.
He cared for Lynnie so much, but what was he to her,

really? A comfort, a reminder of simpler times. If that was all, it didn't seem like enough—for either of them. So maybe she was right, maybe he should look for someone else.

He started seeing other women, blue-eyed blondes every one of them. He kept hoping that someday he'd look at one of those women, run his eyes across her face, and realize, like Brigham Young and his Mormons: *Here. This is the Place.* It hadn't happened. Meantime, everywhere he turned, there was Lynnie's picture, Lynnie's voice. The world was clamoring for her, the new president. The new *woman* president. She continued to phone him, sticking to their old schedule. And now, after eighteen months, he was finally going to see her again.

It had begun to rain, and the windows of Mike's car had steamed up. He rubbed a hole in the condensation so he could look out at the football field. Thunder drummed in over the mountains, and, a moment later, a sharp pinging of hail started on the roof. Good grief. They didn't have weather in the Adirondacks, they had diseases of the sky.

He wondered how much time he'd have with Lynnie tomorrow. Three hours? Six? A whole day and night? As was their custom, he hadn't asked, and she hadn't told him. However long it was, he wouldn't mention Archie Pascoe's conspiracy theories, nor his run-in with Joy and her recorder. He'd hold Lynnie's hand, tell her some jokes and stories, kiss her, make love to her if he could. He'd wring the most out of every minute.

The force of the storm picked up, hail slashing down on the car and the parking lot. Inside of a minute the football field was covered with dancing white pellets. That maple tree in the park, Mike thought, the one they were using as a backdrop for the stage. All the leaves would be gone now, stripped off by the hail. And the sign, too—"The North Country's First Lady"—shot through, ruined. Mike sighed and started the car. "Welcome home, love," he said.

CHAPTER TEN

Fort Drum Military Reservation was located sixty miles southeast of Blaine. It was a big installation, home to the Army's 10th Mountain Division. In daylight hours it was a noisy, dusty place, with troop carriers rumbling along the wooded trails, and helicopters constantly lop-lopping overhead. But at four thirty in the morning, the post was peaceful. Still, things were moving out there, and Colonel Travis Veck was watching. A fox loped across the road. By the motor pool, a raccoon tried to topple a trash can.

Veck was slouched down in his rented pickup, parked where he had a good view of the motor pool and the road leading to it. It was an isolated area, away from the other buildings of the post. He was sipping coffee from a thermos, listening to music through earphones. He loved these little digital players, great inventions. The song was "Sixteen Tons" by Tennessee Ernie Ford. Veck sang along. He had a good voice, surprisingly deep for a man so small.

The song ended and Veck stared down the road. He tapped his ring on the dashboard, his gold West Point ring with its two-carat blue diamond and "Duty, Honor, Country" inscription. "Come on," he grumbled. Veck hated waiting. That was why he'd left the Army (why, technically, he was Colonel Veck, Retired). If you needed supplies, the Army made you wait. If you needed per-sonnel, the Army made you wait. If you needed to take a dump, the Army made you wait. The Army, on its best days, waltzed; he always wanted to jitterbug.

He may not have liked the Army, but the Army liked him. He'd been in military intelligence, a battalion com-mander. He was a good leader, effective in the field. He found things out, cold facts in hot situations, just what his superiors wanted. At times he was overly aggressive, but, no matter what kind of tangle he got into, he always landed on his feet.

Veck had the gift of gab, too. After each deployment—Somalia, Afghanistan, Iraq—Congress would hold hearings. Endless, mindless bullrag. The Army sent Veck to testify. He would sit in the wood-paneled rooms on Capitol Hill, calm to the waist, but fidgeting madly with his legs, down where they couldn't see. "Yes, sir, interrogations—that was part of our job. Specifics are classified, sir, but torture? No. Never." The whole time he'd be thinking, *I'd like to get you in a concrete ten-by-ten, Congressman Dickbrain.*

Life hadn't been so good since Veck retired. The security firm he started had gone belly-up. Seemed that "Former Colonel, Military Intelligence" didn't have the cachet he expected it would. His wife had left him, too, his third wife to be exact, but this one he really liked. She had a voice like Dolly Parton's. Sometimes they took baths together. She scrubbed his back while they sang duets. And her body—that was a whole other story. Damn, he missed her.

But now, with this job, things were finally looking up. He had a chance for a real score. Megillah-megillah. It was a wild ride, but he'd bring it off. Then there'd be plenty money. He could buy himself a new wife. Hell, he could buy himself an opera singer.

If only Miller would get here. Veck drummed his ring on the dash. *"Come on."* Then he saw lights flash through the trees. He sunk low behind the steering wheel.

Lem Miller was driving a rusted yellow Camero. He parked by the motor pool and sauntered to the side door. He was a big man with rounded shoulders, his head a size too small for his body. He was dressed in camouflage BDUs in desert tan. After fourteen years in the Army, he'd worked his way up to Master Sergeant.

Master of what? Veck thought. Not one thing. Miller
was a dingbat; a poster boy for the "Join the Army, Become a Grunt" campaign.

Veck wished now he'd never ordered Miller to kill Eve
Tessmer. Wrong man for the job. Dead wrong. Veck
didn't really blame Miller for screwing things up,
though. It had been a press job, no margin for error and
no time for Veck to get to Blaine to do it himself. But now
he had to clean up the mess. He had a system for dealing
with mistakes, and that system boiled down to two
words: don't hesitate.

Veck trotted across the field to the motor pool. He
looked through the window. There was only one light
on, throwing a harsh glare on an Army Humvee. Miller
was underneath the big vehicle. Veck stepped over to the
door and tried the knob. Miller had locked it behind
him. Using a key on his ring, Veck opened it.

A breeze stole in with him, riffling the pages of a
maintenance manual sitting on a bench. Veck sang out,
"Miller, you freezing your fanny under there?"

"Who's that?" Miller said. A wrench clanked to the
floor. "Damn."

Veck went over and knelt by Miller's feet. "S'me," he
said sweetly. "Veck." He rapped his ring against the
body of the Humvee. That was something West Pointers
did, a sign of prestige. Ring-knockers, they were called.

"Colonel, what are you doing here?" Miller twisted so
he could see him. "Jesus, you shouldn't be in uniform."

Veck chuckled. "What are you doing here, Miller, this
time of day?"

"Orders. Gotta fix this Humvee by ten hundred hours.
Shit, I wish I was home in bed."

Veck shook his head. Poor Miller—too stupid to realize
Veck had set this up, right down to choosing the vehicle
he'd be working on. If you knew the right channels, you
could finagle anything in the Army.

"We need to talk," Veck said. Miller moved, trying to

sit up. Veck grabbed his leg. "Stay put. Only take a minute. I got the file you left, and I've got your money ready. Just a few questions I wanted to ask. You drove a base car to Blaine the other night?"

"Yeah, one of the unmarked MP cars. It was in here for servicing."

"Not smart, Miller. It had government plates. Those get recognized."

"Hell, Colonel, what was I supposed to do? Take my own car?"

Veck shifted his weight. Since he turned forty, his ankles hurt if he sat on them for too long. "What did you do with the gun?"

"What d'ya mean?" Miller moved again, but Veck held tight. "Colonel, it went like you told me. I put the gun to the old lady's head and made her hold the grip. I stuck her finger over the trigger and pulled it. The gun—I left that on the bed."

"They didn't find it."

"What?" Miller twitched. He definitely was uncomfortable under that big Humvee. "Who didn't find it?"

"The police, idiot. There was no gun when they got there. You think it got up and walked away?"

"No . . . I don't know what happened to it." Miller twitched again. His boots were dirty and scuffed. On top of his other faults, he was a slob.

Veck said, "Let's talk about the papers. You picked up everything that was marked 'Arizona'?"

"Sure. The file folder and the phone index cards, that was it."

"Yeah, the phone cards were fine, but the folder was empty," Veck said. "There should have been a stack of papers in it."

"I found that folder right off, and those cards. There were other folders all over the house, but nothing with 'Arizona' on it. I swear, I looked through everything."

Veck pulled a length of chain from his pocket. He set it

on the floor, link clinking on top of link. "Miller, do you remember Rabb Azim?"

Miller's legs started trembling. "Jesus, Colonel, let's not talk about him."

In the early months of the second Gulf War, Miller had served under Veck. A doofus like Miller in an intelligence group, that was par for the course for the Army. Together he and Veck interrogated dozens of Iraqi prisoners. Usually they used a translator, but not with Rabb Azim. Azim was a captain in the Iraqi army, and he spoke English. Veck was convinced Azim was tied in with the Fedayeen guerillas who were ripping up the Sunni Triangle.

Azim hung tough. Name, rank, date of birth, serial number. Blah, blah. He needed some incentive. Veck could have brought in the dogs, but that always took too long, rounding up a handler, filling out the forms. So he laid his service pistol against Azim's throat and told him—simply—he was going to shoot him if he didn't start talking. Azim turned away and spat on the floor. Arrogant bastard. To teach him a lesson, Veck fired off a round. The bullet missed, but the gas discharge from the barrel tore a hole in Azim's jugular. As he bled to death on the floor of the bunker, he admitted he'd sold bomb components to the Fedayeen (he also said he was Saddam Hussein's cousin, but Veck figured there he was only padding his story). Later that night, under a gorgeous full moon, Sergeant Miller dug a shallow grave and laid Azim to rest. On their next stateside rotation, Miller got himself reassigned from intelligence to maintenance.

"Sometimes you've got to throw the fear of God into people," Veck said to Miller. "Azim thought he was going to die that night. He was right, too."

Veck slipped the chain around the jack holding up the Humvee. "You're in deep kimchee here, Miller."

"Colonel, no," Miller gasped.

"What happened to the papers in that folder?"

"Colonel, I took everything I found to the drop, just like you asked."

"You aren't holding out on me? Maybe going to come back later with those papers, ask for more money?"

"I swear, Colonel, you're paying me fine as it is."

Veck tweaked the chain. The jack groaned.

"Colonel, please," Miller whined. "I'm tellin' you straight."

Veck paused a moment, letting the chain go slack. "You know what, Miller?" He gave the sergeant's boot a kindly slap. "I guess I believe you."

Miller laughed, hysterical with relief.

Veck yanked with all his might on the chain. The jack jumped free. Miller took six thousand pounds of Humvee in the face, without even time to scream. His body convulsed once, and was still.

Veck coiled up the chain, careful to rub off a few spots of gore. He adjusted the position of the jack and checked to make sure the chain hadn't left a mark. A-OK. *This* was an accident. No other conclusion possible. Sergeant Lem Miller, crushed by his own stupidity.

Veck locked the door on the way out, and he began to sing, using his best Ernie Ford baritone. "Saint Peter don't you call me 'cause I can't go. I owe my soul to the Army depot."

Half an hour later, Veck was parked outside the village of Evans Mills. Hard to tell one of these little burgs from another, he thought as he pulled his laptop out of its security case. He powered up and typed in the connection command. He hated this high-tech bullshit. Why not just use the damned phone? Ah, what the hell. His was not to reason why. . . .

When his watch registered exactly five thirty, he hit the enter key. The computer screen flickered and a message popped up. :>This is Star.

"Hello, Twinkle," Veck said. And this codename nonsense. What for? They were using the same encryption software the Secret Service used. The best there was. Nobody could decipher the transmission. But he played along. :>This is Bird. How they hangin'?

Star was not amused. :>Stick to routine. News from NYC. Police still have no ID for Trinity Church body.

"You're joking," Veck said. The Manhattan police had had that body for three days. Sure, the head and hands were blown off, but you'd think they'd have figured out who it was by now. God, cops could be such jerkoffs.

Veck typed, :>Glad to hear it. How about Blaine?

:>BCI sent new team of investigators there yesterday. You talked to sergeant?

:>We had a session. Says he did everything according to plan. Arizona file was empty when he found it.

:>You believe him?

:>Sure. Deathbed confession.

:>BIRD, I DID NOT ORDER THAT.

"Aw," Veck muttered. "Lay off the all caps." He typed, :>I hear you. What's next?

:>Need to find those Arizona papers and keep BCI out of the way. Suggestions?

Veck had thought about this and come up with a plan. He'd even taken a few steps to implement it. The Army called that kind of thing initiative; Star might think he was being uppity.

He began typing again. :>They'll stop snooping when someone is arrested. Let's give BCI a hand, put somebody in the frame.

:>Who? Star wanted to know.

:>Two possibles: Stanbridge or Pascoe.

Veck waited, tapping his ring on the steering wheel. Finally the computer flickered, and Veck broke into a grin.

:>Stanbridge.

CHAPTER ELEVEN

Mike was just rolling out of bed when someone thumped on the door. He checked the clock. Six twenty. *"What?"*

"Police." More thumping. "Open up."

Mike padded over and looked through the peephole. Billy White's face popped into view. "Mikey?" Mike cracked open the door, and Billy pointed and chuckled. "Man, do you look pissed off. I was only foolin'."

Joy Leiffer's door opened, and she stepped halfway out, glancing at Billy, then Mike. Her eyes were pinched and angry. "Sorry, ma'am," Billy said, tipping his hat. "Didn't mean to wake you." He remembered his hair transplant and jerked the hat back down. Joy slammed the door. "Wow, Bridge, did you see the legs on her?"

"I'll bet you wouldn't say that to her face." Mike folded his arms and leaned against the door frame. "Now what the hell do you want?"

Billy pushed into the room and snapped on the lights. "Need your help with something down at my office." Mike started to protest, but Billy interrupted. "Come on. A favor." He tossed Mike his pants.

"Is this about Eve?"

"Sure 'nough. And don't worry. I'll have you back in twenty minutes."

Mike went into the bathroom to get dressed. When he emerged, Billy was talking on the phone. "Right . . . Half an hour, then. Breakfast." He hung up. He had a piece of paper in his hand, which he stuffed quickly into his pocket. "So much going on today. I feel like I'm being nibbled to death by ducks."

Mike's head was still cloudy from sleep, but it cleared as they stepped into the frigid air. It was shortly after dawn. The lake was glassy smooth. Back in the bays, a silken sheet of fog hung a foot off the water.

Billy strode over to a van parked on the street. On the side was a logo, BLAINE LOJ SHUTTLE. "My deputies have got all the department's cars out," he said. He locked the van. "Let's walk anyway. Be quicker with this mess." There was a lot of traffic—station wagons jammed with people, a couple of busses, three trucks labeled with TV station call letters, all creeping along Main Street.

Billy hurried down the sidewalk, so fast that Mike, with his limp, had trouble keeping up. They approached the park. A small army—sixty or seventy people, many dressed in business suits—was at work tearing up the stage.

"What's going on?" Mike asked.

"Moving the damn thing," Billy said. "A bunch of us told the advance people that maple was going to lose its leaves if we had a storm, but they wouldn't listen. Now they're in a tizzy to get set up somewhere else."

Billy pulled up suddenly, scowling at Mike. "Did you go to Eve Tessmer's house last night?"

If his change of mood was designed to throw Mike off balance, it worked. "Yeah, well," he stammered. "Archie and I—"

"Dammit, Bridge," Billy said. "That was Archie I was talking to on the phone in your room. *He's* an old fool. You're a lawyer. You know better than to screw around with a crime scene."

"He told you we'd been there?"

"Yup." Billy shook his head and his grin returned. "What a hoot that old guy is. Look, it's no big deal, but don't say anything about it when we get to my office, OK?"

"And who is it I'm not supposed to say anything to?"

"We call her Lieutenant Dish."

They cut down an alley to the rear entrance to the town

hall. The police department was located in the basement. A woman, sitting at the desk nearest the door, looked up when they entered. She was about sixty and had a tired, doughy face marked by a bright gash of lipstick.

"Patsy, babe," Billy said. "How's tricks?"

"Only trick I know is how to get my girdle off without using my hands."

"Are you alone when you do this?"

"Just me and the brass band that plays the dance music." Patsy tapped a pencil against her teeth and pointed at the back hallway. "She's been here a while, and she's not happy."

The hall led to Billy's office. Seated in a chair in the corner was another woman. She was about Mike's age, early forties. Billy introduced her as Lieutenant Dushaney from the New York State Police. She was from the headquarters office in Ray Brook and was in charge of the investigation into Eve Tessmer's murder.

The lieutenant had a square face with very regular features. Her complexion was Mediterranean-dark, and her hair and eyebrows were raven black. Her eyes were the palest of blue. Some men might have found this combination attractive; from the way he fawned over her, Billy certainly did. Mike had a different reaction. Those were cold, cynical eyes, used to catching out sinners. They made him want to look away.

Dushaney was holding a sheet of paper, which she handed to Billy. He waved Mike into another chair. "Sunday night," Billy said, "where were you?"

"Like I told you yesterday, at home."

"That's—" Billy turned so he could look at a notepad on his desk. "On Key Largo. Someplace called Lime Key?"

"Right." Mike wondered where Billy had gotten his address. Archie Pascoe, probably.

"OK, now—well, let me just give this to you. Maybe you can explain it."

He handed Mike the sheet of paper. It was from a fax machine, and the print quality wasn't good. Mike could see that it had come in at four fifteen the previous afternoon. There was an emblem of some kind, nested triangles. His name was in a column on the left, highlighted, but he couldn't make sense of the rest of it. "I don't understand."

Billy took the sheet back. "This is from Delta Airlines. I've got a friend there, and I asked him to do some checking. A passenger named Michael Stanbridge flew from Miami to New York on Sunday. Got into JFK at one thirty-five in the afternoon."

"No," Mike said. "Let me see that again."

Billy handed it over. Lieutenant Dushaney was watching impassively. "Do you know anyone else in the Miami area with your name?"

Mike smiled. "Only my brother. Mom loved the name Michael."

"This isn't a joke, Mr. Stanbridge." She shifted her position, neatly crossing her legs. "One thirty-five. That leaves plenty of time to drive here by ten o'clock. That's when Ms. Tessmer was killed, between ten and eleven."

Mike looked at the fax. Michael Stanbridge, Flt. 2008, October 22. His smile turned sickly. He hadn't done anything wrong, but with those two uniforms staring at him, he felt as though he had. "Yes, this is hard to explain." Then his face flushed. That was exactly the wrong thing to say. From there, his lawyer's training kicked in: get them off the offensive; buy some time to think. "So there must be another Michael Stanbridge, or—"

"Could be," Billy said.

"Or—" Mike held up the sheet. "This is a phony."

"No." Lieutenant Dushaney flicked a spot of lint off her sleeve. That was how much Mike's arguments meant to her. "I talked to Chief White's man at Delta. That manifest is real."

The clock on the wall behind Mike marked the seconds. Tick, tick, tick. She stared at him with her ice-blue eyes.

Billy cleared his throat. "We only wanted to run this by you, Mike. See if you . . . You know, see what . . ." He looked at the floor, seemingly embarrassed by the whole situation.

Dushaney stood up. "I understand you're one of the special guests for President Connor's ceremony. Congratulations. That's a real honor. How long will you be staying with us?"

"She means at Galston's," Billy offered.

"My room's reserved through tomorrow night," Mike said.

Dushaney nodded briskly. "Good. Please let Chief White know if your plans change." At that, she took the fax from Mike and strode out the door.

Mike rubbed his palms together and stared at the chair where she'd been sitting. He said to Billy, "You knew about this last night, out at Pascoe's place, but you didn't tell me."

"Felt bad about it, too," Billy said, "but it's procedure. I had to tell Dish before I could say anything to you. She was downstate at a meeting. I didn't talk to her 'til late last night. The thing is, Archie's been all over us about you since Eve died, like he's got some pipeline to God. 'Stanbridge knows something! You check him out!' That kind of thing. To shut him up, I called the airlines. It was routine. I never expected that thing to come back from Delta." Billy clapped his hands together briskly. "Mike, listen, there's got to be an explanation. We'll figure it out. Right now, though, I need to get back to work."

When the two of them reached the outer room, Patsy pointed her pencil at Mike. "Boy, she sure must have liked you. Went out of here whistling. *Actually* whistling."

"Wooh-ooh," Billy said. "That *is* something. Maybe next time she'll take you into the interview room, let you flog her with your rubber hose." Patsy giggled and Billy slung his arm around Mike's shoulder. "Come on, don't look so glum. You're among friends."

"You bet," Mike said. But he was thinking, *Like the cat is friends with the canary*.

CHAPTER TWELVE

Billy led the way back to the motel, his uniform cutting a neat path through the crowds on Main Street. As he surged along, he jabbered on a portable radio, checking with his deputies. Someone had found a package in front of the Planned Parenthood office. Turned out not to be a bomb, but a brand new pair of Nike basketball shoes. No one knew how they got there. Traffic was a bear everywhere; all the deputies were complaining. Someone said old Eve Tessmer had been right. They should have made everyone park outside of town, hauled them in with busses.

Mike paid no attention to the chatter. He was fretting about the fax from Delta Airlines. Maybe it was a mistake. Billy's friend at Delta might have hit the wrong computer key, somehow slipped Mike's name into a passenger list. Then again, maybe it wasn't so complicated. Could be there *was* another Michael Stanbridge, someone who flew from Miami to New York the day Eve was killed. That would be some surprise, though. In all his life, Mike had never heard of another person with his name. Or the record was a fake. Lieutenant Dushaney hadn't been impressed with that argument, and now, given a while to think about it, neither was Mike. What reason would anyone have to phony up a travel itinerary for him? Anyway, enough worrying. Right now he wanted to concentrate on Lynnie. She'd be here in a little over an hour.

Then the motel came into view, and Mike pulled to a

halt. "Tell me I'm dreaming." An old white Cadillac was parked by his room, and leaning against the fender was Archie Pascoe.

Billy glanced back, grinning. "Your own private nightmare. On the phone before, Arch told me he wanted to talk to you. Said he was going to bring you some breakfast."

By then, Archie had spotted them. "Morning, Michael," he called. He held up his hand, palm out. "How, Chief."

"How?" Billy said. "Like this." He thrust his hips forward a couple of times.

"Fuck you, Billy," Archie replied, oblivious of the crowd. A couple of teenage boys laughed. A woman clapped her hands over her daughter's ears and steered her across the street.

Billy unlocked the door to his van and hopped in; then he craned his head back out. "If I were you, Mike, I'd do what Dish said. Let me know before you leave town."

Archie arrived at the sidewalk. He and Mike watched the van chug into the slow-moving traffic. "Seems like every time I see that twerp, I tell him to go screw himself," Archie said. He tossed a cigarette down and mashed it out with his heel. "What'd he mean, don't leave town without letting him know?"

"If you're really interested, go ask him," Mike said. He turned and walked toward his room.

"Hey, don't get huffy with me," Archie yelled at his back.

There was a copy of the *New York Times* on the doorstep, compliments of the motel. Mike picked it up. The headline read, CONNOR HINTS AT POST-ELECTION CABINET SHAKEUP. The accompanying photo was not flattering, showing Lynnie with a scowl on her face and her hand chopping the air, giving someone the metaphorical axe.

Mike felt hot breath on his neck. "You want my newspaper, Archie? Here, take it."

"No, I want to go inside, unless we're going to sit in my Caddy, have a picnic." He held up a paper sack. "So what do you like, the reg'lar or the sausage McMuffins?"

Mike let a sigh hiss from his lips. "Come on in, but I don't have time to talk. I've got to get changed and get to"—he glanced down the street toward the park—"wherever this thing is going to be."

"Moved the stage to the Community Church, two blocks up," Archie said. He followed Mike in and closed the door. "Won't be a problem getting there."

To keep warm, Mike always slept in a sweat suit. When Billy White arrived, he'd gone into the bathroom to change out of it, keeping his scars from Billy's prying eyes. Archie was a different matter. Mike didn't give a damn what he thought. Standing beside the bed, he pulled off his shoes and socks, stripped off his jacket and shirt.

Archie was unpacking his breakfast goodies, five Mc-Muffins and two tall paper cups of coffee. He already had one of the sandwiches half eaten when he looked up. His eyes widened, and he made a small gurgling noise as he swallowed. Mike brushed his hand over the tangle of scarlet flesh on his ribs. "Takes some getting used to," he said softly. He coasted into the bathroom.

After that, Mike expected Archie to keep quiet, eat his breakfast, maybe read the paper. Instead, as he was lathering his hair with shampoo, Archie spoke up, from right outside the shower curtain. "Cubs really kicked butt last night, 15–2." Mike peeked out. He was sitting on the toilet, his coffee cup balanced on his knee. At least, Mike observed, the lid was down. Then came the play-by-play: home runs, errors, pop flies, even called strikes and balls. By the time Archie was through, Mike was done with his shower, shaved, and pulling his suit from the closet.

Mike had come out of the bathroom with only a towel around his waist. Now the towel had to go so he could get dressed. Archie had seen enough scars for one day. He went to the window, peering through a crack in the blinds. "That guy that plays shortstop for the Cubs," he said, "he reminded me of something you said when we were at Eve's, 'bout the foreman from Lynnie's ranch in Arizona. Same name, right? Rodriguez?"

If this was supposed to be a segue from baseball to Eve Tessmer's murder, it wasn't very smooth. "Martinez," Mike said. He already had his shirt and pants on and was pulling on his shoes. "The foreman's name was Oscar Martinez."

"Martinez. Rodriguez. Same difference. Anyway, you said you don't know where he is now?"

Mike went to the closet again. He couldn't decide which tie to wear. He'd brought four. "That's what I told you, all right."

"Eve tried to find him. Where do you think she would have looked?"

Mike was concentrating on the ties. "What? Oh. She never said, just that she didn't turn anything up."

"Do you know somebody named Aron Aubrey?"

This got Mike's attention. "Yes. I haven't met him, but I talked to Eve about him."

Archie turned to look at him. "You did?"

"To know Aubrey, you have to start with Jon Ferrar. Ferrar owns a media company, TV stations, newspapers—" Archie was nodding; he knew who Ferrar was. "Ferrar hired Aron Aubrey to write a book about Lynnie, an unauthorized biography. That's what Aubrey does. Lloyd Duncan—remember him? Aubrey wrote the book that killed Duncan's nomination for Secretary of Defense, about how he financed his way through college selling pot."

"That was Aubrey? That scummy book?"

"Right. He's written about Michael Jordan, Liz Taylor,

a slew of people in Washington. Aubrey isn't finished with the book on Lynnie, but Ferrar's going to jump the gun, run some chapters in his newspapers before the election."

"And that won't help Lynnie's chances, I'll bet. You say Eve mentioned Aubrey to you?"

"No, the other way around," Mike replied. "She was looking for someone who knew Lynnie's family in Arizona. Except for telling her about Martinez, I couldn't help much, so I mentioned Aubrey. He was researching Lynnie's life. Maybe he knew someone. But I wasn't all that serious about it. From what I've heard, Aron Aubrey's as mean as his books, not the sort of person you can just call on the phone and chat with."

"Eve thought you were serious. She talked to Aubrey, four different times."

"She told you that?" Mike asked.

Archie scowled. *He* was the one asking the questions here. His irritation was lost on Mike, who'd gone back to his ties. Midnight blue, he decided. Sincere, and less flashy than the red.

"I wasn't sure who Aubrey was," Archie said, "but I decided to give him a call, see what he and Eve talked about. Three days I've tried, but no luck. Nobody knows where he is."

"He's a writer, Arch, probably gone off somewhere, working. Besides, you should leave that stuff to the police. They'll find him if it's important."

Archie looked out the crack in the blinds again. "I'm not so sure. The woman at Aubrey's office said he missed a deadline on Monday, then didn't come in for a big meeting on Tuesday. She seemed worried. Maybe she was worried. She could barely speak English. Damned Manhattan. Tower of Babel, that place is. Somebody ought to organize a cleanup. Flush all the toilets at once, send the whole island out to sea."

"Great," Mike said. "You should take out a patent." He

was finishing up with his tie. Checking, he found that the narrow end was too long. He started over.

"A patent?" Archie said. "Aren't you clever. Anyway, I couldn't get an answer at Aubrey's house. Had to talk to a machine. 'This is Aron. Tell all at the beep.' Only two kinds of people in New York City: foreigners and nutcakes."

"Archie, you're as charming as a tick."

"Getting under your skin, am I? That what you mean?"

Yes, that was exactly what Mike meant. It dawned on him Archie was trying to get him angry, hoping he'd let something slip. What he was after, Mike couldn't begin to guess. One thing was clear, though. Archie knew more than he was letting on, about Aron Aubrey, about the investigation into Eve's death. Mike took another stab at his tie—over, around, through. Again the knot came out wrong. "Fudge."

Archie turned him so they were facing each other. "Aren't you the nervous one. Like a kid gettin' ready for your first dance. Here, let me do this." He adjusted the tie. His hands were pillowy with fat, gentle as they moved. "Big ceremony like this, I suppose nobody'll really get to talk to Lynnie. Just speeches and all." He cleared his throat. "Except afterward at the mayor's reception. You'll be there for that, with the rest of the special guests."

"That's how it's set up," Mike said. "Lynnie and the forty-three guests and their wives and husbands and kids. A couple hundred of her closest friends."

Archie was tying a full Windsor, taking his time so each loop was precisely the way he wanted it. "You get a chance, you should take Lynnie aside, tell her about Eve."

Mike felt his shoulders go rigid, his whole body tighten up. "I'm sorry Eve was killed. I'm sure Lynnie would say the same thing. But there's no reason to drag her into it."

Archie had finished the knot. He snugged it up, then pushed it a millimeter too far. His thumbnail bit into Mike's Adam's apple. His eyes were like black nails. "I *told* you, I think she and Eve talked. Maybe Lynnie knows something that could help." Mike lifted his arm to knock Archie's hands away, but, before there was contact, Archie backed off. He dropped his voice, even smiled a little. There was a slyness here that Mike was beginning to recognize. "Anyway, be interesting to see how Lynnie reacts when she hears the news. Interesting, that's all."

Mike tucked his wallet and keys in his coat. He paused, listening. Far away, coming across the lake from the south, was the eggbeater whirl of a big helicopter. Archie had his head cocked, too. "Hark! Her Majesty's chariot!"

Mike stepped to the door. "Enjoy your breakfast. Be sure and lock up when you leave."

"Michael, humor me. An old man's request. Ask Lynnie about Eve. You might be surprised at what she says."

"Not on your life, Archie."

CHAPTER THIRTEEN

Every face on Main Street was turned up, following the helicopter. It pounded up the belly of the lake, banked at the park, and disappeared over the hills to the west. Headed for Black Pond, Mike decided, the golf course out there. The crowd, excited now, poured off the sidewalk into the street, bringing traffic to a complete halt. Mike was swept along, past Ralph's Tavern, toward the pink sandstone spire of Blaine Community Church. A sign for "Participants" was mounted on a car parked there. An arrow pointed to the basement entry to the church. Mike fought his way out of the crowd and down the slope.

Five men stood at a table, three campaign advance men, two Secret Service agents. The campaign people were easy to pick out: tweedy suits and muddy Rockport half boots, manic expressions on their faces. One was talking into his sleeve, like Dick Tracy. "Stolz here, go." He listened to his earphone. "Dammit, no. Bike rack. Close it in with bike rack." He signed off, then on again. "Stolz here, go." Mike recognized the Secret Service agents by the color-coded pins in their lapels, worn so they could sort out the good guys from the bad in an emergency. The two men were rocks in this storm, motionless except for their eyes. Their eyes were everywhere, swinging, locking, swinging, like guns on a battle cruiser.

"Is this the check-in point for the stage guests?" Mike said to one of the advance men.

"Right. Driver's license, please." Mike handed over his license and the man ran his pen down a list. He then fished through a box of orange admission passes. "No. No Stanbridge." Without a flicker, he handed the license back and moved on to the next person in line. "Ma'am?"

Mike said, "But wait—"

One of the Secret Service agents appeared at his elbow. "Step away from the table, please." Mike hesitated. "Please, sir?" He put his hand on Mike's back, nudging him along.

"Stop!" a woman's voice shouted. "He's innocent, Sheriff. Don't string him up!" Claudia Sung came diving through the knot of people gathered at the church door. Mike smiled; the Secret Service man muttered a curse. Sung was Lynnie Connor's chief of staff. She was barely five feet tall, her body and face both round as apples. She walked on the balls of her feet, arms flapping, scurry-scurry. "You making trouble again, Michael? Here, I've got his pass." She pressed the orange card into Mike's hand. "Go on," she said to the Secret Service man. "Go do your job." She tugged on Mike's shoulder, bending him so she could kiss the air next to his cheek. "How're you doin', sweetcakes?" she whispered.

Claudia had been Lynnie's chief of staff since she became vice president. Before that, she'd served three terms in Congress. She was from Hawaii; it was her house on the Big Island where Mike and Lynnie had stayed eighteen months ago. Claudia had arranged everything, right down to installing a special door so Mike could come and go without being seen by the Secret Service. As far as Mike knew, Claudia was the only person in the world who knew he and Lynnie were lovers.

She led him into the church, nodding to people she recognized, smiling at those she didn't. In the corner of the room was a table loaded with trays of doughnuts and a silver coffee urn. Claudia poured a cup and handed it to Mike. "Don't drink," she said, "or you'll need to tinkle during the speech. Just hold it. Like that. Now people might think you're sophisticated."

Claudia's little barbs were legend. Once, in a very public place, she had asked the governor of California if he'd ever considered using deodorant. Another time, when a reporter asked a particularly obnoxious question during a press conference, she tossed him some change and suggested he call home to see if his mother still loved him. Mike was a target like everyone else. When Claudia met him at the airport in Hawaii, she told him Lynnie had gotten up extra early that morning to make herself pretty for him. Really? Mike said. Claudia nodded. Yep. You must be hot stuff. Yesterday we had a goat and a donkey for her, and she wouldn't even shave her legs. Claudia always got away with that kind of thing. No one complained, or even jabbed back. It was her smile that did it. She smiled with her whole face, 100 percent pure sugar. People treated her insults as tokens of her affection.

Mike held the coffee cup the way Claudia told him. "How's Lynnie?"

"Grouchy as a bear today. That's why I came on ahead—to get away from her. Thought we might get in a fight, cussing each other out in front of the press. They'd love that." Sung moved behind the table and pulled him with her, so they'd have a little privacy. "I need your advice, Michael. Lynnie says it's OK, but I wanted—Well, here it is. There's this local guy, wants his picture taken with her for his campaign. You knew him in school. Billy White. He—" Claudia blinked, then burst into a tirade of giggles. "Michael, your face. Last time I saw an expression like that, somebody'd just stepped in what the cow left behind. He's that bad?"

"A cowflop? Maybe. I played baseball with Billy. Every time he hit a ground ball and had to run it out, he'd try to spike the first baseman in the ankle, put him out of the game. Billy always acted embarrassed about it. 'Gee, sorry. Didn't see your foot there.' No, I wouldn't trust him if I were you."

"No endorsement from us, then. Thanks for the tip."

Claudia worked these affairs quickly, getting in as much glad-handing as she could. Her business with Mike completed, her eyes started skating around the rest of the room. He didn't want her to get away so fast. "So what's the plan for the rest of the day?"

Claudia threw her hands up. "The schedule is falling! The schedule is falling!" she peeped. This was one of her shticks, Chicken Little of the White House. She handed Mike a doughnut and bustled off, without saying goodbye. Moments later, from deep in the crowd, he heard her cry out, "Admiral! What a *glorious* hat! Did you make it yourself?"

Mike never got to eat his doughnut. A campaign worker appeared at the church door and shouted for everyone to listen up. The orange admission cards had numbers on them. Everyone was to line up according to those numbers. *No dawdling*. The woman doing the shouting was six feet tall and had the upper body of a mountain gorilla. No one argued. She checked everyone twice against her master list (this one had Mike's name on it), then gave them their orders: sit when she sat, stand when she stood, applaud when she applauded. Most important, smile. She grinned ferociously. "Remember," she growled, "we *love* Lynnie!"

Mike's seat was at the end of the back row, only a few feet from the lake. His chair, like his orange card, had the number seventeen on it, for the year Lynnie was seventeen, the year of the fire. He looked down the row. The first chair, for the year of her birth, was empty; no one had shown up from Arizona. Number nine was empty, too. Eve Tessmer would have sat there.

The woman next to him was Jane Cleary. Before retirement, she had owned the Blaine Book Loft. She'd been in the Waves, she told Mike. She was the one who got Lynnie interested in joining the Navy. If this was true, Mike had never heard it before. Cleary was nervous, twiddling her hands. She commented on the weather. Such a shame, it seemed sure to rain. She wouldn't look out at the crowd, which was growing all the time. Fifteen thousand now, at least, packed into a tight triangle in front of the stage by lines of bicycle racks. The press was there in force, too, in a roped-off bull pen up the slope from the church. The final group of onlookers was out on the lake, in a flotilla of bass boats, pontoon boats, canoes, and kayaks.

In the crowd in front of the podium, Mike spotted Joy Leiffer. She was talking to a man in a dark leather jacket cut in the same style as hers. While he listened, the man tinkered with a video camera. Closer to the stage Mike saw Billy White. Billy had changed clothes, putting on a gray suit and a narrow-brimmed fedora. The hat rested on his ears, several sizes too big. There was a woman with Billy, her arm looped through his. It took Mike a moment to come up with her name. Sandra Ducharme.

In the eleventh grade, Mike had taken Sandy out to the movies a few times. She certainly had changed. Her baby fat was gone. She was tall and prim, dressed in a knee-length, form-fitting coat. She noticed him and waved. She was the one Mike had seen in Billy's police car the night before, out at Archie's house. It was the same wave, a baby-doll flap of the fingers. He smiled and waved back. Then he sat up. In one fluid movement, the crowd turned. The first wail of sirens had reached them.

They came in around the head of the lake, six motorcycles, three black limousines, too many chase cars to count. Despite the sirens and flashing lights, the stragglers on Main Street wouldn't stand aside. It took five minutes for the motorcade to make its way to the church. The high school band was there, and it jumped into a squeaky version of "Happy Birthday." At the same time, the campaign theme song—a jazzy remake of "We Are Family"—started booming over the loudspeakers.

On the stage, everyone was watching the gorilla-woman, waiting for the cue to stand. The door to the second limo opened and a leg appeared. The crowd leaned forward; there was a feeling in the air of a collective breath being sucked in.

Then there she was, the president, sweeping down into the throng, radiant. Mike stood; everyone on the stage stood. He was the tallest one there, but still he could only see her hair, a golden crown. People were reaching out, not trying to shake hands, only wanting to touch her. Three campaign workers cleared a path, bent over and coming on backward, literally butting people aside. Half a dozen Secret Service agents, all big men, swarmed around her, holding people back, knocking some of the hands away.

Lynnie hit the stage, arms over her head, half waving, half swaying to the music. She walked down and back, giving the crowd a good look at her. Her energy was up; her feet barely seemed to touch the planks. At the podium, she stopped and turned to greet the people behind her. There was too much noise to hear what she was saying, but they all could read her lips. "Thank you. Thank you for coming." Then she reached Mike. Their eyes clicked and her smile mellowed. She tilted her head slightly, the way she did when they were alone and she wanted a hug. Mike felt himself blush. Knowing she'd connected, Lynnie turned away, and Jane Cleary poked Mike with her elbow. "She remembers you, I'd say."

"Yes, I guess so."

Lynnie wasn't introduced by anyone. She simply moved to the microphone, and, after bringing her arms down through the air, asking for quiet, she started to speak. "In twelve days we Americans will make a choice. . . ." The people on the stage took their seats, and the crowd settled down to listen.

As best Mike could gather, the speech was about foreign policy. He heard the phrase "in our neighborhood" a couple of times, and that was Lynnie's constant metaphor for the world situation. In our neighborhood, we benefit from understanding, not from spite fences, not from name-calling. Mostly, though, he tuned out the words, choosing instead just to watch her. She'd had her hair trimmed since he'd seen her on television yesterday. And that was a new suit she was wearing, azure blue, not white as Randy Barchic would have it. She'd put on weight recently, too, not much, five pounds maybe, ten tops, but enough so the cartoonists would soon be getting after her. Lynnie hated that—not just the cartoons, but the feeling that she wasn't in control, especially of her own body.

The crowd grew restless. Geopolitics was a long way from the North Country. Still, Lynnie marched on. Several times she paused, glancing at the sky. Then suddenly she was hurrying, thanking everyone for her wonderful childhood in Blaine, for the life she'd had since then. She reminded them to vote. New York was important to her; *they* were important to her.

At that instant the sun split through the clouds, rolling across the lake and the stage. Her suit seemed to light up, a blue flame against the pink backdrop of the church. A faint "ooo" went through the crowd. Every eye was on her, the restlessness gone. This was why Lynnie had been stalling, hoping for this moment. Her voice surged. "I understand from Mayor Hoxie that this weekend is homecoming. That's perfect. It's so wonderful to be back here, to be home. I love you. I love every one of you. Driving over here a few minutes ago, I remembered something." She put her fist in the air, pumped it twice. *"Run Wolves! Beat Saranac!"*

The people roared their approval, even the ones from Saranac Lake. With everyone else on the stage, Mike came to his feet, laughing, pounding his hands together. The music came up, and Lynnie lifted her arms, sway-waving again. "Thank you. Thank you for coming." In the press pen the cameras went off, whirring and chittering like a horde of insects. That would be the shot in tomorrow's papers and on the evening news. *Lynnie, Adored.* The man in front of Mike, a Navy commander, put his fingers in his mouth and whistled. Jane Cleary was wiping tears from her eyes. Mike felt a tug on his coat. He glanced back and almost didn't see Claudia Sung, she was so short. He had to bend down so she could shout into his ear. "C'mon, sweetcakes. You're riding with us."

CHAPTER FOURTEEN

The inside of the limousine smelled of spilt ginger ale, or maybe Mike only imagined it did, since ginger ale was what Lynnie drank. He was alone, except for the driver, a glum little man so intent on listening to his earphone he didn't even glance up when Mike got in. Claudia was outside, talking on a cell phone. Lynnie was still working the crowd.

The door opened and a woman tumbled into the jump seat. Claudia followed on her heels. "Well, I'm not telling her," Claudia said, putting the phone in her pocket.

"Fine. That's why I'm here," the woman replied. "Jesus, move over." She saw Mike and smiled, embarrassed. "Sorry. I'm Gina." She offered her hand.

Gina Rizzo. Mike had heard of her but never seen her picture. She was head campaign manager. Andrew Hoyt, Lynnie's running mate, had discovered her. Gina had been in charge of Hoyt's Capitol Hill office when he was in Congress. She'd moved up to the big leagues when Lynnie picked Hoyt to fill out her term as vice president. Rizzo read the polls and came up with the campaign's message, neatly distilled into catchy one-liners. From all the focus on women and family issues, Mike expected her to look like a stressed-out suburban mom. Instead, everything about her was scrubbed and sleek, as if she had just stepped out of a Madison Avenue advertising agency.

Claudia was asking the driver, George, what route they'd take to get to the mayor's reception. Alternate route, George told her, up on the hill. Too many people on Main Street. Claudia seemed to like that idea. "You can show us the sights, Mike."

A break formed in the crowd, and Lynnie appeared,

shaking hands, letting people paw her sleeve. One of the Secret Service agents opened the door to the limo and, after a final wave, Lynnie climbed in. Her eyes went straight to Mike. Her smile seemed to brighten tenfold. "Hi." Then the Secret Service man swung the door closed, a fraction of a second too soon. It thumped Lynnie in the hip and sent her sprawling into Mike's lap.

"Uh, happy birthday," he said, helping her up.

Lynnie's face was crimson. "God, how bad was it?" She meant her skirt, the crowd.

"I saw one guy drooling," Claudia said. "Another one went the whole way and threw up."

"Nobody saw anything," Mike put in calmly. "The door was closed."

The Secret Service agent hopped in the front seat, muttering into his sleeve. The sirens started to howl and the car lurched forward. Claudia poked Mike in the knee. "Wave. Like this." She did a good imitation of the Hunchback of Notre Dame waving.

"I'm with the guys up front on that," Mike replied. "No waving."

Claudia shook her head. "Seriously, if you don't wave, the press will think we kidnapped you. Three crones take you into the woods, put you in a pot, and cook you up with eye of newt."

"That's not funny, Sung," Gina Rizzo said. She was waving with both hands, but, instead of looking at the crowd, she was studying a spreadsheet on her lap.

"I didn't say we *were* witches, dearie. Just that certain of our friends in the media might *think* we were." Claudia poked Mike again. "Come on."

The windows were so dark, Mike wondered if anyone could see inside, but he lifted one hand and waved. He left the other on the seat by Lynnie's leg. He was afraid to look at her, afraid he'd give something away in front of Rizzo. Claudia hit a button and a glass screen rose, blocking the passenger's compartment from the front seat.

"Did you see the new sign the Boy's Club had?" Lynnie said.

Mike smiled, simply from the sound of her voice. "Who's that?"

Lynnie moved a little closer. She'd taken a blue rubber egg out of the armrest and was squeezing it, exercising her hand or working off stress. "These three old men. We call them the Boy's Club. They follow us to every stop. The sign said, 'Billions for Breasts but Not—'"

Mike finished for her: "'One Penny for the Prostate.'" He'd seen the sign, purple with orange lettering, far back in the crowd.

Claudia was giggling. "What do you think they mean—*the* prostate? Is there a great big one out there somewhere? The Mother of all Prostates?"

"Forget 'em," Gina said, rolling her eyes. "Those guys are from the planet Loon."

"What's their problem?" Mike asked. He wanted Lynnie to talk.

"They don't think we pay enough attention to men's issues," she said. "Maybe they're right. Claudia, get me the figures, relative expenditures on breast versus prostate cancer."

Gina said, "Remember, that's not the side our bread is buttered on."

"Until election day, *nobody's* bread is buttered," Lynnie shot back. She rubbed her forehead. "All this inside baseball stuff—Mike must think it's pretty boring."

"Not at all," he said. Lynnie could have recited last year's stock market quotes and he would have found it interesting.

The motorcade swung past the high school, leaving the crowd behind. Lynnie unbuttoned her jacket. She was sweating; her hair was matted to her temples.

"Damn vest," she muttered. Mike was waiting for the right moment to strike up a conversation, something just between them, but, before he could speak, Lynnie looked at him. "Sorry," she said. Sorry for what? he wondered. Then he understood. She was apologizing for what was about to happen.

Lynnie turned on Gina. "What the hell is going on with Hoyt?"

Rizzo sunk back in her seat, a cornered animal. "What?"

"Lafferty from ABC nailed me coming off the stage. 'Do you have any comment on Vice President Hoyt's statement about China?'" Lynnie reached over and took the spreadsheet off Gina's lap, tossed it none too gently to the floor. "*What* has Hoyt done?"

"I was going to tell you," Gina said, "after the reception. Andrew was at a restaurant. Chinatown. San Francisco. An hour ago. One of the local reporters asked him about our relations with China, Chairman Lo's statement that America was like a schoolyard bully that needed to be taught a lesson. Andrew'd had some sake or something—"

"He wouldn't get sake in a Chinese restaurant," Claudia corrected.

"Whatever. Andrew put a chopstick on his shoulder and said, 'Go ahead Comrade Lo, knock it off. I dare you.'"

Lynnie dropped her face into her hands. "Ohhh, Andrew. It's not even eight o'clock out there. Sake for breakfast?"

"Have to be a Japanese restaurant if it was sake," Claudia said.

"Shut up!" Lynnie and Gina both shouted. Then Lynnie started to laugh. "A chopstick. First rule of politics: if you can't be good, be funny. That should be on Andrew's tombstone. All right. Look, call him. Tell him—"

"I did already," Gina cut in. "No more statements on

China except that he concurs completely with the president's policy."

"Good. We'll talk later about how to handle it from our end." Lynnie wiped a trickle of sweat off her jaw. She looked around. The motorcade was rolling through a sparsely populated section of Blaine, high on the hillside. "Tell George we need air back here, cold as he can get it. And I've got to get out of this vest."

"Now?" Claudia said. She and Gina both glanced at Mike.

"*Right* now." Lynnie dropped to the floor, to her knees, pulled off her coat and started to unbutton her blouse.

"I should look away, maybe?" Mike offered.

Lynnie's fingers paused between her breasts. Her eyes swung up, sparkling, impish. "It's OK. I've got a T-shirt underneath." The blouse came off, revealing a white denim shell. Mike knew what it was. Kevlar. Bulletproof. Then the vest was set aside and that left the undershirt, damp from sweat, clinging to her. She kept her back to Gina, her eyes on Mike, lids lowered. Her nipples showed, taut strawberry-like lumps nuzzling the fabric.

Was this just an impulse or had Lynnie planned it? Sometimes Mike had trouble telling, but not now. She'd had this in mind all along, a presidential striptease. Well, it worked for him. And Lynnie—there was the smile. Now she was biting her tongue to keep from laughing. One thing was certain about Lynnie Connor: she knew how to cut to the chase.

Claudia was feeling left out. She bent sideways, gazing at Lynnie from behind. "My father was in the restaurant business." She prodded Lynnie with her toe. "This here is what he would have called a number ten can."

"Gee, Claudia," Gina said. "You're one to talk."

Lynnie did a quick gymnastic maneuver to look at her own backside. "She's right. The big red caboose. It's lettuce and water for me after the election."

There was a pause while they all looked at Mike, as if

they each got a comment and now it was his turn. He tilted so he had a proper view. "Nah. The Little Engine That Could."

He was rewarded when Lynnie turned crimson again. She peeked at him through her bangs, her eyes sending him a shower of thank-yous.

Lynnie slipped back into her blouse and, using Mike's knee as a brace, climbed onto the seat. She was light-hearted now, ticking with leftover energy from the speech. She pointed out the window at a new convenience store, then the house where a friend had lived when she and Mike were young. Mike nodded and smiled, basking in her cast sunlight.

But Lynnie's moods were quicksilver that day. As they neared the mayor's house, in the new development west of town, she began to brood. Claudia passed a piece of paper to her. "They're expecting us at Fort Drum in two hours. We can make Detroit tonight if—"

"No," Lynnie said, too loudly. "I want to talk to Mike. Have the Secret Service clear the yard. We'll walk by the lake." She looked at him, and quickly away. "Sorry," she mumbled. Funny how a single word could crush so many hopes.

"You can't stay," Mike said.

"I'm sorry, Mike."

"Stop saying that." They were standing at the edge of the lake, alone—or as alone as they could get. Secret Service agents were milling around just out of earshot. There was a line of boats a half mile offshore, people in them chattering and pointing. They recognized Lynnie from her bright blue suit. Gina and Claudia were up the lawn near the house, watching.

"Some of the troops are coming home from Taiwan today, to Fort Drum. The Army runs the schedule, I don't. I need to be there to meet them. The press will be all over it. We can't pass up that kind of coverage." Lynnie swung around, putting her back to the lake. The tabloid reporters followed her everywhere. There were probably a few on those boats. They used listening devices; they might hear. "Claudia had everything arranged. The mayor was going to let us use his house. You could have stayed, too. Then when we found out about Fort Drum, I told Claudia we couldn't do it, breeze in and out of town, leave you here. We had to bring you with us. Claudia said, 'What for? You going to fuck him in the bathroom on the plane? With the press riding in the back, cheering you on?' She's right, Mike, we can't . . ."

Mike wished he could be angry, let it come flooding out. But what good would it do, punishing her? She was as unhappy as he was. He pursed his lips, swallowed it all down. For a time, they just stared along the shoreline. A boathouse hung out over the water, and one of the Secret Service agents was stationed on the roof. With a pair of binoculars, he was scanning the line of boats. Something must have caught his attention, because he started talking rapidly into his sleeve, his voice a muffled, fluttering sound.

"I'm sorry," Lynnie whispered.

"Shhhh. Enough of that." Mike looked at her, the way she stood, held her hands, the profile of her face. He couldn't deny how lovely she was. He summoned his courage. "Last time we were together, I asked you to marry me. I meant it. I mean it now. I want you that much." He took a step, closing the space between them. His arms curled up, ready to hold her.

She shut her eyes. He could sense the control she was exerting over herself. "Mike, please . . . don't. Not here."

"Right," he said harshly. Then, a heartbeat later, he was gentle again. "You're right. Come on. I'll walk you inside. They must be ready to start the reception."

They plodded toward the house, eyes on the grass, both trying to think of something to say. Gina had left, but Claudia was still there. She came scuttling to the rescue,

Lynnie's court jester. "Ain't love grand?" she cooed. When they didn't laugh, she reached up and patted Mike's tie. "I meant to tell you, that's some knot. Do you keep your lunch in there?" That got a chuckle, at least.

They continued up the lawn, Claudia in the middle. Two Secret Service agents bustled by. A third agent came in from the side. "Ma'am?" He took Lynnie by the elbow. "This way, please." He tugged hard, almost pulling her off her feet.

"What's going on?" Lynnie glanced behind, at where the other agents were converging on the lakeshore. "Mike, is that—" She squinted. "Is that Snooky Pascoe?"

Archie, in a kayak. Mike shook his head, disbelieving his eyes. The ten-foot boat was sunk to the gunnels, wobbling and taking water as Archie windmilled the double-bladed paddle. He was fifty yards out and coming on slowly. It must have been his kayak that attracted the attention of the Secret Service man on the boathouse. They were wading out after him now, six of them, their pistols drawn. It was ludicrous, all that firepower for one obviously exhausted old man. Mike expected Lynnie or Claudia to intercede, but they only watched. "Hey!" Mike yelled. "He's not going to hurt anybody. *Hey!*"

The Secret Service team wasn't about to listen. They grabbed the paddle and rolled the boat, and Archie toppled into the lake, *ploosh*, like a bag of cement. The six men hauled him to his feet and wrestled him toward land, while he cursed and fought as best he could, slipping on the muddy bottom. "*Goddamn* idiots. It's a public lake, you know. Part of a fucking *state* park." He looked toward the house. "*Lynnie!*" He slapped at one of the Secret Service men. "Get your hand off my ass, you little freak. *Lynnie Sheridan, I want to talk to you!*" He was so outraged he used her maiden name.

Mike would have missed what happened next had he not turned to ask Lynnie to call off the men. She and Claudia were exchanging a glance. *Stay out of it*, Clau-

dia's frown and head shake said. Lynnie nodded, almost
imperceptibly. Claudia motioned to the agent at Lynnie's
side. "Ben, escort the president to the house, and make
sure the rest of the grounds are secure. I don't want this
to happen again." Her voice had gone icy; this was not
the grinning, witty Claudia who charmed the wags of
Washington. She performed a smart about-face and
headed toward the shore, almost at a trot. "Ahoy! Com-
modore Pascoe! Is that a new class of submarine you're
testing?"

The Secret Service man led Lynnie away. Apparently
he didn't care if Mike came along or not. They were
rounding the corner by the rear porch when he caught
up with them. Lynnie stopped abruptly, frowning, running something through her mind. She then glanced up
at the porch. "Ben, Mr. Stanbridge and I will go in
through here, so we can surprise the reception guests.
You go ahead and check the grounds."

"But ma'am—"

"Ben, Claudia's already unhappy with you. You don't
want me unhappy, too, do you?"

"No, ma'am." He backed away a few steps, hesitated,
then hurried off to do as he'd been told.

The house was made of gray flagstone, a new-style
rancher. Still, it had the obligatory North Country back
porch, a ramshackle oblong with a sloping linoleum
floor, exposed wood framing, washer and dryer, and, in
the corner, a pair of battered metal trash cans. As Mike
shut the door behind them, he heard Archie roaring
down by the lake, "Get away from me with that. *Jesus.*
Attacking ordinary people with a *dildo.*"

Claudia shouted back, "That's a metal detector, Mr.
Pascoe. If you don't hold still and let Agent Donaldson
finish with it, you and I won't be able to talk."

"How does she know him?" Mike asked Lynnie.

"*He* is a pest," she said. She was standing by the door
that led inside, listening to see if anyone was there. "All

quiet," she reported. "Pascoe's been calling on one of the private lines at the White House—every hour, it seems. Leaving these nasty messages. Yesterday, Claudia called him back—after she had our advance people check out what was going on up here."

"About Eve Tessmer?"

"Yes." Lynnie sighed. "Eve. It makes me sick to think about it." She brooded a moment, then turned to look at Mike. Her frown was gradually replaced by a smile. "Hey, you . . . we finally get a few minutes alone."

She walked toward him, her gait slow, her hips rolling. There was only one small window on the porch, making it dim and dusky-feeling. Still, he could see the heat in her eyes. "After the election, New Year's, I've got a vacation planned, in Idaho. I was thinking I should change that, go back to Hawaii." They moved near the wall, where no one could see. She stood so close her breasts brushed his jacket, a whisper of pressure. "Come here," she murmured. The kiss was gentle, her body leaning into his, her arm draped around his neck.

The door to the inside flew open and Lena Hoxie, the mayor's wife, trundled out, lugging three bags of garbage. She was so shocked by the sight of Lynnie that she didn't notice what they were doing. As the two of them separated, Lena—sixty-five years old, and one of Blaine's leading lights—clutched her trash to her chest and curtsied so low her knee touched the floor. "Oh, Lynnie—I mean Madam President. I'm—we're so honored. I just—" She seemed ready to burst into tears.

Effortlessly, Lynnie went to her. "Hi, Lena." She took the trash bags and put them in one of the cans. "We were just talking, OK? You go back inside, and I'll be right in. And Lena, don't tell anyone we're here. It'll be a surprise when I come in, all right?"

"Oh, yes, dear." Lena's eyes flicked to Mike, but he might have been a hat rack for all the recognition she gave him. "Perfect."

Lynnie closed the door behind her. She didn't make a comment or even smile. Apparently older women curtsied to her all the time. She returned to stand in front of Mike. "Where were we? Hawaii. Will you come?"

His first thought was to say no, not being coy or angry, only realistic. New Year's—that would be twenty months since they'd last been together. He'd always love her, and she him, he hoped, but what good was a relationship like that? Then, while he was thinking it over, Lynnie did something that stole his heart all over again. She laid her head on his chest and stretched open her mouth, a gaping, tears-in-her-eyes yawn. Too late, she covered up with her hand, giggling. She snuggled against him. "Mmmmmm."

How could he refuse someone who trusted him that much? "Hawaii sounds great," he whispered. He put his hand on that special place on her back, his place. "Do you think about it much? Claudia's place, I mean. When we were there."

Lynnie grew still in his arms. "Sometimes it's all I can think about." She pressed against him, closer and closer, more needy than a hug. "It's like . . . it's like the clocks stopped ticking while we were there, it was that perfect. I cried for a whole day after you left."

He closed his eyes and smelled her hair, rubbed his cheek against it, kissed it lightly. "To next time, then."

Inside it had grown quiet. Lena hadn't kept her promise. Everyone was waiting for Lynnie to make her entrance.

"I think you've got to go," Mike said.

She held him tighter but nodded. Then she was on her way, adjusting her coat, touching up her lipstick with the pad of her smallest finger. She couldn't quite raise her eyes to look at him as she took hold of the doorknob. "Four more years!" Her voice was shaky, but her smile was rock solid. The guests broke into a chorus of cheers as she stepped through.

Mike closed his eyes again and listened to the door snap shut. "Is that a promise?" he whispered. "Only four more years?"

He left the porch, and, as he went down the steps, he noticed the tiny wet spot on his suit coat from Lynnie's tears.

CHAPTER FIFTEEN

Mike went back into the yard to check the lakefront. Archie and Claudia were gone, along with the pack of Secret Service agents. In the driveway was a delivery van from a caterer in Lake Placid. Two women were unloading it, sprinting in and out of the house with boxes and trays. Seeing all that food, Mike realized he was ravenous. He left a ten-dollar bill on the driver's seat and walked away with two thick ham sandwiches.

On the street, he let his feet carry him away, south out of the housing development and along the gravel Adirondack Park trail that circled the lake. He ate and concentrated on the scenery. Birch trees. Dragonflies. Purple pitcher plants. A snapping turtle on a log.

He'd been walking about an hour when he heard a harsh rumble. He looked up. Lynnie's helicopter roared overhead, a black egg against the pale sky. It was so near the treetops he felt he could reach up and touch it, but, before he could even lift his hand to shade his eyes, it was gone. For a while after that, he tried to imagine what she was doing. Going over her welcome speech for the troops at Fort Drum. Reviewing the polls with Gina Rizzo. Reading a memo on arms control or some big trade deal. Listening to Claudia Sung tell her about Archie Pascoe. Claudia and Lynnie certainly had acted strangely about Archie, nervous, almost as if they were afraid of him. Maybe that was to be expected. The election was so close; anything out of the ordinary would make them antsy now.

The circuit around the lake was twelve miles, and Mike saw only one other person. It was mid-afternoon and he was walking up East Shore Drive, near Eve Tessmer's house, when a big utility vehicle blew by him. The woman behind the wheel stared suspiciously, then brightened and waved. Mike racked his brain, trying to place her. Patsy, the woman who worked for Billy White at the police department. He remembered the garish shade of lipstick she wore.

Back at the motel, Mike showered and changed his clothes, then sat on the edge of the bed, massaging his feet. His wing tips weren't meant for hiking. He'd left them in the corner, muddy lumps of leather. They'd need to be resoled before he wore them again. He picked up the newspaper. The telephone message light was on, an incessant orange eye, winking. He moved the phone around so it wouldn't bother him, and settled back to read, sticking with the sports section, where there'd be no mention of Lynnie.

As sunset came on, Mike was at an Italian restaurant on a Blaine side street, up the hill from Main. To call it a restaurant was a stretch. There were only three tables, clustered by the front window under a Genesee Cream Ale sign. Most of the business was carryout. A television on the wall was tuned to the network news. Mike watched while he munched his bread and guzzled his beer. He was thirsty from all that walking.

A car pulled to the curb outside, Archie Pascoe's Cadillac. Mike was neither surprised nor irritated. It was dinnertime in a small town; it wouldn't take much work to find him. And he'd spent most of the day alone. A little company—even Archie's—would be good for him. The sleigh bells on the door jingled, and Mike, without turning around, said, "I thought you'd be locked up over in Dannemora by now."

"Dannemora's the state pen," Archie replied. "Those goons were feds. Besides, what were they gonna charge me with? Drowning without a license?" He sat down at one of the other tables and called out, "Beth? Bring me a pitcher, will you?"

The waitress must have recognized his voice. She yelled through the closed kitchen door, "You bet, Mr. Pascoe." She came in with a pitcher of beer and a glass. "You want dinner?"

"Yuh. Pepperoni, bacon, something like that." He noticed Mike was watching the television. There was a spot on about Carl Bryce, Lynnie Connor's opponent. He was in Texas, one of the big universities, at a rally. "What do you think of him?" Archie asked.

"He's going to lose," said Mike.

"Damn shame, too. I almost gave money to his campaign."

"Almost isn't the same as giving, Arch. Besides, what's wrong with Lynnie?"

"Everything," Archie said. "Just—Well there, look." Lynnie was on the screen now, footage shot that day in Blaine. She was on the stage, the sun hitting her like a spotlight. Blonde hair, blue suit, pink sandstone background. A Norman Rockwell painting. "That face, that smile. That's all there is to her."

"Because she's pretty, you hold it against her?"

"Pretty? Hell, no. Her father had the same look, down his snoot at everybody. Pip-pip, tally-ho. Related to Winston Churchill and the God-sarned Queen of England. An innkeeper—that suited him fine. Smooth all the ruffled feathers. I know *just* how you feel, sir. I understand com*plete*ly. Apologize for everything, but don't *do* anything. Just sneer at folks behind their backs." Archie's eyes slid sideways. "You think she's pretty, do you?"

Mike had ordered baked eggplant. He steadfastly chopped it into bits, not answering.

"I was damn tired out in that kayak," Archie continued, "but I'll tell you what I think I saw. I think you were about ready to jump Lynnie's bones down there by the lake. 'M I right?"

"Jump her bones? Great. The ladies around here must be putty in your hands."

"So what did you talk to her about?"

"World peace. Global warming. Pro wrestling. That sort of thing."

"You didn't used to be such a smartmouth, Michael."

The sleigh bells tinkled and they both turned to see who it was. Sandra Ducharme entered, the woman Mike had seen earlier with Billy White. Mike smiled a greeting. He glanced at her hand, saw the wedding ring there. "Evenin', Sandy," Archie said.

She seemed to want to say something, but lost her nerve and hurried back out the door.

"Who was that, Mr. Pascoe?" Beth called from the kitchen.

"Looked like Sandy White. Acted like a kid sneakin' into the drugstore to buy condoms." Archie turned to Mike. "I'll tell you, Lynnie sure brings out the weird in people. You know what that Chinese that travels with her said to me?"

"You mean Claudia Sung."

"Right. She asked did I shop at Big and Tall or just get myself upholstered. For no reason, she said that."

Beth arrived with Archie's food, a medium pizza buried under an avalanche of meat. Archie shook pepper flakes onto it. "So I was asking you, what did Lynnie say about Eve?"

Mike set his fork aside. "That you left—I think the word she used was 'nasty'—messages at the White House. That Claudia Sung returned the calls. That you were a pest."

"Guilty on all counts. But did she tell you I talked to her? To the Queen Bee herself?" The surprise that registered on Mike's face was exactly what Archie was after. "Ho!" he shouted triumphantly. "So she didn't tell you. But what's a little lie between old friends, right?"

"She didn't lie. She must—" Mike was trying to reconstruct his conversation with Lynnie. "She must have forgotten. Or maybe she didn't think it was important. Besides, last night *you* didn't tell me you'd talked to her. But what's a little lie between friends, right, Arch?"

"Just like a lawyer," Archie said smugly. "Change the subject." He took out a cigarette and lit it, unfazed by the NO SMOKING sign on his table. "Anyway, you might wonder, if I talked to her once, why was I so hot to talk to her again today?"

"OK, I'll bite, why?"

"When I spoke to Lynnie, she admitted Eve had been in touch with her. She said they didn't talk about anything particular, just that Eve was looking forward to seeing her at the birthday party."

"So? That sounds just like Eve—"

"The only reason Eve called her was to find out about her family in Arizona. You think Lynnie wouldn't remember Eve asking about that? Bullshit. Lynnie was lying."

Mike glanced at his watch. Fifteen minutes—that's all it had taken for Archie to really start annoying him. "Not lying. She's got no reason to, and she wouldn't do it anyway."

"Everybody around here always thought Lynnie Sheridan was so wonderful. I see her for what she is, a slick little hustler."

"No, dammit, she—"

"You're like all the rest," Archie said. "You always put Lynnie way up here—kingdom come." He waved his hand over his head. "You even put her before your own sister. Hell, you come to town after all these years. You see Lynnie, fine. But do you go out to Jen's grave? Were you going to do that, Mike?"

Mike jumped up, sending his chair crashing over backward. If Archie had been in range, he surely would have hit him. Then the rage passed, leaving a sick feeling in its place. He righted the chair and tossed some cash on the table. "Why are you giving me so much grief? What the hell are you after?"

Archie was all innocence. "I'm the same as always. Just curious about people. All God's little monkeys tell me the truth sooner or later."

Curious George. Archie had kept a cartoon poster in his office at school. The mischievous brown monkey. All the students laughed about it. "Remember, Archie, this isn't some kid's prank. You push too hard, and you might find people start pushing back." Mike turned on his heel, figuring he'd gotten the last word.

"Hold on," Archie called. "What's this Billy White tells me about you flying to New York City on Sunday? You want to explain that to me? Hey! *We aren't done talking here!*"

Mike kept going, leaving Archie to bellow at the *chinka-ching* of the sleigh bells on the closing door.

CHAPTER SIXTEEN

Mike drove away from the restaurant at double the speed limit, a thousand guilty thoughts about Jen yapping in his head. Archie had scored big with that comment about putting Lynnie before everyone else. Mike debated going to the cemetery, but what good would it do? He had no idea where the grave was. Besides, the cemetery wasn't where he remembered Jen. He drove home, to Grove Street.

There was a low fence around the lot to keep out roving children. He hopped over it and stood by what was left of the chimney, looking into the pit that had been the basement. Last night he'd had trouble bringing Jen to mind, but not now. He could see her curled up on her bed, doing her homework, chortling because it was so easy for her. He could hear her voice, nasal and drumroll fast, the way North Country girls talked. He recalled the last time he'd heard that voice.

As with most burn survivors, Mike had forgotten much of what went on in the hospital. Not the tubbings, though. Twice, sometimes three times a day, he was wheeled to a separate room at the end of the burn unit. The staff called it TubbyTown, as if it were a children's playland. TubbyTown had been soundproofed so the screams wouldn't escape. In the center of the room was a large metal whirlpool, the Hubbard tub, filled with warm water and disinfectant. Mike's dressings were removed, and he was lowered in. There were three nurses, and they worked on him with scouring pads, grinding at his inch-deep wounds, tearing loose the dead and dying skin. The nerve endings were right there. He could see them, tiny sprouts in the flesh. The pain was unspeakable, heart-stopping. The first time, Mike thought he might die; in a dark corner of his mind, he even wished for it. Eight hours later, he had to go through it again.

It was at that second session, when the nurses had been at him for a half hour and the pain was near its peak, that he heard Jen's voice. He opened his eyes. Jen plopped down on the edge of the tub, swished her fingers in the water and wrinkled her nose as she sniffed. He knew she was dead, but there she was. All that pain could play tricks on a person's mind, but this was more. This was a living, breathing vision, like the ones old men had in the Bible.

Jen returned every day, thirty-one days in all. They talked (yes, he answered her back, the nurses told him later) about silly, mundane things: school and friends and Mom and Dad. She helped block out the pain. He didn't scream or struggle like the other patients; he didn't even weep—until the last day. When dawn came that morning, and the phones at the nurse's station began to ring after being quiet through the night, he couldn't hold back the tears. They flooded from him. Today was his final trip to the tub, and he knew it was the last time he'd see Jen. She made her appearance. She was charming, a barrel of laughs. When it was over she said, "Gotta go!" just as she did to her friends when she had to get off the telephone.

Mike was haunted by those visions. He hated talking on the telephone because it reminded him of Jen, and the tub. Same for the smell of disinfectant. And the sound of running water. For years, he'd had nightmares. Jen would sit on the edge of his bed, try to strike up a conversation. Even now, he half expected her to walk up and point at the wreck of the house. "Geez, what a mess!"

A leaf scudded across his shoe tops, sending a chill through him. He smiled gamely. Ghosts—just in time for Halloween. He closed his eyes and tried again to remember Jen's laughter, here in the yard or coming from her open bedroom window.

Then there was a real sound, a twig snapping. "Who's there?" he called, turning quickly. The Blaine Loj van was parked on the street. He hadn't heard it pull up. "Billy, is that you?"

She stepped from the shadows at the edge of the lot. Not Billy. Billy's wife.

Sandy Ducharme had been a shy kid. Sandy White was not. She approached boldly, and took his arm. "Hi, sailor." She didn't need to ask if he was new in town. With her toe, she flicked a pebble into the basement. "What are you doing here? This sad old place?"

Mike didn't answer. It was too complicated.

Sandy kicked another pebble. "It's cold. Tell you what—want to go for a ride?"

Mike looked at her. In school, when they'd dated, "going for a ride" meant parking, not riding. She gazed back at him confidently. "Sure thing," he said. "I'd love to go for a ride."

They took Sandy's van. As they cruised through town, she told him she'd been looking for him all day. Old times' sake, she said. That's why she'd stopped in at the restaurant. She hadn't expected to find Archie Pascoe there, though. His glower had scared her off.

"Arch can do that," Mike said. He was watching her from the corner of his eye, wondering what she wanted. Old times' sake wasn't an explanation, it was an evasion.

Sandy smiled and switched subjects, telling him about her family. She had three children, all girls. They went to high school, helped out at the Loj. Next year, the oldest would start college. She mentioned Billy a few times, but not by name, using "the girls' father" or "my husband" instead.

They turned onto an unmarked gravel road that Mike knew. It crossed the forest to the west shore of the lake, to an Adirondack Park fishing access site. They parked in a big dirt lot, empty except for a broken-down boat trailer. Through the trees they could see a concrete boat ramp and a small wooden dock and, farther out, the water. The moon was rising, its disk so bright it was hard to look at. Together, they strolled down the path to the lake. The only sound was the pinging of the van's engine as it cooled in the night air. Sandy moved ahead of him, walking faster than he liked. He put his hand on her shoulder. "So what's up?"

"That rock." She pointed. "Remember?" In the moonlight it stood out clearly, a flat boulder with a two-inch bed of moss on top.

"I remember." Mike had brought her here only once. They necked and stripped and came to the very edge of having sex, but didn't. "We chickened out." His hand was still on her shoulder. He could feel the rise and fall of her breathing, faster now than it had been a moment ago. He turned her and kissed her, not aggressively, his lips inquiring. She didn't resist, but didn't help either, keeping her head down, her hands at her sides.

Mike gave a mellow laugh. "OK, that's not why we're here. It must be Billy, then."

"Yes, Billy. Dammit." Sandy picked up a rock and flung it into the lake. He was amazed at how hard she could throw. "This assembly business. I don't know why he ever wanted to run." She reached for another rock. It was stuck in the dirt so she smashed it with her heel to break it loose. "He's going to lose. Not just lose, he'll be humiliated. He's the wrong party, and everybody thinks he's an Indian, and, oh, goddammit everything." She heaved the stone at the water. "You know that bitch Lynnie wouldn't even let him have his picture taken with her today?"

Mike felt a flash of shame: the picture was his doing. "Sounds pretty rough. You haven't said how I fit in."

"Eve Tessmer," Sandy said. "If Billy arrests you—No, if he *nails* you—that's the word he uses, like some TV cop—for Eve's murder, he thinks he could win. I told him it's nuts. Mike Stanbridge a murderer? We all knew each other as kids, and people don't change that much. But he wouldn't listen. He's got it in his head that if he shows up the BCI, makes it look like he's working harder than they are, then people will vote for him. He doesn't care whether you killed Eve or not."

"He can't arrest me without evidence."

"Don't be so confident, Mikey. He's got something planned. I'm not sure what, but . . . He's bent now, twisted in on himself. Whatever he's going to do is wrong. Otherwise he would have told me about it. It's a game we play. All the bad things he does he keeps from me, so I won't give him hell so much. I do know this, though. Tomorrow morning, he's going to bring you in for questioning. He hasn't told the state cops, but he's going to call a press conference at noon. He's that sure of what he's doing. He said, Mike, once you're in, you're not getting out."

Mike's first reaction was to laugh. Wrong move. Sandy's face crumpled. She stomped another rock loose. Before she could pick it up, he pulled her to him and hugged her. "I'm sorry, OK? Now, why are you telling me?" He aimed his elbow at the flat-topped boulder. "Just a favor for an old friend?"

Sandy pushed him away and looked at the ground. "Not for you, Mike, for me. Damned politics. It's a disease. Billy can't stand the thought of losing. He'll be a laughingstock. I just want him to get through this without doing anything stupid. Then, after a while, my life, my family, can get back to normal." She took his hands and lifted them, beseeching. "Go. Leave tonight. Keep out of the way until the election is over. He can't tell the state troopers to go looking for you or he'll lose all the glory. Whatever dirt he's got planned, he'll have to forget about it."

Mike looked down at her hands, which were trembling slightly. "All right," he said. "I've had my fill of the North Country anyway."

They hugged once more, and Mike gazed at the lake over her shoulder. He could see the faint tracks of water striders etched in the spangled reflection of the moon. It was the calmest he'd felt since arriving in Blaine.

They walked back, holding hands but not talking because it would disturb the night. As they approached the van, a noise cut the stillness. *Haaay-oh*. It was the warning siren from the volunteer fire company. They stopped dead, listening without looking at one another. The siren changed cadence, steady horn blasts. Two long, seven short: twenty-seven. Everyone in town knew the code. "East Shore," Sandy said.

They looked across the lake. The flames were already in view, two arms shooting up behind the trees on Rock

Island. "Archie's place?" Mike's voice had gone shaky on him.

"Archie's. Have to be." Sandy's expression was a mixture of horror and grief. "Billy?" she whispered. "Could—" Then she shook off that idea. No matter what scheme Billy had cooked up, he wouldn't go that far.

Mike's mind was taking a different path. A fire in Blaine, at Archie's place, no less. If there wasn't an easy explanation, they'd be looking for someone to blame. Mike would be suspect number one. Torch Stanbridge.

His impulse was to get back to his car and just drive away, disappear as Sandy had asked. But running now would only make him look guilty. He tugged on her wrist. "Come on. I'd better get over there."

CHAPTER SEVENTEEN

Mike and Sandy arrived at East Shore Drive only seconds after the fire trucks. Two men hopped off each truck and pelted down the bank to the lake, hauling a length of hose behind them. This far from town, the lake was the only source of water. The rest of the crew piled out and began pulling hoses toward the house.

The entire back of the building was afire, and flames were curling out from under the front porch. The air was filled with burning pine needles, tiny flaming parachutes that drifted down like flares in a war zone. Some of them had landed on the garage roof; it was starting to smolder.

Inside the van, Mike could feel the heat, though the windows were rolled up. He looked for Archie. Not in the yard or by the lake. There he was—standing beside the road with one of the men from the fire company. Archie was shouting, waving his arms like a madman. The other man stared at him, taking the tirade full in the face.

"Mike, I can't stay here with you," Sandy said. "Somebody will see us. It'll get back to Billy."

It was already too late. Archie had paused in midshout and was glaring at them. Even at that distance, his eyes stood out, hard black pellets. "Sure," Mike said, opening the door.

Sandy grabbed him by the arm and kissed him quickly on the cheek, then, as quickly, wiped off the lipstick. "You're shaking all over."

"The fire. I haven't seen anything like this since I was burned." He shrugged weakly. "Scares the hell out of me."

She patted his hand. "Good luck."

"You, too. And thanks." He didn't turn to watch her drive away.

The man with Archie was wearing a long rubber coat with BVFD stenciled on the back. He had a cast on his foot, which explained why he wasn't helping to fight the fire. Archie had slowed down enough so the man could get a few words in. "All's I'm saying is you gotta have somethin' to set it off, Arch. Propane won't burn without a spark."

Mike stopped a few yards away, not wanting to interrupt. "I *know* that," Archie said. "Listen, I'll say it again. I heard a buzz. I looked up under the back porch, and I *saw* it start."

"A buzz? The hell d'you mean, a buzz?"

Archie poked him in the chest. "I don't know, asshole. It's your job. You figure it out."

The man didn't like being called an asshole. He pushed Archie's hand away. "Must be one of those pyromaniac bees we've been hearing about." As he sniggered, he noticed Mike.

Archie did the introductions. The man was Pete Bowman, the fire company chief. When Archie spoke Mike's name, a cloud crossed Pete's face. "I know you." His glance shifted to the fire and back. "Did you have

anything to do with this?" Subtle as a slap in the face—
that was Bowman style. Pete's brother, Orin, had been in
Mike's class at school. Whenever Orin wanted to ask a
girl out, he'd slip his hand up her skirt and say, "Movie
tonight?" He didn't get many dates that way, but those
he got were productive.

"Not a thing," Mike replied, trying to sound as casual
as possible.

"Good. Just askin', that's all." One of the other firemen
was hollering about some problem with the smallest
pumper. "Now what?" Pete muttered, and he stumped
away on his cast.

Archie had his arms folded and was watching the fire.
The back porch came loose and crashed to the ground.
The whole building groaned and shifted to the right.
"Damned shame," Mike said.

"Tell me about it," Archie spat out. "My mother's father built this place. Except for college, I've lived here
every day of my life."

"It was the propane, you think?"

"Don't *you* start on me," Archie said. Mike put his
hands up, showing he didn't mean to argue. Archie
calmed down a bit. "I was on my way out to the garage,
and I thought I smelled something, that rotten-egg stuff
they mix with the propane. There was a sound, a buzz,
ZZzzz, like that. I turned and saw a flash under the
porch. Next I knew I was on my keister back about
twenty feet, watching what looked like a damn volcano
come up inside the kitchen."

"There was nothing under the porch to set it off?"

"Nope," Archie said. "Not unless somebody put it
there."

"You mean like a fuse or a timer?"

"Like a fuse or a timer," Archie repeated sarcastically.

"If that's so, they'll find it. They solve most arson cases
now."

Archie gave a snort. "Maybe in Oz they do, but not

around here, not Sir Bowman and his Merry Morons. Look at 'em." Three of the firefighters had tripped and lay in a heap, the hose balled around them like a thick snake.

Mike had a soft spot for Blaine's firefighters. They'd saved his life once. "Arch, don't give them a hard time. They're doing their best."

Their best wasn't good enough. The roof gave a shriek and collapsed onto the upper floor, the upper floor onto the lower. As the house fell, so did Archie, his muscles slackening, his fists dropping to his sides. "There she goes," he whispered, not really believing it. But a good measure of his rage remained. He aimed some of it at Mike. "Funny sort of alibi you came up with, shagging Billy's wife."

"I wasn't shagging anybody."

Sirens. Archie must have heard them a few seconds before Mike, and that's why he made the crack about Sandy. "That'll be him," Archie said. "If Billy hasn't already heard about you being with her, one of these yahoos is bound to tell him." Far down the road they could see flashing lights, bouncing as the car rocketed over the potholes. "Way I see it," Archie continued, "you've got three choices. You can run off into the woods, like a dipshit. You can stay here, wait for Billy to find out about you and Sandy, and then he'll try to kick your butt from here to Japan. Or you can go to Eve's place, make yourself comfortable, and when I'm done here you and me can have a nice talk."

Mike had had his back turned so he wouldn't have to watch the fire. He glanced at it, and instantly his chest felt tight and his mouth went dry. No, he didn't want to face Billy here. "I'll go to Eve's," he said hoarsely.

"Good idea. I've got a truck parked over there. Get in and keep your head down."

Archie's pickup was at least thirty years old. Inside it smelled of cigarettes and motor oil. In the rear window was a gun rack, blessedly without a gun. The truck was on the far side of Eve's house, where Mike couldn't see the fire. He felt less rattled there, and tried to plan out what he should do next. The situation was so bizarre—the police, the fire, Archie stomping around like a mad elephant—he didn't get far in his thinking.

Archie arrived after twenty minutes and stopped to put something in the rear of the truck, under the cap. It was too dark for Mike to see what it was. Archie squeezed behind the wheel and dug in his pocket for his keys. "Drove this old thing over here so I could call the fire station," he said. "It's the only thing I saved, I guess." He looked at Mike. "Billy had a state trooper with him. A woman. Lieutenant Dushaney. She wants a piece of your ass—that's what she said. Do anything to get you in custody."

"Only a piece? That's disappointing."

"They're not fooling around, Mike." Archie wasn't fooling either. He was more serious than Mike had ever seen him. He put the key in the slot and started the engine.

"So where are we going?"

"You'll see."

Archie took a road Mike didn't know, farther down East Shore Drive. They turned up Knob Hill to a rock outcrop that made a good lookout. They could see Archie's place, and downtown, and most of the lake. The house was rubble, a few beams and studs left, embers and sparks. The garage, twenty yards away, was an inferno. An explosion came, a windy *oomm* that blew shingles and tar paper to the tops of the trees. "Snowblower," Archie commented matter-of-factly. "Just gassed that sucker up." That was followed by a much larger boom that shattered the garage walls and sent the fire crew skittering for cover. "The Caddy. Guess I won't have to buy those new tires after all."

Mike didn't like it, Archie's being so calm. Maybe it

was time to reconsider option number one—running off into the woods. But then he saw a state trooper's car pull into the lot at Galston's motel. It stopped in front of his room. They were looking for him already. If Mike ran now, he wouldn't get far.

Archie stepped out of the truck. "Come on. Don't have all night." They went around to the back. It was a big duffel bag he'd put in there, a new one with lots of zippers and extra compartments. He dragged it onto the tailgate and opened one of the side pockets. Mike couldn't read anything on his face. "Billy says you were out on East Shore near my house this afternoon, round three o'clock."

"That's right, I was walking—"

"His secretary, Patsy DeBruhl, saw you." Archie sighed and pulled his hand out of the bag, holding a pistol, blue and scarred and ugly. He waved Mike back from the truck and closed the tailgate. "Seems you were born under an unlucky star, Michael."

CHAPTER EIGHTEEN

From the first moment it was clear that Archie didn't know how to handle a gun. He pointed it at the truck, up in the air, finally at Mike. "Sit. That rock." Mike shuffled backward to the boulder and sat. "Good. Now just listen." But Archie couldn't talk like that, towering over him, a gun in his hand. So he sat, too. He seemed to grow tired, slouching and splaying his legs out.

"I never wanted this damn shitstorm," he said. Then, in a blank monotone, he told Mike about finding Eve the night she was killed. After his angina attack, he went back to her bed and picked up the gun, the same gun he had now. He washed her hands with vinegar to remove the powder residue. He knew about the vinegar from an article he'd read—in *Playboy*, no less. See, he said, some people do read the articles. His voice was so flat Mike missed the joke. Archie put the bedsheets back in place, and tidied up so there was no trace of his having been there.

He did it all to fool the police, to make them think it was murder—not suicide, the way it had looked when he got there. When the BCI men came to talk to him, Archie told them he didn't know anything about what had happened, except that he'd seen a car out on the Drive that night. He thought that would be enough to get them started, but, after a little nosing around, they gave up on the car completely.

That's when Archie got the idea of going to Billy. Billy always had a thin skin, so Archie needled him about how badly he was going to lose the election. And he put it in Billy's head that he might turn things around if he was the one who brought in Eve's killer. Being the fool he was, Billy swallowed it right down, turned Eve's murder into a personal crusade. That was how things got the way they were now: a shitstorm.

Mike was playing catch-up. "You said suicide?"

Some of the starch came back in Archie's voice. "*No way.*" He was shaking his head, waving the gun. Mike reached out and—an act of faith for both of them—pried the gun loose and laid it on the rock. Archie shrugged. That was as good a place for it as any. "You knew Eve. Suicide? Idea's absurd, even if the lunkheads around here would believe it."

Mike thought it over. Archie had a point about the kind of person Eve was. It was true, too, that the people of Blaine might not put too much stock in her after she was dead. "OK. Not suicide. What then?"

Archie's eyes glittered. He'd been thinking and thinking about this, but he'd had no one to talk it over with. "There's *got* to be a reason she was killed. Not rape, we know that. She didn't have any enemies, nobody who'd hold that deep a grudge. No family problems, either. Robbery? The BCI asked Mary Hodges, the cleaning lady, about that. Mary's nosy as hell. Some people won't hire her because of that. She went through the house and said nothing was missing. She was almost right, too.

"The night I found Eve, I did my own search. A few hours before, Eve had been at my house with a stack of papers, the information she'd collected about Lynnie's family, when they lived in Arizona. I told Eve I'd look it over so we could talk about it."

"That's why you kept asking me about Lynnie's ranch," Mike put in. "So?"

"Eve kept a file of index cards in the kitchen by the phone. There was a card for each year of Lynnie's life—two for that first year, Arizona, since she'd had so much trouble finding somebody out there. I checked everywhere, and those Arizona cards were gone. Vanished."

"Index cards? She could have done anything with them, thrown them away, put them aside somewhere."

"No, Mike. That party thing was like religion to Eve. She *had* to get it right. And her memory wasn't good anymore. That meant she had to be careful with everything, not mislay it. She had these tricks she used. The note they found on her nightstand with your phone numbers? She did that every day, wrote a list of things she had to do the next morning and put it beside her bed so she'd remember. She was going to call you, probably to ask you again about Arizona."

"All right, I'll buy that part, that she was going to call me. But a couple of index cards—they could be anywhere."

"No, you don't know Eve, I'm telling you. And it wasn't just the phone cards. She kept her notes in folders, one for every year of Lynnie's life, stacked in order around the house. Eve gave me the papers in the Arizona folder, but not the folder itself. That was missing, too. I searched high and low. Somebody cleaned house, took everything they could find about Arizona. They just didn't know I had most of it."

Mike ground the heels of his hands into his eyes. He was beginning to get a headache. "Why would anybody kill her for some phone numbers and an empty folder?"

"Eve was digging pretty deep. She'd call one person and that would lead her to three or four others. So on and so on. She found out more than I ever thought possible. Lynnie was pregnant once, had a miscarriage. Did you know that?" Mike did know (it wasn't a state secret), but he wasn't about to admit it. Devon Connor had been the father. Mike remembered how Lynnie had cried when she told him. He'd held her and stroked her hair and told her over and over everything would be OK. There'd be another baby. But there hadn't been another, and Lynnie had picked herself up and gone on.

Archie continued, "Eve found out something she shouldn't have. That's why that government car was out there that night. That's why she was killed."

The government car. Mike knew what Archie really meant by that: Lynnie's hired gun. He couldn't let that pass. "You've got nothing, Archie. I'll bet the BCI gave up looking for that car because they were convinced you never saw it."

"Sure. Doddering old man living alone in the woods. Those BCI jerks probably think I need an instruction manual to put on my loafers in the morning. Eve, too, just another old fart, one step short of the nursing home. They'd never believe she could have gotten into something over her head. To hell with the cops anyway."

Then Archie sat up, his expression suddenly smug. "There's a reason I was on my way out to the garage when the fire started tonight. You remember Aron Aubrey, that writer who's doing the biography on Lynnie?"

Of course Mike remembered, but he wouldn't play along. "Say what you have to say, Arch."

"The thing is, he's dead. Murdered. The day after Eve was, the very next morning."

Finally Archie had scored. Mike was stunned into silence. With his books, Aubrey was a big player in political circles; a lot of people around Lynnie would be happy to see him dead. Mike's mind was spinning as Archie rattled off the rest of it. A man named Shaumann had called him, returning the message Archie had left on Aubrey's home phone in Manhattan. He was Aubrey's better half, probably. Aubrey had been killed, Monday morning about five. That was less than seven hours after Eve was shot. Oh, and Aubrey had done some of his research on Lynnie in Arizona. He was planning another trip there this week, had the reservations all set.

"Reservations for this week," Mike mumbled.

"I was packing to drive to New York. That's the only reason I didn't get caught in the fire. I'm supposed to meet with this Shaumann character tomorrow, and I've got some other places to check out." Standing up, Archie patted his pockets. "Too many coincidences, Mike. Too many." He walked away, muttering that he needed a smoke.

Mike leaned back on his elbows and stared at the sky. Eve dead. The government car. The missing folder and cards. Aron Aubrey murdered. Tonight's fire. Archie was right: too many coincidences. Suddenly Mike found himself shivering. Until that moment he hadn't believed it. Someone had tried to kill Archie tonight. Not just kill him, but burn him alive.

The gun still lay there on the rock. Mike carried it to the truck, where Archie tossed it on the seat, carelessly, like a piece of litter. After a drag on his cigarette, he said, "Well?"

"How did they kill him?"

"Aubrey? Shotgun. At Trinity Church, if you know where that is. Way downtown Manhattan. Early morning, nobody was around. Shot him three times—head, both hands. The mob does that sometimes. Makes identification harder. They had his body at the morgue for a while before they figured out who it was."

"The police think it was a mob killing?"

Archie laughed harshly. "The mob, right. Or the tooth fairy." He pulled on his cigarette again. "Well? You see it my way, then?"

"Some of it, maybe. Some not. But let me ask you, why are you telling me all this? Why trust me now?"

"I had my doubts until that fire tonight. Somebody set it, but it wasn't you. Hell, you're such a pansy around fire, you'd faint if you even tried. I've seen you; I know."

A siren slammed through the trees less than fifty yards away, on the main road out of town. Mike hadn't realized it was so close. He flattened himself against the truck and watched until the car passed, one of the midnight blue state trooper's cruisers. Archie didn't even flinch. He'd had his big scare earlier, with the fire.

"A pansy," Mike said. "Thanks. I wish our friends in the police felt the same way."

"They got you in their sights, all right," Archie said. "Too bad about that. Not much help I can give you, either, short of turning in the gun and telling 'em everything I know. That I won't do, because if I did they'd just write it up as a suicide and file it. *If* they believed me. At this point they might think *I* killed her—or you and me together. Who the hell knows?"

"What are you going to do, then?" Mike asked.

"I'm not going to stay here, that's for sure, waiting to get potshot at. I'll go to New York, the way I planned. As for you, you're a celebrity now, all those cops wanting to talk to you. Why don't you let me drive you back to town? We could have a beer at Ralph's, let folks see we're chummy so nobody gets the idea you strangled me and stuffed me in a stump somewhere. Then I'll be on my way. Billy and that Dushaney lady will probably give you a good going over, but they don't have much to hold you on. You'll be out tomorrow morning, no problem. Probably anyway." Nervously, Archie flicked ash off his cigarette. "I'll ask one thing. Don't tell them I found Eve and took the gun. You can if you want, but I'm asking you not to."

Mike stared, then hung his head and cursed softly. He walked away, out to the point of the outcrop. Behind him he heard Archie get in the truck and turn on the radio. The baseball game was on, seventh game of the series. The crowd was roaring, the announcers barely audible over the din. Below, things had quieted down. The fire crew was poking through the wreck of Archie's garage, looking for hot spots. Only one trooper's car was parked at Galston's.

A single phrase kept running through Mike's head. *How did they kill him?* He'd said it; he believed it. *They.* Whatever was happening went way beyond a small-town murder, and somehow it led to Lynnie. A zealot in her campaign? Or the opposition, somebody with Carl Bryce? The possibilities were pretty much endless— politicos and military types and corporate execs. Top-turtle, Lynnie called her job, after the Seuss character, Yertle. King of the mountain. The stakes didn't get much higher.

Mike stared at Galston's, at the trooper's car, and he wondered what would happen if he turned himself in. He'd be in for a hard time, since he wouldn't be able to answer most of their questions. And forget Billy. Lieutenant Dushaney was the one who bothered him. She was the kind of person who'd raise butterflies as a hobby, just so she could pull off the wings.

All that seemed like small potatoes to Mike. He could sort out his own problems. He was really worried about Lynnie. If he was stuck in an interview room with a bunch of cops, he wouldn't be able to find out what was going on. Chances were good that Lynnie would get blindsided by this mess. And somehow, he felt responsible. That last thought made him smile. Hadn't he always felt responsible for Lynnie? Wasn't that his perpetual problem?

He took a deep breath and realized the air reeked of balsam. Everywhere he looked around him there were balsams. By God, how that smell brought back bad memories.

Mike went back to the truck. Archie's eyes were closed and he was shaking his head. The radio was dead. "What's up?" Mike said.

Archie kept his eyes shut. "Chicago. Dropped it in the ninth. Friggin' center fielder lost a fly ball in the lights. Went right off the end of his glove. Damn, I hate the New York Yankees." He shook his head again. "It's been *some* day."

Mike peered past him, to the far side of the cab. "I was wondering. New York City's a long drive. Think you could use a copilot?"

"I know the way," Archie said curtly.

"You got me into this. The least you can do is get me out of town."

Archie pulled out another one of his Marlboros and fired it up. He smoked quickly, annoyed. The cigarette was half gone before he made up his mind. "Fair enough, but one condition. You don't ask to go potty every fifty miles."

CHAPTER NINETEEN

Big Apple

Mike glanced stealthily around the motel parking lot. A man dressed in coveralls was cleaning litter from the shrubbery. Behind the shrubs, commuter traffic swirled down Route 9. The morning was chill and gray, and the drivers were hunched over, moving in their own little bubbles of gloom.

Mike's eyes swung to the front of the motel. Mike and Archie had checked in here—a Best Western twenty miles north of New York City—four hours ago. They'd only gotten one room, to get cleaned up and take a nap. The desk clerk had given a smarmy grin as he reached for Archie's credit card. Yes sir, a *nap*. Archie bent over him, his face livid. Watch it, Sonny, or they'll be fitting you for a body cast. Now the same clerk was staring out the lobby door at Mike. Met with a glare, he slunk into the shadows.

Mike turned back to what he was doing, trying to jimmy open the gate on the rear of Archie's truck. Archie was taking a shower, but his duffel bag was out here. Eve Tessmer's Arizona notes were in the bag. Archie had mentioned them half a dozen times during the trip from Blaine, but he wouldn't let Mike look them over. In fact, Archie had grown grouchier each time Mike asked. Mike figured he'd better get his hands on them before Archie got really angry and booted him out on the roadside.

Mike had found a screwdriver in the truck cab. He slipped it into the gate lock and pried. The lock cover skittered across the blacktop while Mike cursed and danced in a circle. He'd scraped the skin off two knuckles. Then he heard the lobby door thump, and footsteps.

"Swell job, ace," Archie said. His hair was wet and slicked straight back, straggling over his ears. He was wearing a black shirt and a black sport coat above a pair of tight bell-bottomed jeans. Benito Mussolini time-warped to the 1970s.

"You were hiding in there, watching me?"

"Yuh. Had a bet with the Smartiepants Kid whether you'd hurt yourself. I won." He inspected the damage to the truck. "That'll cost you fifty bucks." He stuck out his hand.

Mike waved him off. "I want to see those damned papers you got from Eve."

"Geez, didn't we get up on the wrong side of the bed. All right, here." He pulled a stack of paper, folded lengthways, from the inside pocket of his coat. "Came out and got these while you were showering—just in case."

"In case of what? You think I was going to try to sell them to somebody? Maybe run off to the newspapers?"

"Let's get something straight," Archie fired back. "You didn't burn my place down and you didn't kill Eve. That doesn't mean I trust you. Far as I'm concerned, you've still got a big question mark next to your name."

"Dandy," Mike said. "So what's the plan for today?"

"Plan? How about I lead and you keep your mouth shut and follow."

Archie humped into the truck while Mike glared at the pavement. *"Dandy,"* he muttered.

On the trip down from Blaine, Archie hadn't missed a single turn. His sense of direction didn't fail him as they rolled through lower Rockland County, bound for the George Washington Bridge and Manhattan. From there they continued south, toward midtown. All the while, Mike pored over Eve Tessmer's notes.

She had tiny, frilly handwriting, pretty to look at but difficult to read. She began with a description of the CC Ranch, started in the 1880s by Lynnie's great-grandfather, Charles Craig, a displaced Texas cotton farmer. There was a metes-and-bounds description of the place, and a family-tree diagram for Lynnie's mother's side of the family. Two other pages contained a bio of Lynnie's father, John Sheridan: born and raised in Sussex, England; college at Cambridge; joined the RAF during World War II and wounded; met Mattie Craig, Lynnie's mother, while traveling to Boston; the two married later that year; lived first in England, but returned to Arizona the year Mattie's father died. All good stuff for a history buff, but not much use to Eve—or Mike.

Another three pages contained notes of Eve's phone conversations with Mike. It was eerie reading them, remembering her voice, her throaty laugh. She'd written Aron Aubrey's name down and underlined it twice. The last line said, "Aubrey works out of New York. Could locate through agent or publisher." Mike turned the sheet over. It was blank. "Where's the rest? You said she talked to Aubrey."

Archie kept his eyes straight ahead. "Need to go crosstown now." He made a sharp corner.

"Archie, I want to see all of it."

"Hush. I'm driving here." Angrily, Mike slapped the papers back in order and tossed them on the seat.

They rolled into Union Square. Archie glanced around, checking addresses on the buildings. "There it is." He eased straight into an open parking spot, just vacated by a clanking ConEd van.

"Your lucky day," Mike observed.

"Naw, that's skill," Archie said. He believed it, too.

They moved up the sidewalk with a tide of office workers, to a mid-rise building that fronted the square. In the dingy lobby, Archie stopped to check the tenant register. "Fourth floor."

Mike was reading over his shoulder. "Resurrection Press?"

"Aubrey's office. Let's see what we can find out. And remember what I told you: I lead and you follow."

The Resurrection Press waiting room was as dowdy as the downstairs lobby. There were no chairs for clients, just a banged-up metal desk with no one there to tend it. On the wall was a poster showing an old Bible. The caption said, RESURRECTION—WE PUBLISH *THE WORD*. There was an appointment book on the desk, which Mike and Archie scanned, and a paperback novel, turned facedown. The cover art on the novel was florid; *Highland Fling* was the title. Archie picked it up and started to read as the sound of a toilet flushing echoed from behind a nearby door. A young man appeared, wiping his hands on his trouser legs. He was powerfully built and had a shaved head. A gold cross dangled from one ear. "Wha'chu want?" he blurted. Then he pulled himself together. "We didn't expect you until later, Father. Nobody's in yet, except me, I mean."

Father? Archie's black outfit, and there was a note in the appointment book: *Archdiocese Chicago, 10:00*. Archie nodded slowly. "Is this your book?" he said.

"Yes, Father—"

In a passable Scottish accent, Archie read aloud, "With quivering fingers she pulled down her frock. 'Och, lass,' Angus murmured, 'such beauteous wee dairies.'"

The young man reddened and reached for the book, but Archie held it away. The man looked at Mike, hoping for help. Mike shrugged sadly. "You publish Bibles here?" Archie said.

"Sure, Father, and other Christian works."

"This filth?" He flapped the novel in the air.

"No, that's not ours," he mumbled. "It's a book, is all. Something to pass the time."

Now, his dominance firmly established, Archie moved on. "Tell me, how is it that Aron Aubrey works here?"

The young man was happy to change the subject. He talked in a rush. "Aron doesn't work for us. He's got a book contract with PrimeMedia, our parent company. He needed an office, and they gave him one here because it's close to where he lives."

Lives, he'd said: so he didn't know Aubrey was dead.

"He writes trash," Archie commented.

"Yes, Father, trash." Then, confidentially, he added, "None of us like him much."

There was a pause and the young man smiled feebly. Mike decided to take a chance. "Which office is his?" he said. "I want to have a look." He didn't say why. No explanation was better than a flimsy one.

Archie glared at Mike for interrupting, but the youngster fell all over himself to be helpful. "There." He waved down the hallway behind the desk. "Past the photocopier."

The office was easy to pick out. The wall next to it was plastered with dust jackets from Aubrey's books. They were all unauthorized biographies, and each jacket had two photos of the book's subject, one calm and regal, the other grotesque, piggish. Good and evil. Two pictures of Bill Gates. Two of Prince Charles. Two of Rudy Giuliani. What would the ugly photo of Lynnie Connor have looked like? Mike wondered. He blocked that from his mind, concentrating instead on what he was after here. Aron Aubrey had been digging into Lynnie's past. What he found very possibly had gotten him killed. If there was a manuscript, or computer disks, or even a notebook, Mike might learn what was so important.

He stepped into the office. There was a chair and a desk and a phone, and they looked normal enough, but everything else in the room was brand new. Blotter. Packs of pencils and pens. A ream of notepaper. A card file. A cork bulletin board. A package of storage boxes, wrapped in original store cellophane.

Mike shuffled the things on the desk, hoping something was underneath. Nothing. He opened the drawers. Empty. There was no computer, no appointment book or calendar. It was as if someone had whisked the office clean, gotten it ready for a new occupant.

In the corner was a closet, and Mike opened it. Again empty. He stepped on his tiptoes to see the upper shelf; being tall sometimes had its advantages. There was a hat there, a white felt Panama, very large. He looked at the maker's tag: Binion/Bisbee, AZ. He remembered Bisbee from when he was a boy (it was a name hard to forget): a small town in southern Arizona, about fifty miles from Lynnie's ranch.

That was it—just the hat. He shut the closet door and looked around one last time. The phone. Maybe Aubrey had programmed the speed dial. But before he could check, an argument erupted in the front room. A woman's voice—and Archie. Mike hurried out.

The woman wore an expensive suit. Her hair was flame red, and she had a bodybuilder's figure. Behind her was a man, short but so bulked up he looked like hired muscle. He stayed clear of the argument, watching with a calculating expression, while she went toe-to-toe with Archie. Though he was thundering back at her, Archie didn't look nearly as confident as he had earlier.

"I want to know why you're here," the woman snapped, "and what you want with Aubrey."

Mike's entrance caused a momentary break, long enough for Archie to backpedal a few steps. The woman turned her attention on the young man with the cross in his ear. "Who are you?"

"Mort," he whined. He backed into the corner. "I work here."

The redhead was carrying some file boxes, still in their wrapper, like the ones Mike had seen in Aubrey's office. She set them down with a thump. "You won't work here much longer, Morty, unless I get some answers. Who did these men tell you they were?"

Mort burbled, "Priests. Priests from Chicago."

"Priests from . . . ? Ah." Suddenly she was all chummy. "Father! Sorry. Obviously, a mistake. I should have looked before I started shooting. Hr-hr." She had a dreadful laugh, like the bark of a seal. "I heard you mentioning Aron Aubrey when I came in. Why?"

Mike stepped beside him. "We were checking things out, seeing what kind of place this was."

"That's it, yes," Archie said. He was quickly regaining

his footing. "Checking things out before we do business here. Everybody knows Aubrey's a smut writer."

"Was, I'm afraid," the woman said. She looked somberly at her hands. "Aron died on Monday. I only learned last night. We were just—"

The other man filled in for her. "Stopping by."

There was an awkward lull, and Mike looked at the boxes on the floor. "Stopping by to clean out his office?"

She shifted, trying to hide the boxes with her legs. "A few corporate matters to straighten out, that's all."

"Before the police get here," Mike said.

That was one comment too many. The woman looked at him carefully. Archie put his hands behind his back, making a dignified pose. "Well, I think we're intruding here. Michael, come. Mort, we'll be in touch. Good day." He marched out the door, with Mike right behind.

In the hall, waiting for the elevator, Archie sagged against the wall. The argument and recovery had left him a little breathless. "Find anything?" he wheezed.

Mike held out the hat. "This was in the closet. Made in Bisbee, Arizona. That's near Lynnie's ranch."

The elevator arrived and they got on. Archie took the hat, turned it over and back. "Not much help. That's all you came up with?"

"No, it's not, but you don't hear a word until I see the rest of Eve's notes." It was a bluff, but Mike figured it wouldn't hurt to try.

"Chrissakes, you damn squirrel. You can't pull that kind of shit—" They had reached the ground floor and the elevator doors were open. Two men stood there, both in black suits. "Father, Father," Archie greeted them gruffly. He moved past into the lobby. One of the priests shook his head and mumbled a complaint about the cursing. Without breaking stride, Archie said, "Know what? The Chicago Cubs are a disgrace to the entire National League."

They hit the sidewalk, and Archie grabbed Mike by the elbow. "Now, you tell me—"

"Wait," Mike said. "Look there." Parked across the street was a stretch limousine. The back window was rolled down enough so they could see the man inside. He had gunmetal gray hair and a long face ending in a heavy jaw. He was talking on a cell phone, and, as he finished the call, he turned and stared right at them. Mike hustled Archie along.

"Yuh, what?" Archie said.

"You didn't recognize him? That was Jonathan Ferrar—head of PrimeMedia."

"The one who hired Aubrey to write his book?"

"That's him."

Archie looked back at the limo. "Let's go talk to him." Before Mike could argue, he spun on his heel. Then Archie muttered, "Damn." The limo was pulling away. "What do you think he was doing here?"

"Protecting his investment, I guess," Mike said. "Those were his people inside."

"All right. We'll catch up with him later," Archie said, as if spotting Jonathan Ferrar on the street was something that happened three times a day. "Let's get back to what you found in there."

"No, Arch. Show me the rest of Eve's notes first. That's the deal."

Archie ground his teeth together. He watched a man buying a hotdog at a food cart; he looked across the street at the toddlers and nannies in Union Square—all the while thinking it over. "Nope. No deal." He took off toward where they'd left the truck.

"Aubrey's roommate next?" Mike said, catching up.

"No. Next I'm taking you to the police."

CHAPTER TWENTY

Archie explained about the police as he drove down Seventh Avenue through the West Village. While Mike had been trying to jimmy open the truck, Archie had called to inquire about the investigation into Aron Aubrey's murder. He was put through to the Manhattan South Homicide Task Force and from there to the First Precinct. The murder had occurred in the First, and a Detective Mora had been assigned the case. Mora was due at the precinct house at ten o'clock, right about now.

"What do you think the police will have to say that we don't already know?" Mike asked.

"Whether they've got any witnesses or leads. Maybe they've made a connection between Aubrey's murder and the research he was doing for his book."

"Why should they tell us anything? Because we look like honest citizens?"

"One"—Archie held up a finger—"not us, me. You stay in the truck this time, keep out of my way. And two"—another finger went up—"I hinted I had some information that could help them. They'll talk to find out what I've got."

"This isn't Blaine, Archie. The cops here aren't like Billy White. You'll only make trouble if you stick your nose in."

"We'll see. No, scratch that. *I'll* see."

Again, Archie's navigating was impeccable. The precinct house was on Ericsson Place, near the exit from the Holland Tunnel. He parked in front, in the middle of a row of patrol cars. The building was a three-story fortress of tan stone. A pair of green lanterns flanked the door.

Archie pulled off his sport coat. "Sick of bein' a damn priest." He had a plaid hunting jacket folded on the seat, and he put that on instead. "I shouldn't be long," he said as he got out.

Mike waited all of ten seconds before he locked up the truck and followed him inside.

The sergeant at the muster desk was talking on the phone in Spanish. He slammed it down, irritated, then glanced at Archie. "Help you with somethin'?"

Archie didn't realize Mike had come in behind him. "I'm here to see Detective Mora."

"That so?" the sergeant said. "What about?"

"A murder case—Aron Aubrey."

"That so?" the sergeant said a second time. "Let me call upstairs, see what's what." He dialed a couple of numbers. "Yo, M—" After that he switched again to Spanish. The call was brief. Hanging up, he pointed at the stairs. "Follow the signs for 'Detectives.' You two guys together anyway?"

Archie turned and saw Mike. His face fell. "Together," he growled, "like host and parasite."

Archie had to stop twice on the stairs to catch his breath. He waved Mike ahead. The detectives' squad room was behind a blue door with a big NYPD shield. The place looked exactly like the set of a television police drama: chipped steel desks, overflowing file cabinets, bulletin boards littered with wanted posters and hand-scrawled used-car ads. It was so quiet Mike thought no one was there. Then he noticed a woman sitting behind the door. She was tall and well built and was wearing a low-cut red dress. "Detective Mora?"

"No." She lifted her arm, revealing that she was hand-cuffed to the radiator. She gave a laugh at his surprise. "Don't worry, hon, it's all a mistake. Mora you wanted? In there." She nodded at the office beside her. "Everybody else is gone. Some big drug bust, I heard. This place is like a tomb, don't you think?"

The office was a box, three sides made of glass. The sign on the door said LIEUTENANT DIAZ. Two people were inside: a man, seated at a desk, and a woman, standing with her back turned.

Archie had caught up with Mike. "Diaz?" he said, looking at the door. "You'd think they'd have Americans in charge here."

"Listen," Mike said, "let's not make any enemies—" He was cut off as the lieutenant's door swung open and the policewoman came out.

She was chunky and had ruddy dark skin with a sprinkling of freckles. Her hair was reddish and kinky, buzzed off in a flattop. She had a blocky pistol in a holster on her belt, where she rested her elbow as she spoke. "I'm Detective Mora. The note I got says you're Archie Pascoe, that right?"

She had a Spanish accent, clear enough to Mike, but Archie seemed to have trouble understanding. "Yuh, Pascoe, OK."

She glanced at Mike but didn't press for his name. "You got something on the Aubrey hit?"

"We wanted to talk to you about it," Archie said. Maybe he thought he was being sly, not answering her, but it only made Mora scowl.

She said, "Talk? Maybe. First off, why you interested?"

"Friends of his," Mike put in quickly, "from out of town."

Mora studied him for a moment. *Friends* hadn't struck her quite right. She pointed at the chairs by her desk, and they all sat down. Behind them the woman in the red dress jangled her handcuffs. "Detective, could you please—?"

"No, I could *not*," Mora snapped. "You'll have to wait for one of the guys who brought you in. So cool your jets." Mora looked at Mike and Archie. "Ms. Boobs-a-Plenty here works for one of our better hotels. They caught her this morning heading out to her car during her break. Limping. Had a pack of fifties stuffed in her shoe."

"I have no idea how that money got there," the woman in red said. She was calm, almost cheerful about this.

"Save it," Mora said. She turned back to the two men. "How long you know Aubrey?"

"A few years," Mike said. "You're in charge of the investigation?"

"No. Homicide Task Force is in charge. I work with a guy from there on it." She twitched at a button on her shirt. "How did you find out he was dead? Won't be made public 'til later today." Her eyes were as black as Archie's, but they moved faster, dart-dart.

"We called his house," Mike replied. "Talked to his roommate."

"Huh?" Mora said. *Roommate*, like *friends*, didn't sit right with her. Her eyes flicked over their faces.

Archie pulled off his coat, and used the opportunity to shoot Mike a look: *Shut the hell up, will you!* "He was shot at Trinity Church?" Archie said. "About five in the morning?" Mora nodded. "Place must have been locked up then," Archie continued. "So there wasn't anybody around to see it happen?" Mora picked at her shirt again, saying nothing. "Was there anybody around?"

Now Mora smiled, and it was a beaut, perfect little teeth all in a row. "Who are you, really? Newspaper guys? Nah. Not grubby enough. Lawyers—that's what you look like. You do." She nodded at Mike.

"Lawyers?" he said, smiling back at her. "That's a terrible thought."

The phone rang and she picked up. "Yeah? . . . Hey, Murch." That would be the desk sergeant. His nameplate downstairs said DELBERT MURCHISON. Mora stared at Archie and Mike. "Yeah, they're sittin' right here." She listened to Murchison, and she became very still. Her eyes shifted to the papers on her desk. Without saying another word, she hung up the phone. "You guys, ah . . . You wait right here. I gotta take care'a somethin', then we'll talk some more." She hurried to the lieutenant's office, rapped on the door, and went in.

"Aubrey's *roommate*?" Archie whispered. "Where the hell did you get that?"

"From you," Mike whispered back. " 'Better half,' that's what you said."

"But I was joking. I don't know who he is." They glanced at the lieutenant's office. Mora and Diaz were huddled together, talking in low tones. The lieutenant picked up the phone and dialed. "Take a look in her desk," Archie said. "See if there's a file on the Aubrey case."

"Archie, all she has to do is look out—"

"Sssst." The woman in the red dress was trying to get their attention. "Hey, sssst." She had her free hand by her knee and was motioning frantically to them.

Archie started to get up. "Arch, don't. Just leave her alone," Mike said.

"Like Mora said—cool your jets." He shambled across the room, past the woman, and down the hall to the drinking fountain. The lieutenant was still on the phone; Mora was squatting beside his chair. Mike snuck a quick look around the desk. Lots of papers, but nothing helpful.

Then Archie came back to the doorway. "Yuh, what?" he whispered to the woman in red. She spoke so softly Mike only caught the hiss of the ess's. It was something important, though. Archie's face became tense. He nodded and touched her on the shoulder, a thank-you. At the same moment the lieutenant's door banged open and Detective Mora bustled out. She was surprised to find Archie there, and she herded him back to her desk.

"All right," Mora said, dropping into her chair. Her hands were fluttering, patting the papers, arranging pens and scissors, too much motion. "Guy I work with from the task force is on his way over here. You can talk to him. Knows more about Aubrey than me, anyway. Great, huh?"

"Yeah, great," Mike said. He glanced at Archie, who was scowling. Something was definitely wrong.

Then Archie leaned forward, elbows on the desk, intruding into Mora's space. "Where you from, Detective?" She was thrown off by this, and didn't answer. "Cuba, maybe?" Archie said. "Dominica? One of those islands."

"Try the Bronx."

"Really? With your accent?" Mike was sending out brain waves: *Stop it, Archie.* He kicked him in the ankle. Archie leaned a few inches more over Mora's desk. "Tell me, what do you think of Official English?"

Mora stopped fidgeting. Her expression was tight. "I don't know. Wha'chu think about herpes?"

Archie considered this, then ducked his head forward, staring hard at her.

"Wha'chu lookin' at?"

Archie put his finger next to her lips. "You said something about herpes. I figured—"

This was too much for Mora. She jumped up, flushed with anger. "You wait here. I gotta— Jus' wait." She stomped to the back of the room, to a coffee station, and started to fill a cup, while she grumbled to herself.

Mike whispered, "Archie what the hell—?"

"Get out, Michael."

"What are you talking about?"

"For once, don't argue. Just get out of here."

"But I don't—"

"Get out. No matter what happens, don't stop. *Now.*"

Mike stood and backed toward the door. Mora noticed before he was halfway there. "Hey, you! Wait!" There was no place to set down her cup. She flung it aside and pelted after him. Then Archie surged up, holding his left shoulder. He moaned and fell in front of her, taking her out with a perfect cross-body block.

Mike tore down the hall. Moments ago he'd been a study in logic, parsing his questions, sorting the facts about Aron Aubrey. Now instinct and adrenaline took over.

Two uniformed officers were on their way up the stairs. Mike dodged down a corridor, past a smashed vending machine. Please let there be a set of back stairs. Yes!

The stairs took him to a darkened garage full of motor scooters. He could hear feet pounding on the stairs behind him. The roll-up door to the garage was closed, probably locked. There was another, regular door at the rear. He burst through into musty-smelling gloom. Thirteen pairs of eyes stared at him. One man. Twelve horses. A police stable—the horses all had blue NYPD blankets.

He swung around the first stall, skidding on the green muck on the floor. The man had a shovel in his hands. He raised it to defend himself, but Mike sprinted right through him, scattering man, shovel, bucket, horse manure. Then he was out on Varick Street. He turned right and ran, turned right again, kept running.

He finally slowed in front of a high school. It was recess. The kids were hollering and playing games, too busy to notice him. Then, back up the street, a siren sounded. Mike's heart leapt, but he held himself in check, not glancing over his shoulder. A patrol car scorched by, doing fifty and accelerating. Mike rounded the corner and ran head-on into another swarm of high schoolers. He disappeared, swallowed up by the screaming, laughing throng.

CHAPTER TWENTY-ONE

Mid-afternoon found Mike at Trinity Church, sprawled on a bench in the small cemetery. It was a pretty place, a sanctum of grass and trees and smooth-weathered headstones. But it was noisy, too. Broadway was only twenty yards away, a river of southbound traffic.

Aron Aubrey had been shot on the church steps. Mike had heard two of the groundskeepers complaining about how hard it had been to clean up the bloodstains. Aubrey wasn't the reason Mike was here, though. He'd chosen this spot because, in all of Manhattan, he could think of nowhere else to go. He was exhausted—from lack of sleep, from running, from the gnawing uneasiness that rippled through him every time he heard a siren. He wanted to sit and rest, then start planning his next move.

The woman on the next bench was reading a newspaper, a color tabloid with a bold headline, CONNOR COCKY. The photo, covering most of the front page, showed Lynnie sliding a hot dog into her mouth. Her eyes were wide and shimmery. A double entendre: *Connor Cocky*. The article, Mike was sure, was about how confident her staff was of winning the election.

In the last few hours, Mike had been thinking a lot about Lynnie. Months ago she'd given him a number at the White House where he could reach her. He'd never used it, but he'd programmed it into his cell phone. But if he called, what would he say? "Hi, hon, it's me. Listen, I'm on the lam in New York. Could you help out? Federalize the National Guard or something? By the way—love ya!"

The sun was out, and the heat was making Mike drowsy. He stared down the way at the newspaper photo. Lynnie was wearing red, something she rarely did. The last time he'd seen her in red was in Hawaii, in the silk robe he'd brought her, ruby colored with a silver dragon on the back. No buttons—a skinny belt instead. She made him close his eyes while she put it on. "Not yet. Don't look." But he couldn't help himself. They laughed as he pulled the robe right back off her shoulders. She moaned softly as he laid her on the bed.

Mike sat up with a start. He'd dozed off, and everything was dazzling, overbright. Out on Broadway, a horn was blasting away. A gray pickup was stopped in the right-hand lane, trapping a white Jaguar behind it. Someone got out of the truck on the far side, screaming, "Hey, buddy, why don't you take that noise and shove it!" The driver of the Jag hammered the horn again as he swerved into traffic. Archie nonchalantly turned and spat on the windshield.

Archie?

Mike rubbed his face. Archie. He was waving to Mike. "Hurry up before somebody gets really pissed off and shoots me."

Mike dodged through the gate and over to the truck. "How did you find me?"

"Said to myself, now think. If you were a lawyer, where would you go?" He pointed down the block, to a sign: Wall Street. "Where all the money is. Naw, actually I figured the church was the only place we might connect up. Get in. Let's go somewhere we can talk."

The somewhere Archie had in mind was Battery Park, at the lower tip of Manhattan. "What happened back there—with Mora?" Mike said as they drove.

Archie tapped the steering wheel. "It was the truck that got us in trouble." The spot where they'd parked at the police station was reserved for official vehicles, though there was no sign. A traffic cop had decided to have it towed. First he'd called in to see if there were any warrants on it, and, lo and behold, there was an all points bulletin.

"On the truck?" Mike said.

"Courtesy of Billy White and his pal Lieutenant Dushaney. They found your rental car by your old house in Blaine, but they couldn't find you or me. So with nothin' more than that, they decided you must've killed me or somesuch and run off with the truck. They put out the APB. That's what the desk sergeant called up to tell Mora. She would have arrested us both right off, but her boss wanted some more facts first. That's how you got away. Lana—the nice lady in the show-all dress—heard 'em talking on the phone to Dushaney's office. From that, Lana figured out what was going on and gave me the warning."

"But why'd they let you go? You didn't steal your own truck, but you helped me get away."

"You know that, but they don't." Archie pulled out his vial of nitroglycerin tablets. "Angina attack, they think." He gave a smirk. "Mora wouldn't go for it. She was all whiny about the bruise on her keister. Wanted to toss me in the clink just for that. But her boss believed me, that Lieutenant Diaz. He was afraid I was going to sue. Even got me to sign a release."

They'd reached the Battery, and once again Archie found a parking space with no problem. His luck was close to amazing. Before they got out, Archie looked across the park. Three men were banging on a set of steel drums. A line of blue-shirted Asian tourists shuffled by toward the waterfront. Behind the tourists came two women on rollerblades, dancing and holding hands. "Lord, this place gives me the willies," he muttered glumly.

They picked a bench close to the water, near where the Statue of Liberty Ferry was tied up. On the way down, Archie had stopped at a cart and bought four bratwurst sandwiches and a root beer. Mike got a couple of brats for himself, and for a while they ate in silence, looking across the bay at Lady Liberty and Ellis Island and the

Jersey shore. "So," Mike said, licking mustard off his finger, "how much trouble am I in?"

"A boatload." Archie sighed. "First, there's Eve's murder. Right now, you're only wanted for questioning, but tomorrow they're goin' before a judge for an arrest warrant."

"What have they got on me now that they didn't have before?"

"That's what I asked Billy. Dushaney was gone from her office and couldn't be reached. I talked Lieutenant Diaz into calling Billy to check out my story." Archie took a long pull on his root beer. "Billy ran your credit card numbers and found out it was your card those plane tickets were charged to, the ones for the round-trip from Miami to Kennedy Airport. There was a car rental, too, and enough miles on the car to go from Kennedy to Blaine and back. All right around the time Eve was killed."

"Billy?" Mike asked. "The state cops would look into that, and they'd need a court order."

"Not the way Billy tells it. You let him have your credit card numbers. Gave them up so they wouldn't have to go to a judge."

Mike flopped back on the bench. "That's what Sandy meant. Billy's wife. She told me he was up to something. Billy was in my room at Galston's yesterday. I went in the bathroom to get dressed, left him alone with my wallet. That's when he got the numbers. Skunk."

"Yep. Skunk."

"These are computer records Billy was talking about?" Mike said. "Not the real papers?"

"Don't see how he could have gotten his hands on any paper records, not that fast. Why?"

"I'm beginning to believe what they say—computers aren't as reliable as they're cracked up to be. Anyway, you said Eve's murder was first. What's second?"

"Maybe you don't want to know." Archie took a break from his food, wiping his mouth with the cocktail napkin the sausage man had given him. "Aron Aubrey. They want you for that one, too."

Mike should have been surprised, but he wasn't. "Why?" he said dully.

"Simple, really. We went to Mora asking about Aubrey's murder. Makes sense that she'd wonder why we were interested. Then Billy tells them about those credit card records. Mora put it together from there. The rental car Billy mentioned was dropped off at Kennedy at six thirty Monday morning. That's an hour and a half after Aubrey was shot. Work backwards. You could have been at Trinity Church then. And you've got no alibi; you said so yourself. Add to that that you lied about the plane tickets and all."

"I *didn't* lie. Besides, what motive would I have? Did they think of that?"

"They're a long way from talking about motives, Mike. Maybe they figure while Eve was looking into Lynnie's background, she found out something about you. Your families all knew each other. Aubrey tumbled to the same thing. A secret big enough—could be reason for murder."

"Archie, I—"

"I know. You didn't do it. I told them so, but they only smiled their little smiles. To them, I'm just an old bumpkin you conned into taking you to the big city. What could I do?"

"What could—?" Mike's voice was choked with anger. "You could tell them the truth, for one thing. That you found Eve that night. That it looked like suicide. That you screwed up all the evidence. Damn you, Archie, without your meddling I wouldn't *be* in this mess."

"You're right," Archie replied quietly. He laid his hand on Mike's shoulder. "Listen, you're right about the meddling. In fact, you've been right about a lot of things. Right about the fire at my place. They've decided that was arson. Found the fuse, an Army design, Billy said, but you can buy them mail order. And now, them putting you up for Aubrey's murder. They never would have tied Aubrey to Eve if it hadn't been for my foolishness."

"Damn right," Mike muttered. Both of them were too deflated to speak for a while.

"Anyway," Archie eventually said, "I guess you've earned the right to see this." He reached into his back pocket. "The rest of Eve's notes."

Mike snatched the paper and unfolded it. His shoulders sank in disappointment. There was only a single sheet, and it was a scribbled mess.

"Those are her original notes," Archie said. "The other pages you saw, the ones that were so neat, she copied over after she did her book reading or phone calling or whatever. This part—I see Aubrey's name a few times, probably what she wrote while she was talking with him. Don't ask me why she didn't transcribe this like the others. Maybe she didn't get around to it, or she thought it wasn't worth the time."

Mike did see Aron Aubrey's name. The rest was barely legible, and what he could make out didn't mean much—offhand references to the CC Ranch and the foreman, Oscar Martinez. He shook his head. "Dammit all, this is useless."

Archie said, "No, hold on. Look at this." He pointed. "'M.recs.' That could be 'Medical records.' Remember, that was the idea Eve hit on, to try to run down a doctor or nurse who knew the family from back then."

"So what?" Mike said. He was too exhausted, too much on edge. His anger felt like something molten inside him.

"I said *look*. See how this is all together?"

Eve had drawn a circle around "M.recs." and three more lines of chicken scratchings:

Tucson: Doc Denis—Beaupre? Daughtry? Daugherty?
AAubrey Oct.22/6pm Treated John? Lynnie once?
Call Mike

Archie said, "That last night she was alive, Eve told me she'd had a lead on somebody, but it fizzled out. Could be this fellow in Tucson she was trying to find—Doc Denis Beaupre or whatever. That's the only name in all these notes that isn't linked up with the rest of it. And she told me she'd called Aubrey that day—the twenty-second. She said he owed her a favor, but he wouldn't help her; was rude about it, too. Maybe she was trying to get more information on this Doc person."

"Could be," Mike said. "This 'Call Mike.' You thought Eve planned on phoning me the day after she died. But I don't know anything about the rest of this. I've never heard of a Doc Denis Beaupre or any doctor in Tucson." He turned the sheet over. More scrawls. *Martinez on internet? What other people work at ranch? Where were cattle sold? Run down neighbors?* Questions, but no answers.

There was one thing written clearly, at the top of the sheet. "What's this?"

Archie didn't answer. He stepped away to a set of coin-operated binoculars, moving fast for him.

Mike said, "What's this mean—'Love Boat'?"

Archie ducked his head behind the binoculars. "Those questions were for me."

"You're—?"

"Love Boat."

And in less time than it took to draw a breath, Mike saw it all. Archie and Eve out on East Shore Drive. Alone, no family to speak of. Shut in most of the winter. Not much to look forward to except each other. Mike knew what was coming, too—the story, the whole mess. Softly he said, "It doesn't matter. Some things are better kept secret."

But Archie was already into the telling, still hiding behind the binoculars. In his growing uneasiness, Mike only heard part of it. ". . . Eight years . . . Held hands and watched the TV at first . . . Don't know exactly when we started going to bed. . . . People in Blaine never suspected. Evie was always so open about things. Not possible she'd have a man on the sly . . . She wanted to get married, but I wouldn't. . . ."

Mike felt a tangle of emotions, sadness and resentment on top of the strain of the day. "Stop, Archie."

Archie kept talking. "My heart attacks, we couldn't really do it anymore, except for the oral, and Evie wasn't too hot on . . ."

Deep inside Mike, something snapped. He was suddenly furious. "All right, *listen.* I'll tell *you* something. Turnabout's fair play, right? Yesterday you asked me about Lynnie and Jen and the fire. Putting Lynnie first. Remember?"

Archie stood up from the binoculars, nodding. He seemed almost frightened, hearing the jaggedness in Mike's voice.

"When I think of that night, here's what I see. Jen and Lynnie in the two beds. Lynnie's in a Mickey Mouse T-shirt, a red one. Up around her waist, you know? Nothing else on, and the covers thrown off. Sure there's a fire, but I'm not worried yet. What do I know about fires? I'm only seventeen, a kid. I want to touch her, that's all I'm thinking. I just want to touch—"

Archie came toward him, patting the air with his hands. "Hey. Enough of that."

Mike went on, shouting now. "And your Evie. Remember how she used to preach? There's a reason for everything. A plan. Well you tell me, goddammit, what was the reason for what I did that night? What's the plan there? It's why I can't stop—"

But Mike did stop then, lips snapped shut. He'd never told anyone that much about the fire. Not a single friend. Not his parents. He hadn't even formed the words in his own mind, though he'd run the scene through his head countless times—since that day in the hospital when the psychiatrist broke off their usual banter about sports and said to him, point-blank, *Cut the crap. What's eating you, Mike?*

Archie was embarrassed, fidgeting. "Let's you and me . . . We can just forget all that, OK?"

"Sure," Mike mumbled. "Forget it." But the stunned look on his face told a different story. He wouldn't forget. Ever.

They sat together on the bench, finishing their food while they watched the tourists trundle up the gangplank onto the Liberty Ferry. Archie checked his watch and stood up. "That Shaumann fella is expecting me in twenty minutes." He waited a beat, but Mike said nothing. "You coming?"

"I'm coming."

They were tossing their trash into a bin when the two women rollerbladers zipped back past, arms around each other's waists. Archie stared after them. "If those two start smooching, I'm gonna puke."

An hour ago, Mike would have told him off, but since Archie's outburst, and his own, Mike was feeling different, willing to cut him some slack. Besides, yelling at him wouldn't do any good. He wasn't going to change anytime soon. So Mike gave a dry smile and said, "If it bothers you that much, don't look."

"Good point."

They headed for the truck, but, after only a few paces, Archie stopped abruptly. "Oh, *Jesus!* I forgot my coat. At the police station. Left it on the floor in Diaz's office."

Mike kept moving, his legs leaden with fatigue. "Too bad. We'll stop somewhere later so you can get another one."

"No, you don't understand. I didn't want to leave it sitting around in the truck so I had it with me, in the pocket."

Mike looked back now. Archie's eyes—there was fear in his eyes. "What was in the pocket?"

"The gun. The gun that killed Eve."

Mike slowed, and stopped. In his whole life he'd never felt so tired—too tired even to curse. He stared down at his hands. His fingerprints were all over that gun.

CHAPTER TWENTY-TWO

Patchin Place, where Aron Aubrey had lived, was a cobblestone mews not far from Washington Square in the West Village. It was a tiny street, forty yards deep, barred from auto traffic by an iron gate. Mike stared into the shadowed recess as they drove by. He hadn't said a word since they left Battery Park. He was afraid if he did start talking, he'd soon be screaming at Archie about the gun. Archie wasn't doing any better, shaking his head and silently cursing himself as he drove.

Archie's parking luck held, so they only had to walk a few short blocks. Mike brought along the white hat from Bisbee. He figured if Shaumann didn't feel like talking, the hat might break the ice.

They arrived at the gate at the same time as another man, coming out. He was a wiry elf with a military posture, bobbing his shoulders to the beat of music on a pair of headphones. "Watch it," Archie grunted, as the man bounced off him and into Mike. In classic New York style, he kept moving, looking through them as if they were vapor.

The houses were all tan, flat-front Federals. The first-floor windows sported paper cutout ghosts and witches. Mike had nearly forgotten—Halloween was just around the corner. He was sorting that out, getting his dates straight, when he heard a voice say, "Mr. Pascoe? It is you, isn't it?"

Jacob Shaumann was nearly as tall as Mike, and even thinner. He used every inch of his height, standing perfectly erect, though he was older than Archie. The creases on his face were dignified, not craggy. His hair was swan-white. He'd been tending the flowers in his window boxes, and he tugged off a pair of chamois gloves before he offered his hand. "Good to meet you." He led them inside, Archie first. Mike glanced back as he pulled the door closed. The man with the headphones was still out there, popping his fingers to the beat of his secret music.

"E. E. Cummings and Theodore Dreiser both lived here," Jacob was saying. "Not in this house, but on this street." He was in the kitchen, making tea. Mike and Archie were installed in the parlor. It was a peaceful room, warmly furnished. On the coffee table was a copy of *Time Out New York,* open to the arts section. Over the sound of running water, Jacob said, "Aron was so proud of the history here. He thought someday his name would be in the guidebooks with the rest of them." His voice became sonorous. "Patchin Place, home to many literary giants . . ." Mike glanced at his lap, where he was holding the hat. It looked as though the conversation was going to roll along fine without it.

The coziness of the room had drawn Archie out of his funk. "How long did he live here?" he asked.

"Forever. By New York standards, forever. He was, let's see, fourteen when we moved in."

Archie's head snapped toward the kitchen. "What about his parents? They let him do that?"

Jacob appeared in the doorway. "You assume I was his lover, Mr. Pascoe. You're not the first." He tapped his shirt over his heart. "I'm Aron's father. Aron couldn't stand the name Shaumann. Said it suited a circus act." He held his arms out—"Introducing The Great Shaumann!"—and let them fall. "Not the name for a serious writer. So he changed it to Aubrey, his mother's name." He gave them a kindly smile. "Aron wasn't gay. He hated it when people thought that of him. He was a monk, actually, neither one way or the other." The smile became pained; his eyes dropped to the floor. "No one was good enough for him, I suppose."

Archie was sorry for his mistake, but not enough to apologize. Besides, this back-and-forth had proven there was no roommate here. That was why Detective Mora had first become suspicious of him and Mike.

Jacob returned to the kitchen, calling back out, "Now me, I'm definitely one way and not the other. Aron's mother was, well, something *truly* out of character for me." His tone was mocking, like a man looking back on the incredible recklessness of his youth.

Archie gave a huff, and Mike shot him a warning look. He said, "People liked Aron's books."

Jacob came in bearing a tray with a pewter teapot and simple white china cups. "His readers did, but Aron didn't. Hurting people that way. He said it made him feel like the Grim Reaper. He was fair about it, though. Always gave people a chance to comment before he went public with the dirt. But what good is being fair when you're ruining people's lives? That was the argument we always had." Jacob shook his head. "Aron wrote good poetry. He should have stuck with that."

There were cookies on the tray, and Archie took one. "What do you know about how he was killed?"

An indelicate question, which Jacob answered delicately. "The police haven't been forthcoming, so I know only what I told you on the telephone. It was a shotgun, fired three times at close range."

"What was he doing at Trinity Church at five o'clock in the morning?"

"Work of some sort, I'd guess. He was always meeting people at strange times, strange places." Jacob looked at them both in turn. "Now, my friends, I think we should lay our cards on the table. Jonathan Ferrar sent you here, yes?"

"No," they both said.

"Then explain where you got that." Jacob nodded toward the hat.

Mike didn't lie, but he kept the story short, starting with Eve Tessmer and skipping to their visit to Resurrection Press. Jacob listened politely until he was sure Mike was finished. "This woman you saw at Aron's office, she had red hair? Body like a steroid queen?"

Mike laughed. "That's her."

"She's one of Ferrar's lawyers." Jacob fished behind him on the sideboard, coming up with a sheet of paper on which he'd written a name and phone number. "Lea Zedia—some name. The PrimeMedia news bureau got a tip from the medical examiner's office that Aron was dead. She came by last night. I already knew what had happened. I'd been in yesterday afternoon to identify his body. She just started in: 'Mr. Shaumann, I'm sorry to have to tell you, but Aron's gotten himself shot.' As if it were his fault. The kind of thing you'd say when somebody's cat got run over.

"She wanted to pick up all his things—notes, manuscripts, pictures. They had a deadline to meet, she said. Legally they owned everything anyway. If I refused, she could make things difficult—go to a judge. On and on like that, arguing with me when I wasn't saying anything. I was upset, though, and, I'll admit, I didn't like her attitude. So I shut the door in her face. What's more, later on I went down to Resurrection and cleaned everything out of his office. I knew it was all still there. Ms. Zedia didn't have keys to the building and was going to have to wait until this morning to get in. She told me so."

"At the office, you replaced everything you took," Mike said. "I saw it all there, in fresh wrappers."

"I didn't want them claiming I was a thief. I must have missed the hat, in the back of the closet."

Jacob held the plate of cookies out for Archie to take seconds. "You believe this neighbor of yours was killed

because of something she found out about President
Connor?"

"That's right," Archie replied.

"Aron was secretive about his work, rarely let me in on
anything. He couldn't hide how he felt about Lynnie
Connor, though. He adored her. Not the people around
her—they're reptiles, he said. But Connor, he adored. He
thought with her he finally had a chance of writing
something good, all the way through." Jacob had set the
paper with Lea Zedia's phone number on the coffee
table. He picked it up again and stared at it. "A couple of
nights before he died, we watched *60 Minutes* together.
They had a piece about Connor, and Aron got the sad-
dest expression, just like when he was a boy and one of
his toys broke. I asked what was the matter and he said,
'She's not real, DaDa.' 'DaDa' is what he called me. 'A
fake from the start. The book is going to kill her.'"

"Sorry about all the clutter in here," Jacob said. He was
leading them up the stairs to Aron's home office. Mike's
step quickened. He imagined heaps of notes and manuscript pages. He was wrong. The only clutter was on the
walls. Three sides of the room were covered with photos
of Aron Aubrey, advertisements for his books, newspaper clippings about him. The fourth wall, in front of the
desk, was a big mirror, floor to ceiling.

Archie let out a whistle. "Did he have a complex or
something?"

"Aron enjoyed his own company," Jacob answered
dryly.

There was a cot by the window, and, on it, two boxes.
Those were the things from Aron's office at Resurrection
Press, Jacob said. Mike started going through them.
Blank desk calendar. A pack of CDs, still in its wrapper.
Pads, unmarked. Pens, unused. Frustrated, he muttered
a curse.

Jacob sat on the cot. "Aron hated paper. Said it was a

thing of the past. He did all his work on a laptop computer—his notes and appointment book, typed all his drafts straight in. A lot of important things he just carried around in his head. As I said, he was secretive. He had to be, hoping for a big scoop with each book. I haven't been able to find the computer, so I suppose he had it with him at the church when . . . That it was stolen along with his wallet."

"Did he keep a separate copy of what he was working on? A flash drive?" Mike asked.

"A backup drive, yes," Jacob said. "But not separate. He carried it with him. He thought it was safer that way, never out of his sight."

Mike continued to sort through the boxes while Archie looked in the desk and the closet. Mike had given Jacob the hat, and he was touching up the brim, smoothing the felt. "He phoned me the night he bought this, from his hotel in Bisbee. The Copper Queen—a name I'm not likely to forget, right, Mr. Pascoe?" Archie's face reddened, but he said nothing. Jacob smiled. "He'd gone to Connor's ranch that morning to see that little log cabin where she was born."

"It's adobe," Mike put in. "And it isn't little, either."

"Log cabin—that's the story you always hear. Anyway, about a mile before they got there, they saw a jaguar run across the road. A jaguar, mind you, not a mountain lion. Amazing. It must have come over the border from Mexico. There are some pretty rugged mountains there. I don't think I've ever heard Aron sound so happy. 'It's amazing, DaDa, the Wild West! I bought a hat and boots so I'll fit in!' "

"They?" Mike said. Jacob looked at him, not understanding. "You said 'they.' "

"I did, didn't I? So did Aron. I mean 'we saw a jaguar,' was what he said. He must have hired a guide. He'd do that, if he wanted help getting around somewhere." Jacob guessed what Mike was about to ask and held up his hand. "No, I have no idea who it was. Not an official guide, though, somebody you'd find through the Chamber of Commerce. Aron would go to a restaurant or bar, pick out a likely-looking local. He was good at it, too, always finding a diamond in the rough."

Mike had reached the bottom of the second box without seeing anything interesting. There was a card file next to the telephone, and he shot Jacob a look before he opened it. Jacob nodded for him to go ahead. The cards were all blank anyway. "His computer," Jacob said. "Addresses, phone numbers—they would all be on there."

Archie sat on the edge of the bed. "Eve—my neighbor—called Aron the day she died. She said she had a lead on someone who might come to the birthday celebration in Blaine, but she'd hit a dead end."

Jacob touched Archie's arm. "You shouldn't count much on anything Aron might have told her. I remember him mentioning your friend Eve. He said she was stubborn—too stubborn for her own good." Jacob turned away, shamed by what he had to say. "Aron didn't like people calling to get information out of him. I heard him on the phone. He'd lie through his teeth and laugh about it later. A big joke to him, extra work for someone else."

Archie said, "Something has to tie them together, something from those phone calls."

"You won't find anything in here," Jacob said, nodding around at the room. Then he frowned thoughtfully. "But there is one other place. Downstairs."

He led them to the front hall closet, where there was a battered storage box. Inside were three pairs each of underwear and socks, a spare computer battery, an English-Spanish phrase book, a half-pound chocolate bar, a package of Lorna Doone cookies. "This was his traveling kit," Jacob said. "Before he went on a trip he'd get this box out. When he'd think of something he needed to take, he'd toss it in and pack it all before he left." Jacob knelt and removed the candy bar and cookies. "He wouldn't go anywhere without his treats."

In the bottom of the box was an expensive day planner, folio-sized with side pouches and snap locks. It was so new the leather still smelled. Jacob said, "I bought this for him on his last birthday. I didn't really think he'd use it—paper records, you know?" He handed it to Mike, who unzipped it and held it open for Archie to see.

The calendar pages were empty except for the last twenty days, where there were a number of entries, each abbreviated—maybe names, maybe places—and each abbreviation followed by a dollar amount. Mike would have gone through it carefully, but Archie wanted to see what was in the pouches. He clicked open the two on one side: empty, empty. The largest was locked.

Jacob was still kneeling on the floor. "Go ahead," he said.

Archie grabbed the latch, and, *snap*, broke it. Dozens of receipts and envelopes and papers poured out on the floor. Before everything came to rest, Archie was sifting through it.

One of the envelopes contained a fresh stack of cash, traveling money, no doubt. Mike took it from Archie and set it in the box. There was also an airline itinerary and a plastic sleeve with Aron Aubrey's passport.

Jacob wouldn't touch any of it. It seemed to make him anxious, these last scraps of his son's life. The phone rang, and, almost gratefully, he said, "I should take that."

The receipts were clipped together in order of date. Mike picked up a bundle and flipped through: car rental, gas and food purchases, bookstore, dry cleaning.

"Look at this," Archie said. He'd found a business card, an odd deep red color. The name on it was Denis DuPree. Directly underneath the name, it said, YOU'LL NEVER FEEL A THING! There was an address in Tucson, Arizona, but no phone number.

"Denis, spelled with one *n*, like Eve's notes," Archie said.

"Find something?" Jacob said. He'd finished his phone call, and something clearly was bothering him. His voice quavered, and his eyes seemed to have lost focus.

"Nothing, really," Archie answered, slipping his hand down by his side.

Mike wasn't going to steal anything here. He pried the card from Archie. "This name. Eve wrote down something like that in her notes, right next to Aron's name." He pulled the last page of Eve's notes from his pocket and showed it and the card to Jacob. "See—'Denis' and 'Tucson.' What do you think?"

Jacob wasn't even looking where Mike was pointing.

Mike handed the card and paper to Archie. "The phone—was there a problem?"

Jacob gave a distracted shrug. "No problem. Just . . . just the funeral home."

"What's this mean?" Archie cut in. He'd turned the business card over. On the back was written, *Paymt $2k down, total $10k, rest paybl on publi.*

Jacob twisted to look. "Receipts. Aron kept records for his taxes, and he was reimbursed sometimes for expenses." He lost his train of thought for a moment. "I'm not . . . sure what his arrangement was with PrimeMedia for the Connor book."

"That '10k' would be ten thousand. Paying that much for an interview or some other information?" Archie said. "That was normal?"

Jacob smiled, but it was clearly an effort. "No. That would not be normal."

Archie dropped to his knees next to the pile of papers. "Let's see what else is here." He picked up the flight itinerary—"Newark to Tucson, later tonight"—and put it in the box.

"No," Jacob said. Then, with a touch of guilt at having raised his voice: "I've got no use for that."

Archie turned back to the pile. "Sure. You can get a refund from the airline."

Jacob's eyes suddenly filled with tears.

Mike, seeing this, stepped forward to block his view of the closet. He could guess what was wrong. Aron Aubrey's death was public now; they'd heard about it on the radio. Still, the only call was from the funeral home. Jacob was beginning to understand how little his son would be missed.

"We don't want to be a bother," Mike said.

"What's this?" Archie broke in from behind him.

Mike didn't turn around. "Maybe there's someplace out of the way where we could—"

"I said, what's this?" Archie poked him in the leg.

Mike took it—a sheet of paper that had been folded into quarters. He gave a shrug to Jacob, a silent apology.

"Looks like an X-ray," Archie said. "A photocopy of one, anyway. Do you know anything about it?"

Mike turned, exasperated, "Archie, dammit—"

Jacob came to his senses. "No, please. I'm the one who's being rude." He knelt next to Archie and began putting the papers back in the day planner. He worked too fast, crumpling, tearing some. "There, done."

He waited for Archie to get to his feet, then handed the planner to him.

"No, we don't need the whole thing," Archie said.

Jacob pushed it on him. "Otherwise Ferrar's people will get it."

Archie wasn't going to argue, and neither was Mike. Jacob put out his hand and Mike shook it. "Arizona is the next logical step for us. We'll probably take that same plane tonight." Mike looked at Archie, whose face was noncommittal. "Before we leave, is there anything we can do? Anybody you'd like us to call?"

"No," Jacob said stiffly, "but thank you." He looked past them at the door. "Well—"

"Thanks," Mike said. He would always remember his

last view of Jacob, as he pulled the door closed on him. He was standing over Aron's travel box, holding a pair of socks in one hand, the package of Lorna Doones in the other.

CHAPTER TWENTY-THREE

"I got a mule and her name is Sal. Fifteen miles on the Erie—" Travis Veck broke off, disgusted with himself. Singing flat. All day he'd been flat. Hated it when that happened. Bad karma.

He was sitting on a concrete stoop at a side entrance to the Jefferson Market Library. From there he could look straight up Patchin Place. He still had his headphones on, but he wasn't listening to music. His boy had done an A+ job bugging Aubrey's house. Place had ears like Alfred E. Neuman. Veck had caught every word they said: Stanbridge and Pascoe and Shaumann. Now it looked like their little clambake was about over. "Arizona is the next logical step for us. We'll probably take that same plane tonight. Before we leave, is there . . ."

Veck grabbed his satchel and strolled toward Avenue of the Americas. They'd seen him once today, and that was once too many. If he'd had things his way, he'd have left someone else on stakeout here, but there wasn't anybody he could spare. That had been the story with this gig all along. Lots of money for travel and gadgets and diddling computers, but not enough manpower. The whole thing was way too hush-hush for his taste.

Through a third floor window across the Avenue, he could see a forest of raised arms, twirling and waving. JOFFREY BALLET SCHOOL the sign up there said. It didn't hold his attention long. Too scrawny. He liked his women with a little meat on their bones, muscle to fight back with when he wanted to go bump in the night.

Behind him, the gate clanked. He glanced back. Mike and Archie had stopped to make a phone call. The airlines, Veck thought, making reservations to Tucson. Might as well make reservations to the moon, for all the good it'll do you. He waited until they had hung up and moved on, and then he reached into his pocket for his own phone.

Someone answered on the first ring. "Yes, Colonel?"

Good. Cutter was manning the phone. Cutter was a professional-warrior type, always cool. Gerbil, the other man, knew his gizmos, but he could be a real chucklehead sometimes. "How's everything?" Veck asked.

"A-OK," Cutter said. "We're about half a block back from the truck. Clear view."

"All right. Let me talk to Gerb."

Cutter handed over the phone. "What's happenin', buddy?" Gerbil yelped.

Veck counted to three to let his irritation pass. He could hear a moist *chonk-chonk*. Gerbil was eating—again. "How's the signal?" Veck asked.

"Got 'em both, five-by," Gerbil reported. "The transmitter on the truck was easy, but how'd you plant the other one?"

"Bumped into Stanbridge on the street, dropped it in his pocket."

"Hooha! Slick."

"What do you hear from Dowd and Longtemps?"

"Aubrey's office has been quiet since Ferrar's people left this morning. Dowd says they're getting ear rot over there from listening to dead air. Wants to know can they go get a beer—" There was a gargling sound, and a thump.

"Gerbil? You there?"

Cutter came on the line. "Fucker choked on his chow mein, Colonel. No, don't sneeze!" More noise in the background. "Now you got soy sauce coming out your nose. Here, get a napkin. Wipe yourself off."

"Shut up and listen," Veck said icily. "Our two friends

are on their way back to the truck. They should be headed out of town, Newark Airport probably. I want—"

"Right, Colonel," Cutter interrupted calmly. "I see them, rounding the corner on Tenth Street."

"Good. I want you to follow. Stay out of sight. Use the transmitters. And tell Gerbil—if he loses them I'm going to make chow mein out of his dick."

"Got it," Cutter said, and he broke the connection.

Veck put the phone away and took out his wallet. He rearranged his IDs, slipping a new one into the plastic sheath on top. It was an FBI identification card, for Special Agent Jaron Lewis. Veck had met Lewis six years ago at a training session at Quantico. It was weird how much they looked alike. That was why Veck cozied up to him, so he could steal his ID. You never knew when something like that might come in handy. The picture was a little out of date, but good enough. Leastwise a geezer like Shaumann wouldn't know the difference.

Veck slipped the wallet into his back pocket. Sumbitch. *His knife.* Damn thing was hanging out back there like the stripe on the monkey's ass. Lookee-lookee! See what Papa brought home from war surplus! He hauled his coat down so the knife was concealed and headed toward Patchin Place. Hoo, boy. Bad, bad karma today.

A housecleaning—that was Veck's first goal. Collect all the bugs Gerbil had planted and any papers of Aubrey's he could lay his hands on. As always, Veck was in a hurry, but, before he knocked, he ran over in his mind what he knew about Jacob Shaumann. Before he retired, he'd worked for the city in child welfare. Never got promoted because he didn't like to draw attention to himself. There was a reason for that. He had a couple of drug convictions. Old Jacob was a gentleman pot farmer. With that kind of background, he'd react one of two ways when he saw Veck's FBI ID: belligerent or afraid. He was a polite old fart, not likely to make a fuss. So afraid, then.

Veck hit the door with the side of his fist, *blam blam.* When Jacob opened it, he shoved the ID in his face— "FBI"—and bulled inside.

"Yes, come in," Jacob said, stumbling back so fast his feet got tangled and he bounced off the wall. Veck looked down to hide his grin.

Once the introductions were over, Veck asked if he could have a glass of water. Needed to wet his whistle before they talked. While Jacob was in the kitchen, he swept the parlor. The two audio mikes were where Gerbil said they would be. There was a bug on the phone, too, a nifty Travers transmitter clipped to the wire where it went into the junction box. OK, all clean. Nothing for the local cops or anybody else to find.

Jacob was still fooling around in the kitchen, getting ice from the refrigerator, so Veck called out that he needed to use the restroom. He scurried up the stairs. Two more bugs in Aubrey's bedroom and another in the bathroom. (That was a Gerbil trademark, the mike in the can. Made Veck wonder about Gerb's sanity.)

All this might have seemed like overkill, but with Aubrey it was necessary. The guy was a complete spook, kept every detail secret, and all for his silly books. Four days ago Veck had killed him, and they still hadn't cracked the encryption on his laptop. The bugs, by comparison, had been golden. That's how they knew as much as they did about Aubrey—and about that old broad who'd kept phoning him, Eve Tessmer.

Leaving the bathroom, he collided with Jacob, who'd come looking for him. He was holding his glass of water, and Veck checked it to see if his hand was shaking. Not a bit. So he'd overcome his initial fear. Veck would need to change tactics, drop the bluster and show some sympathy. He took the glass and thanked him. "Let's talk about your son. Did he have an office here at home? A workroom? Yes? Let's go in there."

Jacob asked a few questions: Why the FBI and not

NYPD? Did it have something to do with Aron's book? Veck gave vague replies and got him to talk about Aron's work. He needed to find out how much Jacob knew. Meanwhile, he scooped a pen off a bookshelf (another mike). That's it, finished—except for the papers.

Veck knew all about Aubrey's preference for his computer, but everybody, even a complete spook, kept *some* paper records. From what he'd heard through the bugs, he knew Stanbridge and Pascoe hadn't found anything in this room. Still, it deserved a look. He went through the desk drawers and flipped through the card file next to the phone.

"Huh?" Veck said. The old man was still talking— something about Lynnie Connor's ranch in Arizona.

"Aron was going out there again. He had a plane reservation for Tucson tonight."

"Right." Veck already knew about that, right down to the flight and seat number. "He must have packed some things for the trip. Where would they be?" Veck had heard Jacob mention a box to Stanbridge and Pascoe.

"Yes. Downstairs." Jacob led the way.

Veck kicked the box into the hall and knelt over it. Spanish translation book. Cookies and socks and a big candy bar. Passport and three hundred bucks in cash. Flight itinerary. No other papers at all. But he'd heard them talking: receipts and business cards and X-rays.

"Is there something in particular . . . ?" Jacob said.

Veck looked up at him. How to play this? The papers could be anywhere around here. Couldn't just ask straight up or the old man would—

Then it hit him, dead between his eyes, what Shaumann had said a few seconds before Stanbridge and Pascoe left: "Otherwise Ferrar's people will get it."

Veck could have kicked himself. If only he'd let Gerbil bug this place with video cams along with the mikes. Then he would have seen what was going on, not just heard it. Shaumann giving things up to Stanbridge and

Pascoe to get them out of his hair. Still, luck ran in rivers, and sometimes what you had to do was drift with the current.

"I've got to take care of something," Veck said, and he breezed out the door before Jacob could reply.

In the courtyard, he ducked into a quiet spot next to the gate. Patchin Place was very dark now, and the ghost and goblin cutouts glowed in the windows. He punched in Cutter's number on his cell phone. It took a few rings for him to answer. "Yeah, Colonel?"

Veck could hear traffic noise in the background. "Where are you?"

"Entrance to Newark Airport. There's a problem."

Another problem. Veck held back a curse. "What's that?"

"Those pigeons stopped on the Pulaski Skyway. Just *stopped*. We had to drive by or they'd have spotted us."

"Car trouble?"

"Hell, no," Cutter answered. "They just seemed to be arguing."

"Isn't that cute," Veck said. "Has Gerbil got them on his screen?"

"Sure thing, Colonel. They're still sitting there, same spot."

"OK. Maybe it's not so bad. When they left here, did you see them get in their truck?"

"Yeah, why?"

"Was either of them carrying anything?" Veck asked.

"Pascoe was. Had a black leather case. One of those executive organizers."

"*Damn!*" Veck said. "I was up the street. That bastard's so fat I didn't see it on him."

"Important, Colonel?"

"Could be the end of everybody's troubles. There's no paper left here. I think your two pigeons took it with them. That X-ray copy, for sure, and I think maybe an address for Doc Denis, out in Tucson."

Cutter gave an appreciative whistle. That was about as much emotion as he ever showed. "What do you want us to do, Colonel?"

"Are you parked where you can—?"

"They're on the move again," he heard Gerbil say in the background. "Heading . . . yeah, heading toward us."

"You got that?" Cutter said.

"Right," Veck answered. "Let them come to you—the parking lot. Take them down."

Cutter's response was typically clinical. "Confirm, Colonel. Take them down."

For the briefest moment, Veck felt a pang of remorse. It wasn't going to be pretty. Cutter had earned his nickname in a street fight in Somalia. After that, the troopers sang whenever he came into the room. "She cut off their tails with a carving knife . . ."

"You heard right. And take every scrap of paper they've got on them. Especially that damned X-ray."

"Will do," Cutter said calmly, and he signed off.

Now Veck had to decide what to do about Shaumann. Be better for everybody if he didn't have to grease him. First Aron gets taken out, then Jacob. Even the clowns from the NYPD would start wondering what the connection was. Still, Veck was worried. Shaumann was no idiot; he could cause trouble. And Veck couldn't see spending the rest of the night playing Eddie FBI, running some kind of phony interrogation to see how much Shaumann knew. He'd go batty, shit-can the old duffer anyway. Might just as well get it over with.

He went back to the door and quietly tried the knob. It opened right up. Jacob hadn't thought to relock it. Veck checked his knife but didn't draw it until he was inside.

Water was running in the kitchen. Veck stole across the parlor for a peek. Jacob stood at the sink, washing teacups. All hunched over. Poor guy's played out, Veck thought. And look there. Damn turkey neck. Could see the blood popping away in his carotid. Veck was getting psyched now, ready for it.

Jacob heard the floor squeak and turned. His hand went behind him, to the counter, where there was a wood block filled with good quality butcher knives. "I thought you'd left."

Veck barely had time to hide his own knife behind his back. "No. Just making a phone call." They stood very still. Jacob's eyes were dead level on him, and his hand stayed where he could snatch at the knives. He knows, Veck thought with something like amazement. The old poof somehow sussed me.

Veck had no doubt how it would end if he made his move. But those knives—if he got cut, if his DNA ended up here, that could mean a shitload of trouble. Thank the Army for that. They took a sample from all the GI Joes now. Decide, decide, he told himself.

Jacob looked at him through his eyebrows. "Anything else?" he said. Blunt-like, not a tinge of fear in his voice. His hand slipped closer to the knives.

Veck smiled. The tension went out of his body. "Not today, but we'll talk again. Keep the faith, old-timer." He marched straight out the door.

CHAPTER TWENTY-FOUR

When Archie hit the brakes, Mike was looking through Aron Aubrey's calendar. As dark as it was, he had to hold it close to see, and it bounced into his nose. The Pulaski Skyway was a long, rickety bridge over a swamp, no place to stop on a lark. "What's wrong?" Mike said. Archie was clutching the steering wheel in a death grip. Traffic was already piling up behind them. "Arch, what is it?"

"I'm lost."

"How can you be lost? There's no place to turn."

"Never been here before." He had a terrible look on his face—forlorn, fuzzy-eyed, a man without a gyroscope. "This far south . . . never been." His breathing wasn't good, and he kept hitching his left shoulder in a circle.

"Is it your heart?"

"No, damn you. I'm *lost*." He nodded at the horizon. New Jersey. Terra incognita.

"The airport's right over there." Mike pointed at a jumbo jet coming in for a landing. Behind them, horns were blaring. "For God's sake, you can't just *stop*."

That got Archie's attention. His eyes snapped into focus. "Don't you raise your voice to me, you punk."

So they argued, covering old ground and new, and continued arguing until Archie got so mad he jammed the truck in gear and boiled off in a haze of burnt rubber. Twenty minutes later, when they reached the airport, they were still arguing. Archie missed the turn to the main parking lot, so they had to leave the truck in a satellite lot and take a shuttle bus. That, though they would never know it, was the only reason they made it into the terminal alive.

Once inside, Mike had his guard up. Would his name be flagged, the airport cops on the lookout for him? Apparently not. They got their boarding passes and made it through the security checkpoint without trouble.

As late as it was, most of the shops and restaurants were dark and shuttered. Archie spotted a fish bar that was still open and snapped, "Hungry. Get some grub."

"Fine," Mike snapped back. So they piled Archie's duffel bag and Aubrey's day planner and everything else they had on the floor. Archie dropped onto a stool in front of a big ice bed of oysters and steamed shrimp. Mike wasn't hungry, so he said he was going to stretch his legs. He strolled away down the long concourse.

Soon he'd left everyone else behind. The lounges were vacant, the gates buttoned up for the night. He did see a guard and a maintenance worker tinkering with one of the gangway doors. The guard stared at him, for so long that Mike felt a cold burst of adrenaline. Then the man yawned widely, and smiled. Late-shift work, turning him into a zombie. Mike nodded to him and continued on his way.

A hundred yards from the end of the concourse, he slowed and looked around. Four—no, five years ago, he'd run into Lynnie at that same spot. He'd been in New York on a client matter and was on his way back to Miami; she'd been getting off an inbound plane. She was a senator then, surrounded by a gaggle of staffers and reporters. They passed, going in opposite directions, and he wasn't sure she'd seen him. Then she flipped her hair out from her collar, a flashy semaphore. *Hiya!* Her walk changed, too, her hips spiraling, showing him she could feel the pull he exerted. He smiled, reliving the moment.

Out of the corner of his eye, he caught a flash of movement—a man. Close-cropped hair, blunt body, moving low like a jet trying to avoid radar. Mike's mind was still with Lynnie, but instinct made him shuffle-step to the side. From nowhere a knife appeared in the man's hand, a conjurer's trick. Mike arched out of the way. A searing jolt shot up his arm, and, impossibly, for he still couldn't grasp what was happening, a faint spray of blood. Then he saw the knife emerge from the back of his shirt sleeve, a curved blade sharpened to a needle tip, white, dipped in red.

The man had overcommitted. His momentum was carrying him on. Mike snarled with rage and pain. He had a height advantage and leverage and, now, an instant to gather himself. He brought his fist down on the side of the man's head, a crushing blow that reverberated like a splitting maul on soft wood. Mike hadn't hit anyone since he was twelve years old. Dead, he thought as the man collapsed. *I've killed him.* He didn't stop to check. He moved off, slowly at first, clutching his arm. Then he began to run. If they'd come after him, they'd try for Archie, too.

Mike could see him from far up the concourse, still sitting at the fish bar, a black-clad Humpty Dumpty. Someone else in black was next to him, their heads bent together in conversation. *"Archie!"* He kept running until he was on them. "Archie, we've got to go."

They turned, Archie and a nun. "Mike, great!" he said cheerfully. "This is Sister Anne."

Mike was gasping for breath. "We've got to go. Get everything—"

"Sister's been helping me figure out what this is." He motioned at the X-ray photocopy on the bar. "See, the writing on it's in Spanish."

Mike ran his eyes over the crowd. Everything seemed normal. People chatting, eating. Then he spotted a man across the bar. Slope-shouldered with a receding chin. An uneven buzz-cut hairstyle. Overall, not a striking specimen. But his eyes were glued on Archie. Hungry, wolf-like eyes. He glanced at Mike, and there was a flicker of recognition. Mike grabbed Archie by the shirt collar. "Let's go. *Now.*"

"Michael, back off," Archie snapped. He saw the blood on Mike's sleeve. His jaw dropped and he breathed, "Jesus H. Christ."

Together, they snatched the paper off the bar and their other things. Sister Anne seemed not to notice their frenzy. "Nice meetin' ya!" She slapped Archie on the shoulder. "Good luck!" She spun her stool around and tucked into her shrimp cocktail.

"What happened?" Archie burst out.

"Someone with a knife. Let's go—" The man from the counter was moving, cutting off the route into the terminal. There were two more men with buzz cuts by the security checkpoint. Mike couldn't tell if they were watching him, but he wasn't going to take any chances. "This way." He pushed Archie toward the deserted end of the concourse. Out there, without the crowds, they could at least tell who was after them.

Every few yards Mike glanced back. The slope-shouldered man was following, but at a distance. He seemed to be alone. Good. One man they could handle, even if he had a knife.

The pace was more than Archie could take. He stumbled, and his breath came in wet gurgles. Then he grabbed Mike and pointed. Jogging toward them from the far end of the concourse was the man who'd attacked Mike. The side of his face was fiery red, punctuated by a big lump. He wasn't even trying to conceal the knife in his hand. Behind them the man from the fish bar also had pulled out a knife and begun to jog.

Mike cast around for a weapon. There was nothing; even the trash cans were too large. There was no one in sight, either. But that security guard was working on the door up the way. They'd have to take their chances there. Mike prodded Archie. *"Move!"*

By the time they reached the gate area, the two pursuers had closed to fifty yards. The lights were low here, everything still. The maintenance man and guard were gone.

There was a waist-high wall in front of the exit door where the men had been working, forming an alley where passengers would line up to enter the gangway. Mike herded Archie across the lounge. In the alley, protected on two sides, they'd have the best chance of defending themselves. The two other men converged in the concourse. Archie wheezed, *"Somebody. Help us here."* He was so out of breath it sounded like a whimper.

They edged down the alley to the door. Archie reached out to try the handle, but Mike pushed him away. He'd seen something move through the glass panel. He peeked in, then flattened himself against the wall so he couldn't be seen. The maintenance man was in the gangway, working on the lock from the other side. No one seemed to be in there with him.

In the lounge area, the two men were moving slowly, taking the measure of the place. Mike rapped lightly on the door. "Hey, it's me," he said, keeping his voice just above a whisper.

Archie didn't know anyone was behind there. "Michael, what—?"

Mike put his finger to his lips and mumbled, "Hey, let me in."

"Use your swipe card," came a voice from the other side.

The other two men had made it across the lounge to the alley, one on each end.

Archie understood what Mike was up to now. His eyes flicked over the top of the half-wall, down the concourse. The message was unmistakable. *If we don't get through, hop the wall and run. I'll hold them as long as I can.*

Mike said to the door, "Card won't work. Open up."

"Oh, hell," the man on the other side said. "Wait a minute."

The slope-shouldered man was only a few paces away. He didn't know yet about the man behind the door. Mike turned to confront him, readying for the first lunge. His eyes. He wasn't looking at Mike, but at his hand, the X-ray copy. Mike moved. The man's eyes stayed on the paper. Wolf eyes.

From the gangway came a hiss and a blast of cold air. Archie, who was closer now, tumbled through. Too late for Mike. The slope-shouldered man was within striking distance. Mike whipped his hand up. The man lurched, trying to grab the paper, but missed. Mike leapt backward into the gangway and slammed the door.

The maintenance man was laid out and Archie was rubbing his hand. "Had to hit him."

Mike grinned and clapped him on the shoulder. He'd

let go of the door, expecting the lock to catch. Now it squeaked open, surprising them all. He just had time to grab the retention bar before the men outside were on the handle, pulling with all their might.

Mike held on, bracing with his feet. "Back there," he said. "See if there's a way out." The men yanked and snarled, but Mike had a good grip. He could keep them out—for now.

Archie retreated down the gangway. The door to the exterior stairs was locked and chained. He disappeared around the corner. The two outside let go of the handle and started whispering to each other, making plans of some sort. From the other direction, Mike heard Archie. "No. I won't . . . Sorry." Then he shouted, *"Michael, come on!"*

Mike had no choice but to trust him. He let go of the bar and ran. The men bolted through, after him. With Mike's limp they were able to take two steps for every one of his. He rounded the corner, saw the jet, the open hatch. He dove in and Archie slammed the door. The other two crashed into it. The *whump* shook the whole plane, and they howled with rage.

Mike sat up and looked around. The plane was empty except for a man in blue pants and a pink-and-white striped shirt. He lay in a heap on the floor, a broom and dustpan next to him. "Had to hit him, too," Archie said.

That seemed more than reasonable under the circumstances, so Mike said, "Good job." He looked at Archie and scrambled to his feet to give him a hand. He'd seen Archie pale before, but never gray like this. He was clutching his left shoulder up high, near his neck, and was grimacing with pain.

Archie pushed him aside. "This way," he huffed. He dropped Aubrey's day planner, but Mike grabbed it, and they hobbled to the rear of the cabin. Thin yellow light was filtering through the service door. Parked outside was a catering truck, its lift jacked up so the cargo box was level with the plane. The tiny door was a tight squeeze for Archie, but he made it. On the metal bridge, he collapsed. Mike reached to help him up, but again Archie shook him off.

The only light came from an arc lamp on top of the terminal, and that was dimmed by a misting rain. They lowered the lift and hopped to the ground. Not ten yards away, a baggage tractor was parked, its motor running. Mike jumped into the driver's seat, Archie onto the lone trailer. Then they were off, following a courtesy bus through a field of parked commuter planes, toward the far end of the terminal. They rumbled through a tunnel, under a simple sign: THIS WAY OUT.

Mike felt a strange light-headedness, the same feeling he'd had as a boy after going on one of the big kids' rides at the county fair, the Rock-O-Plane or the Kamikaze. He wanted to laugh and whoop. He glanced back, and his smile crumpled. Archie was stretched out flat on the trailer. His chest was heaving, and he was mumbling to himself. Worse than that, his vial of nitroglycerin pills lay next to him in the trailer bed, smashed to bits.

Forty-five minutes later, Travis Veck was sitting in a van on the top level of the Terminal C parking garage. The other men were there: Dowd and Longtemps, Cutter and Gerbil. On the outside Veck appeared calm enough; leastwise he wasn't screaming or kicking or threatening to turn anybody into chow mein. Inside he was mondo ticko.

Dickbrains. Using their fake creds to follow Stanbridge and Pascoe into the terminal—OK. But trying to take them down in there? Absolute clusterfuck. And Cutter *knew* better. What was wrong with him anyway? Too tired, that's what. They were all too tired. Wanted to get this over with, get home, get some sack time.

He glanced around. The four of them, half-asleep sitting up. And Cutter, poor boob. He was one tough trooper, but look at him now. Eyes half-crossed, ear like a mashed strawberry. Bastard Stanbridge. One thing for sure. They wouldn't underestimate him again. Next time they'd just shoot the fuck, ask questions later.

All right, a royal screwup, but there was an upside. The transmitter in Stanbridge's pocket was still working. Or Veck guessed it was. "You got 'em, Gerb?" he said.

"Sure thing, Colonel." Gerbil had his computer on his lap. "They took the monorail around to the other side of the airport, Gate 20 or thereabouts. Not moving now."

So what to do next? Veck asked himself. He was too muzzy-headed to work it out. "Dowd, whatcha think they're up to?" Dowd had this knack. Spooky-like, clairvoyant. That, plus the fact that he was smart, got him in trouble when he was in uniform, but now, working with Veck and the boys, he was a real asset.

Dowd hitched his foot up so he could pick at his bootlace. He closed his eyes for a moment. "Let me see a map of the airport."

Gerbil hit a few keys on the computer. "I loooove this device."

Dowd stared briefly at the screen. "OK. A list of all the flights leaving from the concourse they're on now."

Gerbil's hands flew over the keyboard. "I loooove this—"

Longtemps whirled around and shook his fist under Gerbil's nose. "Once more and it's pow, zoom, to the moon, Alice."

That wasn't a good sign. Longtemps was a die-hard Jackie Gleason fan. That "to the moon" line was one of his favorites, but Veck had never heard him say it in anger. "Keep it down back there," he ordered quietly. What he was really thinking was, We don't get some sleep, the wheels are gonna come right off this buggy.

Dowd scanned the screen, then seemed to go into a trance. "Miami, Colonel," he said after a while. "They took the monorail to Terminal A, as far from where they had their dustup with Cutter and Gerb as they could. Got off and looked for a plane to catch. There's a UA 757 headed for Miami by way of Atlanta. Leaves in twenty minutes." A few more clicks by Gerbil confirmed it.

"What, then?" Veck asked. "Is Stanbridge going home? Got some Florida babe'll give him and Fatty a place to hide out?"

Dowd considered. "No, I doubt they're thinking that far ahead. Just leave us in the dust, that's all they want for now. But give Stanbridge a day or two. He'll move on to Arizona. He's got to try to figure out the squeeze he's in if he wants to clear himself. Arizona is the only place to go for that."

Veck made a decision, one of those snap judgments that served him so well in the Army. "Gerbil, get me Olivas on the scrambler. He can beat them to Miami, take care of them when they get off the plane." This was followed by startled silence. Olivas had been Veck's partner in his security business. He was a former Marine whose hobby was raising fighting dogs. He was as mean as his pit bulls, a good man to have on your flank. But Olivas knew nothing about this operation. Bringing him in would mean cutting everybody's share of the fee. There would be other complications, too. Veck's orders were to keep the detail to four men—*these* four.

Dowd said, "You think, Colonel, you ought to check with Star first?" His eyes were closed, and his voice was soothing. He wasn't looking to start a fight.

Veck laughed. "What, you worried Mommy's going to spank us?" Silence again, this time restless, the men on pins and needles. There were a lot of things they weren't supposed to know about this job, including who Star was, or even that she was a woman. "Or Daddy," Veck added lamely. There were a few uneasy chuckles.

Veck quickly moved on, pointing at Gerbil's lap. "Give me that machine. You get the other one, make us some reservations. We've still got work to do in Arizona."

Longtemps groaned, but Veck shut him down with a glance. "*Tomorrow*, Arizona. Tonight, we go back to Philly. I want to spend a few hours in my own rack."

They cheered, and Veck sat back, smiling. Eleven more days until the election. They'd make it—with a little luck. He started to hum, feeling better with each passing moment. Then Dowd had to go and spoil the mood. "Our own beds. Maybe she'll come and tuck us in. Mommy, I mean."

CHAPTER TWENTY-FIVE

Boarding the flight for Miami, Mike kept a sharp eye out for airport security. They'd left two men unconscious in the other terminal. Sooner or later, alarm bells were going to sound. On top of that, he was a mess, soaked from the rain and spattered with blood. Archie looked even worse, wet and pale and shuffling along like a zombie.

As it turned out, no one seemed to notice them. It was late October on the New York to Miami run. Most of the passengers were snowbirds heading south for the winter, white-haired, creaky, and cranky. Two dozen boarded in wheelchairs; the others were grumbling loudly about being kept waiting.

Mike's eyes flicked back over the crowd. No security guards. No men with knives. Not even anyone with a crew cut. At long last they were through the door and down the gangway.

He began to think ahead, to Florida. First, he'd have to do something about the way he looked. Even in Miami (where "formal wear" meant black sandals instead of tan) people would think he was a bit too creepy. There was a store in Little Havana, sort of a twenty-four-hour combination Cuban-American Wal-Mart and indoor swap meet. They could rent a car and drive out there, do some shopping, then spend the night with Randy Barchic in Coral Gables. In the morning he could decide what to do next—like maybe convince Archie to see a doctor.

Enough planning. Mike was looking forward to some peace and quiet on the plane. Something to eat, maybe even a beer. Sanctuary. Then he heard a squeaky voice say, "Whoa, there. You're gonna need a seat belt extension, aren't you?"

He was in the window seat in their row, a man so short his feet didn't reach the floor. He'd boarded earlier, one of those who arrived in a wheelchair. Archie was too tired to reply, so Mike spoke for him: "We'll take care of the seat belt. Meantime, shut your yap."

The man either had an amazingly thick skin or a hearing problem, because he grinned and said, "Nice to meet you, too. I'm Jan Halstrom. Wonder if they'll need to shift the cargo to balance him out." He made a teeter-totter motion with his hands. "We'll be late if they do."

Mike ignored him and helped Archie get settled. When that was done, Jan Halstrom said, "Reach me a couple of pillows and a blanket, will ya?" Mike obliged. Jan stuffed them in his carry-on bag. "Make great souvenirs." He caught Mike's frown and added, "The airlines budget for it. I saw that in the *Kiplinger's*."

Jan turned to Archie. "My wife was fleshy. Two years ago she went just like that—" He pointed his thumb and forefinger. "*Pow*. That's the way God does it, you know. Looks down and *pow*. Small person like me gets missed, but somebody your size—you're a mighty big fish in God's barrel."

Archie leaned over, squashing Jan into the bulkhead. "Like the man said, shut your yap."

"OK, then," Jan said slowly. He put his head back and appeared to go straight to sleep.

They did have some trouble with Archie's seat belt but, with help from one of the flight attendants, got it hooked. Within seconds Archie was snoring peacefully. It was a good thing. The weather had worsened, and it was a rocky takeoff. This was Archie's first-ever plane trip. Mike was glad he didn't have to feel those gut-twisting drops and bumps.

Mike's arm wasn't bleeding anymore, but it had begun to ache. If he closed his eyes he could see the knife coming at him. A white blade. Something about it—he was sure it was made of some kind of super-stiff cardboard, a technology he'd never heard of. That would explain how they got the knives through the security checkpoint. Maybe Mike shouldn't be so surprised. These were the same people who'd doctored the airline and car-rental and credit-card records. He was sure now that's what accounted for his mystery trip to Blaine. Someone had tapped into the companies' computers and made the changes.

High-tech knives and computer hacking. Bad enough, but that wasn't all. Eve and Aron Aubrey had been killed within hours of each other. Their deaths had to be linked, but how? They were murdered shortly after their last phone conversation. Maybe—it made sense—one of the phones had been tapped. That would likely be Aubrey's because he was the big player here.

A tap on Aubrey's phone could explain a lot. The men who attacked Mike and Archie knew they'd be in New York. Archie had talked to Jacob Shaumann on Aubrey's phone line, setting up their meeting. Someone had listened in on that call and had been waiting for them.

Mike angled his seat back a notch, getting more comfortable. Wiretaps—if they could bug Aubrey's phone, they could probably do it to anyone. He remembered all the calls he'd had over the years from Lynnie. The times she'd said she loved him, the things she wanted to do to him the next time they were together.

His mind began to drift. The things Lynnie wanted to do to him—and Lynnie always lived up to her promises, didn't she? In spite of how tired and jangled he was, he smiled.

Mike woke as something brushed across his knee. Jan Halstrom had hopped over his legs and was scuttling toward the restroom, agile as a squirrel. The flight attendant who'd helped with Archie's seat belt was standing in the aisle. He touched Mike on the shoulder. "Do you need something for that cut?"

"No, thanks. It's OK. Tell me—" Mike waved toward Jan's empty seat. "I thought he used a wheelchair to board."

"Lourdes!" the flight attendant said, chuckling. Mike looked confused, so the man explained. "We call this the Lourdes Flight. All these snowbirds get on in wheelchairs, but, miracle of miracles, they don't need them when we land. The idea is, they board first so they can get all their bags in the overheads. Then in Miami, they don't have to wait to get off. Crafty bunch of toots. But I should tell you, keep an eye peeled. A few of them have sticky fingers."

"I've seen," Mike said. He told him about the pillows and blanket.

The man chuckled again. "That's an improvement. Yesterday somebody took half a dozen life preservers from under the seats. Good luck with that arm."

Halstrom came back and hopped into his seat. Mike was listening to Archie's breathing. It was steady, no more ragged gurgling.

Mike let his mind turn to Arizona. That's what Eve and Aron Aubrey would have talked about. Mike was surprised by how much he remembered about his visits out there as a boy, to the CC Ranch. Oscar Martinez, the foreman, showing him how to ride and fly-fish for trout. Oscar's horse—Jack? No, Zack, that was it. The slat-board barn and long sweep of pasture next to it. The cabin where Oscar lived and, above it at the base of the mesa, the adobe ranch house. The cot and chair in Mike's room, both smelling of leather. The food—tortillas with every meal. Playing hide-and-seek in the peach orchard. Mike always left the orchard and hid in the little cemetery on the mesa top because Lynnie and Jen refused to go there.

All those memories, so vivid, but none of them gave him a clue as to what Eve and Aron Aubrey might have been killed over. What about the things they'd taken from Aubrey's house? There was that red business card, with the name Denis DuPree in Tucson. That was awfully close to Eve's notes. *Tucson: Doc Denis—Beaupre? Daughtry? Daugherty?* That might just be what Aubrey and Eve had talked about. So tracking DuPree down seemed like a good place to start, if he and Archie ever managed to get to Arizona in one piece.

And the rest of the day planner? Not much interesting there except for that photocopy of the X-ray. Mike took the sheet out and looked it over. Sister Anne had been right. The few words he could read were in Spanish, *Calle* and *Octubre*. The rest of it was murky and out of focus, the quality so poor that toner powder came off on his hands. He could vaguely make out a human torso and part of the head.

Jan spoke up: "Whas'at you got?"

"Nothing," Mike mumbled, trying not to lose his train of thought. How did an X-ray fit in? Archie had said Eve was looking into doctors who might have known Lynnie's family in Arizona.

"Whas'at?" Jan said again, like a whining child. "C'mon, lemme see." He reached across Archie to turn the page toward him.

"Dammit," Mike said. "If I give you fifty cents, will you shut up?"

"Wouldn't hurt—the fifty cents, I mean," Jan said.

Mike dug in his pocket for his change. "Take it. Take it all."

Jan grabbed, but Mike jerked his hand back, staring at

it. Four quarters, as many dimes and pennies, and a green plastic disk with a maze of printed circuitry on both sides.

"Geez, you're a cheat," Jan squealed.

Mike didn't take time to answer. He already had his seat belt undone and was reeling down the aisle toward the bathroom. He thought he might be sick.

Mike knew exactly what the disk was: a tracking beacon. He'd seen these used by customs agents in Miami, part of a shipboard sting operation one of his clients had suffered through. The client had been innocent, no conviction, not even any charges brought. But he and Mike had learned a lot about the not-so-fair tactics the government sometimes used.

He whisked into the restroom and slammed the door. He held the disk at arm's length, as if it had fangs and claws and might strike at him without warning. His mind was racing. So they were being tracked. The men in Newark—they almost certainly knew what plane he and Archie had boarded. They might already have people on the ground in Miami, waiting.

But why? Who was behind it? It was the same model of beacon the government used, and Archie had seen a government car the night Eve was killed, and wouldn't it make sense that someone in the government could change flight and car-rental records? And who was top-o'-the-government-heap? Top turtle? Lynnie. "Imagine what she can do," Randy Barchic had said. "Start a war. Make or break people . . ."

Mike shook his head. He wasn't ready to head down that path—questioning Lynnie.

He glanced in the mirror and his expression hardened. A wave of rage swept through him, giving back all the energy that had been taken in the last twenty-four hours. He wanted to smash that green disk to dust. He held back, talking himself down. His hand stopped shaking. He slipped the beacon into the wastepaper bin, all the way to the bottom where it wouldn't be found by another passenger. "Happy trails," he whispered.

He dashed cold water on his face and wiped away the sweat and grime of the day. Outside he heard the pitch of the engines change and a gong sound. A voice came over the PA system. "The captain has illuminated the seat belt sign . . ."

Back in his seat, Mike prodded Archie in the side. "Wake up, pal."

"Wha'?"

"We're coming into Atlanta. We have to get off."

CHAPTER TWENTY-SIX

Borderlands

"Why'd they kill all the trees?" Archie said. The jet had touched down in Tucson, and he was peering out at the fawn-colored mountains.

Mike yawned. "Nobody killed them, Archie. It came that way."

They both were worn out from a long day of traveling. After a few hours' stay in an Atlanta hotel, they had tried to catch the first flight west in the morning. The East Coast was socked in; every airport from Jacksonville to Boston was shut down. So they waited and paced until the storm broke. Now it was mid-afternoon, Arizona time. On the runway the sun was achingly bright, casting coal-black shadows.

Archie sat back in his seat. "Just jokin' about the trees. Not much to look at, if you ask me. To think good folks gave their lives to steal this ugly place from the Indians."

"Oh, they're going to love you here," Mike sighed.

Inside the terminal, Archie headed into one of the boutiques, while Mike went to find a rental car. When they met up again, Mike had a hard time not laughing. Archie had traded his black shirt for a tie-dyed T-shirt with a University of Arizona logo. The best part was the large snarling wildcat on the back. Archie's hands were full, too, with maps and guidebooks, a water bottle, even a compass.

"Looks like you're prepared," Mike said.

"I don't intend to get lost again. Say, you think they've got rattlesnakes around here?"

"Not inside the terminal, Archie."

Neither of them had speculated much about the tracking beacon. It seemed too touchy a subject. Driving away from the airport, Archie said, "Don't see anybody following. No bugs in this car, I hope."

"Keep an eye out anyway. Did you find South Sixth Avenue on the map?" That was the address on Denis DuPree's business card.

Archie said, "Only a couple of miles from here. Turn left at the next light." He glanced at the dashboard clock. "Wonder when Aubrey and DuPree were supposed to meet up. Didn't say anything in that calendar of Aubrey's, did it?"

"No," Mike said. "And we aren't even sure they were going to meet."

Archie snorted. "With ten thousand dollars on the line? They were going to meet, all right."

The place they were looking for was in a rattletrap strip mall close to the Tucson Rodeo Grounds. The buildings in the mall were made of whitewashed adobe, and the one with the right address had a carved sign over the door: LITTLE TED'S SALOON. A man was slumped on the ground nearby. As they drove up, his head sagged forward, and he vomited into his lap.

Archie nodded sagely. "Looks like a nice place."

The inside of Little Ted's was so dark they bumped into each other twice while crossing to the bar. The bartender was a scrawny man, prematurely bald. "What'll it be, gents?" His voice had the passive, empty sound of someone whose mind was elsewhere.

"We're looking for Doc Denis DuPree," Mike said. He passed him the red business card.

The bartender held the card under the lamp by the cash register. "Wait here," he said, and he walked to the end of the bar where another man sat. The second man was small and burly and heavily bearded. Little Ted? It seemed likely from the way the bartender talked to him, like a servant, handing him the card with a little bow, then nodding toward Mike and Archie.

Mike's eyes had adjusted to the gloom. Several men were playing darts in the corner. Another man was knocking back shots of vodka at a table by the door. All the other tables and booths were empty. "Great place to pick up chicks," Archie muttered. Mike laughed quietly. On the wall by the dart players was a big Confederate flag, and, next to it, a poster of a Latino boy grinning, gap-toothed, through the windshield of a lowrider. The caption said, THIS RISING TIDE LIFTS NO BOATS. Mike directed Archie's attention to it. Archie, after staring for a moment, said, "Riiight." From his tone, Mike couldn't tell what he was thinking.

The two at the end of the bar broke into laughter, and the bartender came back. Handing the card over, he said, "He's one of the buzzards playin' darts. Just goes by 'Doc' in here."

"He doesn't work here?" Archie said.

The bartender grinned. "That maggot doesn't *work* a'tall."

"Why'd he use this address, then?"

The bartender gave a shrug that said, *Do I look like his mother?* He went back to polishing beer glasses, and they made their way across to the darts players.

"Doc?" Mike said as they approached.

"Yeah, what?" one of the men answered. He was the

oldest in the group, older than Archie, and he had the look of a gargoyle who'd been spending too much time in the sun. Beaky nose. Snaggletoothed. Crispy brown skin that clung too tight to his skull.

"We'd like to talk to you." Mike flashed the business card.

Doc's eyes zeroed in, and he snatched the card. "Where's Aubrey?" He didn't wait for a reply, but turned to the others. "Fellas, have to excuse us." He motioned as if counting out money. "Got to talk a deal here. Earn me some happy cabbage." His friends gave him a round of joshing about "happy cabbage," and they took their beers and headed for the bar. Doc dropped his darts on a table and waved for Mike and Archie to sit. "Where's Aubrey?" he said again.

"You're Denis DuPree?" Archie asked.

"Could be," Doc parried. "This card's mine anyway." He settled into a chair across from them. He moved slowly, his joints arthritic, but his gaze was nervous, dancing from one spot to another like a hummingbird.

"We're Aubrey's editors," Mike said. On the airplane he'd come up with this story. "Before we go to print, we have to check out a few things. You're one of those things."

Doc relaxed a little. "You're from, whatcha-call-it, PrimeMedia?" Mike nodded. "The deal's still the same? I get the money?"

"Aubrey made the deal," Mike said. "We've never known him to go back on his word."

Doc took a swallow of his beer. His eyes flicked from Archie to Mike, to the corner of the room, the bar, nervous energy in every twitch. Mike let him sweat. Sure, he wanted Aubrey, but if he didn't talk to them, he might not get paid. His fingers moved unconsciously, still counting imaginary bills.

Archie picked up a dart and tapped it on the table. "So you're a doctor?"

"That's not really important. What I know is important." He puffed himself up as he said this, bold and self-satisfied.

Archie dropped the dart and crossed his arms. "Well, please, don't keep us in suspense."

His sarcasm was lost on Doc, who took another suck on his beer. His gaze went to Mike, to his throat. "That's a burn scar."

Mike stared back at him. "Sure is."

Doc giggled. " 'The burnt child, urged by rankling ire, can hardly wait to get back at the fire.' Guy named Ogden Nash said that."

Mike smiled. " 'He lit a match to check gas tank, that's why they call him Skinless Frank.' Guy named Burma Shave said that."

Doc slapped his thigh and howled with laughter. "Skinless Frank! Hot dog, that's funny. You're all right. Yessir. All right." He calmed down. His eyes went flick-flick. "Even if you are from New York." He said it like the name of a slaughter yard, not a city.

Mike's smile seemed set in stone. "So what is it that's so important, Doc? Tell us what you told Aubrey. That's all we need to hear."

"It all started with a scar." Doc paused, teasing them.

"Whose scar?" Archie rumbled.

"A little white scar, about as long as this." Doc held up his middle finger, a purely obscene gesture. Seeing that seemed to push him over the edge. He continued without more prompting.

"Lynnie Connor, our fearless leader? Her mama was from an old-timey Arizona family. Mattie Craig her name was. Then she got married and it was Mattie Craig Sheridan. Well, years ago, I knew Mattie. *Knew* her"—he grinned—"like Adam knew Eve."

"So?" Archie said. "Get to it, dammit."

"All right. So I knew Lynnie Connor's mama and—Oops! Did I say Mattie was her mama? Well, 'tain't so.

This scar. I was with lovely Mattie, doin' the deed as they say, and I saw it. Down here on her abdomen, just by her bush. A white line, up and down. 'Whatcha got here, honey-doll,' I say. Mattie was in another world right about then, giggly and happy, but she knew enough to answer me. 'Hyst'rectomy,' she says. At the time, it didn't make no never mind to me. Sterile woman's all the better for a man with a loose Mr. Wiggly. Then, along about two years later, Lynnie Connor gets born out at the ranch, with nobody but family around to see it. Huh, I think to myself. How'd that happen? Mattie couldn't have babies, yet—*pop*—here comes one right here. Answer was pretty clear, then and now. Somebody else was Lynnie's mother. And *that's* what I told Aubrey."

Mike felt a lurch, a brief dizziness as if the earth had shifted a few degrees on its axis. Out of the corner of his eye he checked Archie. He was poker-faced. Doc was quiet, too, letting them think it over.

At the bar, one of the men had tied a piece of twine into a noose and was stringing up a bottle of Corona Extra. Another man whined in an overdone Spanish accent, "No, *Señor*. Don't give me no necktie party."

Doc giggled. "Nice bunch of boys here, but they don't know a thing about what I told you. I want to keep it that way. My name stays out of it. That's my offer, take it or leave it."

You worthless piece of shit, Mike thought—but he smiled. "I suppose you've got proof?"

"Aubrey said the same thing: 'I suppose you've got proof.' Prissy little fuck. Well let me tell you something. Old men forget a lot, but one thing they remember is every piece of jellyroll they've ever had." He winked at Archie. "Right, partner?" Archie just glowered at the table. Doc drained his beer and said, "Anyway, you want proof, go ask Aubrey. He was going to poke around, see what he could turn up. He must have found something, because he was supposed to show up today with my money, the first two thousand, then the other eight is on account."

"Poke around where?" Mike said.

"At the ranch, for one. Place is shut up, but—" Doc grinned. "All the old ghosts are still there. Aubrey was going to Douglas, too, down on the border, and—" Now Doc's eyes flicked away, for the first time in a while. "And Bisbee, I believe."

Mike nodded. Aron Aubrey had stayed in Bisbee, his father said. "What was he trying to find?"

Doc shrugged. "Checking the old records, looking for more proof that Mattie had her operation. That's what I figured anyway."

"You've known for years about Mattie Sheridan," Mike said. "Why'd you keep it to yourself?"

There was that flick-flick with his eyes again, a rat looking for a way out of trouble. "Let's say it'd be embarrassing if it came out in public how I found out."

Mike said, "What was it you used—on Mattie, I mean—laughing gas? Give her a little extra so she wouldn't put up a fight when you tried to get in her panties?"

Archie leaned in. "What are you saying?"

"Just a guess," Mike said. "But a pretty good one. Eve was looking for a medical connection, a doctor, maybe, who knew the Sheridan family." He picked up the red card. "See what this says: 'You won't feel a thing!' We had a case in Miami a few years back. I'm thinking this is the same deal. Doc was the Sheridan family dentist. He liked to use laughing gas on the ladies."

Now that the truth was out, Doc was all bravado, chest puffed out again. "I was a practitioner of the real art. Painless Doc Denis, they called me. A nickname, see? Everybody's pal. True pain-free dentistry."

Archie's fists were curled in tight balls. "*Bastard*," he hissed.

Doc went right on talking: "For a while there, Cochise

County was like Eden to me. I knew 'em all. Adam with my pack of dewy-eyed Eves."

Archie stood up and backhanded Doc across the mouth. Mike didn't even have time to say, "No!" There was a lot of mass behind that blow. Doc left his chair like a bird taking wing. He ended in a heap under the dart board.

"What the fuck!" the man sitting by the door roared. He grabbed his vodka bottle and cracked it down on the table, breaking off the bottom to leave a nasty jagged edge. *"The fuck you think you're doin', fat-ass?"* He started across the room, tossing the furniture aside. He was a big man and the tables tumbled like matchstick toys.

Mike snatched up his chair, hoping he could knock the bottle away. He had no idea what the others by the bar were doing. Then something whizzed past Mike's ear. The big man stopped dead in his tracks. The bottle shattered on the floor, and he put his hands down, low and in front. There was a dart stuck deep in his crotch. *"Oh, Jesus Lord. Teddy . . . boys . . ."* His eyes rolled up in his head and he pitched sideways, out cold.

Archie moved in front of Mike, facing the bar, holding up another dart. *"The first one of you that moves'll end up like your asshole friend—or worse."* They all cowered, holding their hands down in athletic-supporter fashion.

Archie motioned for Mike to lead the way. Seconds later they reached the car. The door to the bar cracked open and Archie whipped the dart at it. It thudded into the wood a hair left of the handle. The door snapped shut. "Let's go, bucko," Archie said. He laughed then, a real guffaw. "Burst that sucker's bubble, didn't I?"

"Sorry I lost it back there," Archie said as they rolled north toward downtown Tucson. "Couldn't stand to hear that SOB talking like that: 'dewy-eyed Eves.' "

"No harm done," Mike said. "At least not to me." Archie had one dart left and he was turning it over in his hand, admiring the detail work in the brass. "Are you really that good with those things?"

"Everybody's got a hidden talent. Mine's darts. Elk's Club champion eleven years running. Never thought I'd use one that way, though." He tossed the last of his arsenal into the glove compartment. "He was telling the truth, you know, about Lynnie's mother."

"What makes you think that?"

"A feeling I got from watching him. Eyes and hands, mostly. The way they got twitchy when he tried to cover something up—about being a dentist, about Bisbee. But when he got to the real story—Mattie Sheridan's scar, Lynnie's birth—he was solid as a rock, staring right at you, not moving, not even blinking."

Archie saw the doubt on Mike's face. "I know what I'm saying here. I spent my whole life studying liars and cheats."

Mike tapped his finger thoughtfully on the steering wheel. He wasn't going to argue. DuPree probably had been telling the truth. His version of it. But Mike was a lawyer; he saw truth through a different prism. People's memories weren't all that good. Maybe DuPree believed he'd been with Mattie Sheridan, but it was really someone else. Heaven knows how many women he'd given an extra hit of laughing gas to over the years. Or maybe he had his dates mixed up, about when he saw the scar and when Lynnie was born. That scar was another thing. Hadn't Mike read somewhere that a hysterectomy scar could look a lot like one from a caesarean? Maybe Doc got confused about that, too.

Mike's head was starting to spin with all the maybes, so he was glad when Archie spoke up. "Weird, knowing there are people like that guy in the world." He wiped his hands on his thighs. "Anyway, let's find us a motel. After that, I need a shower."

"All right by me," Mike said. "It's already too late to get to the ranch before dark."

Archie retrieved his dart from the glove compartment. He seemed to enjoy playing with it. "The ranch? I thought that place was closed up."

Mike nodded slowly, remembering what Doc DuPree had said: *All the old ghosts are still there.*

CHAPTER TWENTY-SEVEN

Next morning found Tucson with another sparkling-clear sky and a fickle breeze up from the south. The locals wore sweatshirts and Windbreakers, but not Mike and Archie. To them, the sun was so bright it seemed hot, even if it wasn't.

The evening before, they'd had a leisurely dinner and, after that, found a place where Mike could buy some clothes and a razor and toothbrush. Then they'd turned in for a full night's sleep. They both were feeling human again.

The car Mike had rented was a compact red Chevy. Archie called it the "four-horsepower coffin." He refused to drive it, but he was happy to give directions, and that's how they made their way to I-10 and south. Fifty miles down the interstate, they dropped onto a secondary road. All that time, Archie pored over his maps and guidebooks.

"You like maps," Mike observed at one point. "That's how you knew your way around Manhattan."

Archie didn't look up. "Like to know where I'm going, that's all."

It went beyond that, Mike figured. Archie was used to Blaine, to ferns and dense stands of trees, to a close-in horizon. This desert country—so empty, so long and tall—had to seem like Mars to him. The maps were a safety line. But as the miles mounted, Archie's anxiety faded. He looked up at the scenery, commenting on the trees and rocks, even smiling when he spotted a mule deer browsing in a dry wash.

They passed Tombstone, saw a sign for the OK Corral. A while later they reached Bisbee. Mike decided to get them a place to stay for the night. He chose the Copper Queen Hotel because it was where Aron Aubrey had stayed. They were here to find out where Aubrey's research had taken him. The Copper Queen would be a good home base.

Inside at the registration desk, Archie pulled out a credit card. "No, no," Mike said ostentatiously, "this one's on me, John." He paid with cash and registered them as Andrew Snyder and John Peete, of Santa Fe, New Mexico. Archie smiled as he understood. No credit card meant no record that they were in Bisbee.

They got back in the car. It would take another hour and a half to reach the ranch. First they had to go through Douglas, a flat dusty town backed up flush to the Mexican border. On the other side, in Sonora, was Agua Prieta, a much bigger city with a population close to a hundred thousand. Archie opened one of his guidebooks and read aloud, "There are a number of *maquiladora* assembly plants in Agua Prieta, as well as a fine square and a beautiful old church. With a rich history . . ." He read on silently, then dropped the book to his lap, exclaiming, "Pancho Fucking Villa!" He stared hard to the south, while Mike laughed.

They left Douglas on a wide gravel lane, rocks bouncing *ping-cling* on the undercarriage of the car. Every few miles they passed a side road heading into the desert. Most had signs: KEEP OUT or PRIVATE ROAD or, more ominously, TRESPASSERS WILL BE SHOT ON SIGHT. They met a few cars, then nothing for miles and miles, and finally a Border Patrol truck parked on the roadside in the shade of a mesquite tree. The driver was slouched behind the wheel, drinking from a thermos cup. He saluted them with one finger to his forehead.

Mike almost missed the turnoff to the ranch. Instead of the broad, well-graded road he remembered, it was weedy and pockmarked. The big arched entry gate with the "CC" brand on top was gone, replaced by a simple barrier gate. He did recognize the stands of ocotillo along the fence line and hit the brakes, overshooting by a few yards.

"They must have taken away the markers to confuse the vandals and tourists," Mike said as he got out of the car.

Archie pointed south, where a semitruck was grinding up a hill on the horizon. "There's a road over there, not on the map."

"That's Mexico, Arch. Highway 2. Tijuana to Juarez."

"That close?"

Mike swung the gate open. "See the white obelisk down in that arroyo, about two hundred yards away? That's the border marker."

He tracked Archie's eyes, to the obelisk and the plain beyond. There was water there, from a spring, and the grama grass was heavy and emerald colored. Farther east, ten miles or so, mountains rose up, dry and tawny at the base, but wooded, olive green at the peaks. The breeze was light, ruffling the grass, touching Mike's bare arms and face like warm silk. He could smell dust and bush mint and something vague and musky. Skunk, that's what it was, from some far-off place, not unpleasant, the perfect spice for this scene.

"So what do you think? Still ugly?"

Archie answered quietly, a churchgoer's voice. "Not by a long shot."

The ranch was a fifteen-minute drive down the narrow, weedy lane. On the way, Mike told Archie about the place. Originally it had covered more than seventy thousand acres. Lynnie's father had sold everything except the mile-square area around the main house. There was a barn and bunkhouse, and, behind them, the ranch cemetery, up on a mesa. The pond and orchard were farther east, the prettiest spots of all.

Archie listened carefully but asked no questions. When they reached the end of the line, he cranked down his window. "You go ahead. I want to check a few things in my books." Mike climbed out and stood for a moment looking around. "Funny thing," Archie said. "This place will be on the National Historic Register someday. They'll bring people out by the busload." Mike smiled at him, and strode off around the barn.

Eight years earlier, Mike had visited Arizona with Lynnie, on one of their weekend get-togethers, over Labor Day. They had come out to the ranch for an afternoon, had a picnic, walked around, then drove back to Tucson where they were staying. It was a sad day, really. They spent too much time talking about Jen and the things the three of them had done together. That evening, Mike remembered something he'd wanted to check at the ranch, but had forgotten. Now he had his chance.

He passed the cabin where Oscar Martinez had lived and went on to the main house. The windows were boarded up and bushes were growing in the dogtrot breezeway in the middle of the structure. In back was another, smaller building made of stone and sunk in the ground. This was the milk house. The ranch had never had electricity. Back when people lived there, power lines didn't reach that part of the state. They did use propane to run a refrigerator and small generator, though. Overflow from the refrigerator—vegetables, butter, eggs, and the like—was kept in the milk house, cooled by one-hundred-pound ice blocks hauled out from town.

One of the window boards on the little building was loose and Mike tore it free. Inside it was musty and dark. He climbed in, knocking aside spiders' webs. Along one side was a shelf, mounted up near the ceiling. This was where the ice blocks had been stored. He felt underneath it, moving down the wall. That's it. There wasn't enough light to see, but he could read with his fingertips. *LMJ*. Thirty years ago he'd stood at that spot and, using an ice pick, scratched their initials in the plaster. Lynnie, Mikey, Jenny. That's what he'd wanted to check. Who came first? Lynnie, of course, even then.

Slowly he traced the *L* and the *J*. Another memory came to him, something he hadn't thought of in years. They were thirteen, their last summer here. The weather was always hot, so each evening, as a treat, they'd go out to the milk house to play cards and make ice cream the old-fashioned way: in a tub with a hand crank. They needed ice for this, chipped off one of the big blocks. One night, Lynnie's father and Oscar were gone, so there was no one to help move the ice block to the floor where they could work on it. Mikey can do it, Lynnie said. Jen snorted, He *can't!*

For a while they went at each other—Can *too!* Can *not!*—leaving Mike out of it. Then Lynnie turned to him. She didn't say anything, just nodded and smiled in a way he'd never seen before, demurely, her eyes barely reaching up to his. He stood and, to his own great surprise, pulled the block down with a single, graceful heave. Lynnie threw her hands up in a touchdown signal. "Champ! Champ!"

A cynic might say she'd used him, risking a broken arm or crushed toes so she could have her dish of ice cream. But Mike loved her for it—for making him, for one night at least, her champion.

Mike rubbed his face, as if waking from a heavy sleep. He heard a car door slam, from right outside it sounded like. He knew better. In this thin dry air, any noise seemed to travel forever. He went to look and saw Archie climb the rise below the pond and enter the orchard. A short while later he came into view again, mounting the path to the mesa top.

Mike swung through the window and picked up a rock. For just an instant, he thought he heard the laughter of children. He stared inside the milk house, where Lynnie and Mikey and Jenny had played. It was as silent as a tomb. He nailed the board back in place and left to find Archie.

It was a few hundred yards to the mesa top, and Mike stopped twice on the way to enjoy the view. Archie was in the small cemetery up there. Most of the ground for miles around was basalt bedrock, brown and bubbly, hard to walk on and impossible to dig in. The cemetery was in a special spot, where the soil was rich and deep, overlaid by gravel. It had been fenced so cattle couldn't make a mess of things. There were about thirty markers in all. The majority were simple metal crosses with nameplates riveted to the center joints. Ranch hands were buried there, with names like Ynguez and Barbosa and Salido. The rest of the markers were limestone or granite, most bearing the name Craig, from Lynnie's mother's family. Several of the headstones had big gouges, bullet holes left by crackpots out for a little graveyard target practice.

Archie was kneeling beside one of the stones when he heard the fence gate open. Glancing up, he said, "Where's her mother buried?"

"Lynnie's mother?" Mike said. "Not here. In Bisbee. Lynnie and her dad used to go there a couple of times each summer to visit the grave."

Archie pointed to the marker next in line from where he knelt: "But her father's here."

"Right. John left instructions with his will—" Mike caught himself. How would he know such a private detail? "I guess I saw that in the newspaper."

Lynnie's father had died four years ago, when she was running for vice president. It turned into a big media event, and Devon was at her side throughout, blessing the cameras with his wan smile. Mike stayed away, but

Lynnie phoned him eight nights in a row, to talk about the final hours at the hospital and the memorial service and how the reporters wouldn't leave her alone. She cried some, blew off a lot of steam. She had the body shipped to Arizona but held off on the burial until four months later, when the press wasn't so interested in her anymore.

Archie stood up. "Do you know who this is?" The marker where he'd been kneeling was a simple thing, a name—Graciella Ana Yberri—and a single carved rose blossom.

"One of the women the Craigs hired, I guess. A cook or someone to—" Mike broke off, cocking his head. Archie was listening, too. It *was* laughter, from children. A burst of giggles. A phrase, definitely Spanish. Mike turned, trying to find the source, but it seemed to come straight out of the ground, as if the spirits were playing a joke. Then the wind changed. "A ranch—I remember. In that hollow on the other side of the border. Years ago, when we visited, there were kids living there. We used to go down to the fence line and talk to them. Try to talk—Spanish and English, you know, so we'd pantomime. When the wind was right, you could hear them playing, like this."

Archie came to stand beside him. "I read in my guidebook about a man who kept two wives, one on each side of the border. That way he wouldn't get in trouble with the law."

Mike had heard those stories, about a Mormon who lived in the old days on a nearby ranch. "What makes you mention that?"

Archie looked at John Sheridan's grave and the Yberri grave next to it. "Just a thought, is all." He had a foxy smile, the kind he got when he knew something but wasn't going to tell, or at least wasn't going to tell without a lot of prodding. Mike shrugged and moved off, up through the cemetery. "What are you looking for?" Archie asked.

"Oscar Martinez. He'd be buried here."

Archie shook his head and started to reply, but he was interrupted by a whining sound on the far side of the mesa. It quickly turned into a roar. A dune buggy burst into view, a VW Beetle with the body gone, replaced by an open frame of raw-steel rods. The buggy slewed to a halt, and the driver and passenger jumped out. They wore baggy work clothes, boots, crash helmets, and bandannas over their noses and mouths to keep out the dust. Two other things caught Mike's attention: how blue their eyes were, how big their guns were.

There was no place to hide, nothing to do but wait and see what happened. "And me without my darts," Archie mumbled, sidling up beside Mike. The other two peeled off their helmets and the bandannas, and Archie said, "Jesus. *Women?*"

Mother and daughter would be more precise, Mike guessed. They had the same stark jawline and frizzy brown hair, the same way of standing. The older one— about Mike's age—was definitely in charge, directing the other with twitches of her hand. "Let me guess," Archie said. "You'd be Thelma"—he pointed, his hand cocked like a pistol—"and you'd be Louise."

"A comedian," the mother replied. "Lord, I *hate* a comedian." The younger woman, barely in her twenties, seemed too nervous to speak. "Jana," the older one said, "frisk 'em. And leave that shotgun by the bug. You two, on your knees, hands on your heads."

Mike and Archie complied, and Jana came through the fence and up behind them. She started with Archie, and he chuckled when she ran her hands up and down his thighs. He said, "Reminds me of that story about the woman who was chasing her pastor around the church—"

"She caught him by the organ," the older woman said, rolling her eyes. "Now shut up."

Jana had pulled out Archie's wallet and was leafing through it. "Mom, this guy's from Blaine, New York."

"That right?" the mother said. "You ever meet Lynnie Connor? She owns this place, you know."

"I was assistant principal of her high school," Archie said. "It was me who gave her her only detention—for wearing culottes."

"Culottes. And you're proud of this."

Archie smiled benevolently. "You don't see her wearing such trash nowadays, do you?"

The woman looked at the distant mountains. The expression on her face said, *Why am I having this conversation?*

Jana turned to Mike, patted him down, and checked his wallet. "Miami, it says."

"Oh?" the mother replied. "What's your story, then?"

Mike shook his head. "First, who are you?"

Jana had overcome her nervousness. "We work for Lang Corporation, out of Tucson. Security outfit. We guard the ranch."

Her mother put in, "That's right. And if you gents have damaged anything, you're going to do some time in jail." Her voice was taking on a nasty edge. "Now, Miami, like I said, what's your story?"

Before Mike could reply, Jana dropped their wallets in the dirt in front of them. Archie grabbed her by the forearm and snarled, "Hey, sister, be polite. Pick that up."

Slick-click. The older woman had jacked a shell into the chamber of her shotgun.

"No!" Mike knocked Archie's hand down. "Put the gun away. Let him go back to our car. I'll stay—answer your questions." He kicked Archie in the thigh. "Get out of here. Go."

The older woman sighed and kneaded her forehead. "All right, go on. Down to the car, *but no further*."

Archie stood up, smirking. He ducked behind the Yberri headstone and came up with a small bouquet of roses.

"Where'd you get those?" Jana asked.

"Brought 'em with me," Archie said. He gave a sly wink to Mike and strolled out through the gate.

Twenty minutes later, Mike walked down off the mesa, alone. Archie was leaning against the fender of the car. "Get anything?" he asked as Mike came around the corner of the barn.

"Not the way you're thinking. Dammit, what gets into you anyway? Two women with shotguns, and you come off like the warm-up act at a stag party."

"I know." Archie hung his head sheepishly. "But it's like this. Somebody gets a hand up on me, the littlest thing, and I've got to slap 'em down. It's just the way I am, OK?" He stood up from the car. "So, what did they tell you?"

"A few things. For one, they've only been here five weeks. The security outfit they work for had another guard stationed here, but he disappeared. That's why they're so touchy. They've got no idea what happened—if he got lonely and ran off, or got lost in the desert, or maybe stumbled onto something he shouldn't have and got shot for his trouble. The county sheriff is still looking into it."

Archie sucked his teeth thoughtfully. "Five weeks, you say? That's before Aron Aubrey came out here. According to his father, before he even got interested in Arizona."

"That's right, so maybe whatever happened to that guard has nothing to do with our troubles. That would be another coincidence, though, wouldn't it? Anyway, about Aubrey—when he was here earlier this month, those two women found him and ran him off, just like us. He had someone with him. I figure it was the guide that Aubrey's father talked about. Jana checked their driver's licenses. She couldn't remember the guide's name, but she did recall he was from Bisbee. They gave me a good description of him."

A shout came from the mesa top. "Hey!" Jana and her mother stood profiled against the bright sky, shotguns slung over their shoulders. "Haul out, you two," the mother yelled. "No dawdle-assin'."

Mike and Archie got in the car and started up the lumpy road. When they had gone about a hundred yards, Archie pulled the little bouquet of roses from under his seat. "Where *did* those come from?" Mike asked.

Taped to the flowers was a small envelope with a card inside. Archie fingered it but didn't open it up. "That's a good question," he said, smiling, altogether pleased with himself.

Mike felt a flash of anger, which he suppressed. Archie would tell him in his own sweet time. Meanwhile, Mike wanted to focus on the guide. First thing in the morning, they'd start looking for him. "There was one other thing Jana mentioned," Mike said. "When Aubrey came out here, he and the guide went up to the cemetery to look around."

"Sure they did," Archie put in, as if it were the most obvious thing in the world. He gave his little smile again.

"Archie—what?" Mike said, letting his irritation show loud and clear.

"It was on that X-ray copy we got from Aubrey's father. Sister Anne back in Newark had a pretty sharp eye. She couldn't read the whole word, but the first two letters are obvious enough. 'Yb.' Looked like gibberish to me, but Sister Anne said it happens sometimes with Mexican names."

Archie stretched out, trying to settle into his cramped seat. "Wonder what happened to her." He let it roll off his tongue. "Graciella Ana Yberri."

CHAPTER TWENTY-EIGHT

It was late afternoon when they got back to Bisbee. As they entered the Copper Queen, Archie asked Mike for the car keys. He didn't explain why. Mike handed them over, but he said, "I don't think it's a good idea for us to split up."

Archie shrugged, then steamed away toward his room, jingling the keys and whistling.

Mike went for a walk, wanting to stretch out after the day's driving. When he returned it was dinnertime, so he went to look for Archie. No answer in his room. He checked the parking lot; the car was gone. Mike ate alone, then sat in the lobby, keeping an eye on the entrance. He read a two-week-old *Newsweek* and a two-year-old *National Geographic*. He tried not to think about Archie or tracking devices or space-age knives. Ten o'clock came. Eleven. This wasn't doing any good. He went up to his room, determined to get a few hours' sleep.

In the morning, still no Archie. Mike went downstairs for breakfast. Over grapefruit and coffee, he set a deadline. If he didn't hear from Archie by nine o'clock, he'd go to the police, ask them to start looking for him.

As Mike was leaving the dining room, the desk clerk called out, "Mr. Snyder?"

It took him a moment to remember he was Mr. Snyder. "Yes?"

"There's something for you." From under the counter, he pulled out Archie's bouquet of roses. "It was here when I came on duty this morning." He looked at the floor, embarrassed. "You should have gotten it last night, I'm afraid."

Mike nodded and hurried away. He could see there

was a note stuffed in the florist's envelope. He took it out when he was safely in his room.

Michael—
*   You were out so I'm leaving this with the bubblehead at the desk.*

That explained why Mike hadn't gotten the message. The bubblehead in question had read the note (an open envelope—it was too much of a temptation) and been browned-off enough not to deliver it. *Smooth move, Archie, you nitwit.*

Mike read on:

This was sitting by the grave when I got there. Wanted to try to find out where it came from but ran out of time. Maybe you could give it a go. I'll be back sometime round sundown tomorrow probably.
*   Archie PEETE*
PS—Interesting card, don't you think?

"Be back sometime, probably," Mike muttered sarcastically as he took out the florist's card. It was a simple two-inch-by-three piece of white cardboard, the kind all florists use. In the upper corner was a stencil of a droopy flower, an orchid or iris—it was too small to tell which. Someone had written a message with a fountain pen, green ink, very fancy script:

Para Nuestra Ángel, Mucho Amor
✝
Oscar

Mike grabbed the phone book off the nightstand and flipped open to the yellow pages. He started calling florists. On the fifth call, he scored, at a shop in Sierra Vista, a town about thirty miles away. Mike described the card, the special handwriting. The man on the other end said, "That's ours. My wife does that."

"It's a bouquet, half a dozen red sweetheart roses, with those tiny white flowers—baby's breath. Looks like it's only a few days old. Can you tell me who bought it? Maybe have an address for them?"

The man set the phone down and was gone for some time. He cleared his throat when he came back. "Sorry. My wife doesn't remember. Neither does anybody else. Must have been a cash purchase, not one of our regular customers."

"Would you have delivered it?" Mike asked.

"Could be. Where?" Mike told him and the man laughed. "Hell, no. The Craig ranch is way on the other side of Douglas. Whoever bought that bouquet must have taken it out there himself."

Mike hung up and stared at the card, trying to remember his restaurant Spanish from Little Havana. *Nuestra Ángel . . . Amor.* For Our Angel, Much Love. Something like that. Anyway, one thing was certain: dead men didn't buy flowers. The old ranch foreman, Oscar Martinez, was still alive.

Mike didn't want to sit around worrying about Archie, so he moved on to his other job, trying to find the guide Aron Aubrey had hired. He went to a bookstore first and bought a copy of one of Aubrey's books, an old one as it turned out, about Donald Trump. All Mike needed was the picture of Aubrey on the dust jacket, so he could jog people's memories.

He went back to the Copper Queen and tried everyone there, then to the nearby mining museum and the shops along Tombstone Canyon Road. At each stop he showed the photo of Aubrey and described the man who'd been seen with him by the two women at Lynnie's ranch. Tall and dark, maybe Latino. Had a mustache and was missing two fingers on his right hand. Wore a special belt buckle, a big silver thing with his initials on it—P.D. People gave Mike a funny look when he said "P.D.," but they shook their heads. Sorry. Can't help you.

Eventually, Mike worked his way to a side street, to a shop with a sign over the door. CASA DE CABEZAS. House of Heads. There were wigs in the window, and white panama hats. A bell tinkled as he opened the door. Behind the counter sat a young woman with willowy arms and a long graceful neck. Her dark hair hung to her shoulders. She was reading a newspaper and looked up, smiling. Her name tag said she was Alyxis Nuñez.

She nodded when Mike showed her Aubrey's photo. Yes, she remembered him. Then when he described the man he was looking for—the missing fingers, the belt buckle—she laughed. "No, not his initials. P.D. is Phelps Dodge. The mining company. They used to own most of the town. Now"—she raised her hands to the heavens—"poof. Out of business. I think I know who you mean, though." She turned to the rear of the store. "Mr. Binion?"

A man came through the curtain, short and heavyset and completely bald, an odd duck to run a place that sold wigs. He glanced at Mike. "Seven and a quarter. Buy off the shelf. Save yourself some money." He started back through the curtain.

Alyxis Nuñez was laughing again. "He doesn't want to buy. Remember Aron Aubrey? That writer from New York?"

"Sure. Custom job." Binion put his hands in a big circle. "Eight and an eighth!"

"This man wants to find the guy Mr. Aubrey was with. Joey Leyva, wasn't it?"

A wary look crossed Binion's eyes. "That's right."

"Does he still live up on Adams Avenue?" the woman asked.

Binion shook his head. "Wait." He went into the back, and Mike could see him flipping through a card file. Mike remembered the name Leyva. It had been written in Aubrey's day planner, just the last name with no explanation.

Binion came out bearing a slip of paper with an address. He handed it over and explained how to get there. As Mike turned for the door, Binion said, "Joey does yard work, hauls trash, stuff like that. He's a little funny sometimes. Don't take everything he says too seriously."

Nuñez had gone back to her newspaper. She grinned without taking her eyes off the page. "His own mother says Joey lies so much he's got to get a stranger to call his dog."

Bisbee's business district was in a narrow canyon flanked by tall cinnamon-colored hills. The houses were on the hillsides, old miner's cottages mostly, on minuscule lots, elbowing each other for space. According to the directions Mike had been given, he was to go up the main street about two miles, then turn into a side canyon and go to the end of the road. The weather was warm and, because of Bisbee's mile-high elevation, the air was thin. Soon he was breathing hard and mopping sweat from his forehead. He used the time to think about how he'd handle Joey Leyva. He wanted more than to talk; he wanted to go where Aubrey had gone, see what he'd seen. So Mike would hire him as guide, as Aubrey had done, and hope that Leyva was the kind of man who didn't ask too many questions.

At last he reached the house, a wood A-frame perched in a steep field of boulders and scree. There was only one tree in the lot, in the back corner, and it was dead. Under the tree was a sofa, its cushions pulled off and tossed in a heap. In the driveway was a rusty Toyota pickup. Mike mounted the steps to the porch. Over the door was a steer's skull. The horns had been removed and one of them glued on above the eyes, so it looked like the head of a unicorn. Maybe Joey Leyva was a liar; then again, maybe he only had a unique sense of humor.

The inside door was open so Mike knocked on the
screen. No one came, but he could hear voices in back of
the house—or *a* voice, singsong and repetitious, like a
child reciting a nursery rhyme. He made his way up the
driveway, past a stack of old car batteries.

As he came around the corner, something big and
black flew straight at his face. He dove out of the way.
"*Rawwk!*" It was a crow, and, by the time Mike got to his
feet, it had flapped to a landing on the sofa. Mike felt
something wet, looked down, and saw a nasty streak of
guano on his arm.

"Aw, Spot, behave," called a man sitting in the dust
beside the house. Joey Leyva. The description Mike had
been given was perfect. He was tall and spidery with
chestnut skin. In the hand with the missing fingers he
held a can of beer.

"Bottoms up!" said the crow.

Joey dutifully took a gulp from the can. "Sorry about
your arm. Damn bird thinks he's a Tuskegee Airman or
something."

"Spot," Mike said noncommittally. He looked for
something to clean himself off with and found a rag
hooked over a nail in the clapboards.

"Yep. Son of Jim."

"That would be Jim . . . Crow."

Joey smirked and nodded.

"Bottoms up!" the bird called again.

Joey drained his beer, reached behind him for another,
and popped it open. He was sitting next to the chimney,
under a ladder that was angled precariously against the
roof. It was a long way to the top. Joey noticed where
Mike was looking and said, "Wasps. Gotta clean 'em
out." Mike could see them, hundreds of dots wheeling in
the sun. Joey burped. "Gives me the creeps, goin' way
up there." He took another hit of beer. "Couple more of
these and I won't care, though."

Inside, the telephone jingled. "Phone caw!" cried Spot.

Joey pitched a rock at the bird. "Then answer it, ya dumb cluck." He squinted one eye shut and peered at Mike with the other, the way a pirate might look at his mateys. "So, you ain't with Publishers Clearing House. What do you want?"

"I hear Aron Aubrey hired you to show him around the area. About two weeks ago, something like that."

"Aubrey?" Joey said, rubbing his temple. "Aubrey? That name sounds like . . . money." He grinned broadly.

Mike took a twenty-dollar bill from his wallet and held it up. He heard a rustle of feathers and, in the nick of time, jerked his hand out of the way. Spot zipped by, screaming with rage at having been cheated of his prize. "He'd'a spent it, too," Joey said. "Plays the lotto, you know."

Mike sighed. Joey's banter was starting to annoy him. "You remember Aubrey?"

"Yeah, I remember him. What of it?"

"I'd like to hire you to take me around—the same places he went when he was here."

A wasp had landed on Joey's ear. It cocked its backside and stung him. He didn't flinch, just snapped it away with his finger like a mosquito. "We could do that. Cost a lot more'n that twenty, though."

"How much more?"

A spark came into Joey's eyes. Mike could imagine what was going on back there, the numbers floating to the surface, being rejected. "Four hundred."

That would about wipe out his and Archie's supply of cash, assuming Archie came back at all. "That's a little steep, isn't it?"

"Take us a day and a half. Two days if you fool around and talk to everybody in sight the way Aubrey did. So how much do you make in two days?"

He had a point there. Mike shrugged, debating it, then nodded. "All right."

"Want to leave now?" Joey asked.

Without being too obvious, Mike counted the empties in the pile on the ground. Ten. Not good. "Tomorrow will be soon enough. Where did you and Aubrey go, anyway?"

"All over God's green earth, felt like. A ranch way out east of Douglas, and he wanted to stop at some hospitals—" Then Joey wised up. He didn't want to give too much away. "You'll see tomorrow."

"Hospitals?" Mike said. He had the X-ray photocopy with him, and he took it out. "You ever see this before?"

Joey's eyes flicked at it, and he frowned. "Listen, dude, you're the boss, but not until I'm on the clock. Then you can ask all the questions you want."

"Fair enough," Mike said. "Let's make it early. Seven?"

Joey toasted him with his beer can. "Can do."

"Will we need a special vehicle? Four-wheel drive?"

"Nah. Just bring a passport or birth certificate." Joey slurped his beer. "Need it for the border."

Now that would be a problem. The only ID Mike had was a driver's license. What the hell—play it by ear. Didn't tens of thousands of people cross here illegally each year?

The crow soared over the yard, settling on Joey's shoulder. He blinked at it, a glazed look on his face. Drunk as a monkey, Mike thought. "All right, seven o'clock. And Joey, stay off the ladder. You're liable to break your neck."

"Yeah, yeah." Joey nuzzled the bird with his nose. "My ol' drinkin' buddy," he cooed.

"Bottoms up!"

Mike was happy as he walked down the canyon a few minutes later. Joey was a flake, but chances were he'd hold together for the short time Mike needed him. And he hadn't asked what Mike was up to. That was a plus— no elaborate stories, no windy explanations. Mike had learned some things, too. Aubrey had spent two days with Joey. That would account for visits to Tucson, to the ranch, a couple of other places. And they'd gone across the border.

Mexico. Mike had a few questions about that, things a knowledgeable local could answer. He could wait and ask Joey in the morning, but he had someone else in mind, someone he figured was more trustworthy. If he could only convince Mr. Binion to let her off work early.

CHAPTER TWENTY-NINE

Alyxis Nuñez leaned back against the headboard of the bed, cradling the phone to her ear. They were in Mike's room at the Copper Queen. She wasn't flashy, not a Hollywood head-turner, but still attractive, especially now, with her dress pulled tight around her thighs and one strap dropped low off her shoulder. Dark hair and eyes, though—not his type.

She sat up slightly. Someone had answered. "*Hola. Oscar Martinez, por favor. . . . ¿No? ¿Sabe dónde encontrarlo? . . . Sí, Oscar. . . . ¿No? . . . Sí. Gracias, señora.*" She hung up.

They had been there for an hour. That was after talking for a while in the lobby. At first Alyxis seemed to think it was a date, though certainly an odd one. She was overly attentive, smiling too much, sitting primly with her legs crossed at the ankles. Soon enough she decided Mike was leveling with her. He only wanted help finding someone named Oscar Martinez. Her smile grew more natural then. This might actually be fun.

Mike explained that earlier, before he'd gone out in search of Joey Leyva, he'd called a few of the Martinezes listed in the phone book. Half treated him suspiciously and quickly hung up; the others only spoke Spanish. Alyxis laughed at this. They speak English, she said, most of them, a little at least. They probably thought he was trying to sell insurance or something. She knew some Spanish. She'd taken it in school. Six years! she said, as if it were a jail term. She offered to make the calls for him, and they came upstairs.

She ran her finger down the page in the phone book. "That's the last one, except for the three who didn't answer."

"What about Mexico?" Mike asked. "Oscar might be there. Do they have directory assistance we could try?"

She nodded her head, her hair shimmering. "Yes, they do, but Telmex is—everything's out of date and out of order. It never works the way it should." She looked away, at the corner. It was her way of appearing passive, blunting an argument before it got started. "Besides, if he lives in Mexico now, why would he go to Sierra Vista for flowers? He'd have gotten them where he crossed over, Nogales or Douglas . . . right?"

"Could be," Mike said.

He stared at the floor, trying to think. They could try Telmex, and, if that didn't work, then what? He heard a rustle.

She was putting the phone book away. "I have to go, Mike. My mother needs help with the kids and dinner."

"I'm sorry. I should have realized." He brought her purse to her. "Can I call you if I think of something else to try? The Internet, maybe . . ."

She looked away again and he could imagine what she was thinking. *An old ranch hand on the Internet? Give it up, Mike.* "Sure, call any time."

They heard footsteps and turned to the door. Because it seemed like the right thing to do, Mike had left it ajar when they came in. It swung back now, and there stood Archie, bigger than ever, blocking most of the light from the hall. He peered at them with his beady eyes. "Oh."

"Arch," Mike said, "this is Alyxis. We were"—he took her by the elbow and hurried her to her feet—"trying to find Oscar Martinez."

Archie looked past them at the bed. "Did you check under the covers yet?"

Alyxis laughed, not a bit intimidated. She patted Mike on the arm—"Good luck"—and swished past Archie.

"Hey, I didn't mean to interrupt," he said. Alyxis waved at him over her shoulder.

"If we find Oscar, I'll let you know," Mike called after her. "Alyxis, thanks, really." He sat on the corner of the bed. "Great timing, pal. Where the hell have you been, anyway?"

"Tucson." Archie slumped down next to him. "And my rump aches from riding in that mini-mobile you rented." He leaned near the pillow and sniffed sublimely. "Still warm. Nice perfume, too. Seemed like a sweet girl. So, did she know how to ride a pony?"

"Archie, you make it hard, but I'm still glad to see you."

They went to the small brick veranda in front of the hotel. From there they could watch the traffic on Main Street and see the sunset against the hills down the canyon. Their waitress, a bubbly sixty-year-old with a Marilyn Monroe wig, bustled over as soon as they sat down. "What'll it be, boys?" They ordered beers and Archie asked her to bring something for them to eat—chips, something like that. "Sure thing, hon," she said. At that point she hesitated, studying his face. "You look pooped. Gotta be extra careful with the altitude here, ya know. Not do too much." She seemed genuinely concerned.

"Nah, I'm fine," Archie replied. In truth, he was exhausted. As she walked away he slouched heavily back in his chair. "I take it you didn't have any luck finding Martinez."

Mike explained about the phone calls Alyxis had made. "She's probably right. I doubt he moved to Mexico.

But where he is, I've got no idea." The waitress returned with their beers. Mike waited for her to leave before he continued. "On the positive side, I turned up Aubrey's guide." He told him about finding Joey Leyva. "Tomorrow morning at seven, we meet at his house. I just hope he's sober by then."

Archie stared at his feet, nodding, but not showing much interest. "You sure you're all right?" Mike asked.

"Had a rugged day, is all."

"Your heart?"

"Yuh. Angina's a bitch, that's all I can say. I miss my medicine. And that lady's right about the altitude."

"Why don't you see—"

"A doctor?" Archie said. "I did, earlier today in Tucson. No go, they said. No nitro until I've been in their care a week, or unless I have a heart attack. Swell."

"That's why you drove up there?" Mike asked.

"No. I went up there to see a man about a tombstone."

Before he could continue, the waitress showed up with two plates of potato skins, a small one for Mike and a giant one for Archie. She tweaked him on the shirtsleeve. "That'll help you get your strength back, big fella."

Archie gazed at the mound of food. "Thanks, I guess." She shuttled off to deal with the other customers.

Archie pulled a notepad from his pocket. "When we were at the ranch, I checked the back of that Graciella Yberri headstone. There was a plaque, way down low in the dirt, with the monument company's name on it, a Tucson address." Mike frowned and Archie said, "How did I know? Monument makers do that sometimes. You get old, you learn things like that. Anyway, my idea was to go to the monument company and see if they had any records on that Graciella Yberri. And guess what? I wasn't the only one who'd been there to ask questions."

"Aron Aubrey?" Mike said.

"That's right. He was in a couple of weeks ago, asking about that same headstone." He shook a dash of salt into his beer and watched the foam rise. "That monument we saw was a replacement. The original headstone was all shot up, or so that was the story. The monument company was paid cash, no record of who ordered the new stone. It was finished and picked up six weeks ago. One of the shop workers there remembered it was a guy in a pickup truck who came for it, white with black letters on the side. Lang, he thought it said." He stared at Mike over the top of his beer. "Six weeks—that's about the same time the security guard disappeared at the ranch, and he worked for Lang Corporation."

Mike nodded slowly.

"I had them dig back in their old records, see if they made the original Graciella Yberri headstone. Took some doing, but they found a card on it." Archie tapped his notepad. "The original headstone was ordered and paid for by John Sheridan, Lynnie's father."

Mike said, "He might have done that for anybody who worked at the ranch. There are other old hands buried up in that cemetery."

The head on Archie's beer seemed to be to his satisfaction. He took a quick drink. "Did you notice anything strange about that Yberri monument? Anything missing?"

"No, it was just a simple—" Mike stopped, and nodded. "There weren't any dates."

"Right," Archie said. "No date of birth, no date of death." He spun his notepad so Mike could see it. "But John Sheridan wrote it down on the card when he ordered the original monument. Graciella Yberri died forty-three years ago, the same day Lynnie Connor was born."

A deep frown crossed Mike's face. He looked up at the hills, pink in the dying light of the day.

"That explains the bouquet of roses," Archie said. "Left at the grave on Thursday, the anniversary of her death. The rest is harder to fill in. Back when Lynnie was born, a woman dying in childbirth wasn't that uncommon if she got caught somewhere without a doctor, like at that ranch. Then again, maybe that wasn't how she died. Maybe Graciella had her own ideas about the baby. She got in the way of somebody's plans. Graciella got killed in the process."

Mike said, "Hold on. First, you've got no proof this Graciella was Lynnie's mother, or anybody else's. And now you're talking murder. You knew John Sheridan. Do you think he was capable of that?"

"I don't know what he could have done, one way or the other. There's such a thing as a crime of passion, you know. I'm only thinking of all the possibilities."

"OK," Mike said, "*all* the possibilities. What you're suggesting is that somebody is playing cover-up, trying to hide something about Lynnie's birth. If that's so, why is that creep in Tucson still around and talking? Our dentist friend? Wouldn't they want to shut him up? And why is there a new headstone at the cemetery? Wouldn't it be better if that damn thing just disappeared?"

Archie was too tired to argue. He ran his thumb around the lip of his beer glass. "I've had some time to think the last couple of days. Maybe tomorrow with Aubrey's guide we'll figure out what's going on. Maybe not. Either way, I've had my fill of trouble. After tomorrow, I'm going to the biggest newspaper I can find and tell them everything I know. Then I'm going to get me a cheap motel room, sit back, and watch the hurricane come down on Lynnie Connor's head."

"Don't you think we owe it to Lynnie and to Eve to—"

"Don't talk to me about Eve, Michael. I know my responsibilities there. And Lynnie—maybe you owe her something, but I don't." Archie looked away and gave a flip of his hand, indicating he didn't want to discuss it anymore.

They sat in silence until the waitress approached again. She was hustling for her tips tonight. "Aren't those delish?" She pointed at the potato skins. "We use bacon fat, rather 'n lard." She hit extra-heavy on "lard," and at the same time her eyes fixed on Archie's big belly. Archie caught her doing it. She turned bright red and scuttled back inside.

Mike was studying Archie's notepad, so he hadn't noticed this exchange. He only half listened to the story that Archie told next, about a lawyer he'd once hired to help him with a boundary dispute. The lawyer was a real gem. Listened politely. Didn't waste time running up the bill. When they finished their meeting, he stood up to shake hands. "Mr. Pascoe, if the plat map shows things the way you say, then there's no question we'll win. Ipso fatso."

Archie drained his beer and shoved aside the plate of potato skins. "From pissants I can take grief about my weight all summer long, but a little slip like that from a nice person . . ." He shook his head sadly.

"What? Oh, right." Mike was still bent over the notepad. "You wrote 'B. Agua Prieta.' Does that mean Graciella Yberri was born there—over the border in Sonora?"

"I just copied that off the card they had, but I figure so," Archie said. He was still thinking about that "lard" comment, or maybe he was too weary to think at all. He pushed his chair away and stood up. "Got to get me some sleep now. Make sure I'm up by five thirty tomorrow, will you? There's no alarm clock in my room." He plodded through the bar, making a point to call good night to Marilyn Monroe.

Mike picked up the notepad, clicking it with his finger. Joey Leyva had told him they were going to cross the border tomorrow and visit some hospitals, going where Aron Aubrey had gone. That had sounded like a stretch, blundering around. Now it seemed a lot more promising.

Mike smiled. He suddenly had a huge appetite. He pulled Archie's plate next to his own and dug in.

CHAPTER THIRTY

Colonel Veck rapped his ring against the truck window. *Rat-a tat-tat-tat. Tat-tat. Tat-tat-tat* . . . Morse code with a disco beat. B-i-s-b-e-e. He checked his watch. Ought to be there in another ten minutes. Longtemps was driving, with Gerbil in the shotgun seat. Veck was in the back, in the side-facing jump seat, alone where he could think.

Veck liked Arizona, the bare earth, the big distances. You could see what was coming at you out here. What was coming now was sunset, a sweet, spectacular blaze of pink and orange and red.

Gerbil had his computer on his lap and was giggling about something on the screen. He tapped a few keys, laughed some more. They were all in a good mood, a miracle after the hell they'd been through in Newark. Go home to Philly for the night, then on to Arizona—that was the plan. They got their boarding passes, no problem, but before they got on their plane, a walloping thunderstorm hit and Newark Airport was closed. It stayed closed for fifteen hours. Trouble with the radar system was all anybody would say. By the time they got it fixed, Philly was out of the question. Veck had to get his men to Arizona.

The delay hadn't been a complete waste, though. It had given Gerbil a chance to crack the encryption on Aron Aubrey's computer. Veck started reading as soon as Gerb finished up—an absolute mother lode. Not only did the computer have all of Aubrey's book on Lynnie Connor, but also his background files and address list, all organized and cross-referenced.

Aubrey had been one thorough cat. Lordy, the stuff he dug up on Connor. He had her medical files, every year since she entered government service. He had her school report cards, all the way back. First grade: four straight quarters of unsatisfactory for "works and plays well with others." That fact alone gave Veck a little more respect for Connor. Proved she was no patsy.

When they landed in Tucson, Veck had read only half the files on the computer. Still, he knew what they had to do first: find that coot Doc Denis DuPree. Dentist the Menace, Gerbil called him. Or Doctor Thrilldrill. Gerb had this thing about nicknames.

Veck headed for Little Ted's, the bar where, according to Aubrey's notes, Doc DuPree and his cronies hung out. Who would have guessed somebody like DuPree existed? An old geezer who happened to know Mattie Sheridan couldn't have kids? Who would have guessed that he'd surface now, drawn out from under his rock by Aubrey and that broad Tessmer up in Blaine? The world spun some crazy messes sometimes. Veck just needed to clean them up, one at a time.

Little Ted's was closed. The shopkeeper next door said there'd been some kind of brawl there. Two people were hauled off in ambulances. The owner shut the joint down and skipped town, rather than talk to the police. Seems he was wanted for nonpayment of child support.

So where was this Doc DuPree? They had to find that old toothdrawer. Veck and his boys made the rounds. It took more than a day, but they finally turned DuPree up at St. Mary's Hospital. Veck went in to see him, and when he came out he was popping his fingers and singing a bebop version of "Oh, What a Wonderful World."

DuPree had a cracked vertebra and his jaw was broken in three places. His mouth was wired shut so tight he wouldn't be able to talk for weeks. He was high on drugs, too, his eyes flat and empty. It was perfect. Ironic, but perfect. DuPree knew the first chapter of the greatest story on earth, but he'd have to keep it to himself until after the election. Veck couldn't have paid for it to turn out better. He'd come back in a week or two, about when DuPree was getting out of the hospital. Get the duffer alone and quietly ease him out of his misery. Mess all cleaned up and in a way where nobody would ever connect little ol' Doc with anything. For now, Veck fluffed his pillow and left him there, staring dumbly at a Wile E. Coyote cartoon on the television.

In the front of the truck something beeped. Gerbil had three computers going and he glanced at the one on the floor. "Another message from Star, Colonel."

"Lord give me strength," Veck muttered. "Leave it. I'm sick of being ragged on." Gerbil nodded, then gave a shriek of laughter. Veck bent forward to see what was so funny. On the screen on Gerb's lap was a vague round image, flesh colored. "Did Star send that?" Veck asked.

Gerbil laughed until he drooled. "No, man, no. It's a porn site from Europe. Finnfanny dot com."

"I told you to run Stanbridge's and Pascoe's credit cards again. We've got to find those two."

"Yeah, it's under control. Got the other two machines working on it."

"Colonel?" Longtemps said. He pointed ahead. "Mule Pass Tunnel. Bisbee's on the other side."

Veck turned to look out the back window. Cutter and Dowd were in another truck right behind them. The colonel signaled: finger point left, then palm out. Exit. Stop. Veck settled back for a moment, his eyes closed. He could feel the blood starting to sing in his ears. That's it. Get pumped. Joey Leyva, here we come.

They parked in front of an elementary school on Tombstone Canyon Road. Before he got out, Veck checked Aron Aubrey's computer. Along with Joey Leyva's address, Aubrey had noted a few other tidbits, things only a writer would be interested in: that, except for his mother, Joey didn't have any close family; that he drank too much; that he had a soft spot for animals. Veck had done some research on his own, government sources. Leyva had a couple of juvie arrests for boosting cars. Three more for drunk driving as an adult. A stint in the Air Force (general discharge). Didn't pay income taxes or own property. Had an eleven-year-old pickup truck. All in all, not much of a past. Question was, how much of a future did Joey have?

"All right, listen up," Veck said. "Gerbil, you stay here and work the computers, *all* the computers. I want word on Stanbridge and Pascoe, and I want it yesterday. The rest of you—knives only. I don't want a ruckus. Got it?" The men nodded. "Good. Let's hump."

They went one at a time, with Veck first. There was no sidewalk, so he came straight up the middle of the lane. Once he had the house in sight, he crouched under a neighbor's pine tree and waited. A dog wandered by, sniffed his pants without any real curiosity, and settled down to take a nap in the street. The only sound was the faint drone of a television set from one of the homes down the hill.

When the men were all assembled, Veck said, "My lead. Stay back where you won't be seen." Then he moved up to the porch, casually, as if he were a friend stopping by to shoot the breeze. The front door was open a few inches. He listened. From the backyard he heard someone say something, a sharp word or two, maybe a curse. Veck motioned to his men. Split up and follow. Cutter that side. Longtemps and Dowd the other.

The shadows were so heavy in the rear of the house that Veck had trouble seeing. A porch deck. Boulders in the yard. A . . . what was that? A ladder. And up on the ladder was a man, holding a penlight and doing what? Using a spray can. Veck could hear the faint *sssss*. He took a step around the corner. Something black whizzed past his face, screaming, "Bugger off! Bugger off!" Veck went ass over teakettle into the rocks.

The ladder swayed and rattled. Joey Leyva screeched,

"Damn, Spot. Tree. Go!" The ladder rattled some more. "Hey, who is that anyway?" He started down, one slow rung at a time. "Jesus, he didn't hurt you, did he?"

Veck stood up and dusted himself off. "Hit the road," Spot called. And then, for no apparent reason: "Phone caw! Chuck you, Farley!"

"Oh, Lordy, lookit that," Joey said as he reached the ground. "He shat all over you. Here." He groped at the base of the ladder for a rag.

The bird soared up and fluttered back down onto Joey's arm. "*You* are the damnedest thing ever hatched out of an egg," Joey said.

Veck seemed to be taking it all in good humor. "Spot, you said his name was? That's wild. Remember those books when we were kids?" He held out his hand and the crow jumped aboard. "Spot can hop. Hop, Spot, hop." Veck looped his thumb and forefinger around the bird's neck. He twisted. The head came off as easy as the cap off a bottle. "See Dick decapitate Spot."

Joey opened his mouth like a fish. No sound came out. He swallowed and tried again. "Well . . . gee." Then it sunk in. Something was very wrong here. He whipped up his hand and gave Veck a spritz of bug spray right between the eyes. Veck tumbled backward. Joey started to run, but before he'd gone two steps Dowd and Longtemps had him. They pinned him against the wall, hands over his mouth to muffle his screams.

Once again Veck stood up and dusted himself off. He moved in close to Joey, so close he could smell his sweat and the beer on his breath. Veck cupped Joey's neck in his hands and squeezed—pressure, more pressure—not on the windpipe but on the big arteries in the throat. No blood to the brain. Joey stopped struggling. He sagged forward. "Atta boy," Veck said. "Come to Papa."

Dowd pulled out his cell phone, and a minute later Gerbil drove up in one of the trucks. Cutter and Longtemps brought Joey around, folded up and sandwiched between them like a piece of furniture. Gerb stood aside and watched while they loaded him in. He then flourished some papers he was holding. "Got 'em, Colonel."

"Got who?" Veck said. He was rubbing bug spray out of his eyes.

"Stanbridge and Pascoe. Well, Stanbridge, anyway. He rented a car at the Tucson airport."

"When?" Veck asked quickly.

Gerb stammered, "Yeah, well, that's . . . a little over two days ago."

"Two days? How the hell did that happen and we didn't know about it?"

The other men drew back. This was Gerb's trouble and they wanted none of it. "It was the security clearance for the credit card companies," Gerbil said. "Star gave us the codes, but sometime over the weekend the companies changed them. No way I could know because every time I logged on, their machines shunted me into the archives files, instead—"

"Forget it," Veck snapped. "Did Stanbridge use his cards for anything else?"

"No. He must have switched to cash."

Dowd was looking around at the other houses. "We ought to clear out, Colonel. Somebody's going to wonder what we're doing here."

Veck nodded. "Dowd, you stay with me. We'll walk down. You other three drive back to where we parked and wait. If Leyva starts to wake up, keep him quiet, but don't hurt him. Now roll out."

Dowd and Veck moved side by side down the lane, taking their time. "Underestimated him again, didn't we," Dowd said.

"Let's try to avoid the obvious," Veck shot back. He sucked in a quick breath and blew it out. "Sorry." Veck only had himself to blame. He was the one who had decided Stanbridge had gone to ground in Atlanta, that they didn't have to worry about him for a while. "What do you think he's been up to? Is Pascoe with him?"

Dowd slowed his pace while he considered. "Pascoe's with him, sure. They're joined at the hip now." Then Dowd smiled. "They were the ones who put Doc DuPree in the hospital!"

Veck stopped in his tracks. Slowly, a smile came to him, too. "Timing's right, isn't it. Hell, I almost admire those two guys."

They moved on. Dowd said, "If they talked to DuPree, then they might have heard his story about Mattie Sheridan and the hysterectomy. Now they'd be snooping around down here, looking for confirmation."

Veck pinched his chin thoughtfully. "It's a long way from Mattie Sheridan to the Yberri family."

"It is, but they might make the connection. You know, Colonel, maybe we should let Stanbridge and Pascoe run, see if they turn up anything we haven't. Whatever they come up with, they can't go to the police. And I don't think they'll go to the press without talking to Star first. At least Stanbridge won't—old friends like that."

Veck spun around and jabbed his finger into the base of Dowd's throat. "Don't get cute on me."

"Colonel, I—"

"Word games—trying to find out who Star is. Take it to the bank, Dowd. Star is none of your business."

"Yes, sir," Dowd croaked.

They were in sight of the trucks before either of them spoke again. "So what's next?" Dowd asked.

"We take Joey out to that place you found on the map. What's it called?"

"Escacado Canyon."

"Right," Veck said. "You and me and Gerb can have our parley with him there."

"And Cutter and Longtemps?"

The dog from in front of Joey's house had followed them. Veck squatted and scratched it between the ears.

"We should be able to get a description of Stanbridge's car from the rental company records. License number, all that. Cutter and Longtemps can go around to the hotels and motels, sweep the parking lots, see if they can spot it. These little towns around here—can't be more than thirty, forty places to check."

"They'll be trying to conserve cash," Dowd put in. "Tell Cutter to start with the dives, the el cheapo places."

"All right." Veck gave the dog a swat on the side. "Go on home now. Go on! Dead bird up there for you to eat."

The dog sat and bent round and began to lick his privates. *Lop, lop.* Veck chuckled. "Good thing Gerbil can't do that. We wouldn't get any work out of him." He stood up and leaned close to Dowd, as if to tell him a secret. "All kidding aside now. Star is not a topic for discussion in this outfit. That's book, chapter, and verse. Toe the mark or I'm gonna end up feeding you your own wang." He touched the knife on his belt. "And believe me, it won't feel nearly as good for you as it does for Fido here."

CHAPTER THIRTY-ONE

Mike lay on his bed at the Copper Queen. It was after two in the morning but he couldn't fall asleep. He was staring at his cell phone. He'd brought up the number Lynnie had given him at the White House. His mind tumbled back and forth. *Call . . . Don't call.* It reminded him of when he was a teenager. His sister had played a game. Pull the petals off a daisy. *Loves me . . . Loves me not.* He closed up the phone.

His room was decorated in dark green and gold, cozy Old-West colors. He was going to miss it when he and Archie left. That would be today. The Copper Queen was too nice, too expensive anyway. Between them, they only had a few hundred dollars left. They'd have to find somewhere cheaper to stay.

He wouldn't miss the bed, though. Either it was too short, or he was too tall. He'd even considered doing what Lynnie always did—shove the bed out of the way and sleep on the floor—but he couldn't bring himself to take command of the room like that. A whiff of Alyxis Nuñez's perfume drifted off the pillow. It was an uncomplicated scent, one that could have been called, simply, Rose. It was perfect for Alyxis. Lynnie never would have worn it.

The perfume lingered, annoying him. He opened his phone again and wrote down the number. Then, grabbing his wallet and car keys, he slipped out the door.

The phone booth he found was south of town, next to the highway, by a shop that sold Indian jewelry. He'd decided to go out to a pay phone because he didn't want to risk having his cell traced. Was the cloak and dagger really necessary, or was he just being paranoid? He tried not to think about that.

The jewelry shop was so small it was easy to overlook, but twenty yards behind it was an abandoned pit mine, a mile across and a thousand feet deep, a startling sight in broad daylight, as if Atlas had reached down and snatched away a mountain, roots and all. Now, lit only by the stars, the pit was tar black, a flat, empty oval marked by the breeze sighing over the rim.

He lifted the receiver and dropped in his coins. On the first ring a woman answered brightly, "White House."

"I'd like to speak to the president." That's all Lynnie told him he had to say.

"I can take a message, sir." That same bright, level tone.

"I was told I could reach her at any time on this line."

The woman's voice didn't waver. "Sir, give me your name and number, please. Someone will get back to you."

He almost hung up, had the phone halfway to the cradle before he relented. "My name is Michael Stanbridge. I can't leave a number. I'll have to—"

"Stanbridge?" The woman was tapping computer keys. "Yes, I have your name on the list."

"List? Is that good or bad?"

That got a laugh. "It's good, sir. Please hold while I transfer. It may take a few minutes."

While he waited, he tried to convince himself that phoning was the right thing to do. He wasn't going to ask Lynnie for help. No, he was calling to get something off his chest. She deserved to know what he was doing. It was her past he was digging up.

The phone buzzed and for a moment he feared he'd been cut off, then someone barked, "Hello? Who the hell is this? And you'd better not say trick or treat."

Trick or treat? Right, today was Halloween. And that voice, he'd know it anywhere. Claudia Sung. "It's Mike Stanbridge, Claudia."

"Michael? Oh, brother, it *is* trick or treat."

Her tone—wary, skittish—told him one thing. They knew how much trouble he was in.

She recovered a bit, starting with a shaky chuckle. "Hey, we were talking about you a minute ago."

"Who's we?" Mike said.

"Boss lady and me and Rizzo. On the phone with Jonathan Ferrar and one of his—"

"Ferrar?" Mike cut in. "What the hell does—?" He caught himself. Keep it low-key, otherwise Claudia might get spooked and hang up. "What's up with Ferrar?"

"He's got some half-cooked story he thinks he's going to run in his paper tomorrow. Got his facts all futzed up."

"Something about Aron Aubrey?" Mike asked.

Claudia hesitated. "Were you at Aubrey's office on Friday? Disguised as a priest?"

Mike smiled. "I was there. Archie Pascoe was the priest."

"Well, Ferrar called in the police, and they were the ones who figured out it was you. Fingerprints on the office door, Ferrar says. He thinks you stole Aubrey's notes or computer files or something. He's blaming Lynnie, claiming you're some kind of spy for us."

Mike rubbed the spot between his eyes, fighting the tension there. "I'm sorry about that. Aubrey's notes are gone. They were on his computer and it was stolen. Claudia, listen, I need to speak to Lynnie."

He heard a rustle and a soft clunk and he guessed that Claudia was chewing her nails. "I know. I know," she said, trying to sound soothing, but there was that edge in her voice that she couldn't get rid of. "Look at it from our side, though. If Ferrar finds out Lynnie talked to you, he's going to eat us for lunch on this campaign-spy thing. And there's a warrant out for you, you know. FBI. Unlawful flight to avoid prosecution."

Mike had figured as much, but knowing for certain it was true was something else. He came out with a string of curses.

"Did you say pigshit, Michael? How rural. Anyway, back to the point. Wouldn't it make a great story for the papers? An old friend calls in on one of the president's private lines. They talk, maybe exchange a few recipes. Problem is, he's a fugitive in two murder cases, and we forget to mention the call to the police."

"Let's be straight with each other," Mike said. "Do you think I killed Aron Aubrey and Eve Tessmer?"

"Do I? Sweetcakes, I doubt you'd kill your own toe fungus. But like the family therapist says, it's not what *I* think that's important. Your name's in play now, a squib in the *New York Times* yesterday about the investigation into Aubrey's death. A few other papers picked it up. So far, except for Ferrar, nobody has connected you with Lynnie. We need it to stay that way. We need—here's something to put in your 'nasty words' file—distance. Be patient. A few days, that's all. Try again after the election."

"Claudia, I'm getting a little sick of fencing with the palace guards here. Now get Lynnie, please."

"Don't order me around, Mike. You aren't holding a good enough hand for that."

Maybe his hand wasn't so good, but that didn't keep him from bluffing. "Claudia, if you don't let me speak to her, I'm going to hang up and call Ferrar. I'm going to tell him I *have* been working for Lynnie, and that I'd be happy to chat about it, on the record."

Claudia was quiet for a few seconds, nibbling her nails again. She laughed. "What kind of courses do you lawyers take in school, anyway? Kick-Ass 101? It's like this kid who works for Rizzo. She's with us on this conference call. Not thirty yet, and Gina hired her to be the campaign's head lawyer. So she was going head-to-head with this tart of Ferrar's. Couple of tough broads—"

"Claudia?"

"Yes, Michael?"

"Quit stalling."

And so he finally got to talk to her. He heard her come into the room and lift the phone, listened to her pause while everyone else cleared out. A door thumped shut. Still she waited. "Lynnie?"

"Hi, Mikey," she said, gentle as velvet.

He closed his eyes in relief. "Where are you?" they both said.

"Arizona, a pay phone."

"Columbus, a big hotel."

"I miss you," he said, and instantly he wished he could grab the words back. Whenever they'd talked before, the phone line was secure. Lynnie saw to that. Now, since he'd placed the call, he wasn't sure.

She brushed right over it. "Mmmm. What are you doing in Arizona?"

He knew he wouldn't have much time, so he plunged

ahead. "You know about Blaine and New York City,
about how Archie Pascoe and I—"

"Yes," she broke in. "Claudia's been in touch with
people at the FBI. But all that happened back east."

"The murders were back there, yes, but it started here.
Aron Aubrey came to Arizona, looking into your past.
Something about your mother, we think."

"My mother? Why would he have been interested in
my mother?"

"Do you know—" He took a breath to slow them both
down. "Did she have a hysterectomy?"

"Hyster—Mike what's this about?"

"There's a man who claims he was your family's
dentist. He says your mother had the—She had a hysterectomy scar."

"A dentist? What dentist?"

Mike recognized the pattern here, every question answered with a question. He'd seen Lynnie do that in
press conferences, tie reporters in knots. *Could you clarify
that? What do you mean by . . . ?* It was one of her great
gifts as a politician. Now he knew what it felt like to be
on the receiving end. "Have you ever heard of someone
named Graciella Yberri?" he said.

There was a muffled bang and Lynnie said to someone
on her end, "Out. No, later. Go."

He stared at the ground between his feet, waiting.

"Yberri, you said? Is that someone from out there?"

"Lynnie, please answer me. Yes or no. Graciella Yberri.
Do you know that name?"

She lowered her voice a note, as if she were disappointed with him. "The phone, Mike. We shouldn't . . ."

So the line wasn't secure. Or maybe that wasn't the
problem at all. Maybe she didn't want to answer him and
was using the phone as an excuse. The thought pushed
Mike into silence. Did he really believe that? That she
was just making excuses, waltzing him around? Maybe,
yes. Maybe his trust for her was slipping.

"Mike? Are you still there?"

"I'm here. Archie and I went out to the ranch. I think Oscar was there recently. Do you know where he's living?"

"Oscar Martinez, you mean? Why would he go to the ranch?"

Mike sighed loudly.

She said, "I'm sorry. I don't mean to be difficult. It's the campaign. You know how much I hate the traveling and the food, everything. We've been up most of the night here. Now listen to me—complaining, when you're the one with all the trouble."

"It's all right. You sound like you've got a cold."

"My sinuses, from being on the plane so much, and I never can sleep in these hotels."

"Sometimes . . . sleep is overrated," Mike said, chuckling.

"Ha-*ha!*" It was a private giggle she had, childlike, unbridled. He could at least do that for her still. Her voice took on that velvety tone again. "Mike, I am worried about the phone line."

"All right," he said. "No more questions, then. There's one thing I have to tell you, though. It's Archie. He's decided to go to the newspapers tomorrow, tell them what we've learned. It isn't much, but it'll start them digging."

"That wouldn't be good. Not now, not with Ferrar already nosing around. Can you talk to him, tell him to wait?"

"Lynnie, we're in a real box. We have to find a way out."

"Maybe I can help. I can speak to Grearson at the FBI. She could order the field offices to lay off for a while. A few days anyway, through next week."

"No," Mike said, "sooner or later it would get out that you interfered. And then where would you be? Let it ride for now." He stared at the sky, at the blackness, trying to imagine what she looked like right then. "How are the polls? I haven't seen anything in the newspapers in a couple of days."

"Good. We always want more, though." She hesitated; he could hear her playing with the telephone cord. "I never would have guessed how important it is to me, a big win. And there's so much to worry about—things that could go wrong." Another pause. She was waiting for him to speak.

"I won't do anything to hurt you, Lynnie."

"Of course you won't," she said, trying to be cheerful and breezy but not quite bringing it off.

Mike shuffled his feet. He switched the phone to his other ear. He'd had so much to say, but now the words all seemed to have deserted him. "I should let you go. Get some rest, OK?"

"No. No, please." Suddenly there was a note of desperation in her voice. He'd heard it in Blaine, at the end of the few minutes alone they'd had together; he'd heard it in Hawaii, the last morning in bed before he had to leave. "Claudia's got my vacation scheduled," she said.

"Hawaii?"

"Right. Her place. New Year's."

Mike smiled: message received. "Terrific. I hope it works out."

"Yes, it will," she replied eagerly. Then silence, awkward silence.

He said, "Well, take care."

"Don't go yet. I wish there were something I could do to help you. Anything. I've thought and thought about it." The sentences came in little bursts, as if she were trying to hold back but couldn't. "I feel so far away from you."

"I know. Just hope for the best, and—" He laughed. "Think about New Year's. All the clocks will stop."

"I believe that. Mikey, I miss you so—" The phone went dead.

For a long moment he stood listening to the hiss on

the line. Maybe she had just run out of things to say and hung up. Maybe Claudia had cut her off. Maybe, either way, it was for the best.

The breeze rose from the pit behind him, snaking around his ankles, drawing him out of his reverie. He shuffled over to his car. Her last words filled his mind. *Mikey, I miss you so*—He was sure he had never heard her sound so sad.

CHAPTER THIRTY-TWO

"No," Joey Leyva croaked, "Aubrey and I didn't see anybody at the ranch." He was propped on a pile of rotting railroad ties. His face was cardinal red and bloated, like a big tomato.

Colonel Veck squatted in front of him. He had a squirt bottle in his hand, filled with water and ground chilli pepper seeds. "Buddy, you don't understand the rules here. This ain't the *Kama Sutra*. We don't want every variation you can think of. Now, who was at the ranch?"

"We saw a woman there, maybe," Joey said.

"A woman? A while back it was *two* women." Veck gave him a long squirt in the eyes. Joey blinked and licked the juice off his lips as it dribbled down. "A woman and a jaguar."

"Jaguar? For God's sake," Veck muttered, looking at the bottle. "There's somethin' wrong with this stuff." He sprayed a few drops on his own hand and an instant later was dancing in a circle, howling. "*JesusJesusJesus*." It felt like lava, and yet there sat Joey, swollen up a little, but placid as a damn cow.

Dowd was sprawled on top of the railroad ties. "Nah, it's him. Joey-boy's fried his nerve endings, drinking so much."

Veck had stopped his dance. His face was taut with

rage. He flung the bottle at Joey and coiled his fist, ready to strike.

Dowd jumped between the two men. "Cool off, Colonel. Punching his lights out won't help. Go outside for a while. I'll see what I can do with him."

Veck stomped out to the dirt track at the mouth of the cave. They were high up in Escacado Canyon, only a few crow-flies miles from Bisbee, but an hour's driving time because the road was so bad. It was an old mining site, with a couple of broken-down shacks, heaps of rusted machinery. It was a lonely place, perfect for an interrogation. If Joey would just cooperate.

Veck was only interested in two thing: Where had Joey taken Aron Aubrey? What people did they talk to there? Simple, but Joey had to go and make it complicated. For every question, he had a half dozen different answers, and every version came out the same way, mumbled, partly joking, like maybe Joey himself couldn't tell if it was truth or lie. Dowd was probably right: Joey had fried his brains in booze. Then again, could be the shag-ass was being foxy, playing for time, hoping somebody would show up to save him. No joy there, bud, Veck thought. Ain't no cavalry coming up this road.

It was cold, and Veck jammed his hands into his pockets. The stars were fading, the hilltops beginning to turn purple. Dawn. Time to get it in gear, or they'd end up wasting the whole morning. That wouldn't do, not with Pascoe and Stanbridge and all the other garbage they had to deal with. But first, Joey. Veck still had a trick up his sleeve, something he'd been saving for the big finale. Looked like it was time to use it.

On the ground nearby, a two-way radio squawked. Veck picked it up. "Yeah, Gerb, what is it?" Gerbil was in the truck two miles down the canyon, in an open spot where he'd set up a communications link.

"It's Star, Colonel. Got three transmissions from her in

the last ten minutes, all marked 'Urgent.' You want me to unscramble, or at least send a 'message received'?"

"Yeah, sure. Send her one of your fanny pictures."

"Really?"

Veck glanced up at the heavens, shaking his head. "No, *not* really. Don't respond. Hold the messages for me. And Gerb, don't bother me again. Out." He tossed the two-way down and strode into the cave.

"Joey, come here," Veck said. "Want to show you something." Dowd climbed back up on the woodpile out of the way, and Leyva tottered to his feet, stiff from sitting so long. He wasn't tied up. Veck always left his prisoners like that, figuring the hint of freedom helped loosen their tongues. He put his hand on Joey's shoulder. "Back here." They moved deeper into the cave, to the edge of the ring of light cast by the lantern. There was a mine shaft in the middle of the floor, straight down. Veck picked up a rock and tossed it in. Silence . . . silence.

"Deep," Veck said. "Real deep."

Joey tried to shuffle back, but the colonel held him where he was.

"You don't like heights, do you?" Veck said. Joey didn't answer. "Come on, son. I saw you on that ladder at your house. Creep, creep like an old lady. Scared shitless. It's in your Air Force jacket, too."

Joey looked at him, startled, peering with his puffy, aching eyes. "Who are you? *Who?*"

"Sky Pilot, that's what you can call me. Remember that song? Eric Burden? All about nasty ol' 'Nam?" Veck knocked out a few bars, adding a little tremolo. "No? Maybe you're too young. Anyway, I had somebody pull your service file. They booted you out of the flyboys because you decided you didn't like airplanes anymore. That's right, isn't it?"

Joey nodded slightly, then shrugged, then shook his head: three answers all at once.

Veck gave a mean laugh. "The way they wrote it up, you saw some fighter jock eject. Chute didn't open and he went splat on the runway, about ten feet from where you were standing. Ooo, the sound he must have made when he hit. Bet you still have dreams about it." He nudged Joey toward the hole. "So let's quit screwing around. I want to know about Mexico. About Agua Prieta. You took Aubrey there, didn't you?"

Joey made his three-stanza reply: nod, shrug, shake of the head.

"Don't fuck with me, son." Veck gave him a knee in the seat of the pants, sent him reeling toward oblivion, then jerked him back.

"*Yes!*" Joey shouted. "We went there."

"And you met with a woman."

"Yes. No."

Veck shook him like a rag doll.

"*No,*" Joey said. "Look, I'm trying to be straight. I found her for Aubrey. He gave me the name and—"

"What name?" Veck asked.

"Yberri. Dolores Yberri."

"All right. And you talked to her?"

"No. Aubrey did. We found her house and he went in alone. I stayed outside."

"The whole time?"

"Yes, yes. I don't even know what she looks like."

"Aubrey didn't tell you why he wanted to talk to her?"

"No, nothing."

"Good, Joey, good." Veck relaxed his grip slightly. "Where else did you go?"

Joey swallowed. "The hospital. That was all."

"Who did you see there?" Veck asked. Leyva hesitated. "*Who?*"

"Castillo," Joey said quickly. "I forget his first name. He worked there. Not a doctor but some kind of office job."

"And you were there when Aubrey talked to him?"

"No," Joey said. "I waited outside again."

Veck twisted him around so they were face-to-face. "Castillo couldn't speak English, and Aubrey couldn't speak Spanish." Joey wet his lips, his tongue flicking out like a lizard. "You speak Spanish, don't you Joey?"

"No."

"¡*Cuidado!*" Dowd shouted suddenly.

Joey threw his hands up to protect his face.

Dowd chuckled. "Means 'watch out,' Colonel. He speaks Spanish."

"Right," Veck murmured ominously. "Said so in his jacket, too. The *truth*, Joey."

"Sure, sure. Aubrey knew Castillo would be at the hospital—how, I don't know. I asked for him at the front desk, and introduced the two of them when he came out. I translated a little—good day, how are you, what can I do for you—that kind of thing. Then they went into a back room together, to look at some files. I didn't see what was in them. Honest, I didn't."

"Jooeey," Veck murmured.

"OK. There was an X-ray. I saw that. Castillo made a photocopy and gave it to Aubrey. The rest—I was too far away. They talked. Aubrey had a dictionary with him, so he could put together a few phrases. Castillo used it, too. They passed it—one, then the other. It took a long time. Then Aubrey gave Castillo some money. They shook hands. That was it."

"No one else was around?" Veck asked.

"No. Castillo sent everybody away. He was nervous, scared like."

"Did Aubrey tell you anything about the files? Why they were so important?"

"Not a word. I swear."

"Did he show you the X-ray?"

"The copy? No. He just put it away—a leather case he carried."

"All right, so what'd you do after the hospital?"

"Nothing. I wanted to stop for dinner, but Aubrey said

no. We came straight across the border, and I dropped him at his hotel in Bisbee. Last I ever saw of him."

"Great, kid, that's great." Veck eased him away from the precipice a few steps. "What do you think, Dowd? We about done here?"

"Pretty near," Dowd said. "Who have you told about this, Joey?"

"Nobody. Aubrey said that if I kept shut up about it, he'd pay me extra. Two thousand. For that kind of money, Jesus could be camping in my bathtub and I'd keep quiet about it."

Dowd laughed. "You see Jesus in your bathtub often, do you?"

Joey laughed too, a nervous titter. "Once, when I got into the malt liquor real good."

Veck massaged Leyva's neck, gently, gently. "You know what Aubrey was researching, don't you?"

"Something about politics, he told me. President Connor." Joey swallowed hard again. "But I never understood what."

Veck looked into the darkness for a moment, then up at Dowd. He beckoned him down. Before the other man reached the ground, they heard the sound of a truck engine, and a set of headlights flashed past the mouth of the cave. Dowd moved in to hold Joey, while Veck went outside to see what was going on.

It was Gerbil, boiling to a halt in a cloud of dust.

"Thought I told you not to bother me," Veck called.

Gerb hopped out. "Fannies, fannies, fannies. You sure must like the taste of mine, the way you chew it all the time."

"If you've got something to tell me, spit it out."

"Had a call from Cutter and Longtemps. They couldn't find Stanbridge's car anywhere in Bisbee. The two of them are headed for Sierra Vista now, to check the motels there. They did pick up one thing, though. Stopped for gas and asked the attendant if he'd seen anybody who looked like Stanbridge or Pascoe. Yeah, he said. A guy like Stanbridge was in yesterday. He was trying to find somebody, fellow with a couple of fingers missing on his right hand. Must be Leyva he was talking about."

"When was this?" Veck asked.

"About noon, maybe a little after."

Veck thought for a moment, staring at the hills. "Righty-o. You done good, Gerb." He waved toward the cave. "Come on in and join the party."

Dowd had his arm draped over Joey's shoulder and was chuckling, telling him something. Veck rushed in, a blur of forward motion. He spun Leyva around and drove him back until his heels reached the lip of the mine shaft. He whipped Joey's hands up and clapped them together, as if to make him pray, then took a half step forward so Joey's body was angled back over the hole. The only thing that kept him from falling was Veck's grip on his wrists. It was over and done before Joey could make a sound.

"You've been holding out on us, kiddo," Veck growled. "Did a tall guy come to see you yesterday? Had a scar on his neck, was asking about Aubrey?"

"Y-yes."

"You lying son of a bitch."

"*No!* I'd'a told you, but you didn't ask."

"Oh, that's cute, Joey. Real cute. What'd he want? And tell me everything, now."

"Wanted me to show him around where Aubrey went."

"And you agreed, of course."

"I did, yes." Joey peered back over his shoulder at the pit, then clenched his eyes shut. He spoke in a frantic whisper. "Aubrey said I—I only had to keep quiet for a couple of weeks. His book or magazine article, I don't know, whatever was going to be published and he didn't care what I did after that."

"Now, this tall man, did you tell him where you were going to take him?"

"No. We didn't get into that. Except I said something about bringing his passport, to get across the border, you know. That was all." Veck let him slip a bit, then reeled him back up. "*Really, that's all!*"

"All right, Joey. Last question. Final Jeopardy, like on TV." Gerbil giggled, but Veck shut him up with a glare. "When were you going to meet him and where?"

"This morning," Joey whispered. Tears leaked out of his tight-shut eyes. "At my place. Seven o'clock."

"You're sure?"

"Yes, dammit, I'm sure."

"Good for you, son."

Veck glanced at Dowd, who nodded and mouthed, "That's it."

"Joey, friend . . ." Veck smiled and patted him on the cheek. "You just think about Jesus in the bathtub now." He let go.

The scream went on and on. Gerbil leaned over to look into the pit. "*Man*, it's like what those paratroop boys say: 'Airborne, All the Way.'"

Far, far below they heard a thud.

"Well, almost all the way."

Fifteen minutes later the three ex-soldiers were down the canyon at the spot where Gerbil had set up his communications link. Veck put through a call to Cutter and Longtemps. "Where are you?" he asked.

"Ten miles east of Sierra Vista," Cutter replied. "What's up?"

Veck related what Joey had told them. "We can't get out of this damn canyon in time. Can you make it to Leyva's place by seven?"

"We can try," Cutter said. He spoke to Longtemps, and Veck heard their brakes come on, tires whining on the pavement. Then Cutter was back on the line, his voice stone cold. "What's the plan? Take them both out?"

"I want to talk to one of them. The other—I don't care."

"Which one?"

Veck thought it over. He imagined Cutter stroking his ruined ear and the big purple welt on his cheek, all that pent-up hatred he had for Stanbridge. "Your choice."

Cutter laughed. "Righteous, Colonel. On our way."

CHAPTER THIRTY-THREE

The waitress thumped a platter down in front of Archie. "Breakfast Supremo for you"—she splashed coffee into Mike's cup—"and more go-go juice for you." They were in a café around the corner from the Copper Queen. They had already checked out and loaded their things in the car.

Mike dipped his spoon in the coffee and ran it in a lazy circle. He was staring at the television over the bar in the next room. The morning news was on, a piece about a flood in Brazil. They hadn't started on the campaign coverage yet.

"Something on your mind?" Archie said.

"Not really."

Archie dashed salt over his food, a supersized tortilla rolled into a tube and curled around a pile of runny scrambled eggs. "Last night I got up to use the can. Looked out the window to check the weather and saw the car was gone from the parking lot. You want to tell me about that?"

"No."

"Let me rephrase. *Tell* me about that. What were you doing?"

Mike looked at his coffee, the vortex in the middle where he'd been stirring. "I went out to use a pay phone to call Lynnie. She said there's an interstate flight warrant out for the two of us. There's nothing she can do about it. And the other things we found out—the dentist, her mother, the gravestone, all that—she couldn't help there, either."

Mike watched Archie's face, reading the changing expressions. Surprise. A flash of anger. Then a crinkling around his eyes, a calculating look. They held each other's gaze; Mike braced for the inevitable question. *You call in the middle of the night, just like that. And she answers, just like that. President of the United States. You want to tell me about* that, *Michael?*

But Archie didn't ask. He blinked, and made a faint smile, and cut into his tortilla. Out slithered a mess of sliced green olives. "Can of worms," he said quietly.

Except for the sound of a rooster crowing, the neighborhood where Joey Leyva lived was quiet. Joey's pickup was out on the street, and Mike would have parked by it, but there was a big dog sleeping there. He pulled up in front of the next house, past an old camper with three flat tires.

As it had been yesterday, the front door to Leyva's house was ajar. Mike stuck his head in. "Hey, Joey, you awake yet?" Heavy silence came in reply. Mike went in, holding the screen open for Archie. They checked the bedrooms, then the bathroom and kitchen. The light was on over the stove. On the table was a knapsack, unzipped. Mike poked through the contents: a pint bottle of tequila and a can of orange drink, packages of cheese and crackers, Joey's wallet and passport, a map. Everything he needed for a day trip to Mexico. So where was Joey?

There was also a notepad in the knapsack, and Mike started flipping through it. Grocery lists. Car parts. A few addresses, phone numbers.

Archie drifted over to the back window. "What the hell is that?"

Mike came to take a look. He spied the can of insect spray first, then the crow, body here, head over there. "His name was Spot," he said. He still had the knapsack in his hand, and he tugged on the zipper. *Joey's crow killed and left in the yard to rot . . . Joey gone . . . Wallet left behind.* "I think we'd better get out of here."

"What's the matter?"

Mike grabbed the notepad—he wanted to finish looking through that—and shoved it in the knapsack. Then he hesitated. A vehicle was coming up the street, a big truck from the sound of the engine. He hustled into the living room, Archie tight on his heels.

It was an oversized Dodge pickup, rolling along slowly, the two men in it checking out the cars parked on the street. They couldn't see Mike's rental, hidden where it was behind the camper. Directly opposite the house, the truck stopped, and the man in the passenger seat cranked down his window.

"Criminy," Archie said. "The guy you walloped in Newark."

"Exactly," Mike breathed. "Criminy."

The man turned to stare at the house, and Mike and Archie jerked back out of sight. "Have you seen the other guy before?" Archie asked. "The driver?"

"I don't think so. What do you want to do?"

Archie was already moving toward the kitchen. "Find something to fight with."

Earlier, Mike had spotted a gun propped next to the fireplace. He scuttled over on all fours and grabbed it. An air rifle. Terrific.

Someone was coming up the front steps. The door was still ajar. There was no place for Mike to hide so he knelt where he was, clutching the gun, not even knowing if it was loaded.

The footsteps turned and paced. There was a creak and a thud. The man had jumped down to the ground.

Mike started to crawl across the room again, behind

the lone chair, but before he got there Archie came chugging out of the kitchen, holding up a butcher knife nearly as big as a machete. "They're around on the side," Archie said. "Go now." He didn't break stride, right out the door.

That seemed like a good idea to Mike, since most of the rear of the house was glass, and, if the men got back there, everything inside would be in plain view. Making as little noise as he could, he plunged onto the porch and down the steps.

The timing was perfect. In a matter of seconds, Mike and Archie were crouching in the street behind Joey's truck. Part of the house was held up on cement piers, leaving six inches or so of clearance. A pair of feet came into view in the backyard, then another. Mike pulled out his car keys.

"They'll hear the engine start," Archie warned. He gestured toward their big pickup. "We can't outrun them."

Mike stuffed the keys into Archie's hand and took the knife. "You get the car. I'll take care of things here."

Archie nodded and hurried off, while Mike turned to their truck, using the knife to cut open the valve on the rear tire, glancing over his shoulder as he worked. So far so good. The feet had stopped moving. The men were standing together, talking.

The valve split and air came out in a high-pitched *whoosh*. Mike hadn't noticed the dog. Startled by the noise, it rolled to its feet, growling, then began to bay. Mike whispered, "*Shhh. Hush.*"

In the rear yard, the men moved, hurrying toward the driveway. Archie had the car going and was turning around, but too slowly. He wouldn't get there in time.

Mike could see only one option. He stood in plain view and aimed the air gun at the spot where the men would appear. He only hoped they didn't have real guns to shoot back with.

It worked. They stepped out, saw the rifle, and flew back behind the corner. Mike grabbed the knife again and drove it deep into the other rear tire. The explosion of air sent the dog to a new level of frenzy, howling and bouncing on its front legs.

Archie was still jockeying the car, having trouble because the seat was too tight to the steering wheel.

The two by the house had split up. One was ducking through the boulder field in the yard. The other—the man who'd attacked Mike in Newark—was sprinting around the rear of the place, aiming to come in from the far side. Mike stood and aimed the gun again. The man in the boulders kept coming. He pulled the trigger. *Ffft.*

Big mistake—like slapping a tiger in the face. The man touched the corner of his lip, the streak of blood where he'd been hit. "Goddammed *pellet* gun!" he roared. He lurched to his feet and came on at a dead run. The other man pelted into sight by the porch.

Mike wrenched the knife free from the tire and backed into the road, figuring he'd fight better in the open. But again he hadn't counted on the dog. Set off by all the noise and movement, the dog surged at the man in the boulder field, low to the ground, snarling, sinking its teeth into his ankle. The man screamed and went down, flailing at the dog's head. And now the second man hesitated, unsure whether to go after Mike or stop and help his mate.

Archie rolled up, bellowing, *"Get in! Get in!"* He flung open the door. Mike hopped in the open doorway, riding standing up like a character in an old gangster movie.

The man in the boulders was still tangled up with the dog, but the other one sprinted after them. The car was so underpowered it seemed he might catch them. They were headed downhill, though, and soon picked up speed. The man broke off the chase, drifted to a halt. He stared, locked in on Mike, eyes sparkling with rage. As they disappeared around the corner, he turned and raced back to his truck.

When the call came in, Veck and the other men were still in Escacado Canyon, grinding down the pocked dirt road in their pickup. The colonel answered. "Cutter? What ya got for me?"

"Nothing, Colonel. We missed them."

As always, Veck's first reaction was to get angry, but he sensed the bitterness in the other man's voice. He decided to go easy. "Lay it out."

Cutter told him.

"Whoa," Veck cut in. "Longy's been *shot?*"

"It's nothing—split lip. Bastard Stanbridge boobed us with a pellet gun."

"A pellet—?" Veck had to laugh.

"Yeah, it'd be funny if it weren't so pathetic," Cutter said.

"Which way did they go? Did you see?"

"Made a left at the bottom of the hill. North, for Tucson."

Dowd was sitting behind Veck in the pickup. The colonel turned to him. "Says they're headed for Tucson."

Dowd frowned briefly, then gave a brisk shake of his head. "No. Can't see it. Not now."

Veck spoke into the phone. "We'll be there in fifteen minutes, help you get your truck back on the road."

"Sure, Colonel," Cutter mumbled.

Veck chuckled again. "C'mon, trooper. Suck it up. You still got those maps I gave you?"

"Yeah, why?" Cutter said.

"It's time to go over the fence, down Mexico way. Protect our assets. Hang in, buddy. Payback time's a-comin'."

Archie stomped in a circle, kicking at pebbles. "Clay-headed fool," he muttered. They were on a ranch road a few miles north of Bisbee, just off the main highway.

The car was parked under a cottonwood tree, and Mike was leaning against the door, chewing on a twig, deep in thought. Archie spun around and slugged him in the shoulder.

"*Ow!* What the hell was that for?"

"For calling Lynnie, you yo-yo. For bringing those two apes down on us."

Mike rubbed his shoulder. "No way. I didn't tell her what we were planning. I didn't even tell her we were in Bisbee. Those goons found out from Joey. He was the only person who knew we'd be at his house this morning."

"Lynnie didn't know?" Archie grumbled. "Bullcrap. Probably got people out all over the place looking for us. We leave for Tucson now. That *Daily Star* newspaper— somebody there'll talk to us." He tried to shove Mike out of the way so he could get in the car.

"No, Arch. Aron Aubrey went to Mexico, and Joey was going to take us there." Mike had already looked through Joey's notepad and hadn't found anything useful. The map, though, was more promising. Joey had marked a few places around Bisbee and Douglas, including the CC Ranch. He'd put two big stars on Agua Prieta, on the other side of the border. "That's where we go next."

"For what? So we can get a whole new set of cops after us?"

"We do two things," Mike said. His tone was measured. He'd thought it out. "First, we try to find somebody related to Graciella Yberri, and see what they can tell us about her. Then we see if we can track down that X-ray, figure out how it fits in."

"X-ray? Why that all of a sudden?"

"A hunch, but a pretty good one. Joey was going to take us around to the hospitals on that side of the border. And you said yourself there's something on that X-ray that looks like the beginning of the name Yberri."

"Pah," Archie fumed. "Fine. You want to go off on that

kind of goose chase, be my guest." He flung the keys at Mike. "You rented the car anyway." He reached into the back seat and hauled out his duffel bag. "I'll find my own way from here." He marched toward the highway.

Mike called after him, "You know, it wasn't me who started all this—or you. It was Eve."

Archie kept going.

"That was why they killed her."

Archie scuffed to a halt. The sun was still low in the sky and his shadow was cast backward up the lane, tangling with Mike's legs. "How so?" Archie said grumpily.

"Aubrey never would have told Eve anything. She dug up something on her own, and must have called him to talk about it. Maybe Eve didn't know it was important. Something about our dentist buddy in Tucson, I'll bet. Aubrey's phone line was tapped. One conversation would have been enough. The wrong people got scared and had Eve killed."

Out on the highway a pickup cruised by, a big Dodge, enough like the one that had been after them that Mike and Archie both jumped out of sight behind the cottonwood. But the truck was much older, not the same at all.

They came back out in the sun. Mike spoke quietly. "You said yourself how stubborn Eve was. I think she'd want to see this through to the end, figure out what it was she started. There's only one way we're going to do that: follow the trail Aubrey left. That means over the border."

Archie kicked another pebble and gave a long sigh. "*Damn.* Nothing is easy with you is it?"

"No, I guess it isn't," Mike grinned. "And just so we're straight, we've got another problem. We need special ID to cross into Mexico. I might be able to get along on Joey's passport, but that won't do for both of us—"

"Passport?" Archie said morosely. "I got that OK."

"What do you mean?"

"I've *got* a passport."

Mike couldn't hide his surprise. "Why?"

"Walleye, that's why. Best fishing in the world is in Ontario. I get up there four, five times a year." He glanced at Mike and shook his head. "Maybe I've got a little more foresight than you give me credit for, Michael. When I left Blaine, I figured I might end up out here." He gazed around at the weeds and scrub trees. "Godforsaken hellhole."

Archie walked into the shade again, facing south. "Imagine what my poor daddy would say. Messico? With all those Messicans? Son, you need your head examined."

CHAPTER THIRTY-FOUR

On Pan American Avenue there was a billboard, facing south toward the border. Mike looked back at it as he drove by. DOUGLAS, ARIZONA—BIRTHPLACE OF PRESIDENT LYNNIE CONNOR. BIENVENIDOS/WELCOME. Above the words was a portrait of her, a poor likeness, the expression stiff, the eyes staring belligerently. Someone had nailed a Halloween decoration to the bottom of the sign, a witch on a broomstick. The witch had blonde hair. Even in Douglas, where they had so much reason to be proud of her, there were people who hated her. Lynnie always shrugged off that kind of thing. Loony-tunes, she said. Down deep, though, it had to hurt.

Archie was hunched back in his seat, his eyes darting at everything that moved. "It's Mexico, Arch, not the Heart of Darkness," Mike said. "And you better stop looking like that."

"Like what?"

"Like a toad trapped in the snake house at the zoo. The border guards will think we're smuggling something."

"What would anybody want to smuggle *in* to Mexico?"

"Stairmasters. Mexicans want *all* our Stairmasters."

While Archie pondered that, they rolled up to the inspection point. The guards, dressed in snappy black uniforms, circled the car and one of them glanced at the passports. "You stay in Agua Prieta?" he said. Mike nodded. The guard twitched his thumb, the universal symbol to move on.

"That's it?" Archie asked.

"Except for the body cavity search," Mike said. "Wait'll you see the guy who does that—no hands, just a couple of brass hooks."

"Very funny."

Mike pulled over down the block, in front of a brick building with the word *Aduana* on the front. At the Chamber of Commerce in Douglas, they'd picked up a tourist map of Agua Prieta. He wanted to look it over. Archie glanced around, still nervous. The map had a listing of businesses in the downtown area. "*Abogado, abogado*," Mike mumbled. He pointed at a side street. "There's a lawyer's office over there. He probably speaks English, could give us some advice."

"A lawyer?" Archie said. "Sheesh. Now we're really in trouble."

"Hey, *viejos*," a voice called from the sidewalk. It was a boy, about twelve years old, dressed in black jeans and a Phoenix Suns sweatshirt. His face was all angles—chin, jaw, cheekbones, two dark slashes for eyes. "Yeah, you two. Can't park here. Say you give me the keys, uh? I'll take care of your car for you."

With him was a younger boy, dressed much the same, holding a plastic trumpet in his hand. He thought what his friend had said was hilarious. He giggled and blew a quick bullfight call on his horn. Down the way three old men were leaning against the *Aduana* building fence. Embarrassed by the spectacle, they pulled their straw Stetsons down to cover their faces.

"What's your name?" Archie said to the older boy.

"Manlio Chamor." He made a deep bow and added sarcastically, "*Para servile.*"

Archie harrumphed. "Shouldn't you be in school, *Boy*-lio Chamor?"

The younger lad tooted his trumpet: score one for Archie. Manlio snatched the trumpet and gave the other kid a scornful shove. "School. *Me vale madre.*"

Mike had been sizing him up and decided to ask him a real question. "We need to find a couple of people. The map says there's a tourist information office around here. You think they'd be able to help us?"

"If they ever open up," Manlio said. "Closed most the time." He wandered up to Archie's door, a little peevishly, as if this were taking a big chunk out of his busy schedule. "What people you want to find?"

"Get in," Mike replied. "I'll tell you about it."

Archie's head whipped around. "Hold on. I was just warming up to that lawyer idea."

But already Manlio was in the back seat, grinning out at his friend, comfortable as a pasha.

Mike eased into a legal parking space down the street. He began telling the boy about Graciella Yberri, the few things they knew.

Manlio cocked his leg up, playing the bored executive. "Yberri?" he said. He was chewing gum and he popped it between his teeth. "Born here, you say?" Mike nodded. "Way back, 1940s?" Mike nodded again. Manlio began to smile. "You guys need confession?"

"Why?" Archie said suspiciously.

"Two birds, one stone." Manlio tooted the trumpet and waved so long to his friend. Then, for Mike's benefit, he motioned backhanded down the street. "*Vamos.* That way."

Guadalupe Church was next to the main plaza of Agua Prieta. It was an old-fashioned building, dazzling white, with flat facades and a tall, rounded bell tower. The plaza was hard-packed dirt, home to a bandstand and a few dozen spindly orange trees.

Manlio hopped out as Mike came to a stop. "Wait," was all he said, and he disappeared into the gloomy interior of the church.

Immediately, Archie began to grouse. "That kid won't help. Probably on his way out the back door right now, snickering at us."

"He speaks both languages," Mike replied, "and, any way you cut it, we're going to need someone like that. Besides, have you got a better idea?"

Archie grudgingly shook his head, and Mike settled in to wait. The stores around the plaza were opening up for the day. Every shop had something familiar about it, something a tourist from the states would recognize. A restaurant with a sign ¡VIVA BUDWEISER! An office supply store with COPIAS CON EQUIPO XEROX. A music store with the sound system cranked up, Jennifer Lopez blasting out at the street. Mike closed his eyes and could imagine himself back in Miami, at a Dolphins game or watching the volleyball players at Lummus Park.

Somebody snapped a finger next to his ear. He turned and almost bumped noses with Manlio. "Ten bucks."

"What for?" Mike asked.

The boy nodded toward the church. "Collection plate."

Mike gave him the money while Archie sputtered under his breath. A priest had appeared in the church door, dressed all in black, a simple guayabera and slacks. He was using crutches and had close-cut, pure white hair. Though the crutches made him stoop, he kept his head up and looked steadily at Mike.

Manlio strutted toward the church, but once he reached the sidewalk his demeanor changed. Apparently he saved his wise-ass routine for the gringos. He approached the padre respectfully and held the money out so it would be easy to reach. The priest slipped the bill into his shirt pocket, then patted the boy on the shoulder. Manlio trotted back, playing a little air guitar to match the beat of the storefront music. "Hey-hey, dudes! Les' rock-an-roll!"

Manlio didn't tell them what he'd learned from the priest. His grin said he was saving it as a surprise. He gave Mike directions in cryptic bursts. Go there. Turn right. Now straight.

For Mike's part, it all seemed natural. Since their escape from Joey Leyva's house that morning, he'd felt a certain inevitability about the day. Finding Manlio, visiting the church—it was as though he were on a conveyor belt moving toward some predetermined destination. Now he drove quietly, taking in the scenery.

They were headed east, parallel to the border. At the intersections he could look left and see the fence, a ten-foot-high wall of corrugated steel. The shops of downtown gave way to a residential area. It was a lot like Douglas on the other side of the line, but then again different. Agua Prieta had a more muscular feel to it, more like the Wild West. The houses were smaller, lower to the ground; the yards were dusty and had few trees. Most of the people they saw were men, dressed in cowboy boots, tight jeans, snap-button shirts.

Archie had less patience than Mike. They had gone only about a mile when he twisted in his seat and grabbed Manlio by the sleeve. "Where are you taking us, Boy-lio?"

"Don't call him that," Mike said.

"Yeah, don't call that to me." Manlio took out a fresh stick of gum. He slipped it into his mouth while he muttered something.

"*What?*" Archie snapped. "Bulls in a roar?"

Mike was chuckling. "Bowels. He meant bowels in an uproar. He's right. Cool it. So Manlio, what's up."

The boy tossed the gum wrapper out the window.

"Like this. Agua Prieta's a big place now. A hundred thousand? More? Who knows? That's from the *maquilas*—manufacturing plants—and all the people headed over the border."

A dump truck had come up behind them and wanted to pass. The driver tooted his horn. Manlio reacted in a flash, shoving his trumpet out the window and blowing a short tune of his own. Shave-and-a-Haircut, that old ditty. The truck driver honked back, the same five-beat tune, angry now.

Mike pulled over and let the truck by. "What the hell was that all about?"

Manlio grinned and shrugged at the same time, a disarming combination. "*Chinga tu madre,*" he sang, using the Shave-and-a-Haircut rhythm. "Ta-ta, your mo-ther." He laughed and punched Mike in the arm. "Be Mexican, man. Don't let people push you around!"

Mike gave him a look that said, *You'd better cool it, too.* He got underway again.

Manlio said, "Anyway, about here. Way back, the sixties, this place was nothing. Ten thousand, maybe. Before that, only a dirt road. The church, they keep records—baptisms, funerals, weddings. Father Vega looked it up. Oh, hey, stop. Yeah, here. Father thought he could remember her, too."

"Remember who?" Mike and Archie both asked.

"Graciella Yberri." Manlio pointed at a house across the street, a stucco bungalow, neatly painted white with turquoise trim.

"I don't understand," Mike said. "She lives here?"

"No." Manlio climbed out of the car. "You wanted a relative, right? ¡*Orale amigos!* Come on!"

Crossing the street, Archie whispered, "If it's as easy as this, I'll bet dollars to doughnuts Aron Aubrey found it, too."

Over the door was a plaque that said 1934—FAM. VASQUEZ CUELLAR. Manlio tugged his shirt down, composing himself. He knocked. A few moments later a curtain inside moved. Then the door swung open and a woman stepped into the morning sun.

She was thin and short, her dark gray hair swept straight back from her face. Her eyes were turned down at the corners, as were her lips—a mark of sadness or fatigue. She wore a plaid apron over a paisley dress. Her hands and arms and the apron all were dusted with flour. The smell of baking bread drifted out from behind her.

As he had with the priest, Manlio ducked his head respectfully while he spoke. The words tumbled out so fast that Mike only caught a few. *Perdón, señora. Nosotros . . .* Then he heard a name: Dolores Yberri de Cuellar.

"*Sí*," the woman replied. "*Soy Lola.*"

Her eyes swept from Manlio to Mike and Archie. She recognized them, not by name, but their clothes and hair and the way they stood. *Norte Americanos.* She didn't seem surprised, but she brought herself to full height, as if bracing for something. "Graciella—you find her?"

Archie rushed to speak, but Mike interceded. "Let's go in and talk."

She was so tiny, her head barely came to his chest. She stared up, searching his face, seeing the sadness in his eyes.

"Dead," she whispered. "Graciella is dead, no?"

"Yes, *señora*, I think so."

She gestured to the door, the inside of the house. "*Pase, pase*. Talk, yes."

CHAPTER THIRTY-FIVE

Lola Yberri's kitchen was painted the same brilliant turquoise shade as the trim on the outside of the house. In spite of the color, it was a dim, shadowy place, lit only by the sunlight breaking through a small window in the corner. There was a propane stove, plank counters, open-faced cabinets, a red-tiled floor. Everything was worn to a sheen from having been cleaned again and again. The air was warm from the oven, ripe with the smell of bread yeast.

She directed them to sit at the long trestle table in the center of the room, then asked their names. After repeating them to make sure she would remember, she said, "Coffee." She wasn't asking if they wanted any, but simply stating the natural order of things. She turned to the stove to heat water.

Archie was tapping his foot nervously, brimming with questions, but Mike signaled to him. *Relax. Don't rush her.* "Vasquez is your husband?" Mike asked.

"Was. Dead—" She paused to convert the number to English. "Twelve year. My place now, and my daughter, her husband. They work to the coffee plant. *Maquiladora*. Lotta hours, lotta days. Busy all the time. Good money, though."

"And Graciella?" Archie said, unable to hold back.

"My sister," Lola replied softly. She turned to Manlio. "*¿Refresco, grillo?*" He nodded and she retrieved a tall bottle of Fanta from the pantry for him.

"*Grillo?*" Mike said. "What's that?"

"Cricket," Lola replied. She crossed her arms and smiled at the boy. "Looks like a cricket, you think?" Manlio, grinning, wiped orange soda off his chin. Then he rubbed his legs together and burped. The three adults chuckled.

Lola's English was improving with each sentence she spoke. "You talk pretty good," Archie said. "Where'd you learn your English?"

"Thank you," Lola said with a wry smile. "I learn in Douglas, in *el todo* store."

"Toto?" Archie said. "Like the dog in the movie?"

Manlio giggled so hard Fanta sprayed out onto the

table. "No! Not Dorothy, not the dog! *Todo* is everything— like a department store, only cheap."

Lola, nodding, cleaned up the table with her rag. "I worked there years and years. My English needs practice, now, but so." She put her hand by the boy's shoulder. "You go in the other room, OK? Leave us talk."

"Aw," Manlio said.

"Rodrigo, my son-in-law, he has some magazines in there. American . . ." She tried, but couldn't come up with the English word. "*Deportes.*"

"*Sports Illustrated*?" Manlio said. He didn't seem much interested.

"Yes, that's it." Her voice grew cold; she'd had enough argument. "Go now."

He took his bottle and left, but she kept an eye on him through the open door. She recognized him for what he was: a street kid, maybe just rough around the edges, maybe bad to the core. Either way, he might be tempted to steal something.

The kettle was whistling. Lola spooned Nescafé into the cups, added water and a liberal splash of evaporated milk. She brought a bowl of brown sugar to the table, too. To be polite, both men helped themselves to a little. Only after they'd each taken a sip did she speak. "Now, Graciella. Tell me."

"We don't know much," Mike said. He started with what Archie had found out in Tucson, the date of Graciella's death. Tears filled Lola's eyes. "*Ay, Dios,*" she whispered. "So long ago?"

"When was the last time you saw her?"

"The year before, when she was nineteen. We didn't hear from her after that, but all these times, I thought she was alive. Hoped. She—" Lola broke off, her voice choked with emotion. The cuckoo clock in the other room came to her rescue, sounding the half hour. "My bread," Lola said, and she went to the oven to retrieve it.

There was no space on the counter, so she put the pan on the table, on a stack of newspapers she had set out as a hot pad. Mike and Archie leaned in to look at it, then sat back, surprised. The pan was flat, the loaf on it shaped exactly like a skeleton. Lola, watching them, gave a gentle laugh. "For you, Halloween. For us in Mexico, *Día de los Muertos*. Yours is to frighten—ghosts and witches. Ours is for family spirits—" The irony came through to her then. Her voice caught again and she glanced away. "Our dead ones come back to visit. We pray for them and leave them treats—candy, bread. Mostly we just remember. Happy and sad all rolled up together."

She started to decorate the skeleton, using raisins and cinnamon and colored sugar. The work was a balm, soothing her emotions. She began to talk, telling Graciella's story.

Lola and Graciella were both born in Agua Prieta, a year apart, with Graciella the eldest. From the beginning Graciella was popular, but she was never a happy girl. She was restless and starry-eyed, always making big plans, wanting to do outrageous things. There was a statue of Pancho Villa in town, riding a gelded horse. Graciella decided the great Villa deserved better, so, with two balls of clay, she made the horse into a stallion. A policeman caught her at it, and she was forced to clean the statue in broad daylight, while the townspeople watched and jeered. That was typical of Graciella. Her escapades always seemed to come to a bad end.

When she was sixteen she started sneaking across the border to go to dances in Douglas. How she loved to dance, especially the fast songs! She was small and she liked the bigger boys, who could swing her and throw her in the air. One time, a boy gave her a ride in his car all the way to Tucson. She was gone for two days, and when she came home their mother burned her favorite dancing shoes and locked her in her room for a week. Their mother was the disciplinarian in the family.

Soon after that—a few days after her nineteenth birthday—Graciella left town, taking only an overnight bag. A month later they got a letter from her. She was in Los Angeles, settled in an apartment with friends, she said, working in the office of a meat-packing business.

She wrote regularly for a few months, glowing accounts of Hollywood and the beach and all the stores. Then, for a while, they heard nothing. Finally, another letter arrived, addressed to their father. Graciella was pregnant, and alone. She wanted to come home and have the baby.

"When was this?" Archie broke in. "Do you remember exactly?"

Lola shook her head. "Exactly, no. Winter sometime, or spring maybe."

Mike counted up the months. Archie was counting, too. A winter pregnancy could work out to an October birth. Lynnie was born in October.

Lola had finished decorating the skeleton. The crust was still soft; she'd taken the loaf from the oven before it was fully cooked. She began reshaping it, poking one part, smoothing and stretching another. She started up her story again.

Their father was a government worker, not highly placed, a shy man, easily embarrassed. Their mother was always looking out for him. The two of them talked it over, and they agreed. It was bad enough that Graciella had gone to L.A., but to have her return to Agua Prieta pregnant, that was too much. Mamá was the one who wrote back. Graciella could come home on one condition: without the baby. They were good Catholics, so it wasn't an abortion she was suggesting. Graciella should have the baby in California, then give it up for adoption.

Lola was done with the skeleton. Under her skilled touch it had taken on a whole new appearance. What had been a male figure was now female, the hips rounded and cocked to the side in a dancer's pose, the head up, jaunty and proud. She stood back to study her work, and tears flowed freely down her cheeks. "Graciella never answered my mother's letter. We never saw her again. All these years, I see the TV—O. J. Simpson in Brentwood, *Knots Landing* and *The O.C.*—and I think maybe she married some American. Maybe she lives there, a place like that, where it is so pretty."

She sat down. "Where is she?"

"A ranch cemetery," Mike replied, giving a vague wave in the direction of the border. "It is pretty there."

"Ranch? In L.A.?" Lola said.

"No. Outside of Douglas."

"*Douglas*?" Lola gasped. She covered her face with her hands and rocked to and fro, whimpering, "*Dios . . . Dios mío.*" It was some time before her grief subsided. She dabbed at her tears and drew herself up in her chair, but her thoughts still were turned inward. "She came back then, home from California. Nearly home. But why not send word to us? All of us, even Mamá—" She fell silent and, after a moment, reached for her coffee. Sipping, she made a face. "Uy, cold. I'll make fresh."

"No, this'll do fine," Archie said, laying his hand over his cup. "Did her letter mention who the father of the baby was?"

"Not plain, but . . ." She frowned, frustrated with the language barrier, and made a gesture with her hands, writing between her fingers.

"Between the lines," Mike offered.

"Yes, that's it. He was already married. A gringo, I think." Gringo—an angry word, the way she said it. Mike wondered if she would apologize, but she didn't. She stared into space, momentarily aloof.

From the other room came a muffled crash. Lola got up to investigate. "*¡Qué lío!*" they heard her say. "*¿Qué pasó?*"

"*Nada, señora,*" Manlio sputtered in reply. "*No hay problema.*"

Lola made a low sound, like a growl, and she muttered a final word to Manlio: "*Hombres*." She returned carrying a magazine, which she thumped down on the table, the *Sports Illustrated* Swimsuit edition. "My son-in-law got some fast talk to do. He bring this home, and I tell him get rid of it." She made a quick motion, washing her hands in the air. "But here it is still, on pile's bottom." The men laughed while she glared at them mockingly. "Now, fresh coffee, OK?" She took their cups before they could refuse. While more water was heating, she slipped the bread back in the oven for the last bit of baking.

"Aron Aubrey came to see you?" Mike asked.

"Yes. It was some surprise, you know? He heard about Graciella over the border someplace, in Arizona. Her life would make a good story, he thought, a story people would want to read. Girl goes north from here, what she was like, what happened to her there. He said he would try to find her, that she could be famous if he wrote about her." Lola nodded toward Mike and Archie. "He said others might come to talk to me about her someday. You seen him yet? Tell him about the grave?"

Mike avoided her eyes. "No, we haven't talked to him, but we're following up on his research. Did Aubrey say why he thought Graciella was interesting? Why people would want to read about her?"

Lola shook her head. "No, only that she was born here and went north to live. That was the story he liked."

She turned to rescue her bread from the oven. When she had brought the pan to the table, Archie said, "Did Aubrey mention anything about going to a hospital, here in Agua Prieta?"

"No. Only Graciella we talked about."

"Have a look at this," Mike said. "It's a copy of an X-ray." He smoothed it out on the table. "Does this mean anything to you?"

Lola took the sheet to the window where the light was better. "No, Mr. Aubrey didn't talk about this." She brought the page up to her face, peering at it. "It's got a little note here, *San Juan*. You see it?" Mike said he had noticed it, but didn't know what it meant.

She stared out the window momentarily, thinking, then turned to the low cupboard behind her. She had to kneel to look inside it. "This one. I thought I remembered." She pulled out a newspaper from a stack, more hot pads.

She spread it on the table between the two men and ran her finger down the page to a short article: "*Último Adiós*." The photo above showed a burial scene, with a crowd of mourners straining on tiptoes to watch a coffin being lowered into the ground. "Martin Castillo," she said, "his funeral. He worked there the—the *jefe*, the—uy, I can't think. Head administrator, that's it."

"Worked where?"

"Hospital San Juan del Noroeste. Right here, Agua Prieta. The oldest hospital around. Big problem since Señor Castillo died. No one to take his place, and they can't pay much—"

Archie said, "He's dead?"

"Yes," Lola replied. "He drowned." She checked the newspaper. "Two weeks ago."

"Drowned," Archie said. "It was an accident?"

"Yes, sure." Lola bent backward and threw her hands up. "Bad luck. Fell in the bath."

Archie sat back, balancing his coffee cup on his stomach. "The head man at the hospital dies in a freak accident, a few days after Aron Aubrey came to see him. It makes you wonder, doesn't it, Michael?"

Mike didn't reply. For a moment he seemed to be in a trance. Then he took the X-ray back from Lola. "I have to make a call." He remembered his manners. "Sorry. Excuse me." He took out his cell phone. "Can I use the other room?"

"Here," Lola replied, indicating the way past the front door. "The bedroom."

When Lola came back to the kitchen several minutes later, Archie was finishing his coffee. He had the newspaper open in front of him. "He is a nice man," she said, going to the sink.

"For a lawyer," Archie grumbled.

"Ah, that is who he talks to then."

"Who?" Archie asked.

"Other lawyers. He called to his office in Miami."

Archie lifted his eyebrows. "Huh," he said. Then he rattled the paper. "This thing's full of pretty blondes."

Lola came to look over his shoulder. "Yes, you see, Mexico is like the U.S. Blondes have more fun. Or so they get the best husbands. Get rich; get their pictures in the *Sociales*."

"Your sister, was she blonde?"

Lola smiled and bobbed her head. "I have a book." She disappeared into the room where Manlio was and came back lugging a leather-bound photo album. "*Recuerdos*, we call them," she said, patting the cover soberly. "Memories."

The album seemed to have no particular order, but it didn't matter. Lola knew it by heart. This one, Graciella as a baby. That one, a toddler. Then holding a tea party for her dolls. Then taller, slimmer, outdoors somewhere. First communion. A teenager. Her hair was light, but not quite blonde. Her eyes were pale, blue or green or gray—in the black-and-white photos it was impossible to tell which. She rarely smiled, and often turned away from the camera as the shutter snapped, blurring the picture.

They came to the end, her eighteenth birthday. Archie pored over the three photos, all formal poses. Graciella stared blankly up at him, her skin creamy, her face unformed, not a woman yet. Did she resemble Lynnie Connor? Perhaps a little, around the eyes and mouth, but there was nothing definite.

Mike was on his way back, his footfalls brisk on the

tiles. Archie turned and lifted the album to show him the pictures, but he hesitated when he saw the expression on his face. "Trouble?"

Mike looked straight at Lola. "We need your help. Can you come with us for an hour or so?"

"Yes, I can come, but where?"

"To the hospital."

CHAPTER THIRTY-SIX

Mike and Archie stood in the Hospital San Juan waiting room, looking out at the street. They were alone, except for an old woman dozing on a sofa in the corner. Lola had gone ahead to the hospital records office. Manlio was outside, sharing a cigarette with a young man in farmer's clothes. The man had been drinking, enough to give him the giggles. He turned and mugged at Mike and Archie. "Hey, Yankee! Wanna take my picture?" Manlio laughed and clapped him on the shoulder, then distracted him by pointing at a pretty girl across the street.

Archie began to pace, swinging his head like a bear in a cage. "Forty bucks, she took?" he said, motioning down the hallway where Lola had gone.

"*La mordida*," Mike replied. "The bite."

"Bite, baloney. That's money the tax man'll never see."

Mike shrugged. "We've got our way of doing business, they've got theirs."

Archie wrinkled his nose. "Peas and rubbing alcohol. These goddamned places always smell like peas and rubbing alcohol."

"You're Little Mr. Sunshine all of a sudden."

Archie rubbed the spot over his heart. "Don't like hospitals, that's all. Give me the heebie-jeebies."

Lola hissed at them from the hall. "Come. This way."

The man outside called again, "Hey, Yankee!" Mike glanced back, intending to give Manlio a good-bye wave, but the two of them were looking around the corner, at some other poor Yankee.

A stocky woman in a white pants suit was waiting with Lola. She led the way, past a ward with ten full beds, past two private rooms, both empty. Lola hung back a few paces so she could whisper to Mike and Archie without the other woman hearing. "She's a secretary only. Works for the records man. He is in a meeting. Everyone I talk to is nervous—Castillo dead, no one really in charge. We won't have much time."

The hospital was all one level. From the outside it appeared quite small, blocked in by the neighboring buildings, but it snaked around in the back, a warren of narrow halls and small dark alcoves and rooms. They reached an unmarked door, which the woman in white unlocked. She flicked on the lights, revealing a long space with a dirty skylight, a black linoleum floor, and banks of military-green file cabinets. She went to one of the cabinets and unlocked it. Heading for the door, she flashed her fingers at them. "*Diez minutos sólo.*"

The cabinet she had unlocked covered a single year, the year Graciella Yberri had died, the year Lynnie Connor had been born. The manila files, two drawers' worth, were stuffed in in no apparent order. The bottom drawer was in worse shape, with thousands of loose scraps of paper. They'd never get through the whole mess, so they stuck with the files, dividing them into three equal stacks. Archie and Lola took seats at the lone table; Mike worked standing up at the cabinet.

Some of the files in Mike's stack had names on them. Some were blank, and he had to check the contents to find out who the patient was. It was a tedious process, searching through the faded scrawl. Jiménez, Salazar, Sosa, Colón. The papers inside were a jumble: small yellow slips—payment receipts; white sheets—lab results;

and long blue cards—patient charts. And X-rays, lots of X-rays. Someone, way back when, must have loved his X-ray machine.

Mike was halfway through his stack when he found a file with Graciella's name. The top sheet was a hospital admission form. It was dated the same day Graciella died, so she'd only been there the one day. Her address had never been filled in. In fact, most of the form was blank, and what was there was just a brief jot here or a box checked there, as if it had been done in a great hurry. The next sheet was a yellow payment receipt. The bill had been paid in cash by John Sheridan.

Mike turned the admission form over and saw there was an official-looking document clipped to the back, filled out and stamped. A death certificate, he guessed. He crossed the room and set the forms and the rest of the file in front of Lola.

For a moment she seemed not to understand, and then she murmured, "*Ah, sí.*" She began to read, starting at the top, taking in every word. With her knuckles she dug the tears from the corners of her eyes.

Archie leaned over for a look. "Does it say what she died of?"

Lola picked up the death certificate. "Yes, lose the blood. What word? The—"

"Hemorrhage?" Archie said.

"Yes, I think. Hemorrhage." Lola went back to her reading, and Mike took the remainder of her stack to finish off.

The woman in white had promised only ten minutes, but that had passed long ago. Mike flicked quickly through the files, shoving them back in the cabinet as soon as he finished with them. Then Archie stood up, holding something down at his side. "Have a look," he whispered, making sure not to disturb Lola. He set down a file: "*Bebé Yberri.*"

The top sheet was an admission form, and, like Graciella's, it was mostly blank. There was also a patient chart and several sheets of lab results, all too complicated for Mike to understand. He set those aside and took out the single X-ray film. Archie crowded in to look.

The X-ray was the same as the copy they had, but, when Mike held it up to the light, much easier to read. The date, the hospital name, and the doctor, all were clear to see. Given the size of the head relative to the body, it was obvious this was a baby. The problem was obvious, too—a fracture in the collarbone, the two jagged ends of bone spearing past one another. It made Mike wince, thinking of that long-ago pain, and the baby who couldn't be made to understand that it would heal, that the pain would go away. Then he gave a wistful smile. Not just any baby. Lynnie Connor, her first day on earth.

Archie had turned back to the file, digging in the corners for any last pieces of paper. He came up with a small form, simpler and easier to understand than the death certificate. He jabbed his finger down the columns. *Nombre de Niño/a:* Carolyn Jean Yberri. *Madre*: Graciella Ana Yberri. *Padre:* John Stephen Sheridan. A birth registration card. It was signed by a Dr. Ruiz Elidad, the same name as on the X-ray and throughout all the files. "Jackpot!" Archie whispered.

Mike looked sharply at him, irritated by the smugness in his voice. He slouched over, resting his elbow on the cabinet, his forehead on his hand. "Arch, you don't have a clue, do you?"

"What?"

"Here." Mike turned and beckoned. "Come on." Once in the hallway, they swung the door shut most of the way and kept their voices down, so Lola wouldn't overhear.

"Don't have a clue to what? She's a bastard, with a Mexican mother to boot. Lynnie's damaged goods if it gets out. Kaput."

"Maybe in your crabbed little world, Archie, but thank

God not for the rest of us. Graciella Yberri was her mother, not Mattie Sheridan. Big deal. There's nothing Lynnie could have done about it. She'd still win the election in a heartbeat if that was the only problem. But it's not. It's here—" Mike pointed at the ground between his feet. "This place. *Where* she was born that's important."

Archie glanced around at the pocked floor, the stained, chocolate-colored walls. "Yeah, it's a dump, so what?"

"President of the United States. Think about the requirements for the job. You have to be thirty-five years old and—"

Archie had been frowning, but now his eyes shot wide open, his expression as surprised as if Mike had hit him.

"That's right," Mike continued. "A natural born citizen." He tapped the papers in Archie's hand. "Those say Lynnie was born here, in Mexico. If that's so, she's not qualified for the job. Not constitutionally qualified."

There was a chair in the hallway and Archie slumped into it. He scratched his ear in a distracted way. "Natural born," he mumbled.

"If Lynnie's parents were U.S. citizens, it would be different. But Graciella Yberri was Mexican. John Sheridan was British by birth, not naturalized until after he moved to Blaine. That's why I had to call my office, to have someone check the rule . . ." Mike broke off. Archie couldn't care less about the legal niceties.

The legend was that Lynnie had been born in a tiny cabin on a lonely Arizona ranch, her mother trapped there by a harsh storm and rising creeks. It made a wonderful story. Lynnie was the heir to Lincoln, an independent spirit, lionhearted from birth. She cultivated that image. But it wasn't true. She was born here, in a Mexican hospital, a hundred yards south of the border. She couldn't legally be president. Simple. Kaput.

Archie tipped his head back until it was resting against the wall behind him. "Remember what Aron

Aubrey told his father? 'A fake from the start. The book will kill her.' Aubrey knew about her being born here, and that it would put her out of the race. That's what got him murdered, not all his other mucking around."

"Yes," Mike said. "And whoever killed Eve must have decided she might eventually figure it out, or put somebody on the trail."

They heard Lola sniffle in the file room. "What do you think we ought to tell her?" Mike said.

"Everything," Archie answered without pause. "Lady's got a right to know she's the aunt of the president"—he held up the patient chart and birth record—"even if it's only going to last a couple more days."

After that the two men were quiet for some time. The hospital gave him the heebie-jeebies, Archie had said earlier, rubbing his heart. Mike's heart felt cold in his chest, a frozen lump. He remembered what he'd said to Lynnie on the phone: *"I won't do anything to hurt you."* A lie. He had snooped until he reached the end of the road—the Mexican birth record.

Mike had seen Lynnie before when she felt betrayed. She showed no anger, but there was a flash in her eyes, a cutting off, a door slamming shut. He'd have to tell her what they had found. He'd have to look her in the eye and risk seeing that door slam shut on him.

Archie sat forward, elbows on his knees. "A few grubby pieces of paper." He shuffled them, one on top, then the other. "Think what they'd be worth to some people—a villa in France, a yacht, or maybe a quick trip out of town inside a cement mixer." His voice was soft, hypnotic. "Worth that much to Lynnie and the people around her. It's a real temptation, isn't it?"

Mike stared down at the top of Archie's head. He hadn't gotten around to thinking about this yet, but he would have soon enough. Take the file, get rid of it. Be Lynnie's hero. If there were other papers somewhere, find them and destroy them, too.

Archie gave a melancholy sigh. "These go back where we found them, agreed?" When Mike didn't reply, Archie stood up, full height, implacable. "If you've got something else in mind, you're going to have to go through me to get them. Don't disappoint me, Michael."

Mike swallowed the lump in his throat. He glanced at the sheets of paper. "Sure, Archie. It's Lynnie I'm going to disappoint."

CHAPTER THIRTY-SEVEN

They had to lie to Lola to get her out of the records room, telling her the hospital secretary had returned and told them they had to leave. They put the files away, then slipped quietly past the patient rooms and through the lobby.

It was early afternoon now, and the sun was blinding. There were no cars moving on the streets, but several pedestrians were ambling in the direction of the city plaza, presumably on their way to lunch. Manlio and the man he had been talking to were nowhere to be seen.

Lola plodded along in a daze, her lips moving in silent conversation with herself. When Mike unlocked the car, she finally spoke up. "There was a baby. I saw in Graciella's form."

Mike and Archie looked at each other. It was such a complicated story. Where to begin? "We know," Mike said. "Get in. We'll talk about it while we drive."

As Mike reached the key into the ignition, he saw Manlio come sprinting out of an alley. "*Hey, hey, espera!*" the boy shouted. "You got my horn!"

Archie held the trumpet out for him, but Manlio hopped into the back seat beside Lola. "Wow, unbeliev-able." He was looking at the alley. The man he'd been with stumbled into view, holding his nose with both hands and shouting curses. "*Está loco*," Manlio said. "He mouth off to some dudes. Pick a fight. Ay!" He stretched back in the seat, putting his hands lazily behind his head.

Archie dropped the trumpet in his lap. "Son, we appreciate your help—really. But we need to talk with Lola now." He popped open the door.

Manlio shot another glance at the alley. The man was slumped on the ground, still holding his nose. There was blood on his shirt. Manlio clicked the door shut. "Hey, I'll be quiet like a bug. No trouble. Get me out of here, OK?" He huddled down, trying his best to act small and vulnerable.

Archie scowled at him. "So you did some mouthing off of your own, did you?"

Manlio grinned. "Well, a little, maybe. They deserved it, though. *Gringo mariposas.*"

Archie looked at Lola. "Take him back to your place?" She nodded. So Archie motioned to Mike. "*Ándale, ándale.*"

"Where'd you pick that up?" Mike said, smiling. He made a U-turn.

"*Bonanza* reruns," Archie confessed.

The route they took was only a block from the border. The houses were ranch style, surrounded by low fences, many with small shrines in the yards. The streets were so empty the place had a ghost-town feel. Archie asked why. Nowhere to go now, Lola explained. All the businesses are closed. Everybody's inside eating.

Mike was thinking about the hospital. He wondered if Dr. Elidad was still alive. Not likely after forty-three years. Maybe Lola would know what had happened to him. And Mike wanted her to tell him what she'd seen in Graciella's file. Probably wasn't anything important, but it was worth pinning down.

"*¡Carajo!*" Manlio barked. He was cowering, peeping out the back window. "That truck from the hospital, they're after me!"

The truck had come roaring up from behind, so close that Mike, glancing in the mirror, could see only the grille. Archie turned and jacked himself up high in his seat to get a better view. He spoke quickly, his head near Mike's ear. "Arizona plates. The same model of Dodge we saw at Leyva's this morning." Manlio was still trying to hide. Archie laid a hand on his shoulder, steadying him. "There were men in it?"

"Yes. Americans. Three."

"Was there another truck? The same, only red?"

Manlio shook his head. "I didn't see. Only this one, green."

Without thinking about it, Mike had hit the gas. The pickup stayed tight on his tail.

Archie touched Manlio's shoulder again. "It'll be all right. They're not after you."

"Who, then?" Lola demanded. She was sitting up straight, clutching the back of Mike's seat.

No one had time to reply. The red truck they'd seen at Joey Leyva's place in Bisbee burst from a side street right in front of them. On the left was the municipal baseball stadium, the only large building in that part of town. Mike whipped the steering wheel over and they careened into the deserted parking lot. The truck following them overshot, and the driver jammed on the brakes, spinning in a one-hundred-eighty-degree skid.

The red pickup came on unobstructed, bouncing over the curb into the parking lot. A man was crouching in the cargo area, the one who'd been bitten by the dog at Leyva's house. He stood up, feet spread for balance, holding a snubbed-off shotgun at port arms.

Mike had run too close to the stadium. There was a long walkway with a railing, and he had to stop and back up to get around it. He snatched at the shift lever, trying to get into reverse, missing gears.

"*Hold it!*" Archie screamed. He shoved his door open. "I've got him."

"Got him?" Mike yelled back. "What are you talking about?"

The green truck was just entering the parking lot. The red was nearly on top of them. The man in the cargo area was clutching the cab so he wouldn't be thrown out when the driver hit the brakes.

Archie was still bellowing, "*Hold it, hold it!*" He had the glove compartment open, and he snapped the door off with his knee as he lurched out of the car.

Mike pawed at his hip, trying to drag him back. "Archie, *No!* Don't be a fool!"

Archie's arm moved in a tight arc. There was a flash of brass in the sunlight—Archie's dart. Straight through the truck's open window.

It caught the driver high on the cheek, just below his eye. He screamed and the truck bolted forward. The man in the back had turned to bring his shotgun up. He flew across the bed, shoulder into the tailgate. The shotgun went off, a harmless blast, straight up. The driver was still screaming, pawing at his face and slamming on the accelerator to get them the hell out of there.

Archie bounced into his seat and Mike stomped on the gas. They shot past the other truck and out of the parking lot. By the time the two pickups got untangled and after them, they had a lead of about a block. With their small car, it wasn't nearly enough. In less than a minute the two vehicles were closing in. Then, without warning, they backed off, one staying directly behind about fifty yards, the other paralleling on an adjacent street.

It soon became clear what the game was. They were forcing Mike south and east, away from the city center. "What's out there?" he asked, pointing.

"*Colonia, desierto—nada,*" Lola said, her English erased by fright.

"The shacks, then desert—nothing," Manlio translated.

Mike slowed to ten miles an hour, hoping for an opening but seeing none. There were other cars and trucks out now. Siesta was over. The two pickups rumbled along, the drivers brazenly blowing their horns whenever anyone got in their way. South and east, south and east. It was like a chess match, two knights running down a lone king, the beaten player too stubborn to resign. The minutes wore on, and the sun bore down, and in the car they all were on edge, shouting, cursing. The streets turned to gravel. The houses were tiny, cobbled together out of raw wood and tin.

A dust cloud appeared on the left, and out of it roared a white bus, so big and bright it seemed an impossible thing out here. It had a Safeway emblem on the side and the words TRANSPORTES GRATIS. Mike fell in behind, while the trucks continued to shadow him.

The break came when the bus turned and lumbered up a narrow lane between rows of chicken coops. Mike saw a gap and scooted past, his bumper clipping an old Plymouth parked there. Brakes screeched; the bus driver yelled. Then the horn on the truck following them sounded, a long beautiful wail. Another car had come up behind it. The truck was trapped in the lane.

Mike put the pedal to the floor. He wasn't sure where the second truck was, but he'd deal with that when he had to. He didn't have a specific plan, except to get to some place where there were people, lots of people. He passed through a manufacturing district with broad concrete-block warehouses, then turned onto a wide street heading north, toward the border.

He should have been reading the signs and watching where he was going, but instead he kept checking his mirrors. Suddenly, the street he was on came to an end, right at the border fence. He had no choice but to turn onto Calle Internacional, the route to Douglas. Fair enough, he told himself. Take it easy.

By then, Agua Prieta had long awoken from its midday rest. It was five o'clock, the busiest time at the crossing. After a few blocks, traffic slowed to a crawl, with a hundred cars and trucks, maybe more, jammed into three tight lanes. Mike was trapped on the far right, the border fence on one side, vehicles all around on the others. The U.S. customs station loomed ahead—tall, ultramodern buildings of desert brown.

Behind him horns blared and Mexicans cursed. The two pickups had come racing in from a side street, cutting into line. Mike kept his eyes on his mirror. Three men climbed out and started sauntering up the street. They were carrying coats over their arms, and he was sure that under the coats were shotguns.

Mike looked everywhere for a way out. Ahead there was a gap in the fence, a separate entrance to the customs compound for commercial vehicles. Except for a small cargo truck, the checkpoint was empty. Mike twisted the wheel and tapped the gas, and they bounced onto the sidewalk. They cruised past the other cars in line and through the fence opening.

A customs agent came jogging out to meet them, waving both arms. "¡No! ¡No entrada!"

Mike rolled down his window. "I do somethin' wrong?" he said, putting on an innocent smile.

"Commercial only," the inspector said. "Turn it around. Back in line."

Manlio jumped in. "Aw, come on, man, don't be a hard-butt. Pass us through."

The inspector's face grew angry. "I said turn it around. *Now.*"

A horn honked again up on the street, and the inspector glanced that way. The three men had gotten back in the pickups, and the trucks were now trying to cut across the lanes, to get to the commercial entrance. The Mexican drivers, most of them young and middle-aged men, refused to budge or even look. Someone in one of the pickups yelled, "*Hey, estúpido. Mueve un poco.*"

"Idiot better be careful," the customs man muttered. He rapped on Mike's door. "Get it out of here, buddy. Go."

Before Mike could reply, Manlio hopped out of the back. He'd seen Archie's heroics with the dart and Mike's behind the wheel. Now he figured it was his turn. He skittered up the street, quick as a fox. "Hey! Yankee!" he yelled at the trucks. "Screw off!"

"What's that kid doing?" the customs man said.

Manlio reached the lead truck and pounded on the hood. "You think you own this place? Maybe I'll kick your ass!" A gap of a few feet opened up in front of the truck, and the engine rumbled, but Manlio stood his ground. Then the driver slipped out, coming after him.

"Oh, Jesus," Archie said.

Manlio was much too quick. He skipped sideways around the man, and reached in through the open driver's door. The horn sounded. *Baa-te-te-ba-bop.* Shave-and-a-Haircut.

The customs man stared, shocked. "What's wrong with that kid? He want to start a riot?"

With all the buildings and noise from the traffic it was hard to pinpoint which horn it was, but the Mexicans in the cars thought they knew: those shiny *Americano* pickup trucks. Gringo bastards acted like they were kings. Butt in line, expect everybody else to get out of the way. And now this with the horn—"fuck your mother" in vulgar Mexican morse code.

Heads turned, brown Latino eyes tight and glowering. Get with the program, paleface. *Everybody* waits.

The driver had jerked Manlio from the truck, but he twisted free and darted in again. He was so small, he was hidden from view by the door. The driver looked to be the one with his hand on the horn. *Baa-te-te-ba-bop.*

Up and down the line, men boiled out of their cars, closing in on the pickups, a silent, stone-faced horde. "God A'mighty," the inspector moaned. He grabbed his two-way radio and started chattering into it, already moving, running through the checkpoint and around the corner of the customs building, apparently to get reinforcements.

Manlio came racing back to the car. "Go," he said as he jumped in. "Through there." He pointed to another gate at the end of the compound, leading to the streets of Douglas.

Mike took a final glance back at the pickup trucks. A small man who looked vaguely familiar had stepped out and was holding his hands up, as if to surrender. "No trouble, boys," he shouted to the crowd. "Come in peace."

Six customs agents came sprinting through the checkpoint. They had nightsticks in their hands and grim looks on their faces. Mike rolled right past them, keeping his eyes averted, praying that none of them would yell for him to stop.

There was a speed bump by the far gate, and Mike went over it faster than he should have. He heard a sickening clunk, but left it to Archie to look back to see what it was. "Geez," Archie said. "Must have knocked it loose on that Cuda."

"Cuda?" Mike said.

"Barracuda. That Plymouth you hit. Our bumper—just fell right off."

"Leave it," Manlio ordered. "Turn here. That's it, right. Now drive, *paisano*." He slouched back comfortably and picked up his trumpet, smirking as he toyed with the keys. "When you mess with the bull, you get the horn, eh?"

Lola took the trumpet and told him to be quiet. She arranged her hair and sweater, and then she sat forward. "*You*"—she poked Mike angrily in the shoulder, then Archie—"got some 'splaining to do, busters!"

CHAPTER THIRTY-EIGHT

The football bounced across the brown grass, coming to rest in front of Lola and Mike. He tossed it back to one of the boys who'd been playing with it. "What an arm!" the kid yelled. "Sign 'im up!" They were in a small park a few blocks from downtown Douglas. So far, they'd made three slow trips around, talking quietly. Archie and Manlio were in the car, by the town library across the street.

"You can't go home for a while," Mike said. "It won't be safe. I'm sorry about that."

Lola gave a shrug with her hands, an acknowledgment that it wasn't his fault. "I have friends here. Don't worry."

It wasn't six o'clock yet, but there were already youngsters out in Halloween costumes, converging on a house festooned with black and orange crepe paper. On the porch, a man was filling a galvanized tub with water while a little girl dressed in a vampire suit dropped in apples. Lola stopped walking so she could watch. "Mrs. Connor, Lynnie—what was she like as a girl? Pretty?"

"Beautiful," Mike replied. "Prettiest girl in town."

"A troublemaker?" Lola asked.

Mike grinned. "She liked to keep things stirred up."

Lola tipped her head back, fighting her tears. "I see Lynnie Connor on TV, and every time she makes me smile. She glows, you know? She just glows. Graciella would have a daughter like this, I think." Lola giggled then, a girlish sound, and looped her arm through Mike's. "It's better than I had thought for her, no? Brentwood and Malibu—ha! Mother of a president!"

They made one more circuit of the park before returning to the car. "You want to walk with me to the Knights of Columbus?" Lola called to Manlio.

"Sure." He scrambled out of the car, giving Archie a playful slug in the arm. "*¡Nos vemos, amigo!*"

Archie made a thumbs-up sign. "*Hasta la vista, grillo.*"

"He learns quick for an old guy," Manlio said, smiling at Mike. Mike offered his hand and they shook, and then the boy and the old woman started up the street. Lola was very bowlegged and tottered as she walked. Manlio held out his arm for her to take, and she rested her hand on his wrist. For a moment, as they moved through the shadows, they looked like nobility, an aging Spanish countess out for a promenade with her young nephew. Then Manlio had to break the spell, lifting the trumpet to his lips and blowing the first few bars of "Jingle Bells."

"I asked him what citizenship he was," Archie confided to Mike.

"And?"

"The scamp said, 'Who cares?' "

"Doesn't seem to affect his life one way or the other."

"Scamp," Archie said again, following their progress around the corner, out of sight. "What'd Lola mean about the Knights of Columbus?"

"She knows people there," Mike said. "When it's safe for her to go home, we're supposed to call. They'll get word to her."

Archie ran his tongue around his lips. They were chapped and pale. He had one foot out of the car and tried to lift it back in, but he didn't seem to have the strength. He collapsed back, massaging his shoulder.

Mike bent and helped with the leg. A week ago that would have been unthinkable, but now the intimacy didn't faze them at all. "Heebie-jeebies?" he said, laying his hand on Archie's chest. The heartbeat was shifty and distant. *Ump . . . whu, whu . . . whump.*

Archie closed his eyes so he wouldn't have to see the apprehension on Mike's face. "No hospital, Michael, no matter what happens. I'm riding this trail now. Might s'well see where it's going to take me."

"Riding a trail?" Mike laughed. "You aren't turning cowboy on me, are you?"

"Hell, I hope not." Archie took a deep breath through his nose. "Smell it? Burning leaves. The whole month of October, it smells like that in Blaine. When I was sitting here talking to Manlio, I was thinking about that. I'll bet there hasn't been anybody anywhere more homesick than I am now." He ran his tongue over his lips again. "Get me out of here. Down somewhere where there's some air to breathe."

"Already on our way, pardner."

Mike kept to the back roads, heading away from the border, vaguely toward Tucson. Archie fell quickly asleep. Sunset came, followed by a soft, purple dusk. About then, Mike's arms began to ache. He was squeezing the steering wheel too hard. It was an old habit, from when he'd been in the hospital after being burned. His hand was seared to the bone. To keep it from stiffening, he had to exercise while it healed. Squeeze and release. Every millimeter of movement was agony, stretching and tearing the raw tissue. The physical therapists had a saying: The Position of Comfort is the Position of Deformity. Fuck you and fuck your stupid saying, Mike said to himself a hundred times each day, working the hand until it bled, so consumed by rage he barely felt the pain.

That rage was back now, a scarlet, sickening feeling. Pictures flew through his head: Archie's house burning; Jacob Shaumann sorting his dead son's socks; Lola Yberri wandering the streets of Douglas, cut off from her family and home. Squeeze and release. Squeeze and release.

Three hours into the drive, the lights of Tucson came into sight. Mike knew he needed to come up with a plan, at least a next step, but, like quicksand, his thoughts kept slipping away. He made a snap decision and swung onto a dirt road, avoiding the city. He'd gone only a mile when a huge, black form loomed up in front of him. He slammed on the brakes, almost sliding off the road. The steer—he could see what it was now—trotted into the weeds.

Archie had woken up and was staring at him with round eyes. "Almost hamburger there, ace. Maybe you'd better slow down." Then, with a *hmmph* he curled sideways to go back to sleep.

"Maybe," Mike muttered. But Archie was right. Why hurry? There was no place they had to be. He drove on, taking his time, and some of the anger drained out of him. He was finally able to think.

He worked through the steps: the old dentist, the graveyard at the ranch, the border, Lola Yberri, and finally the documents at the hospital. Together, those things told the story of Lynnie Connor's birth in Mexico. If someone was trying to cover that up, they weren't doing a very good job of it. To the contrary, the pieces were all there, almost in plain sight. All somebody had to do was start down the path. So—there wasn't a cover-up. But that didn't make sense. Otherwise, why were Aron Aubrey and Eve Tessmer dead? Why had a bunch of thugs been chasing him and Archie for the past five days?

He ran it all through the mill a couple more times and kept coming up with the same answers, the same contradictions. He checked Archie—snoring peacefully— and clicked on the radio. Mariachi music, then country-western, then a bible discussion. Eventually he hit a news broadcast. A Chinese nuclear scientist had defected. The Pentagon was pleased; the State Department was concerned. Next came the election coverage. Lynnie was holding her lead in the polls. Bryce had switched strategies, pulling out all the stops, letting his spokesmen turn up the heat. Connor had pantywaist ideas. She got no respect from foreign governments. America needed a real president, a leader. Carl Bryce was the only man for the job.

"Rah, rah," Mike murmured at the radio. "Like they said about Nixon: 'We need Dick in the White House.'"

"Tomorrow," the newscaster said, "President Connor will campaign in San Diego, Los Angeles, and San Francisco, hoping to sew up a California win. Senator Bryce will follow her with stops in each of those cities and another"—the announcer stifled a chuckle—"in Rancho Cucamonga."

Mike looked out his window. Though the sun had set long ago, there was still a ghostly indigo streak behind the mountains. His mind flew that way, west, over the sand and tumbleweed. *The coast. Carl Bryce. Lynnie.* He switched off the radio and moved his speed up a notch. Now, at last, he had a plan.

CHAPTER THIRTY-NINE

"Where are we?" Archie asked groggily as Mike parked the car.

"A truck stop, north of Tucson."

"Yuh, good." Archie unhooked his seat belt. He was coming awake quickly. "No lunch today. I'm so hungry I could eat tofu."

It was a sprawling place with an eighteen-pump fuel station, a convenience store, and a gravel parking lot with room for a hundred tractor-trailers. The lot was mostly empty, and, inside the restaurant, business was slack, the dozen or so diners each sitting alone.

The hostess, a teenager with long corn-silk hair and a diamond stud in her nose, seated them by the front window. She splashed coffee in the waiting cups before hurrying away. Mike tipped his head toward the entrance to the convenience store. "I've got to get a couple of things. I'll be right back." Nodding, Archie picked up his menu and started to look it over.

When Mike returned a few minutes later, bearing three newspapers and a new road map, he found Archie chatting with their waitress. She was dressed for Halloween, in a blonde fright wig, a too-tight tank top, and even tighter cutoff jeans. "Used to be Mexicali," she was saying, indicating the buffet table in the corner of the room, "but you ever try to eat a taco been sittin' out on a steam table for four, five hours? Could use those things for a heat shield on the space shuttle. Just the twenty-four-hour breakfast bar now. Scrambles 'n cakes 'n muffins 'n—"

Archie tapped his menu. "What about this chimichanger thing? What's that?"

"Chimichanga. A deep-fried burro."

Archie squinted at her. "You feed people donkeys?"

"What? No! Flour tortilla stuffed with shredded beef. Guac and sour cream over top."

"Oh. All right, I'll take that."

"Whatever you want, honey. It's your cholesterol."

"And a plate of home-fried potatoes."

"Comes with rice and beans."

"That figures. I'll take the potatoes."

She turned to Mike. "How 'bout you, hon?"

"Sure," he said. He was studying the map, not following the conversation much. "The chimichanga sounds fine. No potatoes, though."

She wrote down the order, then jabbed her pen at the map. "Where ya headed?"

"San Diego, I think," Mike replied. He looked up. "How long does it take to get there from here?"

"Five hours if ya scoot. Six if ya lollygag. Be there by sunup, easy. Say, I better warn ya if you're in a hurry. Cook's in a foul mood. Might take a while to get your orders up." She laughed then. "Was a guy in earlier going to San Diego. Vacation trip. Gonna go to that big park they got by the ocean, watch the girl rollerskaters. He kept on and on about it—how perky they all are back here." She touched herself on the rump, hefted and jiggled, as if to test it for ripeness. Then she realized what she'd done. "Oops. Guess I'd better wash that hand."

"Yeah," Archie agreed. "Guess you better."

He watched her walk away, admiring her tight shorts. "So," he said to Mike, "you've got something in mind."

Mike had folded up the map and moved on to the newspapers, checking the political stories. "Something," he muttered. He slowed, scanning carefully through several paragraphs, then took his phone out of his pocket. "Archie, I need to make a call, and I'd feel more comfortable if you—"

"Sure, whatever you want, honey," Archie said, mimicking the waitress, annoyed, but joking, too. He shuffled into the convenience store.

Mike clicked through the list on his phone until he had the White House number. He got an operator who sounded a lot like the one he'd talked to the first time he called. After the usual song and dance—her saying he'd have to leave a message, him telling her who he was, her finding his name on the magic list—she transferred the call. Someone came on after a pause of a few seconds, a female voice he didn't recognize. "I'll put you right through, Mr. Stanbridge," she said.

It was only then that Mike realized his heart was running fast. He played a game with himself, trying to guess what Lynnie's first words would be.

"Dammit, Michael, what did you *do* to her this morning?" Claudia Sung barked.

Mike pulled the phone away from his ear, it was so loud. He gathered himself for a counterattack. "I didn't *do* anything to Lynnie. I need to speak to her again."

"Ha! Not in this lifetime. She's been a basket case all day. Blew off two appearances. *Two.* Hasn't done anything like that since last March. Botched an interview with Jerry Loeb from PBS, too. Gentleman Jerry! He'd give a good interview to goddammed Jack the Ripper.

Have you seen the press for tomorrow? The *San Francisco Chronicle*'s headline is 'Connor Stumbles.' *Stumbles,* for God's sake!"

"Claudia, get a grip. How would I know what tomorrow's headline is? I need to talk to her, about her mother."

"*Her mother!*" Claudia cried. "Oh, that's too low, bringing her mom up now. The poor woman's an orphan; isn't that enough for you?"

"Lynnie's forty-three years old. You can't be an orphan when you're forty-three. Besides, you're babbling. Just get her on the line for me, please?"

"Or what?" Claudia said.

"What do you mean, 'or what?'"

"This morning you told me you'd go to the newspapers. Cockamamy nonsense. 'I'll call Ferrar,' you said. I told Lynnie later, and she laughed right in my face. 'Mikey'd never do a thing like that,' she says, so sweet. She's right; you bluffed me, right up the garden path, you damned—You, you—*Ahhhhhgh,*" Claudia shrieked, unable to come up with a cuss word that was strong enough. "*Oh, bulldoody!*"

In spite of everything, Mike laughed, all the way up from his belly. Soon Claudia was laughing, too. "All right," she said, "that feels better. Woo-hoo. What a day." She chuckled a bit more. "I've got a thousand things going on here."

"You're in Denver?" Mike said. He'd read in one of the newspapers that Lynnie was spending the night there.

"Right, but only for a few more hours. Listen, can we call you back?"

"We?" Mike said.

Her voice became silky. "You heard right."

"I won't be here long," he said.

"No problem. Ten minutes at the outside. What's the number?"

He hesitated, but only momentarily, then gave her his cell number. Brightly she said, "So long, Sweetcakes," and hung up. He set his own phone down and stared at it. He felt a tightening in the pit of his stomach, a silent alarm bell going off. Something about Claudia's tone didn't set right. She'd been too cheerful all of a sudden.

Archie returned, carrying a paper sack. "Got a pinball arcade back there and showers and a print-your-own-T-shirt booth, even a bar with a lady dancing in a cage."

"Oh," Mike said, still watching the phone.

"I take it the call didn't go too well."

"Not too well, no."

The waitress arrived with their food. Once it was served, she said, "Anything else I can get you?"

Archie opened the sack and took out a crop-top T-shirt. "Got this for you," he said. On the front was a preprinted logo: I SURVIVED BOOT CAMP AT . . . He moved his hands around so she could see what he'd had silkscreened on the back. SAN DIEGO, LAND OF THE PERT PATOOTIE.

She squealed and hugged him. "You sweetie, that's *so* bad!" She put it on right there, over her other shirt, modeling it for him, then hurried off to the kitchen to show her friends.

Archie sighed contentedly. "No better class of people in the whole world than restaurant people."

"You're pretty chipper all of a sudden," Mike said. He was eating already, ravenously, though the food tasted like cardboard to him.

Archie grabbed his knife and fork. He inhaled through his nose. "Can breathe again. Must be lower altitude here. Makes a difference in my disposition, all right."

"And you're not smoking," Mike observed.

"Not since we left New York." Archie prodded him with the butt of his knife. "And you didn't even notice. You're a sorry excuse for a wife."

They ate and said little, and exactly ten minutes after Claudia Sung hung up, the phone chirped.

Mike slowly set his silverware aside and wiped his mouth. The phone rang a second time. "Well?" Archie said.

Mike picked it up. "Hello?"

"Mr. Stanbridge," a male voice said, "this is Justin Reynolds. I'm Ms. Sung's chief of staff."

"Chief of staff to the chief of staff?" Mike said. He had no idea such a position existed.

"Quite," Reynolds replied.

Archie had stood up and was starting to move away from the table to give him some privacy. Mike grabbed his wrist and motioned for him to sit down again.

"What can I do for you, Mr. Reynolds?" Mike said.

"Very little actually." Reynolds gave a bland chuckle. The connection was startlingly clear, as if the call were coming from that very dining room. It made Mike uneasy, a feeling of being spied upon. "Just stay away from us. No more phone calls. We're so busy now, you see."

"The royal 'we,'" Mike said, heat coming into his voice.

"Yes, the royal 'we.'"

"If I'm not supposed to call anymore, I'll need to be told that by someone a little further up the food chain than you," Mike said. "Like the president herself."

Reynolds chuckled again. He kept his voice perfectly modulated, like a radio announcer. "I'm about as far up the food chain as you're likely to get, Mr. Stanbridge. You see, people like you are my stock-in-trade. I'm Ms. Sung's pipe cleaner. Her plumbing snake, if you will."

"Ah, the"—Mike stammered—"Official Mr. Goddammed Roto-Rooter."

"Charm," Archie said to his chimichanga. "Charm'll get 'em every time."

Mike kneaded the back of his neck, trying to control his temper. "If I can't speak to Lynnie, then I'd like to leave her a message."

"So sorry, out of the question."

"Listen, you supercilious moron, I'll speak to the president, or you'll lose your damn job."

"This conversation is over, Mr. Stanbridge."

"*Wait*, wait," Mike said. His mind was spinning, trying to come up with any bit of leverage he had. "A message for your boss then, for Claudia. Do you have a pen?"

Impatiently, Reynolds said, "Everything is being taped. Say what you have to say."

Mike closed his eyes so he could concentrate. Every word had to be exactly right. "Tomorrow morning at seven o'clock, Archie Pascoe and I will be at Lindbergh Field in San Diego, outside the USO club. Lynnie knows where that is; Claudia can find it. We'll wait for an hour to be taken to meet with the president. One hour. If no one shows up by eight o'clock, we'll take our information and documents to the Bryce campaign. I know a woman who works in opposition research for them, Joy Leiffer."

Reynolds jumped in, his voice agitated. Mike had hit a nerve. "Leiffer? How do you know Joy Leiffer?"

"I met her in Blaine, the night before Lynnie's birthday party. I know she's following Lynnie around the country. She'll be in San Diego tomorrow."

"Tell me," Reynolds said, regaining his composure. "What information do you have that's so interesting?"

"That's none of your business, but it has to do with Lynnie's family, and with her qualifications to be president."

"Qualifications to be president? That's pretty broad, isn't it?"

"It's all you need to know."

"Just so, Mr. Stanbridge. Just so. Good night." Abruptly, Reynolds hung up.

To see how bad things were, Mike dialed the White House again. The operator was pleasant, but firm. "Yes, Mr. Stanbridge, I understand . . . No, no, I don't see your name anywhere here. You can leave a message, but it might be some time before anyone can—"

Mike's hand was shaking as he put the phone down.

So quick, so efficient. His name was off the magic White House list, his only link to Lynnie gone.

Archie had finished his meal and was sitting with his elbows on the table, his coffee cup in front of his lips. "Sounds like you just burned some bridges."

"I probably burned them a long time ago," Mike mumbled distantly. He closed his eyes again so he could think. Another bluff? Was that all this was? No, this time around, he'd play out the hand. He started flipping through one of the newspapers.

Archie set his cup down. "Whatcha lookin' for?"

"That phone number for the Bryce campaign," Mike said. "The one they advertise all the time."

Archie nodded, his eyes shimmering with satisfaction. He sang the ditty from the radio commercials. "That's 1-800-Rite-Way. Do something right for your country to-day."

CHAPTER FORTY

The people with the Bryce campaign weren't as efficient as those who worked for Lynnie. After half an hour of being shuttled from one sleepy-voiced staffer to another, Mike finally was connected with a man named Bates, who said he was Assistant Director of Communications Strategy. Bates had a Texas farm-boy accent, earthy and impatient at the same time. Joy Leiffer? Sure, he knew her. She worked in his shop. Was out of town now, though. What about her?

Mike said, "I figure she'll be in California tomorrow, following President Connor. I'd like to arrange a meeting with her."

"And who the hell are you, the Czar of all the Russias?" Bates snapped.

Mike gave his name and spelled it. He heard computer

keys clicking and Bates said, "Unh, sure, we know you, Mr. Stanbridge. Joy filed a report on you from Blaine, looks like. You want to tell me what's going on?"

"Nope, I don't."

"OK, then. I can patch you through to her voice mail. She's on her way to San Diego now. After she gets to her hotel, she'll check her messages. That be all right?"

"It'll have to do," Mike said. "Wait a minute. Before you transfer me, can you tell me where she'll be staying?"

Bates laughed. "Do I sound like an idiot? You say you're Michael Stanbridge, but you could be Ted Bundy's twin brother for all I know."

So Mike left a message, asking Joy to meet him at the San Diego airport at eight o'clock in the morning. He said he couldn't tell her why over the phone, except that he had information about Lynnie Connor that was critical to the election. After he was done, he stayed on the line a moment. He heard a squeak and a click. Bates had been listening in and, Mike imagined, was now phoning Joy's hotel in San Diego. If she wasn't there yet, Bates would leave a message of his own to make sure she knew about the call from Mike and the plan for them to meet at the airport. Mike snapped the phone shut and said to Archie, "That's it, I guess. Now we get there and see what happens."

As Archie had pointed out, the truck stop had showers, and he and Mike took advantage of them to scrub off the grime of the day. They shaved and changed into clean shirts. They gassed up the car and checked the oil and, thus prepared, headed into the night.

It was an uneventful trip. Scruffy desert, most of it flat. Star-spangled sky. Few cars. They took a break at a rest stop, and, as they crossed the parking lot, saw an owl drop like a rock out of the darkness fifty feet away. A cry cut the air, a squealing whistle, eerie and frightening. "Lord," Mike whispered, intimidated by the sound and the vast space around them, "was that a rabbit?"

"Yuh," Archie replied. "Only noise they ever make."

Once back in the car, they were quiet for a long time. They were thinking the same thing as they watched the pale, distant lights of the desert hamlets flash by: how easy it would be to pull off the interstate, find a motel, hunker down until the election was over.

Mike drove the final leg, letting Archie sleep. As their waitress from the truck stop had predicted, they reached San Diego shortly before dawn. Mike knew the city well. He'd been there a dozen times on business and twice on weekend get-togethers with Lynnie. He stopped at a round-the-clock diner on Hotel Circle so they could get some breakfast. Even after coffee and toast and pancakes and grapefruit, he felt empty. It was something he recognized, a looking-forward-to-Lynnie feeling, an anxious hunger that food wouldn't satisfy.

The sun was rising when they reached the I-5 interchange and turned south. The airport came into view, backed by the pearl waters of San Diego Bay and the dense greens of Coronado Island. "Look," Mike said. "There." He pointed at the big blue-and-white plane sitting at the far end of the tarmac. "Air Force One."

Archie began jiggling his leg, an outlet for nervous tension. "And all those cop cars around it."

They parked by the commuter terminal, under a four-story-high mural of Charles Lindbergh. The sky was robin's-egg blue now. It was going to be a gorgeous day. A few minutes later they strode up to the entrance to Terminal Two. The USO club was inside, but Mike wanted to wait out here, where they could clear out in a hurry if they had to.

They were both edgy, glancing at every person who passed by, hoping for a flash of recognition, a wave, a beckon. Nothing happened. Several groups of servicemen went into the terminal; an airport security car cruised by, turned around and went past a second time. Archie sat on a bench, chewing his lip and jiggling his leg. At ten minutes before eight, he came back to stand beside Mike. "Looks like Madam President isn't interested in talking to us."

"If Claudia even told her we were going to be here," Mike replied.

"On to phase two, then," Archie said. "What's this Joy Leiffer look like?"

Mike smiled. "Keep your eye on the men. They'll let you know when she's here."

And that's how it happened. Archie was watching the access road, the line of traffic snaking past the terminals, when he said, "There?" Men on the sidewalks and in cars were turning to stare at the figure in the back seat of a taxicab. Mike recognized her hair first, that lovely buttery color, twisting in the breeze of the open window. She wore the same dark leather coat she'd had on in Blaine. The cab stopped and she stepped out, scanning the crowd.

The next few seconds were a jumble. A woman appeared near the cab, pulling a big wheeled suitcase, moving faster than she should have been. She turned at an odd angle, and the suitcase rolled on, striking Joy in the back of the legs, knocking her headlong to the ground.

Just then a hand came down on Mike's shoulder. He turned to find a large man hovering behind him, his other hand grasping Archie by the forearm. "Gentlemen," he said in a voice so cool and neutral it sounded machine-made, "this way quickly if you would, please." He was dressed in a frumpy sport coat and wrinkle-free slacks, ankle-high Rockport clodhoppers. Campaign worker's clothes.

Mike cast another glance at Joy Leiffer. She was sitting up now, holding her fingertips to her mouth. The woman with the suitcase was bent over her, expertly blocking her view of the terminal.

"Gentlemen, please," the man repeated. Two other large men had moved in to join him.

Mike quit thinking, gave in to the feeling in his gut. "Come on, Archie. Let's go."

"*You* go. I'm not leaving this spot."

"All right," Mike said. He started to walk away.

"Oh, bullshit," Archie grumbled. He hurried after him.

They entered the terminal and rode up the escalator. They caused quite a stir, five big men swinging along in such a tight group. Mike expected them to head for a meeting room somewhere, a quiet place to talk. Instead they went into the food court.

There sat Claudia Sung.

She wore a plain purple dress and large, round sunglasses. Her shoes were off, her feet tucked underneath her. She'd been talking on a cell phone, and she laid it aside on the table. In front of her was a cinnamon roll, as big as a salad plate and drowning in sugar glaze. It was so warm steam was rising off it. She picked up a plastic fork and knife and was about to dig in when she saw the men approaching. She jabbed the fork toward Mike. "Hey, if it isn't the original bad penny."

"Claudia," Mike greeted her curtly. "Was that your circus we saw downstairs?"

She ignored him and turned to Archie. "Mr. Pascoe, how 'bout joining me?" She reached beside her and lifted up a large box of the rolls. "Put on an extra love handle or two."

"See what I mean about her?" Archie complained to Mike. "She says stuff like that, with no call a'tall. Is she just trying to piss me off?"

"Oh, please, no," Claudia said, cooing. "Anyway, my circus, you asked? Yes indeedy, my circus entirely. Sorry about that, too, but I had to see if you were bluffing me again, Michael. If you had been, you'd still be cooling your heels out there. And, by the way, don't worry about Ms. Leiffer." She nodded toward the phone. "Already had a report. She's fine, except for a chipped tooth. I wish that hadn't happened, but you know what they say: politics ain't beanbag."

"So, do we get to talk to Lynnie?" Mike asked.

Claudia gazed at the two of them. Her glasses were so big they couldn't read anything in her expression. Then, with great deliberation, she cut a piece off her cinnamon roll and laid it on her tongue. She chewed slowly, swooning her head back. "I . . . am . . . in . . . heaven."

Archie pulled out a chair and sat. "Enough shenanigans," he said in his assistant-principal voice. "Answer him."

Claudia was unmoved, staring him down from behind her shades. She started to cut into the roll again.

Archie hit the red line. "*Take* those damn things off when you talk to me. They make you look like a fool." He snatched the glasses off her face.

Claudia turned away, but not fast enough to hide the bruise under her right eye. It was a nasty one, sharp around the edges and very dark. She lifted her hand to cover it.

"What happened?" Mike said, embarrassed because she was so embarrassed.

"An argument," Claudia mumbled. "The boss."

"Lynnie?" Archie honked. "She *hit* you?"

Claudia shrugged. "There's too much going on. Too much traveling, never any sleep. That last debate's coming up. Lots and lots of pressure."

She saw the skeptical look on Mike's face and turned away again. "Devon's meeting us in San Francisco tonight," she said, putting the sunglasses back on. Her voice had lost all its sassiness. "Been planned for a long time, the two of them together for the last run of the campaign. They're going to do a joint interview. You know, loving couple, looking forward to some quiet time together after the election. Rizzo—the whole campaign staff—was behind it. I kept it off the schedule because I knew Lynnie would veto it. She went ballistic when I told her. Chucked a briefing book. Then an Adidas. Was the shoe that got me. My fault. First requirement for my job is being able to duck fast. Maybe I'm getting too old."

She ate another bite of her roll, quickly, not enjoying it nearly as much as before. When she was done she said, "Anyway, that's yesterday's problem. We've got a new one today—the bad penny problem." She pushed her plate aside. The campaign workers stood just far enough away that they couldn't hear what was being said. She beckoned with her head, and the biggest of the three trotted over. "Edgar, put this in the box with the rest and bring it along, will you? And don't you dare eat one. They're for me. The only way I'm gonna get through today is with a screamer of a sugar high." She slipped her shoes on and stood up. "You two, come on," she said to Mike and Archie, and she started to walk away.

"Where?" Mike asked, not intending to move until he had an answer.

Claudia chuckled pleasantly. "The plane, you yutz. Lynnie."

CHAPTER FORTY-ONE

A contingent of Secret Service agents was waiting in a room on the lower level of the terminal. They gave Mike and Archie a thorough going-over—pat-down search, metal detecting wands, the works. They weren't gentle about it either, shoving them around, cursing at them when they didn't move fast enough.

Claudia groused, "Hey, they're not terrorists."

"So you say," one of the agents fired back.

The inspection over, they all loaded into a van for the trip out to the plane. On the way, Claudia gave Mike and Archie sleeveless blue sweaters to wear. She didn't want the press photographers around the airport to notice them boarding, she explained. The sweaters were the kind the stewards on the plane wore. She handed them each a box to carry, on which someone had scrawled, *Mses—Checked/EverGreen*. Go right up the steps and inside, she ordered. Act like you own the place. She'd follow in a minute or so.

Mike was first to board, and, even before he reached the door, he heard Lynnie's voice, shrill and furious. It was coming from behind a wood-paneled wall, her office or stateroom, he figured. A man was sitting in one of the leather swivel chairs in the corridor, dressed in a fashionable pinstripe suit and fuzzy bedroom slippers. Mike had seen him on television and in the papers hundreds of times, Lynnie's press secretary. His name was Jim Logan.

"Ah, Mses!" Logan said, and he took the box from Mike. By then Archie had arrived, and Logan took his box, too. He didn't ask what the two of them were doing there. Maybe he thought they really were stewards. He opened one of the boxes, revealing dozens of small white cartons marked with the presidential seal. He tore the top off one and dumped out a handful of M&Ms, which he tossed into his mouth. "Yum," he mumbled. "Onwy deshent perk abouwt this job."

Claudia came chugging aboard, just in time to hear Lynnie shout from behind the wall, "You *said* you could control him! You *said* there'd be no problem!"

A woman answered, too softly to be understood.

Claudia stopped dead. Her shoulders drooped. "Devon?" she said to Logan.

Logan sighed. "Not this time. Devon is blessedly lost in the wind somewhere." He waved her into the seat next to his. "But watch this." From his coat pocket he took out a remote control. He aimed it at a television in the small cabin across the corridor. The set flickered to life. He hit another button, starting a tape. "Happened an hour ago, in Jacksonville."

The vice president came on the screen, making his

way through a crowd to his car. "Mr. Hoyt!" a reporter shouted. "Would you like to comment on the statements made yesterday in Riyadh by Prince al-Raheem?"

Hoyt gave a sneering smile. Just seeing it made Claudia shudder and cover her eyes. "Al-Raheem?" Hoyt said. "It's like my mother always told me: Never trust a man who wears a doily instead of a hat."

"No, Andrew," Claudia moaned.

Logan switched off the set. "We've already had calls from the Arab-American Anti-Defamation Committee, the Saudi ambassador, even King Abdullah—"

He was cut off by Lynnie's voice. "Three days in a *row* he's done something like this."

The woman with her answered, almost yelling. "I'll handle it. He'll apologize. A press conference. Tonight if you want."

"Are you *crazy?* He doesn't talk to the press anymore. I'm sending him home. He's got laryngitis. Pneumonia. Fucking brain cancer—they'll believe that. Now get out. *Go!*"

Gina Rizzo stepped through a door in the wood-paneled wall, pulling it shut behind her. It bounced back open. She left it and sat down next to Logan. The last time Mike had seen her, in Blaine, Rizzo had been as cool and confident as a bank president, poring over her print-outs and poll figures. Today, she still had the power suit and the perfect hair, but a large bead of sweat trickled down her cheek. The pressure was getting to them all.

Logan patted her arm and, with a gracious flourish, handed her a box of M&Ms. "Eat. Feel better," he said.

They heard Lynnie again. Her voice was steely now, more threatening than angry. "Yes, Andrew, I know I kept you waiting . . . No. Be quiet and listen. You will not say another word to the press. You will not give another speech . . . You *what?* . . . On your own? That's ridiculous. You couldn't get elected sewer inspector on your own . . . Andrew, *shut up.*"

Logan had taken out a rubber exercise egg, exactly like the one Mike had seen Lynnie using in Blaine. He mashed it in his hand a couple of times, giggling. "You know that Zen thing? The sound of one hand clapping? What you hear now is the sound of one hand grinding Andrew Hoyt's nuts."

That comment was more than Gina Rizzo could tolerate. She jumped up and strode off toward the rear of the plane. "Don't go away mad, dear!" Logan called after her.

A phone banged into its cradle behind the wall, and Claudia stood up. "All right, you two," she said to Mike and Archie. "That's your cue. You've got five minutes, and I mean *five* minutes. After that, I'm coming after you with a mob and pitchforks."

Archie glared at her. He wasn't intimidated by Claudia, by the plane, by the Secret Service, by anything here. "We're done when we're done. You just try getting us out of there before then."

The office was cramped, the odd-shaped desk taking up much of the floor space. Lynnie was sitting behind it, turned away, talking on the phone again. Claudia whispered a few words in her ear, then motioned for Mike and Archie to sit on the love seat against the wall. She stepped out and closed the door, but it swung back open an inch or so. The latch was broken for good. Not that Mike noticed. He couldn't take his eyes off Lynnie.

She was wearing a powder-blue sweat suit, one Mike had bought for her maybe ten years ago. It was frayed around the collar, and the rest of the fabric was pilled and rumpled. Her face had a fresh-scrubbed look, as if she had just stepped out of the shower. Her hair was wet, too. She lifted her right hand to tuck a loose strand behind her ear. The thumb and forefinger were bandaged. She'd shaken so many hands lately she had blisters.

Lynnie hung up the phone and turned to them. Mike's heart plummeted. Her expression was as cold and hard as flint. They might have been enemies facing each other across an armistice table. "Yes? You wanted to talk to me?"

Her eyes were on Archie at that point, so he was the one to answer.

"Right. Might s'well get straight to it. We know about your mother. Graciella Yberri, that is, not Mattie Sheridan."

Something crossed Lynnie's face, a dangerous flicker that came and went so fast that only Mike noticed. "Go on. I'm listening," she said.

"And we know you've been covering it up. You've had men out after us—"

"Mr. Pascoe, my hearing is fine. You don't need to raise your voice. My mother died years ago. Everybody knows that. Why would I be interested in covering up anything about her?"

"Because she was Mexican," Archie said. He pronounced it the way his father would have—Messican. "You've known all along and didn't want it to get out."

Lynnie's eyes danced over to Mike and back again. "You seem pretty certain of yourself. What do you plan to do?"

"Bring it all out in the open," Archie said. "Show people what a cheap guttersnipe you are."

Lynnie's face remained blank, and then she laughed.

The anger Archie had been holding in for so long exploded. He lurched to his feet, bearing down across the desk, so huge, so fast, a freight train. His nose stopped an inch from Lynnie's. "Eve Tessmer's dead because of you," he growled, his voice deadly. "You'll pay for that, damn you."

Lynnie didn't retreat a bit. "Mr. Pascoe, when I was sixteen, you could bully me. Not now. Sit down or I will signal the Secret Service. If I do, you will not see the light of day for a very long time. *Sit*."

In his fury, Archie's face had turned purple. "I'm not a dog. You can't say that to me."

"Sit."

Mike moved now, using his height advantage and all his strength to lever him up from the desk. Archie's lips were quivering. He moved his shoulder in a circle and shook his arm in an odd, spastic way. "Hurts?" Mike said. He touched him gently on the chest.

Archie didn't reply, but tilted his head so he could glower at Lynnie.

"It won't work," Mike said. "You can't scream at her and get your answers. She's not a kid anymore. Archie, you have to go outside and wait."

Archie grimaced and moved his shoulder again. "Won't," he said.

Mike maneuvered him toward the door. "We want the same thing. The truth, that's all. Wait. I won't be long."

Archie looked at the floor. He was concentrating, trying mightily to control his heart. But the pain was too much. He could barely breathe, much less hold a conversation. He trudged quietly out of the room.

Mike leaned against the door to hold it closed. He stared at Lynnie; she stared at him. He wasn't sure what his own expression was, but she was studying him, inch by inch over his face. He could imagine her doing the same thing with the Russian premier or the Speaker of the House. Her eyes dropped. "Damn door," she muttered. "Nothing works around here anymore." She came to her feet and stepped through another door behind her desk, into the bathroom. "Come on," she said. "Unless you want everybody out there to hear us."

Mike followed and clicked the inner door closed. Finally they were alone.

It was a tiny room, still steamy from her shower. She had no shoes on and he felt awkward, towering so high above her. "Lynnie, I—"

She cut him off with a blunt motion of her hand. "Have you talked to Bryce's people, told them anything about us?"

"No, I needed some way to get in to see you. Threatening to go to Bryce was the only leverage I had." He smiled, trying to diffuse some of the tension. "And all this running around I've been doing. I had to find out why Eve Tessmer was killed. That warrant out for me—I had no choice."

"Warrant," Lynnie grumbled, tightening her arms over her chest. "That whole thing's a load of garbage. I talked to the FBI director last night. They're out of it. I told her, leave him alone. Local cops, I can't do anything about, but I won't have the FBI chasing you, not on some bullshit charge cooked up by Billy White and the rest of those North Country bozos."

"You called off the FBI? Lynnie, it'll leak. You can't interfere like that. That's dumb."

"Dumb? What the hell was I supposed to do?"

She spun to face him, screeched, and started hopping up and down. The leader of the free world had just stubbed her toe.

Mike laughed softly and gathered her into his arms. She sputtered and squirmed. Then, gradually, she grew quiet.

A glorious sense of calm descended on him. He brushed his fingers through her hair, feather-light. He nudged her chin up. Her face was sweaty from the humidity. Their eyes locked on each other.

"Love you," he said.

"Love you," she whispered back.

They hadn't kissed in eighteen months, and they tried to make up for it all at once. Their noses bumped and they giggled. Her lips parted slightly. He felt her tongue; he felt the ripple of her hand on his spine. They were so lost in each other they didn't hear the door open.

"I knew it," Claudia said. "Leave you alone for one minute and everything gets all sticky-tingly. Stop it. Hey, stop it." She pried them apart. They both blushed. "Sorry, Sweetcakes, but your time's up."

"Nice try," Lynnie said. "Now shoo."

Claudia tapped her watch. "We're already behind schedule and you aren't even dressed."

"Shoo."

Claudia had been smiling, but now she looked peeved. "You're a bad influence, Michael."

"How's the eye?" Lynnie asked, changing the subject.

Claudia hung her head and held out her hands. *"No más. No más.* No more box. Look, seriously, we can't afford to blow off another rally. We can't."

"All right," Lynnie said. "Just another couple of minutes." She swung the door closed in Claudia's face.

Mike pulled Lynnie to him again. Another kiss, holding tight, groping, slipping away in the feeling. But not completely away. He was only halfway home. He still had to tell her about the hospital in Agua Prieta, about those three awful words, *natural born citizen*. Would she kiss him after that? Would she still say, "Love you?"

CHAPTER FORTY-TWO

Lynnie's stateroom was located through another door, beyond the bathroom. Mike led her there, holding both her hands in his one. The curtains were closed, the lights turned down low. They sat on the sofa, nestling together. A jet rumbled into the air from a nearby runway, making too much noise for them to talk. When it was gone, Mike said, "You know about Graciella."

Lynnie had been smiling up at his face. Now her eyes slipped to the floor, to a coffee stain there. She scratched at it with her toe. "Yes, I know." She sank closer against him. "I should have told you about it a long time ago. It probably would have done me some good to talk it over. I tried to bring it up, but I couldn't find a way to get started. I'm sorry."

Mike held up his hand. "No more apologies. We don't have time. How did you find out about her?"

"Oscar Martinez," Lynnie replied. "He told me the day we buried my father at the ranch. His whole life, my dad never said a word to me about it. Oscar didn't think that was right. Graciella was part of me, something I needed to know about."

"How did your father meet her?"

"At a dance in Douglas. He'd brought some of the ranch hands into town for an evening out. He saw her a few times after that, even took her to Tucson for a weekend. Then Graciella tried to break it off. She moved to Los Angeles. Dad couldn't just let her go like that, and maybe she didn't want to. He found her, or she sent word to him. Oscar wasn't sure which. Anyway, it started up again. That's when she got pregnant. Dad couldn't—" Lynnie's voice broke. She'd always adored her father, and it hurt to speak about his biggest mistake and all the lies that came from it. "Dad talked to my mom—to Mattie about it. He told her one of his friends in L.A. knew this girl who was pregnant. The baby's father had died, he said. She wanted to give it up for adoption. It could be their baby. Mattie couldn't have children, so she jumped at the idea.

"Dad arranged for Graciella to come to the ranch right away, months before she was due. She and Mattie didn't get along too well. Mattie started worrying about the adoption not working out, and being embarrassed at having a Mexican baby. Maybe she guessed about my dad and Graciella. Anyway, she came up with the plan to send all the ranch hands away except Oscar. That way, she could say I was her baby, skip the adoption, be a real mom. As far out of town as they lived, if she stayed out of sight for a while, nobody would know the difference. Graciella didn't care. She wanted to get it over with, have the baby, get on with her life.

"Most of the rest of the story my dad always told was

true. The storm and the flooding. Graciella hemorrhaged and died a few hours after I was born."

Mike reached into his pocket for the X-ray photocopy. He'd been carrying it for so long the creases were worn through, and he had to hold the pieces together on his lap. He said, "The original X-ray is in a hospital in Agua Prieta." He pointed out the broken collarbone.

"I don't understand," Lynnie said. "What were you doing in Agua Prieta?"

"Aron Aubrey went there, the same hospital. That's where he got this photocopy. Lynnie, I think this is you, the day you were born."

She frowned and bent for a closer look. Gradually, she broke into a smile. "It is. It *is* me. Remember when I had that MRI? I told you—about three years ago? The radiologist said there was an old break, at that same spot. I had no idea how I got it."

Mike folded up the X-ray, then held her hands again. "That's not all we found. There was a birth record, too. With your name on it."

She looked confused, trying to process the information. "In Agua Prieta?" she said. "How could that be?"

Another jet was taking off. Its engines were so loud the curtains in the stateroom began to vibrate. Mike spoke to her, his lips almost touching her ear so she could hear. Birth record in Mexico . . . constitutional requirements . . . natural born citizen.

Her first reaction was pure disbelief. "That's not possible. I was born at the ranch."

"Oscar told you that? Or was that just part of your father's story?"

"Oscar didn't— It wasn't an easy conversation with him. He didn't say one way or the other." Her resolve was breaking; Mike could feel her hands trembling. "At the ranch," she whispered. He tried to hold her, but she shoved him away and began to sob. He pulled her back, manhandled her when she began to struggle. Finally she collapsed into him, burying her head in his chest. She wept and wept, and all he could do was rock her slowly and mumble in her ear, foolish things. "It's all right . . . We'll work it out . . ."

Lynnie stopped crying abruptly, turning her grief off like a spigot. She curled her legs beside her, and began tapping her fingers against her thigh, as if she were ticking off ideas, counting up her options. This is what Mike had expected. She wouldn't simply give up. There was too much fight in her for that.

Another jet took to the air, and she used the noise as cover to pull herself together. She stood and found a tissue and cleaned her face. "Who knows about this?" she asked.

"Archie. Me. The men he mentioned who've been following us—they know something. How much, I can't say."

"What about at the hospital in Mexico?"

Mike paused. He wasn't sure he liked where this was headed. "I don't think anybody there knows. There was a man named Martin Castillo. He was hospital administrator, and apparently he met with Aubrey. That's how Aubrey came across the X-ray. Castillo's dead now, though. Drowned in his bathtub, the newspaper said."

"The newspaper said," Lynnie repeated slowly. "OK, tell me exactly where the documents are—the X-ray, the birth record, everything you found."

Mike stared at her. Her eyes roved away, sideways and down again to the coffee stain. "Lynnie, no," he said. "You don't want to steal those documents."

"I've got an Arizona birth certificate. I've seen it. I was born there. I know it." From her tone, she was trying to convince herself as much as him. "This whole thing has a smell to it, a dirty-tricks smell. Bryce's people could phony up a Mexican birth record"—she flipped her hand up—"just like that."

"Maybe they could; I don't know. But what about the

X-ray? The X-ray is there, and it's you. You said so yourself. And it isn't phony. I compared it with the others in
the files. It's the same format, came from the same machine. There's a death certificate for Graciella, too. It all
fits. Your father took her to the Agua Prieta hospital to
give birth. No questions asked that way, everything kept
quiet. It was a bad delivery. You had a broken collarbone
and Graciella hemorrhaged. He brought you home to the
ranch, and after a day or two he got some doctor to sign
a clean Arizona birth certificate for you."

Lynnie tapped her foot, frustrated, not agreeing, but
not wanting to argue. "Who are these men who've been
following you? You think they're with Bryce?"

"I don't know," Mike said. "They seem to know where
all the pieces are hidden. They certainly knew about the
hospital in Agua Prieta. Like Archie says, they're covering something up. But if they work for Bryce, a cover-up
doesn't make sense. Bryce's people would be trying to
get this out in the open, especially now, this close to the
election. Lynnie, you've got to consider that it's somebody on your own staff, somebody trying to protect you."

"Protect me?" she said. "If that's so, they're not doing
a very good job of it." Then she asked bluntly, "Do you
think I'm behind it? Eve's death and Aron Aubrey's and
this other man—Castillo?"

"Archie thinks so," Mike said. He shrugged. His voice
wavered. "I—I'll tell you the truth. Those men who've
been after us, they always seemed to know right where
we'd be, before we even got there. And I couldn't get
through to you on the phone. I never stopped believing
in you, but it's hard to—"

"I understand," she said. Her voice was angry, as it
had been when he'd first arrived. Then she seemed to
change her mind, do a complete about-face. "I do understand," she murmured. She bent over him. Her lips
brushed his, a whisper-soft kiss. "Now, Mike, that's what
matters. Do you trust me now?"

All he could see was her eyes, hypnotically close, that infinite blue color he'd loved as far back as he could remember. He stroked her hair and nodded. "You know I do."

She smiled and kissed his palm and sat down beside him, thoughtful. As her mind worked, so did her hand, absently twining their fingers together. "How did you find out about Graciella?" she asked.

"Her headstone in the cemetery at the ranch. It's right next to your father's, and when Archie saw it—"

Lynnie's face registered surprise. "You saw it? You could read it?"

Mike nodded. "Yes, and there's a story behind that. Archie went to Tucson—"

"Graciella's grave is there in the cemetery, but it isn't next to my father's." Lynnie pulled back so she could look at him. "Tell me everything you saw."

He pointed to his leg, as though it were a map: the fence is here; the headstones here and here; Oscar's flowers were here. Then he told her about Archie's trip to Tucson to visit the monument maker. "So I guess the original headstone was shot up. There's been a lot of vandalism out there. The monument company had no record of who paid for the replacement."

"Of course there was no record," Lynnie said. For the first time in a while, there was energy in her voice. "Mike, this is a setup, a stage piece."

"How's that?"

Her eyes drifted away from him again. "I'm the idiot who used that headstone for target practice. That's right. I'm not proud of it, either. It was the day Oscar told me about Graciella. I was upset, angry. How could my dad lie like that? And . . . and I was worried about my career, what would happen if the story got out. So I snuck up there with Oscar's deer rifle. When I was done, you couldn't read a thing on that marker except for a few letters in her name."

"So how's this a setup?"

"Somebody bought the new headstone and put it next to my dad's. Be easy enough—go in at night and make the switch. The soil out there is just gravel and sand. One good rain would wash away any trace. And why do it? A complicated story about documents in Mexico, that's a tough sell. People might believe it, they might not. Most would just be confused by the details. But this—" She motioned toward the spot on his leg where he'd pointed out his invisible map. "Imagine a picture on a magazine cover. The two headstones: my dad and his lover, together for eternity. They almost wouldn't have to write the article, people would catch on so fast." Lynnie's voice was running quickly now. She was nodding. "This is politics, Mike. Pure form. Find some dirt and expose it in the bluntest possible way, but keep your own fingerprints off it. This is Bryce. I smell him all over it."

"All right, but where does that get you? The birth record and all the other documents are still in Agua Prieta. You were born there."

"Fake records, all of them. I was born at the ranch."

Mike paused, considering what to say next. "There's one person who knows for sure. Call Oscar. Ask him."

Lynnie stood and paced. "He won't speak to me, Mike."

"Why? He worshiped you—I remember. You were always his buddy, his little saddlemate."

"It was Graciella's headstone. When he found out what I'd done to it, he got mad. Disgusted, too. Didn't matter that I was vice president of the United States. He cursed me out like some worthless field hand. Then he packed his truck and left. I tried to contact him after that, calls and letters, gifts at Christmas, anything. He wouldn't answer. Not once."

Mike paused again to think. "OK, then I'll talk to him, go to see him if I have to."

Lynnie's emotions were plain to read that morning. He'd seen anger and grief and confusion. Now he saw fear. She didn't want to know the truth, didn't want to know if those documents in Mexico were real. "Lynnie, you can't hide from it," he said gently. "You've got to know for sure."

She was still pacing, but now she stopped to pick something up from the end table. It was a framed copy of a *Time* magazine front cover, the one with a cartoon of Lynnie doing a high-wire act on a unicycle. She stared at it as she spoke, her voice slow and melancholy. "These covers. Sometimes they get them so right it hurts. This one . . ." She brushed her hand over it. "When I was in the Navy, flying the jets, there were times when I felt like nothing could touch me, like Superwoman. I was golden. I could go forever." She nodded at the cartoon. "Now every day is like this. I'm up there, wobbling along, just waiting for the wind to come and blow me off."

"You're not alone, Lynnie. Don't feel that way."

She looked steadily at him, her eyes soft and glowing. "You'll catch me, Mike—if I fall?"

He wanted to touch her, but felt he shouldn't. "You bet."

She smiled, then, putting on a brave face. "But maybe not yet."

Lynnie picked up a telephone and punched in a number. "Hi, who's this?" she said. "Oh, yeah, hi, Mel. Happy birthday. Who's back there? . . . Right. . . . He is? Well, bless his heart. OK, put Sung on." She covered the mouthpiece and said to Mike, "A birthday party in the back. Pascoe's there, telling dirty jokes."

Claudia's voice was so loud that Mike could hear it from across the room. "Somebody here just told me I could file for workers' comp for my eye."

Lynnie chuckled. "Good for you. Do me a favor. Call Meisser at Veterans Affairs. I need to locate somebody I think is in one of his hospitals. Phoenix, probably. His name's Martinez. Arfulno Martinez. A-r-f-u-l-n-o. Low-key, but pronto, OK?"

"Pronto is about right," Claudia barked. "Do you know how late it is?"

"Not too late to start looking for that other shoe," Lynnie said, and she hung up.

"Arfulno?" Mike said.

"His real name. Oscar was, well, sort of a nickname. Ask him about it when you see him. I think you will have to go there. If he'll talk to you about me at all, it'll be face-to-face, not on the phone."

Mike stood and put out his hands. She took them, stepping in close, molding her body to his. She looked longingly at the sofa. "A few minutes, I guess, that's all we've got."

"Not enough time for sticky-tingly," Mike said.

They laughed and nuzzled closer. They were ravenous for each other, and knowing so, they were careful to keep the temperature down. "Did you hear it?" Lynnie whispered.

"What?"

"All the clocks—they stopped ticking." Then they began to sway, not kissing, just hugging, breathing each other in.

There was a sharp knock on the outer door.

Lynnie sighed and called, "Claudia?"

"Yep."

"Did you get through?"

"Arfulno Martinez, the V.A. hospital in Phoenix. Got a room number and phone number."

"Good," Lynnie said. "Slide it under the door."

"Will do." Then Claudia cleared her throat and whispered, "Lynnie we have *got* to go! Now I'm not leaving this spot until Sweetcakes comes the hell out of there."

Lynnie's eyes went to the clock on the wall. "Mike, we really are late. I'm sorry, we—"

"No apologies, right?" He gave her a slow kiss, full of flame and sparkle. "New Year's in Hawaii?"

"Wait'll you see my new hula skirt," she said.

He hugged her one last time and left.

CHAPTER FORTY-THREE

When Mike emerged from the stateroom, Claudia was waiting with Archie near the plane's exit door. She pointed to the van parked below and beckoned over a campaign worker. "Chuck here will drive you to the terminal." She gave Mike a squeeze around the middle and whispered, "Truce?"

He stared coolly at her before he returned the hug. "I'll think about it. First get my name back on that phone list at the White House."

She shoved the three of them out the door. "Already done. Go on now."

It was a short drive, only a few hundred yards. A line of police black-and-whites went whizzing by in the other direction, toward the plane. Silently, Archie watched them pass. He hadn't spoken a word to Mike, hadn't even looked at him. He tilted his head up and said, "You notice that smell, Chuck?"

"What do you mean, Mr. Pascoe?" the driver asked.

Archie swung around, aiming an accusing eye at Mike. "Sex. Smells like sex in here."

Chuck didn't catch Archie's expression, but he laughed boisterously anyway. "Naw. I think that's Ms. Sung's cinnamon rolls."

Chuck led them past a pair of Secret Service agents, into the terminal. Putting on a wide grin, he handed Mike and Archie each a CONNOR/HOYT button. "Everybody gets one. That's the rule." He shook their hands and jogged back to his van.

"I suppose you're not going to tell me what happened out there with Lynnie," Archie said grumpily.

"Some of it I'll tell you, and some I won't. Right now I need to make a call."

"No. Right now you need to tell me what an 'Arfulno' is."

"Where did you hear that?" Mike asked.

"Ms. Sung-of-the-Cinnamon-Rolls. Asked me if I knew what an Arfulno was. Sounds like a Spanish laxative, I told her. So what is it?"

Mike pulled out his phone. "I'll explain, but later. We need to get to Phoenix. Go to the ticket counters over there and find out when the earliest plane is, all right?"

"Phoenix? Sheesh," Archie grumbled. He took a pen and pad from his pocket and went to look at the flight listings.

Before he dialed, Mike thought a moment about Oscar Martinez. Despite all the time that had passed, he stood out crystal clear in Mike's mind. Oscar didn't make much of a first impression: a short man, blade-thin, with basset eyes and pocked, olive-brown skin. It was what you noticed later that made him memorable. Everything about Oscar was dead certain, no wasted energy—his hands, his walk, his voice, even his laugh. Tell him a joke that wasn't funny and he wouldn't crack a smile. Get out a baseball and ask him to play catch, and he'd say, "What for?" Come across a rattlesnake in the cow pasture, and he'd grab it by the tail, smack its head on a rock, and leave it for the birds to eat, all without a word of comment.

Mike tapped in the number for the room at the Phoenix V.A. hospital. A nurse answered. Mike spoke Oscar's name, and she said, "OK, sure. He just woke up." She handed the phone over and Mike heard her footsteps moving away.

The voice that came on the line sounded dreadful, like a file pulled across wet wood. "Ye-ss? Wh-a-a-at i-ss?"

"Oscar Martinez?" Mike said, hoping there was a mistake and this wasn't really him. "Arfulno?"

There was much coughing and labored breathing. "W-ai-t." He coughed once more and spat noisily. "That's better. Yeah, I'm Martinez. Who's this?"

"Mike Stanbridge. I'm a friend of Lynnie Connor's. We were kids together. My sister and I used to visit the ranch with Lynnie and her father."

There was a pause. "What're you talkin' about? You nuts?"

Mike raised his voice, the way people do when they're speaking with someone senile, using volume when what they need is patience. "Lynnie Connor. Lynnie *Sheridan*. And her dad, John Sheridan. Do you remember them? The CC Ranch?"

"Yeah, I worked the CC for a while." Oscar took a long breath, which sounded like a broken harmonica. "You sellin' burial plots? That what this is?"

"No. You know me. You took us all fishing once, at San Carlos in Mexico. I wasn't much at casting. I put a treble hook right through your ear. Remember that?"

Oscar didn't reply. Archie was coming back. Mike nodded to him and held his hand out for the notepad.

"Oscar, listen, I have to come to see you, talk to you. About Lynnie's mother. About Graciella Yberri."

Oscar's breathing came down the line, wet and steady now, like the ocean surf.

Mike gnawed his lip, thinking. There had to be some trigger for Oscar's memory. "You rode a horse named Zack. We came every summer for a while. My sister's name was Jen. We lived in Blaine, in New York. Do you remember—any of it?"

"It's all right," Oscar said calmly. "I know who you are. You're the one pulled Lynnie from the fire. Her daddy told me all about it. Only testin' you, was all." Oscar spat again. "So you want to talk about Graciella?"

Quickly Mike said, "Yes."

"Did Lynnie tell you to call?"

"No. She got your phone number for me, but it was my idea to talk to you. I've been out at the ranch. I saw the roses you left at her grave. I need to find out some things. It's important. With the election only—"

"Election, *crap*," Oscar said, suddenly angry. He burst out coughing again and almost dropped the phone. Then he cursed viciously, and Mike was afraid he might hang up. Instead, when he got his breath back, he said, "Yeah, why not. We can talk."

"There's a man traveling with me, a friend," Mike said, glancing at Archie. He looked at the notes Archie had made. "We can be there in about three hours."

"Not at the hospital," Oscar said. "Too many people. Luis, my nephew—he's the one left those flowers at Graciella's grave—comes to take me for a ride Wednesday afternoons. Only time all week I get out. Him and me were gonna go to a park. Easy to find. That do ya?"

"Are you sure?" Mike said. "You sound sort of tired."

Oscar chuckled. "Tired is right. Plumb wore out. But I'll do fine." He gave Mike directions. "Meet there at one o'clock?" he said.

"Right, we can be there by then. Oscar, there's something else you should know. I said it was important that we talk to you. It's more than that. People are dead over this. Murdered. Two that we know of for sure, probably more. A man I met with in Bisbee disappeared. Makes us feel like a couple of Typhoid Marys."

"Good God A'mighty," Oscar sighed. "Always wondered if it would come to this, all the sneakin' around and lying. Why'd she have to go into politics, huh?"

"Good question," Mike said. "It's been a while since we last saw each other. How will I recognize you?"

Oscar laughed again. "Don't worry 'bout that. I'm a *unique specimen*, that's what Luis always says. One o'clock." He rang off.

Archie took his pad back. "Guess I know what an Arfulno is now. Where'd he get that name instead of Oscar?"

"Lynnie says we should ask him," Mike replied.

"Speak of the devil," Archie said, looking over Mike's shoulder.

There was a television set in the gate area across the concourse, showing the local news. They were running a live shot of Air Force One. Lynnie had come out at the top of the steps, waving to the crowd of a few hundred people assembled below, mostly reporters and staffers. Her cream-colored suit was perfect, same for her hair and makeup. Her smile, her whole face, was aglow, lustrous in the slanting morning sun.

Archie said, "Hard to believe that's the same twerp who just told me to *sit*, like I was some old spaniel who'd mussed her carpet. Wonder how many people she's got in that one body of hers?"

Mike stared at the screen, captivated. "It's just her job," he mumbled.

Lynnie blew a kiss, not only for those below, but a bigger kiss than that, thrown at the sky, to all of San Diego. Every person in the gate area was looking at the television; every face had a smile.

"Oh, and look at this now," Archie groaned, "Ahab the A-rab." At the bottom of the airplane steps, a man in a gray business suit and a kaffiyeh headcloth was waiting to greet Lynnie, holding a bouquet of daisies. He seemed totally confused about what he was supposed to do. "What'd'ya call it—damage control," Archie said. "Hoyt's doily shenanigans. They probably snagged that guy off some inbound flight. Ten minutes ago he was on his way to Sea World, now he gets to meet the president. Goddamned creep show, that's what it is."

Mike grinned. "Know what, Arch? For once, you're pretty close to right. Come on. Let's see if we can both get aisle seats this time."

CHAPTER FORTY-FOUR

Valley of the Sun

Encanto Park was in one of the older sections of Phoenix. The streets around it were flat and beeline straight; the houses were tidy brick bungalows with red-tiled roofs. In the middle of the park was a meandering man-made watercourse called the Lagoon. Mike asked the taxi driver to drop him and Archie off in a parking lot near the north end of it. They were to meet Oscar Martinez by the boat rental house.

Oscar was right when he said they'd have no trouble spotting him. He was in a wheelchair, and across the seat back was a bumper sticker, slapped in place, wrinkled and off kilter: LATINOS/LATINAS POR CONNOR. He wore a baseball cap, turned backward so the bill covered his neck. It had a round logo, and, as Mike got close, he saw it was the presidential seal—a gift from Lynnie, then.

Oscar heard their footsteps and turned. Mike slowed almost to a halt. An instant sadness fell on him.

Oscar had always been thin, but now he didn't top one hundred pounds. He was tiny everywhere, birdlike, except for his chest, which was swollen obscenely, like a great bellows. There was a green metal tank in a long pouch on his chair. From it ran a plastic tube, up under his shirt, to a cannula in his nose. His nostrils were raw and cherry red, slathered with some kind of clear jelly.

"Hi, Oscar. Good to see you."

"Hey, you got tall," Oscar squeaked, offering his hand. The effort of speaking made him cough. Still, he grinned. And he was as economical as ever with his words. He touched his chest and said, "I got emphysema." Somehow, he made it clear that was all he had to say about his health.

Mike introduced Archie and asked where Oscar's nephew was. "Sent him to get some lunch," Oscar replied. "Figured if we were going to talk about Lynnie, we should be alone." He waved his hand at a boy standing by the Lagoon, fishing. "Was showin' him how to cast. He picks it up faster than you did." Grinning again, Oscar touched his ear, the one Mike had hooked years ago. "You a fisherman, Mr. Pascoe?"

"Call me Archie. I've got into a bass or two in my day."

Oscar was watching him carefully, taking his measure. His eyes were clear, unsullied by his disease. "I'll bet you have," he murmured. "You folks seem kind of jumpy. You know, we got rid of the wolves and bears around here, long time ago."

"Wolves and bears wouldn't be so bad," Mike said, laughing.

Oscar studied them both for a moment more, then said, "Tell ya what. Wheel me around the lake. We can see the sights while we talk."

So Archie pushed the chair while Mike walked alongside. The path was concrete, lined with tall date palms and bushy acacias. In the shady spots the air was fresh and cool; out in the sun it was warm enough to make all three of them perspire. "You've seen Lynnie?" Oscar asked after they were started.

"A few hours ago," Mike said.

"That'd be San Diego."

"Yuh," Archie said. "How'd you know?"

"Some guys follow baseball. I follow Lynnie. Might say I've got to be a political junkie in my old age."

"But you won't speak to her?" Mike said.

Oscar glanced quickly at him, then ahead again. "No, I won't." He shifted his position in his chair, trying to ease the load on his uncushioned bones. "So you want to know about Graciella. How'd you find out about her?"

"The flowers on her grave, for one thing," Mike said. "Your nephew put them there?"

Oscar nodded. "I promised Lynnie's dad I'd do that every year, long as I was alive. I can't get out there anymore, though, so Luis does it for me."

Mike said, "What we wanted to talk about was—"

Archie cut him off. "We know John Sheridan brought Graciella to the ranch, and that she was pregnant then. And we know about the hospital in Mexico. The only thing we want to clear up—"

Now Mike interrupted. "Arch, let him tell us. His own words. The day Lynnie was born, that's what we need to know about. What happened?"

Oscar looked down at his hands, bony and blue-veined and scarred. "Damn nightmare," he said darkly. "Worst friggin' day of my life." Then he brightened. "Say, buy me a sno-cone. I'm kind'a dry."

There was a vendor's cart up ahead, and Mike sprung for three cones, all raspberry. They continued their way around the Lagoon.

Oscar said, "If you talked to Lynnie, then you know Mattie and John were trying to keep the birth a secret. Back then, it happened a lot more often than anybody'd admit. Anglo couple wants to adopt a baby but don't want all the messin' around it takes in the States. They go to Mexico, to a poor village, find a girl willing to give up hers. They wait around and bring the baby home with them. Fake papers at the border—nobody really checks. Instant family."

They were crossing a footbridge, and a man was standing there, dressed in jeans and an Army field jacket, too warm for the weather. He had close-cut hair and wire-rimmed glasses that glinted in the sun. Mike and Archie glanced warily at him, and so did Oscar.

"Screwballs hang out here," Oscar said when they had gone far enough so the man could no longer hear. "Druggies mostly. Act like they're vets—Iraq, you know? Get some sympathy. Hell, last time Luis and me was here, one of 'em followed us around screamin', 'Hey, Paco! Welcome to America!'"

"Oscar," Mike said gently. "We need to know about Graciella."

The old man stared at his hands again. "Yeah, Graciella." He slurped a little of his sno-cone, then settled back to tell about the worst day of his life.

"Mattie had sent everybody away, the cook and all the hands, to live on the other end of the ranch. When we figured Graciella was due, we brought in a midwife, an old lady from Janos, south of the border. Not really 'we.' It was John that found her. Mattie stayed completely out of it, like at that point she didn't know what was going on, or care. The midwife, Leonor, was a take-charge type at first. Told us what to do, how to get ready. But Graciella was late to start the labor. A week or more late, Leonor figured, and time kept goin' by. Leonor got real nervous. She wanted to take her to a doctor. John talked to Mattie about it, then Graciella, and they decided to stand pat, wait it out at the ranch."

Oscar paused to catch his breath. He looked blankly at the tall buildings to the east, along Phoenix's central corridor. Softly he said, "I don't know how we all could'a been so dumb." He adjusted his oxygen line and continued.

"Leonor must'a guessed something bad was comin'. She lit out right after John told her we weren't havin' no doctor. Left her stuff and everything. Probably walked all the way to Douglas. We didn't have much time to worry, though, because—wouldn't ya know it—that's when Graciella finally started gettin' her pains. And those stories about Lynnie bein' born in a near hurricane—true, all true. Damnedest rain I've ever seen, and I served three years in the Pacific, right through Korea and all.

"For a long while, most of that night, the contractions were real regular, then they slacked off. Almost nothin'. I didn't know what to do; not John either. Mattie got drunk, sat out in the breezeway of the big house and cried her eyes out. Graciella was so weak she couldn't lift her head. Couldn't push, couldn't talk, couldn't do anythin'. It was the peak of the storm then, 'round dawn. I begged John to start for town, for the hospital. We could take the tractor, be there in a couple of hours. He hemmed and hawed, then finally said OK, but we'd have to go in the pickup, not the tractor. He couldn't see havin' Graciella out in the open with the weather like it was.

"John did the driving. There was a cap over the back of the truck, and I was in there with Graciella. We made it four miles, then hit a wash with ten foot'a water in it. No way was we gettin' across. I told Graciella and I think she understood. She nodded anyway. She was in a world of hurt. She pushed me down, down by her belly. I could see the baby. Lynnie. The crown of her head was right there, and a little peek of her shoulder." Oscar looked up at Mike, as if for confirmation. "I had to do somethin', didn't I?"

His gaze was so piercing that Mike glanced away, but he touched him on the shoulder and nodded.

Oscar said, "I put my hand there, one side of Lynnie's head, and twisted. Only a little. She popped right out, clear to her feet. I was so surprised, I squawked like I'd been snakebit. I cleaned her off and she started to cry. The noise seemed to roust Graciella. She smiled and motioned to the knife we'd brought, so's I'd cut the cord. I did and she took Lynnie and cuddled her right up. Then John started laughing and shouting. The rain was clearin' off; there was blue sky out to the west, even a rainbow. I sat down in the blood and mess and thought, *A miracle, Jesus God, a miracle.*"

"No," Archie said abruptly. "That doesn't make sense."

Oscar grabbed the wheels on his chair, bringing them to a halt. "What doesn't make sense?"

"The way you tell it. The way you say she was born," Archie said. "We saw the records. We know better."

Oscar held up his hands, trembly and fragile, like large butterflies. "*You* know better? Listen here, these were the first hands to touch her. You think I wouldn't remember it right? Lynnie Connor—your president, Mr. Pascoe—was born in the back of a '41 Willys pickup truck. I can take you to the exact spot, show you the marker John and I built, later that week, after we buried Graciella."

Archie tried to stare him down, but Oscar had too much fire in his eyes. "Told you, call me Archie," he mumbled.

"What happened with Graciella?" Mike said, strolling on. Archie, still scowling, pushed the chair along behind.

Oscar started to speak, but was immediately seized by a fit of coughing that lasted nearly a minute. He moaned when he was through and wiped his face. "These hands again," he wheezed. "That's what killed her. So the doctor said."

"What doctor?" Archie asked sullenly.

Mike flashed him a warning glance: *Keep quiet.*

"Elidad," Oscar said. "Ruiz Elidad. It was right about the time we saw the rainbow that Graciella noticed something was wrong with Lynnie's shoulder. Bones stickin' up funny. And I'll say somethin' for her here. Graciella could light up a room with her smile. She was an easy person to like. Too easy, almost. Never serious about anything. But she was a tiger about that baby. 'We're goin' to the hospital,' she said. John made to argue, but she cussed right in his face. 'Bastard. Take us or we walk.'

"We waited for another hour for the water to run out of that wash, then headed for Douglas. By the time we got there it was midday. Town was a mess. They'd had a lot of flood damage. Graciella was asleep in the back, and Lynnie, too. John turned south. I knew what was up, and it seemed OK to me. We took our ranch hands over to the Agua Prieta hospital all the time. The illegals, that is. Broken bones and stitches. No paperwork that way, nobody to call in *la Migra*. Why not do the same for Lynnie? Keep the birth a secret. That'd been the idea all along."

Oscar held the wheels of his chair again, stopping them. Up ahead, some people were having a party. They had tied a piñata to a tree, and two little girls were whirling around, flailing with long sticks. Oscar watched intently, ducking his head right and left, as if he were at a boxing match. One of the girls struck home, and he applauded as candy flew everywhere.

He said, "We crossed the border, no trouble, and got to the hospital. Was really only a clinic then. They were busy. A nurse took Graciella and Lynnie into a room and told us to go outside. We waited and waited, damn near all afternoon. I went back in to check but couldn't find out anything. Then, finally, the nurse come out, pale as a ghost. 'Doctor will see you,' was all she said. I looked at John and he looked at me, and I think we both almost cried.

"Graciella was gone. Bled to death. She'd been bleeding the whole time after the birth but never said a word to us. The doctor thought . . ." Oscar was looking at his hands again, rubbing them slowly together. "When I told him how the baby had come, he said it was my twisting her that probably did it. Her shoulder was hung up and when it came loose it tore something down there inside Graciella. He was pretty good about it, didn't ride me or anything. Just said, 'Baby lives, mother dies, that's the way it is sometimes.'"

"Lynnie had a broken collarbone?" Mike said.

Oscar cleared his chest, a long bubbly sound. "Yeah. Doc took an X-ray, then wrapped her arm up and pinned it to her side. Said she'd be fine, and she was. We took her back to the ranch. Used an old smuggler's track out in the desert I knew. Didn't see a soul the whole trip.

John had Graciella's body sent over a couple days later. She didn't have any family we could find, so we buried her up on the mesa."

He took his cap off and jammed it back on, right side to. "And that's the whole story. Most I've talked all week put together." He got them moving again, wheeling his chair along to a trash can so he could throw away his sno-cone cup. That short bit of exertion left him gasping. There was a kink in his air line, too, which didn't help matters. Mike freed it. "Thanks . . . buckaroo," he panted. Archie caught up and started to push. Oscar drew oxygen deep into his lungs. "Now . . . that's better. Say, tell me somethin'. You said you found out about Graciella from her headstone. How's that? Can't read the damn thing anymore."

"Yes, you can," Archie replied gruffly. He was still smarting from their earlier exchange. So he told Oscar all about the tombstone—where it sat in the cemetery, the inscription, what he'd found out from the monument company that had carved it.

Mike cut in, "Lynnie thinks somebody replaced the stone, moved it next to John's. Your nephew didn't mention things were changed around? From when he was out there with the flowers?"

Oscar laughed, *har-har*. "Luis? His dog died once. Three days it laid by the door in the front hall before Luis figured out somethin' might be the matter. But tell me: Why would anybody want to mess around with that stone?"

Mike motioned for Archie to stop, then knelt in front of the wheelchair so he and Oscar were at eye level. "That's what we've been wondering. Why would anybody be messing around with this old stuff. Oscar, we went to the hospital in Agua Prieta and looked in the files. We saw the X-ray you mentioned, the one of Lynnie's shoulder. There were patient records for her and Graciella, and Graciella's death certificate. There was a birth record, too, an official form. According to that, Lynnie was born there, in that hospital. It was signed by Dr. Elidad, dated the day she was born. Mother, Graciella Yberri; father, John Sheridan."

Oscar was shaking his head. "A birth record?"

"Lynnie thinks it's fake," Mike said.

"Baloney," Archie snorted.

Oscar twisted around in his chair. "All right, you, tell me what's on your mind. What the hell do *you* think's goin' on?"

"Lynnie. It's her. She's up to something with all this. Maybe she was born in the truck like you say, north of the border, but there's nothing to prove that. All there is is that birth record. And we looked it over. It's the real McCoy."

"Oh, brother," Oscar muttered. "OK now, I'll go real slow for the puddingheads. I was *there*. I *know* what happened. There wasn't a birth record. Couldn't'a been. Here, you tell me, what was the name on that paper? The name of the baby?"

Archie said, "Carolyn Jean Yberri."

Oscar broke into a smile, pleased with himself. "Lynnie didn't get that name 'til five days later, back at the ranch, from Mattie. There was no possible way Doc Elidad could have known. So how did it get on the damn birth record? It's a fake, like Lynnie said. And unless you want to call me a liar, right now, to my face, you'd better start believing it."

For a moment Archie seemed totally befuddled, like a man who'd looked out his window and seen a horse fly by. Then he shrugged and dipped his head, almost a bow. "No, I don't think you're a liar. And I guess I'd better stop arguing."

Mike had watched this with amusement, but at the same time his mind was clicking along. "If that birth record is fake, somebody had to put it there. It's only a guess, but I've got a good candidate." He told Oscar about Martin Castillo. "As hospital administrator he had access to the files. If he planted the birth record, that would be a reason for somebody to want to kill him, to keep it quiet."

"But why would he do it?" Archie asked.

"Maybe for money. Or maybe somebody blackmailed him into it. Something like that," Mike said. "I don't think Castillo came up with the idea. He was somebody's tool, somebody who wanted that birth record there so they'd have an extra-big lever on Lynnie, or a way to keep her out of the election altogether."

"Explain something to me, then," Archie said. "Lynnie was Graciella's baby. Isn't that the end of it? I mean, Arizona or Mexico, wherever it happened, Lynnie can't be a 'natural born citizen,' not if her own mother was a Mexican."

Oscar jumped in. "That's not the way it works. If you're born here, you're a citizen. That's it. Doesn't matter who your parents are."

"Oh, right," Archie said, frowning. "Sheesh. We need a bigger fence." When Mike and Oscar both looked at him, he chuckled brightly, as if he'd taken a hand in a card game. "A joke, guys, that's all."

They strolled along, back past the boat rental house and the end of the Lagoon, each of them thinking about what had been said. Finally Archie spoke up. "Tell us about your name. How Arfulno got to be Oscar."

"Lynnie," Oscar said. "When she was four years old, she came out to the ranch for a visit with her dad. John still owned most of the place then, had all the hands workin'. She tried and tried, but she couldn't say Arfulno. Got it turned around. Arnulfo. Farnolo. So one day at dinner—everybody'd just started to eat—she stands up in her chair and pats me on the head. 'You're Oscar!' Don't know where she got it from, but that was it." He reached up, as if to recreate Lynnie's touch on his head. "Four-year-old tadpole flicks her hand and *poof*. I've been

Oscar since, to everybody, everywhere—even my own family."

Mike looked into the distance and smiled. In his mind he could see Lynnie standing outside a Cuban restaurant in Washington. She was lifting her hand to flag down a taxi. In a moment, the two of them would be heading for a motel in Arlington, and their first night together. "That's Lynnie, all right," he said. "Make a whole new man out of you."

Archie was thoughtful, too, mulling over something else. "I'll bet not everybody thinks you're Oscar. I'll bet it's Arfulno on your driver's license, and at the V.A., and with the Social Security."

"Yeah, so?" Oscar said.

"That's why nobody's come to visit you about Graciella before," Archie replied. "The first time I asked Mike about Lynnie's days in Arizona, he mentioned you. Since then it's been Oscar this and Oscar that, always Oscar who'd have all the answers—if we could just find him. I'll bet there've been other people out trying to find you, too, people you'd rather not meet. But like us, they were looking under the wrong name."

Oscar murmured, "Well now." He gave his face a brisk rub. "So what do we do?"

Mike said, "Knowing the things you know—that's like being radioactive right now. We may have to get you into a new hospital for a while, under a new name. Lynnie might have some ideas. We can call her, see what she thinks."

Archie was looking around them. "Meantime, I don't much like being out in the open like this."

"Luis can drive us to his place," Oscar said. He chuckled. "Don't worry. He's not usin' the dog for a doorstop anymore. If you don't mind wheelin' me, he's at the Kentucky Fried, a couple blocks from here."

Mike took over for Archie behind the chair. They left the park and, following Oscar's directions, cut across the street to an alley flanked by a board fence on one side and tall hedges on the other. It was very hot now, and they hugged the fence, taking advantage of the shade. "You didn't know Graciella's family lived in Agua Prieta?" Archie said.

Oscar squinted up at him. "Agua Prieta? She was born there, she told us. But her folks, the whole family, moved down to Guaymas when she was little. John tried to find them, let them know what had happened, but no luck."

A panel truck had turned into the alley behind them. Archie edged closer to the fence to let it pass. "No, we talked to her sister. Graciella grew up right there on the border. Her family was still there when she died."

"Huh," Oscar said. And again: "Huh. Had no idea. Sounds like everybody had lies to tell."

The truck stopped and the rear door rumbled open. It took them a moment to recognize the man who stood there—close-cut hair, Army field jacket, shiny spectacles. "What the hell's this?" Oscar said.

"*Archie!*" Mike shouted. He didn't have to say anymore, because Archie was already turning and starting to run. Mike followed, heaving against Oscar's chair.

A pickup truck spun into the mouth of the alley and stopped. Three men hopped out. Archie ran right at them, screaming and flailing his arms. The man Archie had thrown the dart at in Agua Prieta was in the lead. He slipped sideways, agile as a bullfighter, and swung with his left fist. The punch landed so hard on Archie's chin that he bounced into the fence before he went down. He didn't move after that.

The men closed in quickly on Mike and Oscar. Mike was yelling. He could feel the sound in his lungs and throat, but he had no idea what he was saying. He moved in front of the wheelchair, trying to protect Oscar.

The man who'd hit Archie was still at the head of the pack. Mike feinted, as if to run, then turned into him, swinging efficiently, a straight right that broke his nose.

Before Mike could swing again, someone grabbed him from behind. He twisted to get free and never saw the punch that laid him out. It came from the man Mike had slugged at the Newark airport.

He hit Mike a dozen more times before Colonel Veck pulled him off. By then Mike's face was a pulp. He couldn't feel anything. For a second or two he drifted, his eyes fixed on the wheels of Oscar's chair. Then cold blackness settled over him.

CHAPTER FORTY-FIVE

Mike came awake with a sound echoing in his head, like the squawk of a bird. There was a tattered train of thought attached to it, something about Lynnie and Claudia Sung. Something. It slipped away from him. He opened his eyes, not far because they were badly swollen. He'd been awake twice before. Both times, he drifted a while, then went back under. Now, fully conscious, he could feel every bruise, every aching muscle.

Around him it was inky dark, but he could make out forms. A ceiling of corrugated tin. Rafters in a curved shape. A Quonset hut. Outside, the wind was blowing. That accounted for the noise. Two sections of the roof were rubbing together in the breeze. *Oyt, oyt.*

He heard another sound, a brief moan, and turned his head an inch or so to see where it had come from. It was even darker back there, at the far end of the hut, but he picked out a figure, a shadowy mound. The moan came again. He crawled toward it. The floor was made of rough wood planks, dry and brittle with age. Something skittered across his arm—a chubby rat with a gnawed-off tail. Mike reached the mound and put his hand out, prodding stealthily. "Archie?" he whispered.

"I can adjust my own equipment, thank you very much," Archie said, slapping him away.

Mike was so startled he needed a moment to catch his breath. "Damn, you scared me."

"Scared you? I thought you were one of those big squirrels I keep hearing in here, comin' after the royal acorns."

"They're rats, Arch."

"Even better."

"You don't sound so good. Angina?"

Several seconds passed before Archie answered. "I wish."

"What do you mean, 'you wish.' "

"Not so loud. Somebody'll hear," Archie whispered. "Well, it isn't angina and it isn't indigestion."

If Archie wouldn't call it "heart attack," then neither would Mike. "When did it start?"

"Last evening, after we got here, about the time I came conscious. Not so bad now." He arched his back, stifling another moan. "I'll be all right."

"We've got to get you out of here, to a hospital."

Archie managed to chuckle. "You're a master of understatement, Michael."

Mike looked around the hut. There was more light than there had been a few minutes earlier. Dawn, then. He blinked, trying to clear his head of the massive headache. "Where are we?"

"Oscar said it's an old Air Force base, closed up now. Not the main base either, but one of the auxiliary landing strips. Way out nowhere, cotton fields all around."

"Where is Oscar?" Mike asked.

"They took him a couple of hours ago. There's a big wood shack out that way." Archie shifted position, sitting up against the wall. "I heard him screaming, Mike, over and over. They were hurting him."

"Who are they?"

"I don't have any idea. Five men. There's a little guy in charge, named Veck. They call him 'Colonel' sometimes. Former military, I'd guess. Don't act like they're on the payroll now."

The two were quiet for a while. The wind rose and the roof squeaked again. It was an irritating sound and they both glanced up, frowning. Then Archie dozed off. He woke abruptly after only a few minutes, and looked over at Mike, who'd been watching him.

"I'll *be* all right," Archie said again. His voice did seem stronger now. "How do you think they found us, anyway?" Mike didn't have an answer, so Archie continued. "Been trying to figure that out. First thing I thought of was Lynnie, as usual—that she told 'em we'd be in Phoenix. But I can't see that it's her. She could have gotten to Oscar any time she wanted. So why do it now? And it wouldn't make sense that she'd fiddle that birth record, make it look like she was born in Mexico when she wasn't, ruin her own chances."

"Wait," Mike said. "Wait a minute." He reached into his pocket and pulled out the CONNOR/HOYT button the campaign worker had given him in San Diego. He tore it apart, breaking off the pin, snapping the metal in two, looking for circuitry, an antenna, something that would send out a signal. It was only a button.

By that time Archie had his button out, too. He broke it in half. Pure, shiny metal, no electronics. "It was a good thought anyway," Archie said. He hitched his body down until he was lying flat again. His breathing came easier that way. "The other thing I've been trying to work out is who's behind it all. They got Castillo to put that fake record in the hospital files, but then they kept it quiet, didn't call in the newspapers, didn't tell a soul. They did everything they could to keep it secret, like they were saving it for something."

"That's right," Mike said. As far back as two days ago,

during their dinner at the truck stop outside of Tucson, he'd been thinking the same thing.

"So who'd do it?" Archie said. "Who'd have something to gain from all that?"

From outside they heard a voice, then another. Mike scrambled back to his spot in the middle of the floor and lay still. A door creaked open and Oscar was wheeled in. He was wrapped in a blanket, and his chin lolled down on his chest, as if he were asleep or unconscious. There were three men with him, one carrying a flashlight.

Mike shut his eyes, hoping they'd leave him alone. Footsteps came his way, clunking on the old floorboards. Someone twisted his head around and yanked up his eyelid. He twitched. His tormentor giggled. "Hey, Cutter, you didn't hit him hard enough. He's wakie-poo."

"So's blubber-boy," Cutter said, kneeling over Archie.

"That's enough," the third man said. "Colonel only wanted to know if they'd come to yet." With that, they left, pulling the door closed and, from the sound of it, chaining it shut.

Mike hurried to Oscar. His cannula had fallen out of his nose. Mike rearranged it and checked the air line to make sure it was free of kinks. Oscar opened one eye and looked around, smiling faintly. "Playin' possum," he said. His voice was thick and slow. He focused on Mike. "Goddamn, son, you're a sight. I couldn't believe how that fool kept whalin' on you."

Mike touched his face. "Looks worse than it is. Nothing permanent anyway."

"How you doin', pard?" Oscar asked Archie.

"I'm tops," Archie grumped. "Takes a licking and keeps on ticking."

Mike didn't like the way Oscar was sitting, curled up on himself. He lifted the blanket and breath whistled from his lips. Oscar's hand lay in his lap, swaddled in a heavy towel. The towel was soaked with blood. He reached for it, but Oscar said, quite calmly, "Nah, best leave it alone."

Mike tucked the blanket back around his knees. "What happened out there?"

"Asked me some questions. Didn't care for my answers much."

"What did they want to know?"

"Fix my gas first, will ya?" Oscar said. "My tank run out. They refilled it but didn't get the valve right." Mike made the adjustment and Oscar nodded. "That's it. Right 'bout there." He spat on the floor. "Tastes like rust. What they kept askin' about was documents in Spanish. Did you guys have them. Did I know what was in them. Did I tell anybody about them. Had you guys made any copies. Like that."

"Spanish?" Archie said.

"The X-ray photocopy," Mike said. "And they're not sure what else we might have taken from the hospital."

Archie sat up now, interested. "OK. Did they say why it was important?"

Oscar had to hack up some phlegm before he could answer. "No, but they're plenty mad. Veck especially. First off, he was all smiles. Little creep loves to sing, like when he did this to my hand. 'If I had a hammer, I'd hammer in the mo-or-nin' . . . ' "

Archie and Mike both winced.

"His boys thought it was awful funny," Oscar continued. "Then they got a message and the whole thing changed. Everybody got ticked off all of a sudden."

"A message?" Mike asked. "Somebody called them?"

"No," Oscar said. "Computer message. You should see the setup they got. Machines every which way."

Archie asked, "What was the message?"

Oscar was growing weaker. His voice was down to a chirp. "Dunno all of it. Somebody's comin' here, though, to talk to you two. That's why they left you alone just now. Be back for you later."

Mike tucked Oscar's blanket in tighter. "Can we do anything for you? They left a water bottle. Would you like some?"

Oscar nodded and Mike got it for him. After a single sip, Oscar pushed the bottle away. Then he seemed to go into a trance. His eyes were open but not moving. Mike checked his pulse. It was skimming along, thready and much too quick. But before long his breathing leveled out; his heart rate came down. His eyes closed and his head sagged back. He was asleep. Mike settled down next to Archie.

It was growing lighter by the minute now, and warmer. Outside the breeze had died off, and desert doves were cooing. A shaft of sunlight blazed through a hole high up in the roof, lighting a million spinning dust motes. Mike stared at the tiny sparkles, his mind swirling with them. "Hoyt," he said at long last.

"What?" Archie muttered. He'd been sleeping.

Mike said, "What you said before—who would gain from planting that birth record but not telling anybody about it? The vice president."

Archie heaved himself up. "I'm a little foggy. Take it slow."

"As it stands now, Connor/Hoyt will coast to a win. Then after the election's over, after the inauguration, somebody leaks it to the press: there's a set of documents in a Mexican hospital; check it out. They find the X-ray, the birth record. They look at the Constitution. Lynnie Connor can't serve as president. But it's no problem. There's somebody ready to take her place: the duly-elected vice president, Andrew Hoyt. What Lynnie said was right. Without her, Hoyt couldn't get elected sewer inspector; with her, he wins in a walk. Then with those documents out in the open, he steps right into the Oval Office."

"Could be," Archie said. He was skeptical, still trying to sort it out.

Oscar cleared his throat, surprising them both. "Hoyt?" he croaked. "That poor slob couldn't plan a trip around the block without a compass and three aides to read it."

"Hey, you're still with us!" Mike kidded.

Oscar was crabby after his rest. He didn't smile. "I tell ya you're wrong. I follow politics. Hoyt's a reptile. No style at all. This isn't his kind of deal." Oscar paused for a couple of breaths. "Think of that gravestone. Political theater."

"He's got a point there," Archie said. "A stage piece— that's what you told me Lynnie called it."

Oscar nodded brusquely. "An idiot like Hoyt couldn't have thought that up. His blade's way too dull."

"He's got buildings full of consultants and advisors," Mike countered.

Oscar was having none of it. "Yeah, but if he knew, he'd have tipped his hand. He's just too smug to keep a secret like that. Lynnie'd be on to him by now."

"She's got a lot on her mind—" Mike began.

Oscar cut him off, ending the argument. "Get me a drink, would ya?"

Archie was closer than Mike. He got up and handed over the bottle. It was the first time he'd been on his feet in twelve hours, and he became so dizzy he had to sit right back down.

Oscar used his good hand to take a sip. He looked around the hut. "Didn't leave any food, did they?"

"No," Mike replied distractedly. He was still thinking about Andrew Hoyt.

"I've got some candy," Archie said. He rummaged in the pocket of his Windbreaker and came up with a white box. It had the presidential seal on it. "Got these from your buddy Lynnie." He tore the box open and dumped M&Ms into Oscar's hand.

"Stale," Oscar said as he nibbled on them.

"Well ex*cuse* me," Archie chuckled. "Sorry it's not filet

mignon." He lifted the box to his own mouth, poured down the last few bits.

"So maybe Hoyt doesn't know," Mike said. "The people on his staff—"

"*Damn*," Archie screeched. He started spitting candy into his hand. Candy and flecks of green plastic. Circuit board. Wires. "What is this garbage?" he muttered.

Mike scuttled over for a closer look. "Tracking device. Like the one I found after we left Newark. Where'd you get that box?"

Archie was using his finger to clean his mouth. "Told you—the plane."

Mike was frustrated. "I *know* that. But it wasn't Lynnie. Who? Logan? No. It was Claudia, wasn't it?"

Archie spat once more. "Nope. The other one—the one that runs the campaign. That Gina Rizzo person."

CHAPTER FORTY-SIX

It was late afternoon and Mike was kneeling by the wall of the Quonset hut, peering through a knothole. He couldn't recall ever feeling so hot and dirty. Hours ago he'd quit worrying about the bugs and rats and even the fat white snakes that curled lazily under the floorboards.

He'd spent most of the day in the same spot, watching Veck and his men. He knew all their names now: weird Gerbil; Longtemps with his constant Ralph Kramden jokes; Dowd, always thoughtful, acting a cut above the others; and cool, mean-spirited Cutter. Most of the time, Mike kept his attention on Veck. He'd been in a black rage all day. He refused to talk to the others, except to bark out an order once in a while. He had tried whittling, but after half an hour of that he suddenly flew into a fury and smashed what he'd been working on. Now he was sitting with his back to the others, cleaning his pistol.

His men treated him like a bomb with a lit fuse, keeping their distance and watching with quick, fretful glances.

Inside the Quonset hut, things weren't going well either. Mike's headache was so bad his ears rang and his vision was sometimes blurry. Archie had a bad stretch shortly after noon, when his breathing became quick and ragged. He bit his lip, groaning and shaking from the pain in his chest. He was looking better now, lying on his side and peeking through another hole in the wall.

Oscar was in the worst shape. He'd had a slow decline since morning. Veck's men had twice refilled his air tank, but getting enough oxygen wasn't his only problem. Because of the low humidity, his lungs were drying out. With the tissue so irritated, mucus was building up. He was drowning in his own spit. During one wrenching coughing spell he pitched forward, almost out of his chair. Catching himself, he began to chuckle. He waved at the low, round roof over their heads. "Look at us." He gagged and swallowed noisily. "Three gimps in a tube."

With so much time on their hands, they had plenty of opportunity to talk over their situation. Mike argued some, but ultimately had to agree with Oscar: Andrew Hoyt didn't know about the plan to unseat Lynnie. If he'd been told, he'd have done something stupid, something to blow the whistle on himself.

So the only thing they were sure about was Gina Rizzo. Why would she be involved in something like this? There had been a lot of friction between her and Lynnie; there were rumors Lynnie was going to get rid of her after the election, no plum job at the White House or anywhere else.

Mike remembered an article he'd read, one of Rizzo's rare interviews with the press. She said she thought the most important job in Washington (after Lynnie's, of course) was Homeland Security Director. That made him shake his head. Already so many manipulations, so many deaths. Think of the damage Rizzo could do if she had everyone in Homeland Security working for her. But how could she get there unless somebody at the top gave her the nod? That led right back to Lynnie and Hoyt. Nowhere.

All right, so change directions—what about Aron Aubrey and Eve Tessmer? Mike and Archie bickered about the details, but they saw the same general outline. Eve must have been the one who'd started looking for the Sheridan family dentist. She got as far as the nickname—Painless Doc Denis. She gave what she had to Aubrey, and he ran with it.

Aubrey came up with the last name—DuPree—and tracked him down. Then he followed the leads all the way to the documents in the hospital in Agua Prieta. There Aubrey had the scoop of his life. It was his one decent streak—his fairness as a journalist—that got him in trouble. He called Lynnie's campaign to let them comment on the story before he broke it. And who was it he talked to? Not Lynnie. They'd never let him get that close to the throne. No, Gina Rizzo, as campaign manager, would have been the one to deal with Aubrey. Rizzo was the pin that held it all together. She found out what Aubrey knew and had him murdered to keep him quiet. Eve, too, had to be silenced, the last link between Aubrey and Doc Denis DuPree and Agua Prieta.

That left Mike and Archie and Oscar to deal with. With them sown up, Rizzo was in pretty good shape. All she needed to do was make sure the story about Lynnie's birth wasn't somehow already blown. That's why they'd questioned Oscar about the copy of the X-ray and Spanish documents. Mike and Archie would be up next—their turn with the hammer. That, Mike realized (though he didn't say it out loud), was the only reason they were still alive.

In the meantime, some new problem had popped up on Veck's horizon. That explained his foul mood, and why Mike and Archie hadn't been interrogated yet. Thank heaven for small favors, Mike thought glumly.

There was a commotion in the wood shack across the way. Mike changed positions so he could see. Gerbil came trundling out the door, pushing a hand truck. On it were two tall gas cylinders, one green and one orange. The shack was where Oscar's oxygen refills had come from. The building had once been used as a welding shop. In it, Oscar reported, were dozens of fuel tanks, abandoned when the air base was closed.

"What are you up to?" Veck growled.

"Cookin' dinner," Gerb replied. "You said we couldn't have a real fire." He went to their pickup and came back with a cardboard box. After pawing through it he said, "Can'a corn," with a nasal drawl, the way Little Leaguers call for pop flies. He pulled a big tin can out of the box and set it on the ground. Then he unwrapped the hose from the cylinders and turned on the gas. He was puffing on a cigarette and used that to light the torch.

"That lunkhead's gonna be sorry if he's not careful," Archie muttered.

Mike was spellbound by the flame. It spurted three feet from the nozzle—smoky, oily, an evil yellow color. He was weak anyway, but now he started to feel shaky all over. He pulled away from the knothole, leaning against the wall.

"Jesus, Gerb," somebody shouted. "You got to open the damn can before—"

Whooomp—it exploded. Mike gulped a breath and made himself look out there.

The can had vanished, leaving a dent in the sand. The torch was out, and there was a bloody gash on Gerbil's arm. He wiped his face and pensively licked his fingers. "Supposed to be whole kernel, not creamed."

"Put that goddamned torch away," Veck shouted. He was on his feet, and he had his gun aimed at Gerbil's head.

"OK, Colonel," Gerbil said, scrambling to comply, forgetting about the corn and his bleeding arm. "Sure. No problem. Was only makin' dinner. No problem."

While Gerbil was wheeling the hand truck back into the shack, Longtemps pointed toward one of the cotton fields in the distance, the buffer zone between the airstrip and the main road. "Somebody's coming."

Mike could see the plume of dust, and, before long, two black sedans pulled up across the way. The door opened in the lead car, and Gina Rizzo climbed out.

Archie sighed. "Damnation. And I used to like Cadillacs."

Through their two knotholes, Mike and Archie were watching the welding shack. Veck and Rizzo had been inside twenty minutes. "You know, she doesn't seem like anything special," Archie commented.

"Hmmm," was Mike's reply. He hadn't noticed, but what Archie said was true. Away from Lynnie and Claudia and the bustle of the campaign, without her power suit and briefcase and stack of poll figures, there was nothing at all remarkable about Gina Rizzo. She wore her hair in a ponytail, a few stray ends dangling in her eyes. She had on jeans and cheap tennis shoes and a plain blue top. She was thin and a little humpbacked, not in particularly good shape.

The second car was still there, but no one had gotten out. Mike had been keeping an eye on it. Every few minutes the engine started, ran a bit, and shut down again—using the air conditioning. The windows were heavily tinted, but he could see two figures in there.

"Archie," Mike said, "that monument place in Tucson. Who was it you said had picked up that new head-stone?"

"Somebody from Lang Corporation, the security outfit. Why?"

"Just wondering, is all." Mike went back to staring at the car.

Veck's men were sitting on the ground by the pickup truck. They were anxious, sifting sand through their fingers, rarely talking to each other. Now they turned, as one, to look at the shack. Rizzo was yelling, loud enough for all to hear, even the three in the Quonset hut. "You knew this and you didn't tell me?"

Veck yelled back, his voice at exactly the same decibel level. "Yes. It was none of your damn business. They're my men. My problem—"

"Not when it comes back on me," Rizzo boomed. "Look here. A hundred thousand he wants. A finder's fee."

"What?" Veck shouted. "Where'd this come from?" Then he lowered his voice, and they couldn't hear the rest.

A short while later the two of them came out of the shack. They each had a pistol. Rizzo held hers away from her side, as if she were afraid of it. They marched up to the other men, and, without the slightest warning, Veck jammed his gun against Gerbil's forehead.

Gerb screeched, "*Colonel, what—?*"

Veck pushed hard, snapping Gerbil's head against the truck, keeping the pistol glued between his eyes. "I've been checking your computers, Gerb, buddy. You've been in touch with Star here. Sent her an e-mail, all on your lonesome."

"No," Gerbil said, confused now. "Why would I do that?"

Veck leaned harder on the gun. "The truth, Gerb."

"No. Cross my heart, Colonel. I sent the things you told me to send. That's it."

"You didn't ask her for money? Call it a finder's fee?"

"*No!*"

In a flash, Veck's demeanor changed. He gave a soft chuckle and tucked the gun into his belt. He knelt and patted Gerbil on the shoulder. "Son, you look like you could use a piddle pack. Didn't really scare you, did I?"

Gerbil let out a gasp of breath. He'd been holding it so long his face had turned red.

Veck tousled his hair. "Sorry. Had to check you out, that was all. But now we got a problem. You remember the papers we picked up the first time we were in Agua Prieta?"

"At the hospital when we met with Castillo? The old file he gave us?" Gerbil was beginning to loosen up, his goofy grin starting to return. "You gave it to me that day, Colonel, and told me to put it away with your gear. I haven't seen it since."

"Gerb, I can't find those papers now. The lady needs to know what they said. Do you remember?"

Gerb should have stopped to think before he answered. He might have walked away from the trap. Instead he blurted, "Not all of it, but a little. There was the old patient form, you know, for Connor. The original one we took out—"

"Wrong answer, Gerb," Veck said. He yanked his pistol back out.

"Colonel, what do you want?" Gerbil screamed.

"You weren't supposed to look at that file. You weren't supposed to know what it said, ever."

"I didn't. I do, but not— Jesus, Colonel, I don't even speak Spanish."

"No, you don't," Veck said. He turned and looked down the row of men. "*¡Cuidado!* Right, Dowd? Means 'watch out.'"

Dowd stood up, an inch at a time. He said nothing.

Veck let his gun dangle in his hand. Somehow it was more ominous that way. "You sent Star an e-mail, asked for a finder's fee? Blackmail? How stupid do you think we are—I am? That I wouldn't figure it out; that I wouldn't come after you?" Veck paused but got no reply. "And you had to go and get Gerb mixed up in it, poaching Star's e-mail address, then letting you use his computer. What's the matter, boy? Come on, explain. You're good at that."

Still Dowd was quiet. He slipped his hands into his pockets and shrugged.

Veck clucked his tongue once. "Curiosity does kill the cat, doesn't it?" He raised his pistol and fired.

Oscar had wheeled up behind Mike. "What happened?" he whispered urgently.

Archie answered with a single word. "Dead."

Veck went to Dowd's body and patted him down. He emptied his pockets, then dragged over his knapsack. From inside, he took out a pale green file folder, like the ones from the Agua Prieta hospital.

"I told you to get rid of that," Rizzo said, grabbing it from him.

"Yeah, well, that didn't seem like such a good idea until all the dust settled."

"You were going to come back on me with this?" Rizzo said, waving it in the air.

"Fuck no. Just want to know what I'm dealing with—"

He broke off because Gerbil had jumped up and was running toward the scrub bushes on the edge of the clearing, two hundred yards away.

"Stop him," Gina Rizzo said.

"Gerb," Veck called, "don't be an ass. You helped him out, so what? I know you weren't in on the money part."

"Stop him," Rizzo repeated, her voice rising. "*Do it!*"

Veck made no move.

Rizzo flipped up her gun and fired, limp-wristed, like someone pitching horseshoes at a Sunday picnic. Astonishingly, the bullet hit the target. Gerbil howled and twisted around. He still had his silly grin, but there was a gaping hole in his chest where the slug had exited. He thudded into the dust and lay completely still.

Rizzo stared at the pistol, amazed. Then, slowly, she put on a thoughtful frown. *Huh . . . that easy?* she seemed to be thinking. She smiled and nodded, a happy customer, the way someone might smile and nod over a scouring pad that really did make those pots and pans sparkle.

She turned, pointing the gun at the Quonset hut, at the exact spot where Mike was hidden behind his spy hole. "All right, then," she said. "Let's see what we've got in here."

CHAPTER FORTY-SEVEN

Cutter and Longtemps brought Archie out, dragging him because he couldn't stand on his own. Veck then told Mike to bring Oscar. Gina Rizzo studied the three men, her face blank. "Take them in the other building," she said. On the way, she and Veck huddled together, talking in quick, hushed tones.

The welding shack was shaped like a tiny church, tall and deep and very narrow, with a row of sooty windows high on the walls. Under the windows was a loft of rough-hewn planks. This was where the old fuel tanks were stored. The floor was in two levels: a dirt area by the door, and a low platform that stretched to the back of the building. The air inside was hot and rank with the garlicky smell of acetylene gas.

A ramp led up to the platform, and Veck pointed, indicating Mike should push Oscar up there. Gerbil had left the hand truck with the welding torch in the way, so Mike had to move it first. Eventually Oscar was settled, and there was a folding chair for Mike. Cutter and Longtemps left Archie unattended, propped in a corner. He wasn't going anywhere under his own power.

Rizzo brought another chair to the platform and sat in front of Mike. She had the old hospital file with her and the X-ray photocopy, which someone had taken off Mike while he was unconscious. She'd managed to get a spot of Dowd's blood on the file. With a smile, she wiped it off on her pant leg. Mike had the feeling this was a performance, showing him how unconcerned she was about Dowd's death, and Gerbil's, and others that might follow.

Once more, she studied him. "So here we are."

Mike nodded slowly. He was thinking about who wasn't there—the shadowy figures in the car.

Rizzo waved at the surroundings. "Some place, huh?" She pointed at the welding tanks. "We thought it would be perfect for you."

"We?" Mike said. "You and your friend outside?" He made her wait a split second. "Devon?"

A jolt of surprise crossed her face. Mike smiled. That was all the proof he needed. *"Devon Connor!"* he yelled. *"Come on and join the party!"*

Veck grabbed Mike's hair. "Shut up."

"Fuck you," Mike hissed back. *"Devon, don't hide from us!"* Veck backhanded him across the top of the head. No matter: the damage was already done. A car door opened, and a second. Footsteps approached, stopping just outside.

"It had to be," Mike called out. Rizzo glared at him but let him talk. "Who else would know about the cemetery and the headstones? About Lang Corporation? That's not political; that's the CC Ranch. Off limits to everyone but family. Right, Devon?"

Devon edged through the doorway. He was taller than Mike expected, and a lot stronger looking. His face still had that vague, lost expression from all the photographs, as if his eyeglasses were fogging his vision.

"Holy shit," one of Veck's troopers said, recognizing Devon's face, though he hadn't picked up on the name.

Another man stood behind Devon. He was much bigger than anyone else there, dressed in khaki pants and a too-tight aloha shirt. He wore no Secret Service lapel pin; there was no coil of wire coming from his shirt collar. That made him a rent-a-cop, a private bodyguard for Devon, and he wasn't at all happy about this setup. Looking anxiously from side to side, he said, "Mr. Connor, we should leave—" Devon waved for him to be quiet. The man put his hand on Devon's arm. "Mr. Connor, it's not safe."

"Car," Devon said quietly. "Go."

"Oh, Jesus," the man muttered, and he backed out of sight.

Devon came a few steps into the building, looking at each person in turn. He nodded to Veck—"Colonel"— and to Oscar—"Hello, Oscar. No—Arfulno, isn't it?" He shook his head mildly. "The things we never know, yes?"

Then he turned to Mike, tilting his head to look at him. "And Mr. Stanbridge."

Mike motioned around at the grubby walls. "So, you're running this show?"

"Show?" Devon said. He didn't seem to understand what Mike was getting at.

Mike didn't really care about placing blame, but he hoped to buy some time. He might hit on a way out. At least he could learn a thing or two. "How did you find out about Lynnie and Graciella?"

"Lynnie's father," Devon said. "He knew he was dying. He trusted me with the secret. I suppose he figured I'd find the right time to tell Lynnie."

Archie was watching carefully, his eyes darting about, looking for the same opening that Mike was. Nothing so far.

"And how did you find out about me?" Mike said.

"You? I've known almost since the beginning." Devon drew in the dust with his toe, a circle and a cross. He brushed them away. "Lynnie just changed sometimes. She couldn't hide it, almost floating she was so happy. I followed her one weekend, to an inn outside Philadelphia—and you." He couldn't quite get the dust right now that he'd disturbed it, so he nudged it this way and that. "I was never jealous of you. Lynnie's an extraordinary woman. You scratched an itch I couldn't begin to reach."

"Then why ruin things for her?" Oscar said.

They were all startled by the new voice. Devon looked at him, noticing the oxygen tank, the cannula. A frown of pity came on his face. "No, not ruin things. I want to help—"

"Devon, don't," Rizzo said. "Just wait outside."

He stood behind her, laying his hand on her shoulder. "No, Gina, I want them to know. I wouldn't hurt Lynnie. I only want her to listen, pay attention. We're partners. Marriage, you know? It's supposed to work that way, talking it out, deciding things together. Her work, it should be us together." He was pleading now, frustrated that they weren't all nodding in agreement. "I'm her *husband*. I have to make an *appointment* to see my own wife. It's not right." His voice dropped to a whisper. "I'll never hurt her. No one will know about any of this, if she just listens to me."

Archie gave a dry laugh. "Everybody here knows about it. What happens to us?"

Devon shrugged vaguely. He leaned closer to Rizzo, seeming to take strength from her. His fingers caressed her shoulder, ran softly over her hair.

Mike said, "So you'll blackmail Lynnie with the birth records in Agua Prieta? Make her push for a new secretary-general in the UN? Bring all the orphans back from Africa? Put a Bible and Koran and Torah in every classroom? I've heard all your nonsense, Devon. You can't shove her around that way. She'll resign first."

Rizzo had had enough. She stood up, taking Devon's hand in her own. "And leave things to Andrew Hoyt? No, Lynnie will deal with us before she gives the presidency to that animal." She pointed at Cutter. "Now you—get him out of here." She held out Devon's hand, like a child to be led off at bedtime.

As Cutter pulled him toward the door, Devon looked back at the platform. He seemed totally lost, blinking behind his glasses. "Why did you come here?" Mike said.

"I—" Devon's eyes went to Rizzo. "I wanted to meet you."

Mike said, "OK, you have. That's it?"

Cutter pulled Devon into the sunlight. "Yes, I guess. I'm sorry, Michael, for all of this." They passed out of sight.

Rizzo had returned to her seat. Mike bent toward her. "You made him come here. For what? To tie him in? So he couldn't deny any of it?"

She leaned back and cocked one leg over the other, comfortable now that she was in charge again. "He's weak, but we're working on that."

"It looked like you two are working on a lot of things."

She smiled. "It's all part of my job, keeping the wheels greased."

Mike's headache was gone. There was a new ringing in his ears, his blood pumping hard and furious. "You told Lynnie you could control him, but you only wanted to get close—to use him."

"No," she said. "Devon deserves more credit than that. He knows what's happening. Part of it was his idea— bringing you here." She looked at Veck. "Now tie him up."

"Nah," Veck replied. "No need." Rizzo stared at him, not angry, but determined. "All right," Veck sighed. "It's your party." Cutter had come back in, and he found a roll of duct tape. He jerked Mike's arms behind his back and put a wrap of the tape around his wrists. Outside, Devon was pacing, shooting occasional glances through the door.

Rizzo still had her pistol, and she clicked her fingernail over the sight. "Devon's learned quite a bit about you, Mike, through all those years. You won't turn on the heat in your house. You eat cold meals most of the time. It seems like you've got a problem with fire."

"What do you want?" he snarled, trying to keep his rage up, hoping that would fight the fear growing in the pit of his stomach.

"We ought to do this outside," Veck said.

"No," Rizzo answered flatly. She didn't want to be interrupted again. Her eyes came back to Mike and her smile returned, peaceful and bland. "I need to find out a few things, that's all. I don't want to hurt anybody—unless it's necessary. That's another one of Devon's ideas."

She wagged her finger, a signal. Veck struck the sparklighter—*ritch*—and the torch came alive with a soft *pop*. From the corner of his eye Mike could see the flame, yellow and wavery at first, then changing to a long bluish-white needle as Veck adjusted the gas mixture. Mike's legs begin to shake.

"OK," Rizzo said. "Did you show the X-ray to anybody? Anybody at all?"

Veck moved in with the torch, waving it like a wand over Mike's arm. The flame didn't make contact, but the heat off the tip was so intense his shirtsleeve split open as if cut with a scalpel. Underneath, blisters blossomed on Mike's biceps. He tried to keep quiet but couldn't. "Yes—nobody," he gasped. The torch swung back, hovered an instant, then moved on. "A nun. We showed it to her at the Newark airport."

"A nun?" Rizzo asked. "Why?"

Mike twisted as far from Veck as possible. He could see Archie lying by the door. He wanted to make eye contact, get some reassurance, but Archie was looking at Oscar. Behind the weariness there was a twinkle in his black eyes, a what-the-heck expression. He motioned, just a flick: thumbs-up.

The heat touched Mike's arm again. He jerked, but Veck held him. The torch was closer this time, the pain excruciating. Rizzo said, "Why a nun?"

"She spoke Spanish," Mike groaned.

"She read the X-ray label, then?"

Archie cut in. "The lady's got a plan, you know. She'll kill every mother's son of ya." He pointed out the door, at where Gerbil lay. "Like your buddy."

Rizzo glared at him. "Shut up."

"Kiss my tuna," Archie shot back.

Oscar laughed, so hard he broke into a fit of coughing.

Veck intervened. This was his job, getting information out of people, and he hated to see an amateur like Rizzo screwing it up. "Cutter, Longy, get these two geezers out of here."

Before they could move, Oscar held up his hand, bloody towel and all. "Wait, Veck—" He was still coughing. "Veck, I'll tell you—"

Mike was dizzy from the pain in his arm, but still he saw it all. Oscar's other hand was hanging low, by the floor. He grabbed his gas line as he croaked again, "Veck I'll tell you—"

"What?" Veck said. He took a step closer to the wheelchair.

Oscar kept coughing.

"What?"

Oscar smiled sweetly. "Welcome to hell."

He pitched out of the wheelchair, to the dirt floor below. The oxygen line came with him. For a second or so, Veck seemed rattled, halfway between laughing and cursing. Then he heard the oxygen hissing from the tank. The briefest flicker of understanding crossed his face. He whipped the torch away. At the same instant, the air around him burst into flame.

It was eerie, a ball of pure white light, no sound at all. It swallowed Veck. He was the torch now. He squalled, his voice going up and up and up, the rugged little baritone hitting the first high C of his life.

Rizzo was stunned, unable to move. They all were. Then Cutter and Longtemps jumped into action. Loyal troopers, they fought the fire, pounding Veck's back and head and arms with their open hands. Veck's scream went on endlessly.

Now Rizzo got her wits about her. She yelled too, from rage, and raised her pistol at Oscar. Mike's hands were bound, but not his feet. He kicked her in the ribs hard enough to lift her two feet off the platform. She slammed into the wall and dropped to the dirt below. Mike followed, heaving out of his chair, on top of her. The impact knocked the wind out of him, but it also loosened the tape holding his wrists. He struggled to get rid of it, yanking, twisting. It was too strong. With his arms pinned behind him, he couldn't get up, couldn't even manage to sit. And that, by sheer luck, saved his life.

Oscar's chair had caught fire. His oxygen tank gave an ominous *pinnnng*, then exploded. Shrapnel howled through the air. Veck and his men were cut down, bleeding, screaming. An arm, heavy as a fireplace log, bounced off Mike's back.

The smoke and dust cleared slowly. Rizzo wasn't moving. Groggily, Mike peered into the gloom. There and there: Oscar and Archie. Like him, they were uninjured by the explosion, protected by the lip of the platform. Oscar was inching toward the door, but Archie was too exhausted to move. The fire was racing now, up and across the ceiling. One of the big tanks in the loft made a groaning sound and a low *ping*.

Mike clambered to Archie on his knees. "The tape," he yelled, turning to expose his wrists.

Archie pawed at it. "Can't," he panted.

"Archie, come on!"

Archie jammed his thumb in and threw himself back, using his weight for momentum. The tape snapped.

Mike grabbed Oscar first and dragged him, like a rag doll, into the open. He parked him beside Rizzo's big sedan. Then he sprinted back for Archie. This was harder. He was so big. Together they made it, fighting, uphill it seemed, against their own fatigue and the soft sand. They collapsed next to Oscar.

The rent-a-cop had panicked as he tried to get his car

turned around and out of there. It was stuck axle-deep in the sand, tires screaming as he worked for traction. Devon had abandoned the car and taken shelter on the far side of the Quonset hut where he crouched, helpless.

A *whoosh* came from the shack, and flames flared out of the windows and climbed the outside of the roof. Mike stared for a split second, then started running back toward it.

"Michael, what—?" Archie yelled. "*No!* Leave her. She's not worth it."

Oscar pulled him down. He was smiling, the same happy-sad smile Lola Yberri had given when she described *Día de los Muertos*. "Not Rizzo," he said. "The file. For Lynnie. It's proof."

Welcome to hell. Oscar's dark joke sounded in Mike's head as he approached the shack. Orange flames licked out at him through the cracks in the walls and around the doorway. There was so much heat his skin prickled. He could hear the gas tanks making their menacing *pinnng* sounds. He hesitated a moment, afraid he was going to be sick. No, not sick, just plain terrified. He wanted to turn and race for the bushes, put miles between himself and the fire.

Then a memory flashed in his mind. The milk house at the ranch. The ice block he thought he never could move. Lynnie dancing and cheering, "Champ! Champ!"

Mike drew a final breath, ready now, but, before he could move, Archie shouted, "Watch out!" Devon was hurtling toward him. With only a split second to think, Mike couldn't guess what Devon was doing. The look on his face was pure panic. Maybe he was trying to save Rizzo. Maybe he was after the file. He understood how damning it could be.

They hit the door together, but Devon had no experience with a fire like this. He was sprinting, full height. Mike was low, almost on his belly. The superheated air caught Devon full in the face. He had time to gasp, stumble two steps. Then he began to scream, staggering crazily, wanting the door but not able to find it.

Mike slithered on, away from the worst of the flames, but the smoke was so thick he couldn't see his own hands. He located Rizzo by patting the ground in front of him. An arm, a shoulder. There was a large scorch mark across her stomach. He touched her roughly, but she didn't move. He couldn't feel her breathing, either.

The green folder was under her hip. He rolled her over to free it. Now, the door—back that way. He nearly made it, too, still slithering. Around him, the air seemed cooler, lighter, but there was something in the way. He shoved it, trying to stay down. It moaned. Devon. He was burned from the waist up, his clothing in tatters and his flesh a crimson mess. "You," he croaked. He'd gotten his fingers around Mike's belt.

Mike could hear the blood gurgling in Devon's roasted throat and lungs. He tried to claw his way past.

Devon's hand flopped up. He'd found Rizzo's gun. "The file . . . she . . ." He coughed, and blood sprayed everywhere. *"Get me out of here,"* he screeched in a cracking, half lunatic voice.

Flames had reached the doorway, filling it. Mike shook his head. "Too late."

"Out of here," Devon screamed, and he began to sob. His hair was literally on fire, curling and turning to ash.

The loft groaned and gave way. One by one the fuel cylinders tumbled to the ground. Devon, terrified, cowered in a fetal position. That was enough for Mike to shove the gun aside and dive for the door. Devon shrieked and fired, spraying the ceiling, the loft with bullets. The last shot hit one of the big oxygen tanks.

The explosion tore the roof off the shack, blew the walls to splinters. Like a giant hand, it flung Mike facedown in the dirt. Then came the fireball. It was brilliant white. He could see it even through his tightly closed eyes. The heat was awesome, roaring over his legs and back. He heard other tanks go off, dull thuds through the windy howl. He couldn't breathe. Taking air that hot into his lungs would kill him. Ten seconds. Twenty. Forever. Then, even more quickly than it hit, the fireball was gone.

Debris crackled to the ground around him. He could smell his own cooked flesh, not the bad barbecue smell that people joke about, but something cleaner, fresher, like burned bread. His back was wet and already growing cold. That was his blood, his lymph, his life fluid, oozing out, catching the breeze. He felt giddy, light-headed. Soon, he knew, he would go into shock and pass out.

He raised his head, looking across the clearing to where he'd last seen Archie and Oscar. They were far enough back to be unharmed. When they saw his eyes flutter open, relief came onto their faces. Archie grinned.

Mike edged his hand out from under him. The file was there, crumpled and singed but all in one piece, protected from the blaze by his own body. He held it up, his trophy. Archie shook his head in mock disgust and muttered a joking curse.

Mike looked at Oscar. The old man's face was blue from lack of oxygen, but he was smiling broadly. He said something, too low for Mike to hear. It didn't make any difference. Mike could read his lips—one word anyway. The only word he cared about.

Lynnie.

CHAPTER FORTY-EIGHT

The monitor screen traced the pattern of Mike's heartbeat, a wavering green line. From where he lay, on his stomach, it was the only thing he could see that moved. He watched it, half in a trance.

"Mr. Stanbridge? Are you still awake?" The intrusion came from Will Wynn, an FBI Special Agent. When he'd introduced himself earlier, Mike gave a sloppy grin and said, we'll win what? The government man sighed and answered: the battle against crummy jokes.

"Mr. Stanbridge?"

"Still awake," Mike replied.

"Good." Wynn was wearing a bulky yellow isolation gown. His beard caused his surgical mask to puff out grotesquely from his face. Overall, he resembled a giant party balloon. "Back to Martin Castillo. Did you ever—"

"Could you do me a favor?" Mike broke in. "Adjust my pillow? I'm sick of lying in my own drool. That's it." He gave another loose-lipped grin. "Now tap your heels together and say 'There's no place like home.'"

Mike could joke because of the morphine they had him on. Soon that calm, drifting feeling would wear off. The nerves in his back would begin to fire randomly, like a swarm of bees, crawling, stinging. And later there would be another trip to the whirlpool tub. He'd had two tubbings so far, to remove the dead and dying flesh. They were everything he remembered, sheer agony. But right this minute, he was a pretty happy camper. "Castillo?" Mike said. "What about him?"

Wynn sat back down. "Did you ever meet him?"

"No. He was murdered before I got involved."

"Murdered, yes." Wynn's gown was slick and he

started slipping out of his chair. He pulled himself up-right again. "In the bathtub, you said?"

"I said," Mike parroted cheerfully.

"And you don't know if he was involved in, um—" Wynn shuffled the papers on his lap, all photocopies of the originals. "Switching the hospital files?"

"Make sense if he was. Maybe he was paid off. I'm just guessing, though. Hey, could you turn the television on? I want to hear the news."

Wynn picked up the remote and clicked it at the TV. The screen remained blank. "Maybe your insurance doesn't pick up the cost," he said. "Anyway, let's stick with Castillo. You told one of the other agents—"

Mike interrupted. "Where's the original file? The real hospital records?"

"In Washington at the FBI lab."

"Has the president seen it?"

Wynn became nervous, fidgeting with his pen. "The Justice Department doesn't—we don't have a habit of showing things to the president, no."

Mike smiled. "But you made an exception in this case, didn't you?"

"I can't say, really—" Wynn was saved by the bell, the ringer on his cell phone. He dragged it out of his pocket, tearing his gown in the process. "Yes? . . . He what?" Wynn listened for nearly a minute before he mumbled, "All right." He stuck the phone next to Mike's ear. "It's for you."

There was a crackle of static, then: "Hey, Torch, how's it goin'?"

"Archie? Where are you?"

"Not with the angels, that's for sure. Cardiac unit. And if they'd give me a damn metal spoon instead of plastic, I'd start tunneling my way out of here."

Mike was momentarily choked up, just hearing his voice. That was one of the downsides of the morphine.

His emotions were only a pinprick below the surface. When he could talk again, he said, "What about Oscar?"

"Intensive care. They almost lost him, but he's doin' a little better. Should be OK if he makes it through the next twenty-four hours. He's one tough hombre, Oscar is. Lucky they got such a good Medevac team here. We're all lucky."

"Hombre. Is that *Bonanza* Spanish?" Mike asked.

"You betcha," Archie said. "Hey, you got television in your room? I'd like to know what the hell's going on in the world." Mike said his wasn't working either.

"Huh. That's pretty strange, don't you think?" Archie said. "Anywho, I called Blaine a while ago. The government sure works in mysterious ways. All the charges against us have been dropped. Best I could tell, they don't even want to question us back there. That state trooper dame Dushaney has gone on leave. Oh, and young Billy White dropped out of the assembly election. Nobody knows where he's run off to."

Mike laughed. "Just licking his wounds. He'll be back."

"Sad but true," Archie said. "Say, I did hear some of the people talking here. I guess somebody leaked the story that Graciella Yberri was Lynnie's mother. America's got an honest-to-God *Messican*-American president. Wha'cha think Lynnie'll do to celebrate the news? Give Texas back? I know, she'll start jumping on tables at state functions, doing the flamenco."

"The flamenco's from Spain, not Mexico."

"Do tell? How's your back, by the way?"

Mike moved as if to look, but he couldn't turn an inch with all the tubes and equipment and bandages. "It's toast. It'll heal. The doctor says I should be out in three weeks if the grafts go as planned, then a few months of rehab. How about your heart?"

"They're talking bypass, but I think I can wheedle 'em down to angioplasty. I'm working on 'em anyway. It's weird having all these FBI guys around, isn't it? Mine's got the crabs." Mike heard rumbling sounds in the background, and Archie said to someone else, "Hey, then why are you scratching yourself every damn minute?" Another rumble. "Body wax? Sheesh. That's even worse." He turned to the phone again. "So I was wondering, if you get back on your feet quick enough, maybe you can come on home for some ice fishing."

"Ice fishing?" Mike laughed so hard he snorted. "I'll go ice fishing when you put on a tutu and join the ballet. Why don't you come to the Keys? My neighbor can show you how not to catch bonefish."

"Bonefish? Haven't they got any walleye down there?"

"*What* do you think you're doing?" a woman exclaimed from somewhere on Mike's left, by the door to his room. She was Maggie Pearsall, charge nurse for the burn unit. "Put that thing away. This man can't talk on the phone."

"No, he's—he—" Agent Wynn stuttered. "I think he's doing OK."

"OK?" the nurse whispered. The low tone made it sound like a threat.

"Archie, I've got to go," Mike said.

Through the phone, Archie could hear what was going on in Mike's room. "Is she pretty? Ask her if you can donate some bodily fluids."

"You're always a class act, Archie. So long."

Nurse Pearsall tugged the phone away. "Do you have any idea how easily he could become infected?"

"I don't, I can't—" Wynn said.

"That's enough of you anyway. Out. I have work to do in here."

"But—" Wynn began.

"Out! Or li'l old me is going to put that cute FBI butt of yours in a sling."

"I'm not done yet," he said. But he knew when he was outranked. He shuffled out the door.

The nurse checked Mike's IV lines and his monitor.

She adjusted the heat shield over his bed, a hood-like contraption that kept him warm. She worked quietly and methodically. As she finished, she said, "The doctor's decided it's time to lighten up on the painkillers. We'll step you down to oxycodone later today. No more morphine."

"Oh, goody gumdrops," Mike said with a mild chuckle.

Maggie Pearsall studied him. She'd worked there for thirteen years and never had a patient like him. Always with the jokes. He seemed to take his fear—she knew he was afraid; they all were—and swallow it, put it away somewhere way down deep. But who was she to complain? It only made her job easier. "There were some flowers delivered for you a while ago. Biggest bouquet I've ever seen, four dozen sunflowers. I had to get two men from maintenance to carry them up to the children's ward. I hope that's all right. We can't keep them here, and I didn't want them to go to waste."

"Sure, fine," Mike answered.

"There was a card with it." She moved to the head of the bed and held it where he could see.

Michael Sweetcakes Stanbridge.
> *Thanks! A thousand thanks! Get well, yes? We miss you!*
>> *C.S. (and you-know-who)*

Nurse Pearsall watched his expression change. Gently she said, "You must love her a lot."

"What?" Mike said quickly. He twisted, trying to look at her. "What do you mean?"

"Calm down. I didn't mean anything, but . . . You were talking about her when we had you in the tub this morning. Don't you remember? Not just talking about her, but *to* her. Jen. That's her name, right?"

Mike had blocked it out, but now it all came back. "You brought a chair over so she could sit down. We talked about cheerleader tryouts."

"Mmmm," the nurse said. "Something like that."

"She was worried she wouldn't make the squad, that her ankles were too fat." In his mind, Mike could see her. She was still a kid, still the same old Jen. He puckered up his eyes, fighting back tears. The morphine again. "You're right," he said with a trembling smile. "I love her a lot."

The nurse bent to look at something under his bed. "You know, you've got great kidneys."

"They're proud to serve," Mike droned. He was feeling drowsy all of a sudden.

"If you're up to it, you've got a visitor," she said.

"Who?"

"I think she'd rather tell you herself."

"Sure, OK," Mike said.

A moment later he heard rustling by the door and a few whispered phrases. Someone sat down in the chair where Agent Wynn had been. "Jesus, Sweetcakes, you look like hell."

"Hey, Claudia, how're you doin'?" He tried not to slur, but it just wasn't possible.

"I'm OK." Her voice was weak and shaky. She'd started to cry as soon as she saw him.

"Come on, now," he said. "I'll get through it. Done it before."

"Sure you have." He felt her hand touch the bed. She was afraid to touch him, though.

"So what's the story with Devon?" Mike said. She didn't say anything, so he went on, "I figure that's why we've got a news blackout. No TV. You people are putting together a cover story and don't want Archie and Oscar and me to screw it up for you."

She sniffed loudly. "Can't even blow my nose inside

this thing." Then she was bawling, barely intelligible. "I'm sorry, Mike. Sorry. The campaign people think we've got to come up with something. They want to say it was all of you—Devon and Gina and you and Pascoe and Oscar—went out to that old air base. You were trying to keep that Veck person from blackmailing the campaign. Devon went with you. *With* you, or you went with *him*. I don't know. God, this is awful. Devon was helping, and it all went wrong, and he died. That's the story. Oh shit, I hate this. I hate this."

"Hey, now," Mike said. "Politics ain't beanbag, right?"

Claudia shuddered, trying to bring herself under control. "You know what the worst thing is? I *liked* Devon. I—" Then she was bawling again. "No, that's not the worst thing. The worst thing is how you look right now. I can't believe how awful—"

"You aren't going to be sick are you?" This new voice came from the door.

Claudia stood up, and Mike listened to the faint hiss of sterile booties shuffling across the floor. "Hey, there," Lynnie said, bending where he could see her.

"Hey, yourself." She wore a blue gown, not yellow like the rest. It went well with her eyes, and he told her that.

She smiled—he could see it in those eyes. Her mask covered the rest. "I wish I could kiss you."

"Mmmm," he said. "Nice thought." He was fighting hard against the morphine now. He wanted to savor every second of this. "I'm sorry about Devon. I would have tried—"

"Shhh," Lynnie said, shaking her head. "You don't have to explain anything."

Claudia had moved around next to her. She whispered something, and Mike caught the word *plane*.

"Gotta go?" he mumbled. "It's the debate, isn't it?"

"No," Lynnie said quietly. "Devon—back to Washington."

"She has to travel with the body, Mike." Claudia had already slipped back to her official voice. "The plane's waiting."

"Give me a minute," Lynnie said.

"Now don't—"

Lynnie simply looked at her. "OK, OK," Claudia said. "Just don't throw another shoe at me." She glanced at Mike, wanting to say something pithy, a final joke, but it was all too much for her. She hurried out before she burst into tears again.

"Sit down," Mike said. He was so tired now his vision was closing down, ringing her face in a pale halo.

Lynnie shook her head. "I like it here, where we can see each other. They've had you in the tub?"

"Yes. Remember what it was like?"

"I sure do. I hear they give showers at some burn centers now—no tubbings."

"I don't know. I think I'd rather take mine lying down."

She laughed. "You would, would you?"

He nodded and his eyes slipped shut.

"Mikey?"

There was something in her voice, more than just worry, that made him fight back to the surface. "Still here," he mumbled. He noticed then that she was crying. He wanted to tell her to stop, that everything was OK. He couldn't get the words to form. His eyes closed again, and he dropped off to sleep.

The hands under him were cold and rough. "Mike?" one of the nurses said. "Mike, wake up. We've got to take you to the tub."

"I'm here," he said. He tried to sound brave, but that wasn't how he felt. His back was a thousand torture points—and they hadn't even started yet.

The hands gripped him, four nurses in all, and shifted

him to a gurney. He made a sound, a wet gurgle that would have been a scream if he hadn't kept his teeth clenched. Then he saw a blue pant leg. He craned up. "You . . . your plane?"

Lynnie had a look in her eyes that he'd never seen before. Surprise, maybe even a little fear. She'd been weeping so much the tears had soaked through her mask. "I couldn't—I couldn't leave you."

She was in the way of the door, and one of the nurses pulled her gently aside. Lynnie bristled at the touch, and then she seemed to right herself. "Yes, of course. I'm sorry." She stood as tall as she could. Mike could see the smile in her eyes. "I love you, Mikey."

He couldn't get his hand all the way to her, but he reached anyway. "Did you hear it?" he said.

Lynnie shook her head. "What?"

"The clocks just stopped ticking."

She smiled again. "I'll be here when you get back."

So it was four unnamed nurses who first learned the truth. It made the Internet within hours. The next morning, it was the lead in the tabloids, with headlines like ROYAL CONSORT? By noon, the TV and radio news shows were leading off with it. Randy Barchic was interviewed in Miami. Reporters went through Mike's trash at Lime Key and tried to talk to his neighbors. They didn't find out much, and Lynnie and the White House had no comment.

Aside from Lynnie, the only person allowed to visit Mike's room was Claudia. She smuggled in a tiny digital camera, and, when Lynnie wasn't looking, she snapped a few shots. One of them caught Claudia's attention. Lynnie had changed into a white gown from the blue. She was seated at Mike's bedside, nodding over her hands. She'd actually drifted off to sleep, but she appeared to be praying.

"Here," Claudia told an aide. "Give that to the press. *Nothing* else."

Archie happened to catch a glimpse of that photograph, splashed across the front page of a Phoenix newspaper that a woman was reading in the hallway outside his door. "Sheesh," he said, and he laughed until his belly shook.

Three days later, Lynnie Connor won in a landslide.

JIM KELLY

THE FIRE BABY

An American plane crashes into a remote farm on England's Cambridgeshire Fens. Out of the flames walks a young woman, Maggie Beck, with a baby in her arms—the only two survivors. Now, twenty-seven years later, Maggie is dying. As she lies in the hospital, she gives a startling deathbed confession to the patient in the bed next to hers, Laura, a woman slowly awakening from a coma. The confession would blow open the murder case that Laura's husband, reporter Philip Dryden, is covering…if only Laura could communicate the shocking secrets she's learned.

ISBN 13: 978-0-8439-6001-3

MICHAEL SIVERLING

THE SORCERER'S CIRCLE

Private investigator Jason Wilder was wrapping up another tough day working for his mother, Victoria, at the Midnight Investigation Agency. Then elderly Elijah Messenger came in, claiming that he'd had a premonition that someone would kill him. Jason politely showed him out. But the next morning Jason learned that Messenger was found dead, with a Midnight Agency business card in his pocket. And his mother has taken on a new client—the mayor, whose daughter is the prime suspect in Messenger's murder!

ISBN 13: 978-0-8439-6003-7

"Ruttan has a spellbinding style."
—CLIVE CUSSLER

SANDRA
RUTTAN

One year ago, a brutal case almost destroyed three cops.
Since then they've lost touch with one another, avoiding
painful memories, content to go their own ways. Now Nolan
is after a serial rapist. Hart is working on a string of arsons.
And Tain has been assigned a series of child abductions, a
case all too similar to that one. But when the body of one
of the abduction victims is found at the site of one of the
arsons, it starts to look like maybe these cases are connected
after all....

WHAT
BURNS
WITHIN

ISBN 13: 978-0-8439-6074-7

"The ultimate cat-and-mouse thriller. Nonstop action."
—*Book Crossing* on *African Ice*

Jeff Buick

As the vice-president of a Washington, D.C., bank, Leona Hewitt knows her new position will have greater responsibilities. She doesn't know they may cost her life. Her boss made it pretty clear that he expects her to approve a particular conversion for one of their largest corporate clients, no matter how questionable it may seem to her.

Both the head of the bank and the head of the corporation have a lot to lose if this doesn't go through…and they're not about to let anything or anyone get in their way. If Leona and her conscience prove to be a problem, they know a very effective way of getting rid of her—permanently. As Leona races to stay one step ahead of the killer on her trail, the only man who can help keep her alive is fighting for his own life halfway around the world.

DELICATE CHAOS

ISBN 13: 978-0-8439-6038-9

GREGG LOOMIS

The newest secret is about to be uncovered....

A scientist in Amsterdam—murdered. Another scientist in Atlanta—murdered, and his journal stolen. Lang Reilly worked with them both. And when someone took a shot at Lang, it only made him more determined to find the truth. Lang's search will lead him along a twisted trail to Brussels, Cairo, Vienna, Tel Aviv...and deep into the secrets of the past. What's the connection between the murdered scientists and an ancient parchment, recently unearthed? What revelations does it contain, and what powerful group is willing to kill to make sure its secrets remain hidden? With the balance of power in the Middle East at risk, Lang has to stay alive long enough to find the answer to a mystery that has puzzled historians for centuries.

THE SINAI SECRET

Available March 2008 wherever books are sold.

ISBN 13: 978-0-8439-6042-6

❑ YES!

Sign me up for the Leisure Thriller Book Club and send my
FREE BOOKS! If I choose to stay in the club, I will pay only
$8.50* each month, a savings of $7.48!

NAME: _____

ADDRESS: _____

TELEPHONE: _____

EMAIL: _____

❑ I want to pay by credit card.

❑ VISA ❑ MasterCard. ❑ DISCOVER

ACCOUNT #: _____

EXPIRATION DATE: _____

SIGNATURE: _____

Mail this page along with $2.00 shipping and handling to:
Leisure Thriller Book Club
PO Box 6640
Wayne, PA 19087
Or fax (must include credit card information) to:
610-995-9274

You can also sign up online at **www.dorchesterpub.com**.